LUCY MAUD MONTGOMERY SHORT STORIES, 1909 TO 1922

By
L. M. MONTGOMERY

Lucy Maud Montgomery Short Stories, 1909 TO 1922

by L. M. Montgomery

Copyright © 2023

All Rights reserved.
No part of this publication may be reproduced, stored in a retrieval system, or transmitted in any form or by any means, electronic, mechanical, photocopying or Otherwise, without the written permission of the publisher.

The author/editor asserts the moral right to be identified as the author/editor of this work.

ISBN: 978-93-57486-41-5

Published by

DOUBLE 9 BOOKS

2/13-B, Ansari Road, Daryaganj
New Delhi – 110002
info@double9books.com
www.double9books.com
Tel. 011-40042856

This book is under public domain

ABOUT THE AUTHOR

The best-known works by Canadian author Lucy Maud Montgomery OBE, also known by her pen as L M Montgomery (November 30, 1874 – April 24, 1942), include a number of novels, essays, short tales, and poems that began with Anne of Green Gables in 1908. Along with 530 short stories, 500 poems, and 30 articles, she also authored 20 novels. The novel Anne of Green Gables was an instant hit, and the titular character, the orphan Anne Shirley, helped make Lucy Maud Montgomery famous and earned her a global following. The majority of the novels were set in Prince Edward Island, and those parts of Canada's tiniest province—specifically, Green Gables farm, which served as the inspiration for Prince Edward Island National Park—became literary landmarks and well-liked tourist destinations. In 1935, she received the title of officer of the Order of the British Empire. Scholars and readers from all over the world have read and studied Montgomery's writings, journals, and correspondence. The University of Prince Edward Island's L. M. Montgomery Institute is in charge of doing academic research into L. M. Montgomery's life, works, culture, and influence. On November 30, 1874, Lucy Maud Montgomery was born in Clifton, Prince Edward Island (now New London).

CONTENTS

A Golden Wedding 7
A Redeeming Sacrifice 12
A Soul That Was Not at Home 17
Abel and His Great Adventure 27
Akin To Love 38
Aunt Philippa and the Men 49
Bessie's Doll 59
Charlotte's Ladies 67
Christmas at Red Butte 75
How We Went to the Wedding 81
Jessamine 103
Miss Sally's Letter 109
My Lady Jane 118
Robert Turner's Revenge 126
The Fillmore Elderberries 133
The Finished Story 139
The Garden of Spices 146
The Girl and the Photograph 161
The Gossip of Valley View 169
The Letters 176
The Life-Book of Uncle Jesse 186
The Little Black Doll 195
The Man on the Train 202
The Romance of Jedediah 209
The Tryst of the White Lady 219
Uncle Richard's New Year's Dinner 231
White Magic 235

A Golden Wedding

The land dropped abruptly down from the gate, and a thick, shrubby growth of young apple orchard almost hid the little weather-grey house from the road. This was why the young man who opened the sagging gate could not see that it was boarded up, and did not cease his cheerful whistling until he had pressed through the crowding trees and found himself almost on the sunken stone doorstep over which in olden days honeysuckle had been wont to arch. Now only a few straggling, uncared-for vines clung forlornly to the shingles, and the windows were, as has been said, all boarded up.

The whistle died on the young man's lips and an expression of blank astonishment and dismay settled down on his face — a good, kindly, honest face it was, although perhaps it did not betoken any pronounced mental gifts on the part of its owner.

"What can have happened?" he said to himself. "Uncle Tom and Aunt Sally can't be dead — I'd have seen their deaths in the paper if they was. And I'd a-thought if they'd moved away it'd been printed too. They can't have been gone long — that flower-bed must have been made up last spring. Well, this is a kind of setback for a fellow. Here I've been tramping all the way from the station, a-thinking how good it would be to see Aunt Sally's sweet old face again, and hear Uncle Tom's laugh, and all I find is a boarded-up house going to seed. S'pose I might as well toddle over to Stetsons' and inquire if they haven't disappeared, too."

He went through the old firs back of the lot and across the field to a rather shabby house beyond. A cheery-faced woman answered his knock and looked at him in a puzzled fashion. "Have you forgot me, Mrs. Stetson? Don't you remember Lovell Stevens and how you used to give him plum tarts when he'd bring your turkeys home?"

Mrs. Stetson caught both his hands in a hearty clasp.

"I guess I haven't forgotten!" she declared. "Well, well, and you're Lovell! I think I ought to know your face, though you've changed a lot. Fifteen years have made a big difference in you. Come right in. Pa, this is Lovell — you mind Lovell, the boy Aunt Sally and Uncle Tom had for years?"

"Reckon I do," drawled Jonah Stetson with a friendly grin. "Ain't likely to forget some of the capers you used to be cutting up. You've filled out considerable. Where have you been for the last ten years? Aunt Sally fretted a lot over you, thinking you was dead or gone to the bad."

Lovell's face clouded.

"I know I ought to have written," he said repentantly, "but you know I'm a terrible poor scholar, and I'd do most anything than try to write a letter. But where's Uncle Tom and Aunt Sally gone? Surely they ain't dead?"

"No," said Jonah Stetson slowly, "no—but I guess they'd rather be. They're in the poorhouse."

"The poorhouse! Aunt Sally in the poorhouse!" exclaimed Lovell.

"Yes, and it's a burning shame," declared Mrs. Stetson. "Aunt Sally's just breaking her heart from the disgrace of it. But it didn't seem as if it could be helped. Uncle Tom got so crippled with rheumatism he couldn't work and Aunt Sally was too frail to do anything. They hadn't any relations and there was a mortgage on the house."

"There wasn't any when I went away."

"No; they had to borrow money six years ago when Uncle Tom had his first spell of rheumatic fever. This spring it was clear that there was nothing for them but the poorhouse. They went three months ago and terrible hard they took it, especially Aunt Sally, I felt awful about it myself. Jonah and I would have took them if we could, but we just couldn't—we've nothing but Jonah's wages and we have eight children and not a bit of spare room. I go over to see Aunt Sally as often as I can and take her some little thing, but I dunno's she wouldn't rather not see anybody than see them in the poorhouse."

Lovell weighed his hat in his hands and frowned over it reflectively.

"Who owns the house now?"

"Peter Townley. He held the mortgage. And all the old furniture was sold too, and that most killed Aunt Sally. But do you know what she's fretting over most of all? She and Uncle Tom will have been married fifty years in a fortnight's time and Aunt Sally thinks it's awful to have to spend their golden wedding anniversary in the poorhouse. She talks about it all the time. You're not going, Lovell"—for Lovell had risen—"you must stop with us, since your old home is closed up. We'll scare you up a shakedown to sleep on and you're welcome as welcome. I haven't forgot the time you caught Mary Ellen just as she was tumbling into the well."

"Thank you, I'll stay to tea," said Lovell, sitting down again, "but I guess I'll make my headquarters up at the station hotel as long as I stay round here. It's kind of more central."

"Got on pretty well out west, hey?" queried Jonah.

"Pretty well for a fellow who had nothing but his two hands to depend on when he went out," said Lovell cautiously. "I've only been a labouring man, of course, but I've saved up enough to start a little store when I go back. That's why I came east for a trip now—before I'd be tied down to business. I was hankering to see Aunt Sally and Uncle Tom once more. I'll never forget how kind and good they was to me. There I was, when Dad died, a little sinner of eleven, just heading for destruction. They give me a home and all the schooling I ever had and all the love I ever got. It was Aunt Sally's teachings made as much a man of me as I am. I never forgot 'em and I've tried to live up to 'em."

After tea Lovell said he thought he'd stroll up the road and pay Peter Townley a call. Jonah Stetson and his wife looked at each other when he had gone.

"Got something in his eye," nodded Jonah. "Him and Peter weren't never much of friends."

"Maybe Aunt Sally's bread is coming back to her after all," said his wife. "People used to be hard on Lovell. But I always liked him and I'm real glad he's turned out so well."

Lovell came back to the Stetsons' the next evening. In the interval he had seen Aunt Sally and Uncle Tom. The meeting had been both glad and sad. Lovell had also seen other people.

"I've bought Uncle Tom's old house from Peter Townley," he said quietly, "and I want you folks to help me out with my plans. Uncle Tom and Aunt Sally ain't going to spend their golden wedding in the poorhouse—no, sir. They'll spend it in their own home with their old friends about them. But they're not to know anything about it till the very night. Do you s'pose any of the old furniture could be got back?"

"I believe every stick of it could," said Mrs. Stetson excitedly. "Most of it was bought by folks living handy and I don't believe one of them would refuse to sell it back. Uncle Tom's old chair is here to begin with—Aunt Sally give me that herself. She said she couldn't bear to have it sold. Mrs. Isaac Appleby at the station bought the set of pink-sprigged china and James Parker bought the grandfather's clock and the whatnot is at the Stanton Grays'."

For the next fortnight Lovell and Mrs. Stetson did so much travelling round together that Jonah said genially he might as well be a bachelor as far as meals and buttons went. They visited every house where a bit of Aunt Sally's belongings could be found. Very successful they were too, and at the end of their jaunting the interior of the little house behind the apple trees looked very much as it had looked when Aunt Sally and Uncle Tom lived there.

Meanwhile, Mrs. Stetson had been revolving a design in her mind, and one afternoon she did some canvassing on her own account. The next time she saw Lovell she said:

"We ain't going to let you do it all. The women folks around here are going to furnish the refreshments for the golden wedding and the girls are going to decorate the house with golden rod."

The evening of the wedding anniversary came. Everybody in Blair was in the plot, including the matron of the poorhouse. That night Aunt Sally watched the sunset over the hills through bitter tears.

"I never thought I'd be celebrating my golden wedding in the poorhouse," she sobbed. Uncle Tom put his twisted hand on her shaking old shoulder, but before he could utter any words of comfort Lovell Stevens stood before them.

"Just get your bonnet on, Aunt Sally," he cried jovially, "and both of you come along with me. I've got a buggy here for you ... and you might as well say goodbye to this place, for you're not coming back to it any more."

"Lovell, oh, what do you mean?" said Aunt Sally tremulously.

"I'll explain what I mean as we drive along. Hurry up — the folks are waiting."

When they reached the little old house, it was all aglow with light. Aunt Sally gave a cry as she entered it. All her old household goods were back in their places. There were some new ones too, for Lovell had supplied all that was lacking. The house was full of their old friends and neighbours. Mrs. Stetson welcomed them home again.

"Oh, Tom," whispered Aunt Sally, tears of happiness streaming down her old face, "oh, Tom, isn't God good?"

They had a right royal celebration, and a supper such as the Blair housewives could produce. There were speeches and songs and tales. Lovell kept himself in the background and helped Mrs. Stetson cut cake in the pantry all the evening. But when the guests had gone, he went to Aunt Sally and Uncle Tom, who were sitting by the fire.

"Here's a little golden wedding present for you," he said awkwardly, putting a purse into Aunt Sally's hand. "I reckon there's enough there to keep you from ever having to go to the poorhouse again and if not, there'll be more where that comes from when it's done."

There were twenty-five bright twenty-dollar gold pieces in the purse.

"We can't take it, Lovell," protested Aunt Sally. "You can't afford it."

"Don't you worry about that," laughed Lovell. "Out west men don't think much of a little wad like that. I owe you far more than can be paid in cash, Aunt Sally. You must take it—I want to know there's a little home here for me and two kind hearts in it, no matter where I roam."

"God bless you, Lovell," said Uncle Tom huskily. "You don't know what you've done for Sally and me."

That night, when Lovell went to the little bedroom off the parlour—for Aunt Sally, rejoicing in the fact that she was again mistress of a spare room, would not hear of his going to the station hotel—he gazed at his reflection in the gilt-framed mirror soberly.

"You've just got enough left to pay your passage back west, old fellow," he said, "and then it's begin all over again just where you begun before. But Aunt Sally's face was worth it all—yes, sir. And you've got your two hands still and an old couple's prayers and blessings. Not such a bad capital, Lovell, not such a bad capital."

A Redeeming Sacrifice

The dance at Byron Lyall's was in full swing. Toff Leclerc, the best fiddler in three counties, was enthroned on the kitchen table and from the glossy brown violin, which his grandfather brought from Grand Pré, was conjuring music which made even stiff old Aunt Phemy want to show her steps. Around the kitchen sat a row of young men and women, and the open sitting-room doorway was crowded with the faces of non-dancing guests who wanted to watch the sets.

An eight-hand reel had just been danced and the girls, giddy from the much swinging of the final figure, had been led back to their seats. Mattie Lyall came out with a dipper of water and sprinkled the floor, from which a fine dust was rising. Toff's violin purred under his hands as he waited for the next set to form. The dancers were slow about it. There was not the rush for the floor that there had been earlier in the evening, for the supper table was now spread in the dining-room and most of the guests were hungry.

"Fill up dere, boys," shouted the fiddler impatiently. "Bring out your gals for de nex' set."

After a moment Paul King led out Joan Shelley from the shadowy corner where they had been sitting. They had already danced several sets together; Joan had not danced with anybody else that evening. As they stood together under the light from the lamp on the shelf above them, many curious and disapproving eyes watched them. Connor Mitchell, who had been standing in the open outer doorway with the moonlight behind him, turned abruptly on his heel and went out.

Paul King leaned his head against the wall and watched the watchers with a smiling, defiant face as they waited for the set to form. He was a handsome fellow, with the easy, winning ways that women love. His hair curled in bronze masses about his head; his dark eyes were long and drowsy and laughing; there was a swarthy bloom on his round cheeks; and his lips were as red and beguiling as a girl's. A bad egg was Paul King, with a bad past and a bad future. He was shiftless and drunken; ugly tales were told of him. Not a man in Lyall's house that night but grudged him the privilege of standing up with Joan Shelley.

Joan was a slight, blossom-like girl in white, looking much like the pale, sweet-scented house rose she wore in her dark hair. Her face was colourless and young, very pure and softly curved. She had wonderfully sweet, dark blue eyes, generally dropped down, with notably long black lashes. There were many showier girls in the groups around her, but none half so lovely. She made all the rosy-cheeked beauties seem coarse and over-blown.

She left in Paul's clasp the hand by which he had led her out on the floor. Now and then he shifted his gaze from the faces before him to hers. When he did, she always looked up and they exchanged glances as if they had been utterly alone. Three other couples gradually took the floor and the reel began. Joan drifted through the figures with the grace of a wind-blown leaf. Paul danced with rollicking abandon, seldom taking his eyes from Joan's face. When the last mad whirl was over, Joan's brother came up and told her in an angry tone to go into the next room and dance no more, since she would dance with only one man. Joan looked at Paul. That look meant that she would do as he, and none other, told her. Paul nodded easily — he did not want any fuss just then — and the girl went obediently into the room. As she turned from him, Paul coolly reached out his hand and took the rose from her hair; then, with a triumphant glance around the room, he went out.

The autumn night was very clear and chill, with a faint, moaning wind blowing up from the northwest over the sea that lay shimmering before the door. Out beyond the cove the boats were nodding and curtsying on the swell, and over the shore fields the great red star of the lighthouse flared out against the silvery sky. Paul, with a whistle, sauntered down the sandy lane, thinking of Joan. How mightily he loved her — he, Paul King, who had made a mock of so many women and had never loved before! Ah, and she loved him. She had never said so in words, but eyes and tones had said it — she, Joan Shelley, the pick and pride of the Harbour girls, whom so many men had wooed, winning their trouble for their pains. He had won her; she was his and his only, for the asking. His heart was seething with pride and triumph and passion as he strode down to the shore and flung himself on the cold sand in the black shadow of Michael Brown's beached boat.

Byron Lyall, a grizzled, elderly man, half farmer, half fisherman, and Maxwell Holmes, the Prospect schoolteacher, came up to the boat presently. Paul lay softly and listened to what they were saying. He was not troubled by any sense of dishonour. Honour was something Paul King could not lose since it was something he had never possessed. They were talking of him and Joan.

"What a shame that a girl like Joan Shelley should throw herself away on a man like that," Holmes said.

Byron Lyall removed the pipe he was smoking and spat reflectively at his shadow.

"Darned shame," he agreed. "That girl's life will be ruined if she marries him, plum' ruined, and marry him she will. He's bewitched her—darned if I can understand it. A dozen better men have wanted her—Connor Mitchell for one. And he's a honest, steady fellow with a good home to offer her. If King had left her alone, she'd have taken Connor. She used to like him well enough. But that's all over. She's infatuated with King, the worthless scamp. She'll marry him and be sorry for it to her last day. He's bad clear through and always will be. Why, look you, Teacher, most men pull up a bit when they're courting a girl, no matter how wild they've been and will be again. Paul hasn't. It hasn't made any difference. He was dead drunk night afore last at the Harbour head, and he hasn't done a stroke of work for a month. And yet Joan Shelley'll take him."

"What are her people thinking of to let her go with him?" asked Holmes.

"She hasn't any but her brother. He's against Paul, of course, but it won't matter. The girl's fancy's caught and she'll go her own gait to ruin. Ruin, I tell ye. If she marries that handsome ne'er-do-well, she'll be a wretched woman all her days and none to pity her."

The two moved away then, and Paul lay motionless, face downward on the sand, his lips pressed against Joan's sweet, crushed rose. He felt no anger over Byron Lyall's unsparing condemnation. He knew it was true, every word of it. He *was* a worthless scamp and always would be. He knew that perfectly well. It was in his blood. None of his race had ever been respectable and he was worse than them all. He had no intention of trying to reform because he could not and because he did not even want to. He was not fit to touch Joan's hand. Yet he had meant to marry her!

But to spoil her life! Would it do that? Yes, it surely would. And if he were out of the way, taking his baleful charm out of her life, Connor Mitchell might and doubtless would win her yet and give her all he could not.

The man suddenly felt his eyes wet with tears. He had never shed a tear in his daredevil life before, but they came hot and stinging now. Something he had never known or thought of before entered into his passion and purified it. He loved Joan. Did he love her well enough to stand aside and let another take the sweetness and grace that was now his own? Did he love her well enough to save her from the poverty-stricken, shamed life she must lead with him? Did he love her better than himself?

"I ain't fit to think of her," he groaned. "I never did a decent thing in my life, as they say. But how can I give her up—God, how can I?"

He lay still a long time after that, until the moonlight crept around the boat and drove away the shadow. Then he got up and went slowly down to the water's edge with Joan's rose, all wet with his unaccustomed tears, in his hands. Slowly and reverently he plucked off the petals and scattered them on the ripples, where they drifted lightly off like fairy shallops on moonshine. When the last one had fluttered from his fingers, he went back to the house and hunted up Captain Alec Matheson, who was smoking his pipe in a corner of the verandah and watching the young folks dancing through the open door. The two men talked together for some time.

When the dance broke up and the guests straggled homeward, Paul sought Joan. Rob Shelley had his own girl to see home and relinquished the guardianship of his sister with a scowl. Paul strode out of the kitchen and down the steps at the side of Joan, smiling with his usual daredeviltry. He whistled noisily all the way up the lane.

"Great little dance," he said. "My last in Prospect for a spell, I guess."

"Why?" asked Joan wonderingly.

"Oh, I'm going to take a run down to South America in Matheson's schooner. Lord knows when I'll come back. This old place has got too deadly dull to suit me. I'm going to look for something livelier."

Joan's lips turned ashen under the fringes of her white fascinator. She trembled violently and put one of her small brown hands up to her throat. "You—you are not coming back?" she said faintly.

"Not likely. I'm pretty well tired of Prospect and I haven't got anything to hold me here. Things'll be livelier down south."

Joan said nothing more. They walked along the spruce-fringed roads where the moonbeams laughed down through the thick, softly swaying boughs. Paul whistled one rollicking tune after another. The girl bit her lips and clenched her hands. He cared nothing for her—he had been making a mock of her as of others. Hurt pride and wounded love fought each other in her soul. Pride conquered. She would not let him, or anyone, see that she cared. She would *not* care!

At her gate Paul held out his hand.

"Well, good-bye, Joan. I'm sailing tomorrow so I won't see you again—not for years likely. You will be some sober old married woman when I come back to Prospect, if I ever do."

"Good-bye," said Joan steadily. She gave him her cold hand and looked calmly into his face without quailing. She had loved him with all her heart, but now a fatal scorn of him was already mingling with her love. He was what they said he was, a scamp without principle or honour.

Paul whistled himself out of the Shelley lane and over the hill. Then he flung himself down under the spruces, crushed his face into the spicy frosted ferns, and had his black hour alone.

But when Captain Alec's schooner sailed out of the harbour the next day, Paul King was on board of her, the wildest and most hilarious of a wild and hilarious crew. Prospect people nodded their satisfaction.

"Good riddance," they said. "Paul King is black to the core. He never did a decent thing in his life."

A Soul That Was Not at Home

There was a very fine sunset on the night Paul and Miss Trevor first met, and she had lingered on the headland beyond Noel's Cove to delight in it. The west was splendid in daffodil and rose; away to the north there was a mackerel sky of little fiery golden clouds; and across the water straight from Miss Trevor's feet ran a sparkling path of light to the sun, whose rim had just touched the throbbing edge of the purple sea. Off to the left were softly swelling violet hills and beyond the sandshore, where little waves were crisping and silvering, there was a harbour where scores of slender masts were nodding against the gracious horizon.

Miss Trevor sighed with sheer happiness in all the wonderful, fleeting, elusive loveliness of sky and sea. Then she turned to look back at Noel's Cove, dim and shadowy in the gloom of the tall headlands, and she saw Paul.

It did not occur to her that he could be a shore boy — she knew the shore type too well. She thought his coming mysterious, for she was sure he had not come along the sand, and the tide was too high for him to have come past the other headland. Yet there he was, sitting on a red sandstone boulder, with his bare, bronzed, shapely little legs crossed in front of him and his hands clasped around his knee. He was not looking at Miss Trevor but at the sunset — or, rather, it seemed as if he were looking through the sunset to still grander and more radiant splendours beyond, of which the things seen were only the pale reflections, not worthy of attention from those who had the gift of further sight.

Miss Trevor looked him over carefully with eyes that had seen a good many people in many parts of the world for more years than she found it altogether pleasant to acknowledge, and she concluded that he was quite the handsomest lad she had ever seen. He had a lithe, supple body, with sloping shoulders and a brown, satin throat. His hair was thick and wavy, of a fine reddish chestnut; his brows were very straight and much darker than his hair; and his eyes were large and grey and meditative. The modelling of chin and jaw was perfect and his mouth was delicious, being full without pouting, the crimson lips just softly touching, and curving into finely finished little corners that narrowly escaped being dimpled.

His attire was a blue cotton shirt and a pair of scanty corduroy knickerbockers, but he wore it with such an unconscious air of purple and fine linen that Miss Trevor was tricked into believing him much better dressed than he really was.

Presently he smiled dreamily, and the smile completed her subjugation. It was not merely an affair of lip and eye, as are most smiles; it seemed an illumination of his whole body, as if some lamp had suddenly burst into flame inside of him, irradiating him from his chestnut crown to the tips of his unspoiled toes. Best of all, it was involuntary, born of no external effort or motive, but simply the outflashing of some wild, delicious thought that was as untrammelled and freakish as the wind of the sea.

Miss Trevor made up her mind that she must find out all about him, and she stepped out from the shadows of the rocks into the vivid, eerie light that was glowing all along the shore. The boy turned his head and looked at her, first with surprise, then with inquiry, then with admiration. Miss Trevor, in a white dress with a lace scarf on her dark, stately head, was well worth admiring. She smiled at him and Paul smiled back. It was not quite up to his first smile, having more of the effect of being put on from the outside, but at least it conveyed the subtly flattering impression that it had been put on solely for her, and they were as good friends from that moment as if they had known each other for a hundred years. Miss Trevor had enough discrimination to realize this and know that she need not waste time in becoming acquainted.

"I want to know your name and where you live and what you were looking at beyond the sunset," she said.

"My name is Paul Hubert. I live over there. And I can't tell just what I saw in the sunset, but when I go home I'm going to write it all in my foolscap book."

In her surprise over the second clause of his answer, Miss Trevor forgot, at first, to appreciate the last. "Over there," according to his gesture, was up at the head of Noel's Cove, where there was a little grey house perched on the rocks and looking like a large seashell cast up by the tide. The house had a stovepipe coming out of its roof in lieu of a chimney, and two of its window panes were replaced by shingles. Could this boy, who looked as young princes should—and seldom do—live there? Then he was a shore boy after all.

"Who lives there with you?" she asked. "You see"—plaintively—"I must ask questions about you. I know we like each other, and that is all that really matters. But there are some tiresome items which it would be convenient to know. For example, have you a father—a mother? Are there any more of you? How long have you been yourself?"

Paul did not reply immediately. He clasped his hands behind him and looked at her affectionately.

"I like the way you talk," he said. "I never knew anybody did talk like that except folks in books and my rock people."

"Your rock people?"

"I'm eleven years old. I haven't any father or mother, they're dead. I live over there with Stephen Kane. Stephen is splendid. He plays the violin and takes me fishing in his boat. When I get bigger he's going shares with me. I love him, and I love my rock people too."

"What do you mean by your rock people?" asked Miss Trevor, enjoying herself hugely. This was the only child she had ever met who talked as she wanted children to talk and who understood her remarks without having to have them translated.

"Nora is one of them," said Paul, "the best one of them. I love her better than all the others because she came first. She lives around that point and she has black eyes and black hair and she knows all about the mermaids and water kelpies. You ought to hear the stories she can tell. Then there are the Twin Sailors. They don't live anywhere — they sail all the time, but they often come ashore to talk to me. They are a pair of jolly tars and they have seen everything in the world — and more than what's in the world, if you only knew it. Do you know what happened to the Youngest Twin Sailor once? He was sailing and he sailed right into a moonglade. A moonglade is the track the full moon makes on the water when it is rising from the sea, you know. Well, the Youngest Twin Sailor sailed along the moonglade till he came right up to the moon, and there was a little golden door in the moon and he opened it and sailed right through. He had some wonderful adventures inside the moon — I've got them all written down in my foolscap book. Then there is the Golden Lady of the Cave. One day I found a big cave down the shore and I went in and in and in — and after a while I found the Golden Lady. She has golden hair right down to her feet, and her dress is all glittering and glistening like gold that is alive. And she has a golden harp and she plays all day long on it — you might hear the music if you'd listen carefully, but prob'bly you'd think it was only the wind among the rocks. I've never told Nora about the Golden Lady, because I think it would hurt her feelings. It even hurts her feelings when I talk too long with the Twin Sailors. And I hate to hurt Nora's feelings, because I do love her best of all my rock people."

"Paul! How much of this is true?" gasped Miss Trevor.

"Why, none of it!" said Paul, opening his eyes widely and reproachfully. "I thought you would know that. If I'd s'posed you wouldn't I'd have warned you there wasn't any of it true. I thought you were one of the kind that would know."

"I am. Oh, I am!" said Miss Trevor eagerly. "I really would have known if I had stopped to think. Well, it's getting late now. I must go back, although I don't want to. But I'm coming to see you again. Will you be here tomorrow afternoon?"

Paul nodded.

"Yes. I promised to meet the Youngest Twin Sailor down at the striped rocks tomorrow afternoon, but the day after will do just as well. That is the beauty of the rock people, you know. You can always depend on them to be there just when you want them. The Youngest Twin Sailor won't mind — he's very good-tempered. If it was the Oldest Twin I dare say he'd be cross. I have my suspicions about that Oldest Twin sometimes. I b'lieve he'd be a pirate if he dared. You don't know how fierce he can look at times. There's really something very mysterious about him."

On her way back to the hotel Miss Trevor remembered the foolscap book.

"I must get him to show it to me," she mused, smiling. "Why, the boy is a born genius — and to think he should be a shore boy! I can't understand it. And here I am loving him already. Well, a woman has to love something — and you don't have to know people for years before you can love them."

Paul was waiting on the Noel's Cove rocks for Miss Trevor the next afternoon. He was not alone; a tall man, with a lined, strong-featured face and a grey beard, was with him. The man was clad in a rough suit and looked what he was, a 'longshore fisherman. But he had deep-set, kindly eyes, and Miss Trevor liked his face. He moved off to one side when she came and stood there for a little, apparently gazing out to sea, while Paul and Miss Trevor talked. Then he walked away up the cove and disappeared in his little grey house.

"Stephen came down to see if you were a suitable person for me to talk to," said Paul gravely.

"I hope he thinks I am," said Miss Trevor, amused.

"Oh, he does! He wouldn't have gone away and left us alone if he didn't. Stephen is very particular who he lets me 'sociate with. Why, even the rock people now — I had to promise I'd never let the Twin Sailors swear before he'd allow me to be friends with them. Sometimes I know by the look of the Oldest Twin that he's just dying to swear, but I never let him, because I promised Stephen. I'd do anything for Stephen. He's awful good to me. Stephen's bringing me up, you know, and he's bound to do it well. We're just perfectly happy here, only I wish I'd more books to read. We go fishing, and when we come home at night I help Stephen clean the fish and then we sit outside the door and he plays the violin for me. We sit there for hours sometimes. We never talk much—Stephen isn't much of a hand for talking—but we just sit and think. There's not many men like Stephen, I can tell you."

Miss Trevor did not get a glimpse of the foolscap book that day, nor for many days after. Paul blushed all over his beautiful face whenever she mentioned it.

"Oh, I couldn't show you that," he said uncomfortably. "Why, I've never even showed it to Stephen—or Nora. Let me tell you something else instead, something that happened to me once long ago. You'll find it more interesting than the foolscap book, only you must remember it isn't true! You won't forget that, will you?"

"I'll try to remember," Miss Trevor agreed.

"Well, I was sitting here one evening just like I was last night, and the sun was setting. And an enchanted boat came sailing over the sea and I got into her. The boat was all pearly like the inside of the mussel shells, and her sail was like moonshine. Well, I sailed right across to the sunset. Think of that—I've been in the sunset! And what do you suppose it is? The sunset is a land all flowers, like a great garden, and the clouds are beds of flowers. We sailed into a great big harbour, a thousand times bigger than the harbour over there at your hotel, and I stepped out of the boat on a 'normous meadow all roses. I stayed there for ever so long. It seemed almost a year, but the Youngest Twin Sailor says I was only away a few hours or so. You see, in Sunset Land the time is ever so much longer than it is here. But I was glad to come back too. I'm always glad to come back to the cove and Stephen. Now, you know this never really happened."

Miss Trevor would not give up the foolscap book so easily, but for a long time Paul refused to show it to her. She came to the cove every day, and every day Paul seemed more delightful to her. He was so quaint, so clever, so spontaneous. Yet there was nothing premature or unnatural about him. He was wholly boy, fond of fun and frolic, not too good for little spurts of quick temper now and again, though, as he was careful to explain to Miss Trevor, he never showed them to a lady.

"I get real mad with the Twin Sailors sometimes, and even with Stephen, for all he's so good to me. But I couldn't be mad with you or Nora or the Golden Lady. It would never do."

Every day he had some new story to tell of a wonderful adventure on rock or sea, always taking the precaution of assuring her beforehand that it wasn't true. The boy's fancy was like a prism, separating every ray that fell upon it into rainbows. He was passionately fond of the shore and water. The only world for him beyond Noel's Cove was the world of his imagination. He had no companions except Stephen and the "rock people."

"And now you," he told Miss Trevor. "I love you too, but I know you'll be going away before long, so I don't let myself love you as much — quite — as Stephen and the rock people."

"But you could, couldn't you?" pleaded Miss Trevor. "If you and I were to go on being together every day, you could love me just as well as you love them, couldn't you?"

Paul considered in a charming way he had.

"Of course I could love you better than the Twin Sailors and the Golden Lady," he announced finally. "And I think perhaps I could love you as much as I love Stephen. But not as much as Nora — oh, no, I wouldn't love you quite as much as Nora. She was first, you see; she's always been there. I feel sure I couldn't ever love anybody as much as Nora."

One day when Stephen was out to the mackerel grounds, Paul took Miss Trevor into the little grey house and showed her his treasures. They climbed the ladder in one corner to the loft where Paul slept. The window of it, small and square-paned, looked seaward, and the moan of the sea and the pipe of the wind sounded there night and day. Paul had many rare shells and seaweeds, curious flotsam and jetsam of shore storms, and he had a small shelf full of books.

"They're splendid," he said enthusiastically. "Stephen brought me them all. Every time Stephen goes to town to ship his mackerel he brings me home a new book."

"Were you ever in town yourself?" asked Miss Trevor.

"Oh, yes, twice. Stephen took me. It was a wonderful place. I tell you, when I next met the Twin Sailors it was me did the talking then. I had to tell them about all I saw and all that had happened. And Nora was ever so interested too. The Golden Lady wasn't, though — she didn't hardly listen. Golden people are like that."

"Would you like," said Miss Trevor, watching him closely, "to live always in a town and have all the books you wanted and play with real girls and boys — and visit those strange lands your twin sailors tell you of?"

Paul looked startled.

"I — don't — know," he said doubtfully. "I don't think I'd like it very well if Stephen and Nora weren't there too."

But the new thought remained in his mind. It came back to him at intervals, seeming less new and startling every time.

"And why not?" Miss Trevor asked herself. "The boy should have a chance. I shall never have a son of my own—he shall be to me in the place of one."

The day came when Paul at last showed her the foolscap book. He brought it to her as she sat on the rocks of the headland.

"I'm going to run around and talk to Nora while you read it," he said. "I'm afraid I've been neglecting her lately—and I think she feels it."

Miss Trevor took the foolscap book. It was made of several sheets of paper sewed together and encased in an oilcloth cover. It was nearly filled with writing in a round childish hand and it was very neat, although the orthography was rather wild and the punctuation capricious. Miss Trevor read it through in no very long time. It was a curious medley of quaint thoughts and fancies. Conversations with the Twin Sailors filled many of the pages; accounts of Paul's "adventures" occupied others. Sometimes it seemed impossible that a child of eleven should have written them, then would come an expression so boyish and naive that Miss Trevor laughed delightedly over it. When she finished the book and closed it she found Stephen Kane at her elbow. He removed his pipe and nodded at the foolscap book.

"What do you think of it?" he said.

"I think it is wonderful. Paul is a very clever child."

"I've often thought so," said Stephen laconically. He thrust his hands into his pockets and gazed moodily out to sea. Miss Trevor had never before had an opportunity to talk to him in Paul's absence and she determined to make the most of it.

"I want to know something about Paul," she said, "all about him. Is he any relation to you?"

"No. I expected to marry his mother once, though," said Stephen unemotionally. His hand in his pocket was clutching his pipe fiercely, but Miss Trevor could not know that. "She was a shore girl and very pretty. Well, she fell in love with a young fellow that came teaching up t' the harbour school and he with her. They got married and she went away with him. He was a good enough sort of chap. I know that now, though once I wasn't disposed to think much good of him. But 'twas a mistake all the same; Rachel couldn't live away from the shore. She fretted and pined and broke her heart for it away there in his world. Finally her husband died and she came back—but it was too late for her. She only lived a month—and there was Paul, a baby of two. I took him. There was nobody else. Rachel had no relatives nor her husband either. I've done what I could for him—not that it's been much, perhaps."

"I am sure you have done a great deal for him," said Miss Trevor rather patronizingly. "But I think he should have more than you can give him now. He should be sent to school."

Stephen nodded.

"Maybe. He never went to school. The harbour school was too far away. I taught him to read and write and bought him all the books I could afford. But I can't do any more for him."

"But I can," said Miss Trevor, "and I want to. Will you give Paul to me, Mr. Kane? I love him dearly and he shall have every advantage. I'm rich — I can do a great deal for him."

Stephen continued to gaze out to sea with an expressionless face. Finally he said: "I've been expecting to hear you say something of the sort. I don't know. If you took Paul away, he'd grow to be a cleverer man and a richer man maybe, but would he be any better — or happier? He's his mother's son — he loves the sea and its ways. There's nothing of his father in him except his hankering after books. But I won't choose for him — he can go if he likes — he can go if he likes."

In the end Paul "liked," since Stephen refused to influence him by so much as a word. Paul thought Stephen didn't seem to care much whether he went or stayed, and he was dazzled by Miss Trevor's charm and the lure of books and knowledge she held out to him.

"I'll go, I guess," he said, with a long sigh.

Miss Trevor clasped him close to her and kissed him maternally. Paul kissed her cheek shyly in return. He thought it very wonderful that he was to live with her always. He felt happy and excited — so happy and excited that the parting when it came slipped over him lightly. Miss Trevor even thought he took it too easily and had a vague wish that he had shown more sorrow. Stephen said farewell to the boy he loved better than life with no visible emotion.

"Good-bye, Paul. Be a good boy and learn all you can." He hesitated a moment and then said slowly, "If you don't like it, come back."

"Did you bid good-bye to your rock people?" Miss Trevor asked him with a smile as they drove away.

"No. I — couldn't — I — I — didn't even tell them I was going away. Nora would break her heart. I'd rather not talk of them anymore, if you please. Maybe I won't want them when I've plenty of books and lots of other boys and girls — real ones — to play with."

They drove the ten miles to the town where they were to take the train the next day. Paul enjoyed the drive and the sights of the busy streets at its end.

He was all excitement and animation. After they had had tea at the house of the friend where Miss Trevor meant to spend the night, they went for a walk in the park. Paul was tired and very quiet when they came back. He was put away to sleep in a bedroom whose splendours frightened him, and left alone.

At first Paul lay very still on his luxurious perfumed pillows. It was the first night he had ever spent away from the little seaward-looking loft where he could touch the rafters with his hands. He thought of it now and a lump came into his throat and a strange, new, bitter longing came into his heart. He missed the sea plashing on the rocks below him — he could not sleep without that old lullaby. He turned his face into the pillow, and the longing and loneliness grew worse and hurt him until he moaned. Oh, he wanted to be back home! Surely he had not left it — he could never have meant to leave it. Out there the stars would be shining over the harbour. Stephen would be sitting at the door, all alone, with his violin. But he would not be playing it — all at once Paul knew he would not be playing it. He would be sitting there with his head bowed and the loneliness in his heart calling to the loneliness in Paul's heart over all the miles between them. Oh, he could never have really meant to leave Stephen.

And Nora? Nora would be down on the rocks waiting for him — for him, Paul, who would never come to her more. He could see her elfin little face peering around the point, watching for him wistfully.

Paul sat up in bed, choking with tears. Oh, what were books and strange countries? — what was even Miss Trevor, the friend of a month? — to the call of the sea and Stephen's kind, deep eyes and his dear rock people? He could not stay away from them — never — never.

He slipped out of bed very softly and dressed in the dark. Then he lighted the lamp timidly and opened the little brown chest Stephen had given him. It held his books and his treasures, but he took out only a pencil, a bit of paper and the foolscap book. With a hand shaking in his eagerness, he wrote:

> *dear miss Trever*
>
> *Im going back home, dont be fritened about me because I know the way. Ive got to go. something is calling me. dont be cross. I love you, but I cant stay. Im leaving my foolscap book for you, you can keep it always but I must go back to Stephen and nora*
>
> *Paul*

He put the note on the foolscap book and laid them on the table. Then he blew out the light, took his cap and went softly out. The house was very still. Holding his breath, he tiptoed downstairs and opened the front door. Before it ran the street which went, he knew, straight out to the country road that led home. Paul closed the door and stole down the steps, his heart beating painfully, but when he reached the sidewalk he broke into a frantic run under the limes. It was late and no one was out on that quiet street. He ran until his breath gave out, then walked miserably until he recovered it, and then ran again. He dared not stop running until he was out of that horrible town, which seemed like a prison closing around him, where the houses shut out the stars and the wind could only creep in a narrow space like a fettered, cringing thing, instead of sweeping grandly over great salt wastes of sea.

At last the houses grew few and scattered, and finally he left them behind. He drew a long breath; this was better—rather smothering yet, of course, with nothing but hills and fields and dark woods all about him, but at least his own sky was above him, looking just the same as it looked out home at Noel's Cove. He recognized the stars as friends; how often Stephen had pointed them out to him as they sat at night by the door of the little house.

He was not at all frightened now. He knew the way home and the kind night was before him. Every step was bringing him nearer to Stephen and Nora and the Twin Sailors. He whistled as he walked sturdily along.

The dawn was just breaking when he reached Noel's Cove. The eastern sky was all pale rose and silver, and the sea was mottled over with dear grey ripples. In the west over the harbour the sky was a very fine ethereal blue and the wind blew from there, salt and bracing. Paul was tired, but he ran lightly down the shelving rocks to the cove. Stephen was getting ready to launch his boat. When he saw Paul he started and a strange, vivid, exultant expression flashed across his face.

Paul felt a sudden chill—the upspringing fountain of his gladness was checked in mid-leap. He had known no doubt on the way home—all that long, weary walk he had known no doubt—but now?

"Stephen," he cried. "I've come back! I had to! Stephen, are you glad—are you glad?"

Stephen's face was as emotionless as ever. The burst of feeling which had frightened Paul by its unaccustomedness had passed like a fleeting outbreak of sunshine between dull clouds.

"I reckon I am," he said. "Yes, I reckon I am. I kind of—hoped—you would come back. You'd better go in and get some breakfast."

Paul's eyes were as radiant as the deepening dawn. He knew Stephen was glad and he knew there was nothing more to be said about it. They were back just where they were before Miss Trevor came—back in their perfect, unmarred, sufficient comradeship.

"I must just run around and see Nora first," said Paul.

Abel and His Great Adventure

"Come out of doors, master—come out of doors. I can't talk or think right with walls around me—never could. Let's go out to the garden." These were almost the first words I ever heard Abel Armstrong say. He was a member of the board of school trustees in Stillwater, and I had not met him before this late May evening, when I had gone down to confer with him upon some small matter of business. For I was "the new schoolmaster" in Stillwater, having taken the school for the summer term.

It was a rather lonely country district—a fact of which I was glad, for life had been going somewhat awry with me and my heart was sore and rebellious over many things that have nothing to do with this narration. Stillwater offered time and opportunity for healing and counsel. Yet, looking back, I doubt if I should have found either had it not been for Abel and his beloved garden.

Abel Armstrong (he was always called "Old Abel", though he was barely sixty) lived in a quaint, gray house close by the harbour shore. I heard a good deal about him before I saw him. He was called "queer", but Stillwater folks seemed to be very fond of him. He and his sister, Tamzine, lived together; she, so my garrulous landlady informed me, had not been sound of mind at times for many years; but she was all right now, only odd and quiet. Abel had gone to college for a year when he was young, but had given it up when Tamzine "went crazy". There was no one else to look after her. Abel had settled down to it with apparent content: at least he had never complained.

"Always took things easy, Abel did," said Mrs. Campbell. "Never seemed to worry over disappointments and trials as most folks do. Seems to me that as long as Abel Armstrong can stride up and down in that garden of his, reciting poetry and speeches, or talking to that yaller cat of his as if it was a human, he doesn't care much how the world wags on. He never had much git-up-and-git. His father was a hustler, but the family didn't take after him. They all favoured the mother's people—sorter shiftless and dreamy. 'Taint the way to git on in this world."

No, good and worthy Mrs. Campbell. It was not the way to get on in your world; but there are other worlds where getting on is estimated by different standards, and Abel Armstrong lived in one of these—a world far beyond the ken of the thrifty Stillwater farmers and fishers. Something of this I had sensed, even before I saw him; and that night in his garden, under a sky of smoky red, blossoming into stars above the harbour, I found a friend whose personality and philosophy were to calm and harmonize and enrich my whole existence. This sketch is my grateful tribute to one of the rarest and finest souls God ever clothed with clay.

He was a tall man, somewhat ungainly of figure and homely of face. But his large, deep eyes of velvety nut-brown were very beautiful and marvellously bright and clear for a man of his age. He wore a little pointed, well-cared-for beard, innocent of gray; but his hair was grizzled, and altogether he had the appearance of a man who had passed through many sorrows which had marked his body as well as his soul. Looking at him, I doubted Mrs. Campbell's conclusion that he had not "minded" giving up college. This man had given up much and felt it deeply; but he had outlived the pain and the blessing of sacrifice had come to him. His voice was very melodious and beautiful, and the brown hand he held out to me was peculiarly long and shapely and flexible.

We went out to the garden in the scented moist air of a maritime spring evening. Behind the garden was a cloudy pine wood; the house closed it in on the left, while in front and on the right a row of tall Lombardy poplars stood out in stately purple silhouette against the sunset sky.

"Always liked Lombardies," said Abel, waving a long arm at them. "They are the trees of princesses. When I was a boy they were fashionable. Anyone who had any pretensions to gentility had a row of Lombardies at the foot of his lawn or up his lane, or at any rate one on either side of his front door. They're out of fashion now. Folks complain they die at the top and get ragged-looking. So they do—so they do, if you don't risk your neck every spring climbing up a light ladder to trim them out as I do. My neck isn't worth much to anyone, which, I suppose, is why I've never broken it; and *my* Lombardies never look out-at-elbows. My mother was especially fond of them. She liked their dignity and their stand-offishness. *They* don't hobnob with every Tom, Dick and Harry. If it's pines for company, master, it's Lombardies for society."

We stepped from the front doorstone into the garden. There was another entrance—a sagging gate flanked by two branching white lilacs. From it a little dappled path led to a huge apple-tree in the centre, a great swelling cone of rosy blossom with a mossy circular seat around its trunk. But Abel's favourite seat, so he told me, was lower down the slope, under a little trellis overhung with the delicate emerald of young hop-vines. He led me to it and pointed proudly to the fine view of the harbour visible from it. The early sunset glow of rose and flame had faded out of the sky; the water was silvery and mirror-like; dim sails drifted along by the darkening shore. A bell was ringing in a small Catholic chapel across the harbour. Mellowly and dreamily sweet the chime floated through the dusk, blent with the moan of the sea. The great revolving light at the channel trembled and flashed against the opal sky, and far out, beyond the golden sand-dunes of the bar, was the crinkled gray ribbon of a passing steamer's smoke.

"There, isn't that view worth looking at?" said old Abel, with a loving, proprietary pride. "You don't have to pay anything for it, either. All that sea and sky free—'without money and without price'. Let's sit down here in the hop-vine arbour, master. There'll be a moonrise presently. I'm never tired of finding out what a moonrise sheen can be like over that sea. There's a surprise in it every time. Now, master, you're getting your mouth in the proper shape to talk business—but don't you do it. Nobody should talk business when he's expecting a moonrise. Not that I like talking business at any time."

"Unfortunately it has to be talked of sometimes, Mr. Armstrong," I said.

"Yes, it seems to be a necessary evil, master," he acknowledged. "But I know what business you've come upon, and we can settle it in five minutes after the moon's well up. I'll just agree to everything you and the other two trustees want. Lord knows why they ever put me on the school board. Maybe it's because I'm so ornamental. They wanted one good-looking man, I reckon."

His low chuckle, so full of mirth and so free from malice, was infectious. I laughed also, as I sat down in the hop-vine arbour.

"Now, you needn't talk if you don't want to," he said. "And I won't. We'll just sit here, sociable like, and if we think of anything worth while to say we'll say it. Otherwise, not. If you can sit in silence with a person for half an hour and feel comfortable, you and that person can be friends. If you can't, friends you'll never be, and you needn't waste time in trying."

Abel and I passed successfully the test of silence that evening in the hop-vine arbour. I was strangely content to sit and think—something I had not cared to do lately. A peace, long unknown to my stormy soul, seemed hovering near it. The garden was steeped in it; old Abel's personality radiated it. I looked about me and wondered whence came the charm of that tangled, unworldly spot.

"Nice and far from the market-place isn't it?" asked Abel suddenly, as if he had heard my unasked question. "No buying and selling and getting gain here. Nothing was ever sold out of *this* garden. Tamzine has her vegetable plot over yonder, but what we don't eat we give away. Geordie Marr down the harbour has a big garden like this and he sells heaps of flowers and fruit and vegetables to the hotel folks. He thinks I'm an awful fool because I won't do the same. Well, he gets money out of his garden and I get happiness out of mine. That's the difference. S'posing I could make more money — what then? I'd only be taking it from people that needed it more. There's enough for Tamzine and me. As for Geordie Marr, there isn't a more unhappy creature on God's earth — he's always stewing in a broth of trouble, poor man. O' course, he brews up most of it for himself, but I reckon that doesn't make it any easier to bear. Ever sit in a hop-vine arbour before, master?"

I was to grow used to Abel's abrupt change of subject. I answered that I never had.

"Great place for dreaming," said Abel complacently. "Being young, no doubt, you dream a-plenty."

I answered hotly and bitterly that I had done with dreams.

"No, you haven't," said Abel meditatively. "You may *think* you have. What then? First thing you know you'll be dreaming again — thank the Lord for it. I ain't going to ask you what's soured you on dreaming just now. After awhile you'll begin again, especially if you come to this garden as much as I hope you will. It's chockful of dreams — *any* kind of dreams. You take your choice. Now, *I* favour dreams of adventures, if you'll believe it. I'm sixty-one and I never do anything rasher than go out cod-fishing on a fine day, but I still lust after adventures. Then I dream I'm an awful fellow — blood-thirsty."

I burst out laughing. Perhaps laughter was somewhat rare in that old garden. Tamzine, who was weeding at the far end, lifted her head in a startled fashion and walked past us into the house. She did not look at us or speak to us. She was reputed to be abnormally shy. She was very stout and wore a dress of bright red-and-white striped material. Her face was round and blank, but her reddish hair was abundant and beautiful. A huge, orange-coloured cat was at her heels; as she passed us he bounded over to the arbour and sprang up on Abel's knee. He was a gorgeous brute, with vivid green eyes, and immense white double paws.

"Captain Kidd, Mr. Woodley." He introduced us as seriously as if the cat had been a human being. Neither Captain Kidd nor I responded very enthusiastically.

"You don't like cats, I reckon, master," said Abel, stroking the Captain's velvet back. "I don't blame you. I was never fond of them myself until I found the Captain. I saved his life and when you've saved a creature's life you're bound to love it. It's next thing to giving it life. There are some terrible thoughtless people in the world, master. Some of those city folks who have summer homes down the harbour are so thoughtless that they're cruel. It's the worst kind of cruelty, I think — the thoughtless kind. You can't cope with it. They keep cats there in the summer and feed them and pet them and doll them up with ribbons and collars; and then in the fall they go off and leave them to starve or freeze. It makes my blood boil, master."

"One day last winter I found a poor old mother cat dead on the shore, lying against the skin and bone bodies of her three little kittens. She had died trying to shelter them. She had her poor stiff claws around them. Master, I cried. Then I swore. Then I carried those poor little kittens home and fed 'hem up and found good homes for them. I know the woman who left the cat. When she comes back this summer I'm going to go down and tell her my opinion of her. It'll be rank meddling, but, lord, how I love meddling in a good cause."

"Was Captain Kidd one of the forsaken?" I asked.

"Yes. I found him one bitter cold day in winter caught in the branches of a tree by his darn-fool ribbon collar. He was almost starving. Lord, if you could have seen his eyes! He was nothing but a kitten, and he'd got his living somehow since he'd been left till he got hung up. When I loosed him he gave my hand a pitiful swipe with his little red tongue. He wasn't the prosperous free-booter you behold now. He was meek as Moses. That was nine years ago. His life has been long in the land for a cat. He's a good old pal, the Captain is."

"I should have expected you to have a dog," I said.

Abel shook his head.

"I had a dog once. I cared so much for him that when he died I couldn't bear the thought of ever getting another in his place. He was a *friend*—you understand? The Captain's only a pal. I'm fond of the Captain—all the fonder because of the spice of deviltry there is in all cats. But I *loved* my dog. There isn't any devil in a good dog. That's why they're more lovable than cats—but I'm darned if they're as interesting."

I laughed as I rose regretfully.

"Must you go, master? And we haven't talked any business after all. I reckon it's that stove matter you've come about. It's like those two fool trustees to start up a stove sputter in spring. It's a wonder they didn't leave it till dog-days and begin then."

"They merely wished me to ask you if you approved of putting in a new stove."

"Tell them to put in a new stove—any kind of a new stove—and be hanged to them," rejoined Abel. "As for you, master, you're welcome to this garden any time. If you're tired or lonely, or too ambitious or angry, come here and sit awhile, master. Do you think any man could keep mad if he sat and looked into the heart of a pansy for ten minutes? When you feel like talking, I'll talk, and when you feel like thinking, I'll let you. I'm a great hand to leave folks alone."

"I think I'll come often," I said, "perhaps too often."

"Not likely, master—not likely—not after we've watched a moonrise contentedly together. It's as good a test of compatibility as any I know. You're young and I'm old, but our souls are about the same age, I reckon, and we'll find lots to say to each other. Are you going straight home from here?"

"Yes."

"Then I'm going to bother you to stop for a moment at Mary Bascom's and give her a bouquet of my white lilacs. She loves 'em and I'm not going to wait till she's dead to send her flowers."

"She's very ill just now, isn't she?"

"She's got the Bascom consumption. That means she may die in a month, like her brother, or linger on for twenty years, like her father. But long or short, white lilac in spring is sweet, and I'm sending her a fresh bunch every day while it lasts. It's a rare night, master. I envy you your walk home in the moonlight along that shore."

"Better come part of the way with me," I suggested.

"No." Abel glanced at the house. "Tamzine never likes to be alone o' nights. So I take my moonlight walks in the garden. The moon's a great friend of mine, master. I've loved her ever since I can remember. When I was a little lad of eight I fell asleep in the garden one evening and wasn't missed. I woke up alone in the night and I was most scared to death, master. Lord, what shadows and queer noises there were! I darsn't move. I just sat there quaking, poor small mite. Then all at once I saw the moon looking down at me through the pine boughs, just like an old friend. I was comforted right off. Got up and walked to the house as brave as a lion, looking at her. Goodnight, master. Tell Mary the lilacs'll last another week yet."

From that night Abel and I were cronies. We walked and talked and kept silence and fished cod together. Stillwater people thought it very strange that I should prefer his society to that of the young fellows of my own age. Mrs. Campbell was quite worried over it, and opined that there had always been something queer about me. "Birds of a feather."

I loved that old garden by the harbour shore. Even Abel himself, I think, could hardly have felt a deeper affection for it. When its gate closed behind me it shut out the world and my corroding memories and discontents. In its peace my soul emptied itself of the bitterness which had been filling and spoiling it, and grew normal and healthy again, aided thereto by Abel's wise words. He never preached, but he radiated courage and endurance and a frank acceptance of the hard things of life, as well as a cordial welcome of its pleasant things. He was the sanest soul I ever met. He neither minimized ill nor exaggerated good, but he held that we should never be controlled by either.

Pain should not depress us unduly, nor pleasure lure us into forgetfulness and sloth. All unknowingly he made me realize that I had been a bit of a coward and a shirker. I began to understand that my personal woes were not the most important things in the universe, even to myself. In short, Abel taught me to laugh again; and when a man can laugh wholesomely things are not going too badly with him.

That old garden was always such a cheery place. Even when the east wind sang in minor and the waves on the gray shore were sad, hints of sunshine seemed to be lurking all about it. Perhaps this was because there were so many yellow flowers in it. Tamzine liked yellow flowers. Captain Kidd, too, always paraded it in panoply of gold. He was so large and effulgent that one hardly missed the sun. Considering his presence I wondered that the garden was always so full of singing birds. But the Captain never meddled with them. Probably he understood that his master would not have tolerated it for a moment. So there was always a song or a chirp somewhere. Overhead flew the gulls and the cranes. The wind in the pines always made a glad salutation. Abel and I paced the walks, in high converse on matters beyond the ken of cat or king.

"I liked to ponder on all problems, though I can never solve them," Abel used to say. "My father held that we should never talk of things we couldn't understand. But, lord, master, if we didn't the subjects for conversation would be mighty few. I reckon the gods laugh many a time to hear us, but what matter? So long as we remember that we're only men, and don't take to fancying ourselves gods, really knowing good and evil, I reckon our discussions won't do us or anyone much harm. So we'll have another whack at the origin of evil this evening, master."

Tamzine forgot to be shy with me at last, and gave me a broad smile of welcome every time I came. But she rarely spoke to me. She spent all her spare time weeding the garden, which she loved as well as Abel did. She was addicted to bright colours and always wore wrappers of very gorgeous print. She worshipped Abel and his word was a law unto her.

"I am very thankful Tamzine is so well," said Abel one evening as we watched the sunset. The day had begun sombrely in gray cloud and mist, but it ended in a pomp of scarlet and gold. "There was a time when she wasn't, master—you've heard? But for years now she has been quite able to look after herself. And so, if I fare forth on the last great adventure some of these days Tamzine will not be left helpless."

"She is ten years older than you. It is likely she will go before you," I said.

Abel shook his head and stroked his smart beard. I always suspected that beard of being Abel's last surviving vanity. It was always so carefully groomed, while I had no evidence that he ever combed his grizzled mop of hair.

"No, Tamzine will outlive me. She's got the Armstrong heart. I have the Marwood heart—my mother was a Marwood. We don't live to be old, and we go quick and easy. I'm glad of it. I don't think I'm a coward, master, but the thought of a lingering death gives me a queer sick feeling of horror. There, I'm not going to say any more about it. I just mentioned it so that some day when you hear that old Abel Armstrong has been found dead, you won't feel sorry. You'll remember I wanted it that way. Not that I'm tired of life either. It's very pleasant, what with my garden and Captain Kidd and the harbour out there. But it's a trifle monotonous at times and death will be something of a change, master. I'm real curious about it."

"I hate the thought of death," I said gloomily.

"Oh, you're young. The young always do. Death grows friendlier as we grow older. Not that one of us really wants to die, though, master. Tennyson spoke truth when he said that. There's old Mrs. Warner at the Channel Head. She's had heaps of trouble all her life, poor soul, and she's lost almost everyone she cared about. She's always saying that she'll be glad when her time comes, and she doesn't want to live any longer in this vale of tears. But when she takes a sick spell, lord, what a fuss she makes, master! Doctors from town and a trained nurse and enough medicine to kill a dog! Life may be a vale of tears, all right, master, but there are some folks who enjoy weeping, I reckon."

Summer passed through the garden with her procession of roses and lilies and hollyhocks and golden glow. The golden glow was particularly fine that year. There was a great bank of it at the lower end of the garden, like a huge billow of sunshine. Tamzine revelled in it, but Abel liked more subtly-tinted flowers. There was a certain dark wine-hued hollyhock which was a favourite with him. He would sit for hours looking steadfastly into one of its shallow satin cups. I found him so one afternoon in the hop-vine arbour.

"This colour always has a soothing effect on me," he explained. "Yellow excites me too much—makes me restless—makes me want to sail 'beyond the bourne of sunset'. I looked at that surge of golden glow down there today till I got all worked up and thought my life had been an awful failure. I found a dead butterfly and had a little funeral—buried it in the fern corner. And I thought I hadn't been any more use in the world than that poor little butterfly. Oh, I was woeful, master. Then I got me this hollyhock and sat down here to look at it alone. When a man's alone, master, he's most with God—or with the devil. The devil rampaged around me all the time I was looking at that golden glow; but God spoke to me through the hollyhock. And it seemed to me that a man who's as happy as I am and has got such a garden has made a real success of living."

"I hope I'll be able to make as much of a success," I said sincerely.

"I want you to make a different kind of success, though, master," said Abel, shaking his head. "I want you to *do* things—the things I'd have tried to do if I'd had the chance. It's in you to do them—if you set your teeth and go ahead."

"I believe I *can* set my teeth and go ahead now, thanks to you, Mr. Armstrong," I said. "I was heading straight for failure when I came here last spring; but you've changed my course."

"Given you a sort of compass to steer by, haven't I?" queried Abel with a smile. "I ain't too modest to take some credit for it. I saw I could do *you* some good. But my garden has done more than I did, if you'll believe it. It's wonderful what a garden can do for a man when he lets it have its way. Come, sit down here and bask, master. The sunshine may be gone to-morrow. Let's just sit and think."

We sat and thought for a long while. Presently Abel said abruptly:

"You don't see the folks I see in this garden, master. You don't see anybody but me and old Tamzine and Captain Kidd. I see all who used to be here long ago. It was a lively place then. There were plenty of us and we were as gay a set of youngsters as you'd find anywhere. We tossed laughter backwards and forwards here like a ball. And now old Tamzine and older Abel are all that are left."

He was silent a moment, looking at the phantoms of memory that paced invisibly to me the dappled walks and peeped merrily through the swinging boughs. Then he went on:

"Of all the folks I see here there are two that are more vivid and real than all the rest, master. One is my sister Alice. She died thirty years ago. She was very beautiful. You'd hardly believe that to look at Tamzine and me, would you? But it is true. We always called her Queen Alice—she was so stately and handsome. She had brown eyes and red gold hair, just the colour of that nasturtium there. She was father's favourite. The night she was born they didn't think my mother would live. Father walked this garden all night. And just under that old apple-tree he knelt at sunrise and thanked God when they came to tell him that all was well.

"Alice was always a creature of joy. This old garden rang with her laughter in those years. She seldom walked—she ran or danced. She only lived twenty years, but nineteen of them were so happy I've never pitied her over much. She had everything that makes life worth living—laughter and love, and at the last sorrow. James Milburn was her lover. It's thirty-one years since his ship sailed out of that harbour and Alice waved him good-bye from this garden. He never came back. His ship was never heard of again.

"When Alice gave up hope that it would be, she died of a broken heart. They say there's no such thing; but nothing else ailed Alice. She stood at yonder gate day after day and watched the harbour; and when at last she gave up hope life went with it. I remember the day: she had watched until sunset. Then she turned away from the gate. All the unrest and despair had gone out of her eyes. There was a terrible peace in them — the peace of the dead. 'He will never come back now, Abel,' she said to me.

"In less than a week she was dead. The others mourned her, but I didn't, master. She had sounded the deeps of living and there was nothing else to linger through the years for. *My* grief had spent itself earlier, when I walked this garden in agony because I could not help her. But often, on these long warm summer afternoons, I seem to hear Alice's laughter all over this garden; though she's been dead so long."

He lapsed into a reverie which I did not disturb, and it was not until another day that I learned of the other memory that he cherished. He reverted to it suddenly as we sat again in the hop-vine arbour, looking at the glimmering radiance of the September sea.

"Master, how many of us are sitting here?"

"Two in the flesh. How many in the spirit I know not," I answered, humouring his mood.

"There is one — the other of the two I spoke of the day I told you about Alice. It's harder for me to speak of this one."

"Don't speak of it if it hurts you," I said.

"But I want to. It's a whim of mine. Do you know why I told you of Alice and why I'm going to tell you of Mercedes? It's because I want someone to remember them and think of them sometimes after I'm gone. I can't bear that their names should be utterly forgotten by all living souls.

"My older brother, Alec, was a sailor, and on his last voyage to the West Indies he married and brought home a Spanish girl. My father and mother didn't like the match. Mercedes was a foreigner and a Catholic, and differed from us in every way. But I never blamed Alec after I saw her. It wasn't that she was so very pretty. She was slight and dark and ivory-coloured. But she was very graceful, and there was a charm about her, master — a mighty and potent charm. The women couldn't understand it. They wondered at Alec's infatuation for her. I never did. I — I loved her, too, master, before I had known her a day. Nobody ever knew it. Mercedes never dreamed of it. But it's lasted me all my life. I never wanted to think of any other woman. She spoiled a man for any other kind of woman—that little pale, dark-eyed Spanish girl. To love her was like drinking some rare sparkling wine. You'd never again have any taste for a commoner draught.

"I think she was very happy the year she spent here. Our thrifty women-folk in Stillwater jeered at her because she wasn't what they called capable. They said she couldn't do anything. But she could do one thing well—she could love. She worshipped Alec. I used to hate him for it. Oh, my heart has been very full of black thoughts in its time, master. But neither Alec nor Mercedes ever knew. And I'm thankful now that they were so happy. Alec made this arbour for Mercedes—at least he made the trellis, and she planted the vines.

"She used to sit here most of the time in summer. I suppose that's why I like to sit here. Her eyes would be dreamy and far-away until Alec would flash his welcome. How that used to torture me! But now I like to remember it. And her pretty soft foreign voice and little white hands. She died after she had lived here a year. They buried her and her baby in the graveyard of that little chapel over the harbour where the bell rings every evening. She used to like sitting here and listening to it. Alec lived a long while after, but he never married again. He's gone now, and nobody remembers Mercedes but me."

Abel lapsed into a reverie—a tryst with the past which I would not disturb. I thought he did not notice my departure, but as I opened the gate he stood up and waved his hand.

Three days later I went again to the old garden by the harbour shore. There was a red light on a distant sail. In the far west a sunset city was built around a great deep harbour of twilight. Palaces were there and bannered towers of crimson and gold. The air was full of music; there was one music of the wind and another of the waves, and still another of the distant bell from the chapel near which Mercedes slept. The garden was full of ripe odours and warm colours. The Lombardies around it were tall and sombre like the priestly forms of some mystic band. Abel was sitting in the hop-vine arbour; beside him Captain Kidd slept. I thought Abel was asleep, too; his head leaned against the trellis and his eyes were shut.

But when I reached the arbour I saw that he was not asleep. There was a strange, wise little smile on his lips as if he had attained to the ultimate wisdom and were laughing in no unkindly fashion at our old blind suppositions and perplexities.

Abel had gone on his Great Adventure.

Akin To Love

David Hartley had dropped in to pay a neighbourly call on Josephine Elliott. It was well along in the afternoon, and outside, in the clear crispness of a Canadian winter, the long blue shadows from the tall firs behind the house were falling over the snow.

It was a frosty day, and all the windows of every room where there was no fire were covered with silver palms. But the big, bright kitchen was warm and cosy, and somehow seemed to David more tempting than ever before, and that is saying a good deal. He had an uneasy feeling that he had stayed long enough and ought to go. Josephine was knitting at a long gray sock with doubly aggressive energy, and that was a sign that she was talked out. As long as Josephine had plenty to say, her plump white fingers, where her mother's wedding ring was lost in dimples, moved slowly among her needles. When conversation flagged she fell to her work as furiously as if a husband and half a dozen sons were waiting for its completion. David often wondered in his secret soul what Josephine did with all the interminable gray socks she knitted. Sometimes he concluded that she put them in the home missionary barrels; again, that she sold them to her hired man. At any rate, they were very warm and comfortable looking, and David sighed as he thought of the deplorable state his own socks were generally in.

When David sighed Josephine took alarm. She was afraid David was going to have one of his attacks of foolishness. She must head him off someway, so she rolled up the gray sock, stabbed the big pudgy ball with her needles, and said she guessed she'd get the tea.

David got up.

"Now, you're not going before tea?" said Josephine hospitably. "I'll have it all ready in no time."

"I ought to go home, I s'pose," said David, with the air and tone of a man dallying with a great temptation. "Zillah'll be waiting tea for me; and there's the stock to tend to."

"I guess Zillah won't wait long," said Josephine. She did not intend it at all, but there was a certain scornful ring in her voice. "You must stay. I've a fancy for company to tea."

David sat down again. He looked so pleased that Josephine went down on her knees behind the stove, ostensibly to get a stick of firewood, but really to hide her smile.

"I suppose he's tickled to death to think of getting a good square meal, after the starvation rations Zillah puts him on," she thought.

But Josephine misjudged David just as much as he misjudged her. She had really asked him to stay to tea out of pity, but David thought it was because she was lonesome, and he hailed that as an encouraging sign. And he was not thinking about getting a good meal either, although his dinner had been such a one as only Zillah Hartley could get up. As he leaned back in his cushioned chair and watched Josephine bustling about the kitchen, he was glorying in the fact that he could spend another hour with her, and sit opposite to her at the table while she poured his tea for him and passed him the biscuits, just as if — just as if —

Here Josephine looked straight at him with such intent and stern brown eyes that David felt she must have read his thoughts, and he colored guiltily. But Josephine did not even notice that he was blushing. She had only paused to wonder whether she would bring out cherry or strawberry preserve; and, having decided on the cherry, took her piercing gaze from David without having seen him at all. But he allowed his thoughts no more vagaries.

Josephine set the table with her mother's wedding china. She used it because it was the anniversary of her mother's wedding day, but David thought it was out of compliment to him. And, as he knew quite well that Josephine prized that china beyond all her other earthly possessions, he stroked his smooth-shaven, dimpled chin with the air of a man to whom is offered a very subtly sweet homage.

Josephine whisked in and out of the pantry, and up and down cellar, and with every whisk a new dainty was added to the table. Josephine, as everybody in Meadowby admitted, was past mistress in the noble art of cookery. Once upon a time rash matrons and ambitious young wives had aspired to rival her, but they had long ago realised the vanity of such efforts and dropped comfortably back to second place.

Josephine felt an artist's pride in her table when she set the teapot on its stand and invited David to sit in. There were pink slices of cold tongue, and crisp green pickles and spiced gooseberry, the recipe for which Josephine had invented herself, and which had taken first prize at the Provincial Exhibition for six successive years; there was a lemon pie which was a symphony in gold and silver, biscuits as light and white as snow, and moist, plummy cubes of fruit cake. There was the ruby-tinted cherry preserve, a mound of amber jelly, and, to crown all, steaming cups of tea, in flavour and fragrance unequalled.

And Josephine, too, sitting at the head of the table, with her smooth, glossy crimps of black hair and cheeks as rosy clear as they had been twenty years ago, when she had been a slender slip of girlhood and bashful young David Hartley had looked at her over his hymn-book in prayer-meeting and tramped all the way home a few feet behind her, because he was too shy to go boldly up and ask if he might see her home.

All taken together, what wonder if David lost his head over that tea-table and determined to ask Josephine the same old question once more? It was eighteen years since he had asked it for the first time, and two years since the last. He would try his luck again; Josephine was certainly more gracious than he remembered her to ever have been before.

When the meal was over Josephine cleared the table and washed the dishes. When she had taken a dry towel and sat down by the window to polish her china David understood that his opportunity had come. He moved over and sat down beside her on the sofa by the window.

Outside the sun was setting in a magnificent arch of light and colour over the snow-clad hills and deep blue St. Lawrence gulf. David grasped at the sunset as an introductory factor.

"Isn't that fine, Josephine?" he said admiringly. "It makes me think of that piece of poetry that used to be in the old Fifth Reader when we went to school. D'ye mind how the teacher used to drill us up in it on Friday afternoons? It begun

> 'Slow sinks more lovely ere his race is runAlong Morea's hills the setting sun.'"

Then David declaimed the whole passage in a sing-song tone, accompanied by a few crude gestures recalled from long-ago school-boy elocution. Josephine knew what was coming. Every time David proposed to her he had begun by reciting poetry. She twirled her towel around the last plate resignedly. If it had to come, the sooner it was over the better. Josephine knew by experience that there was no heading David off, despite his shyness, when he had once got along as far as the poetry.

"But it's going to be for the last time," she said determinedly. "I'm going to settle this question so decidedly to-night that there'll never be a repetition."

When David had finished his quotation he laid his hand on Josephine's plump arm.

"Josephine," he said huskily, "I s'pose you couldn't—could you now?—make up your mind to have me. I wish you would, Josephine—I wish you would. Don't you think you could, Josephine?"

Josephine folded up her towel, crossed her hands on it, and looked her wooer squarely in the eyes.

"David Hartley," she said deliberately, "what makes you go on asking me to marry you every once in a while when I've told you times out of mind that I can't and won't?"

"Because I can't help hoping that you'll change your mind through time," David replied meekly.

"Well, you just listen to me. I will not marry you. That is in the first place. And in the second, this is to be final. It has to be. You are never to ask me this again under any circumstances. If you do I will not answer you—I will not let on I hear you at all; but (and Josephine spoke very slowly and impressively) I will never speak to you again—never. We are good friends now, and I like you real well, and like to have you drop in for a neighbourly chat as often as you wish to, but there'll be an end, short and sudden, to that, if you don't mind what I say."

"Oh, Josephine, ain't that rather hard?" protested David feebly. It seemed terrible to be cut off from all hope with such finality as this.

"I mean every word of it," returned Josephine calmly. "You'd better go home now, David. I always feel as if I'd like to be alone for a spell after a disagreeable experience."

David obeyed sadly and put on his cap and overcoat. Josephine kindly warned him not to slip and break his legs on the porch, because the floor was as icy as anything; and she even lighted a candle and held it up at the kitchen door to guide him safely out. David, as he trudged sorrowfully homeward across the fields, carried with him the mental picture of a plump, sonsy woman, in a trim dress of plum-coloured homespun and ruffled blue-check apron, haloed by candlelight. It was not a very romantic vision, perhaps, but to David it was more beautiful than anything else in the world.

When David was gone Josephine shut the door with a little shiver. She blew out the candle, for it was not yet dark enough to justify artificial light to her thrifty mind. She thought the big, empty house, in which she was the only living thing, was very lonely. It was so still, except for the slow tick of the "grandfather's clock" and the soft purr and crackle of the wood in the stove. Josephine sat down by the window.

"I wish some of the Sentners would run down," she said aloud. "If David hadn't been so ridiculous I'd have got him to stay the evening. He can be good company when he likes—he's real well-read and intelligent. And he must have dismal times at home there with nobody but Zillah."

She looked across the yard to the little house at the other side of it, where her French-Canadian hired man lived, and watched the purple spiral of smoke from its chimney curling up against the crocus sky. Would she run over and see Mrs. Leon Poirier and her little black-eyed, brown-skinned baby? No, they never knew what to say to each other.

"If 'twasn't so cold I'd go up and see Ida," she said. "As it is, I guess I'd better fall back on my knitting, for I saw Jimmy Sentner's toes sticking through his socks the other day. How setback poor David did look, to be sure! But I think I've settled that marrying notion of his once for all and I'm glad of it."

She said the same thing next day to Mrs. Tom Sentner, who had come down to help her pick her geese. They were at work in the kitchen with a big tubful of feathers between them, and on the table a row of dead birds, which Leon had killed and brought in. Josephine was enveloped in a shapeless print wrapper, and had an apron tied tightly around her head to keep the down out of her beautiful hair, of which she was rather proud.

"What do you think, Ida?" she said, with a hearty laugh at the recollection. "David Hartley was here to tea last night, and asked me to marry him again. There's a persistent man for you. I can't brag of ever having had many beaux, but I've certainly had my fair share of proposals."

Mrs. Tom did not laugh. Her thin little face, with its faded prettiness, looked as if she never laughed.

"Why won't you marry him?" she said fretfully.

"Why should I?" retorted Josephine. "Tell me that, Ida Sentner."

"Because it is high time you were married," said Mrs. Tom decisively. "I don't believe in women living single. And I don't see what better you can do than take David Hartley."

Josephine looked at her sister with the interested expression of a person who is trying to understand some mental attitude in another which is a standing puzzle to her. Ida's evident wish to see her married always amused Josephine. Ida had married very young and for fifteen years her life had been one of drudgery and ill-health. Tom Sentner was a lazy, shiftless fellow. He neglected his family and was drunk half his time. Meadowby people said that he beat his wife when "on the spree," but Josephine did not believe that, because she did not think that Ida could keep from telling her if it were so. Ida Sentner was not given to bearing her trials in silence.

Had it not been for Josephine's assistance, Tom Sentner's family would have stood an excellent chance of starvation. Josephine practically kept them, and her generosity never failed or stinted. She fed and clothed her nephews and nieces, and all the gray socks whose destination puzzled David so much went to the Sentners.

As for Josephine herself, she had a good farm, a comfortable house, a plump bank account, and was an independent, unworried woman. And yet, in the face of all this, Mrs. Tom Sentner could bewail the fact that Josephine had no husband to look out for her. Josephine shrugged her shoulders and gave up the conundrum, merely saying ironically, in reply to her sister's remark:

"And go to live with Zillah Hartley?"

"You know very well you wouldn't have to do that. Ever since John Hartley's wife at the Creek died he's been wanting Zillah to go and keep house for him, and if David got married Zillah'd go quick. Catch her staying there if you were mistress! And David has such a beautiful house! It's ten times finer than yours, though I don't deny yours is comfortable. And his farm is the best in Meadowby and joins yours. Think what a beautiful property they'd make together. You're all right now, Josephine, but what will you do when you get old and have nobody to take care of you? I declare the thought worries me at night till I can't sleep."

"I should have thought you had enough worries of your own to keep you awake at nights without taking over any of mine," said Josephine drily. "As for old age, it's a good ways off for me yet. When your Jack gets old enough to have some sense he can come here and live with me. But I'm not going to marry David Hartley, you can depend on that, Ida, my dear. I wish you could have heard him rhyming off that poetry last night. It doesn't seem to matter much what piece he recites—first thing that comes into his head, I reckon. I remember one time he went clean through that hymn beginning, 'Hark from the tombs a doleful sound,' and two years ago it was 'To Mary in Heaven,' as lackadaisical as you please. I never had such a time to keep from laughing, but I managed it, for I wouldn't hurt his feelings for the world. No, I haven't any intention of marrying anybody, but if I had it wouldn't be dear old sentimental, easy-going David."

Mrs. Tom thumped a plucked goose down on the bench with an expression which said that she, for one, wasn't going to waste any more words on an idiot. Easy-going, indeed! Did Josephine consider that a drawback? Mrs. Tom sighed. If Josephine, she thought, had put up with Tom Sentner's tempers for fifteen years she would know how to appreciate a good-natured man at his real value.

The cold snap which had set in on the day of David's call lasted and deepened for a week. On Saturday evening, when Mrs. Tom came down for a jug of cream, the mercury of the little thermometer thumping against

Josephine's porch was below zero. The gulf was no longer blue, but white with ice. Everything outdoors was crackling and snapping. Inside Josephine had kept roaring fires all through the house but the only place really warm was the kitchen.

"Wrap your head up well, Ida," she said anxiously, when Mrs. Tom rose to go. "You've got a bad cold."

"There's a cold going," said Mrs. Tom. "Everyone has it. David Hartley was up at our place to-day barking terrible—a real churchyard cough, as I told him. He never takes any care of himself. He said Zillah had a bad cold, too. Won't she be cranky while it lasts?"

Josephine sat up late that night to keep fires on. She finally went to bed in the little room opposite the big hall stove, and she slept at once, and dreamed that the thumps of the thermometer flapping in the wind against the wall outside grew louder and more insistent until they woke her up. Some one was pounding on the porch door.

Josephine sprang out of bed and hurried on her wrapper and felt shoes. She had no doubt that some of the Sentners were sick. They had a habit of getting sick about that time of night. She hurried out and opened the door, expecting to see hulking Tom Sentner, or perhaps Ida herself, big-eyed and hysterical.

But David Hartley stood there, panting for breath. The clear moonlight showed that he had no overcoat on, and he was coughing hard. Josephine, before she spoke a word, clutched him by the arm and pulled him in out of the wind.

"For pity's sake, David Hartley, what is the matter?"

"Zillah's awful sick," he gasped. "I came here because 'twas nearest. Oh, won't you come over, Josephine? I've got to go for the doctor and I can't leave her alone. She's suffering dreadful. I know you and her ain't on good terms, but you'll come, won't you?"

"Of course I will," said Josephine sharply. "I'm not a barbarian, I hope, to refuse to go to the help of a sick person, if 'twas my worst enemy. I'll go in and get ready and you go straight to the hall stove and warm yourself. There's a good fire in it yet. What on earth do you mean, starting out on a bitter night like this without an overcoat or even mittens, and you with a cold like that?"

"I never thought of them, I was so frightened," said David apologetically. "I just lit up a fire in the kitchen stove as quick's I could and run. It rattled me to hear Zillah moaning so's you could hear her all over the house."

"You need someone to look after you as bad as Zillah does," said Josephine severely.

In a very few minutes she was ready, with a basket packed full of homely remedies, "for like as not there'll be no putting one's hand on anything there," she muttered. She insisted on wrapping her big plaid shawl around David's head and neck, and made him put on a pair of mittens she had knitted for Jack Sentner. Then she locked the door and they started across the gleaming, crusted field. It was so slippery that Josephine had to cling to David's arm to keep her feet. In the rapture of supporting her David almost forgot everything else.

In a few minutes they had passed under the bare, glistening boughs of the poplars on David's lawn, and for the first time Josephine crossed the threshold of David Hartley's house.

Years ago, in her girlhood, when the Hartley's lived in the old house and there were half a dozen girls at home, Josephine had frequently visited there. All the Hartley girls liked her except Zillah. She and Zillah never "got on" together. When the other girls had married and gone, Josephine gave up visiting there. She had never been inside the new house, and she and Zillah had not spoken to each other for years.

Zillah was a sick woman — too sick to be anything but civil to Josephine. David started at once for the doctor at the Creek, and Josephine saw that he was well wrapped up before she let him go. Then she mixed up a mustard plaster for Zillah and sat down by the bedside to wait.

When Mrs. Tom Sentner came down the next day she found Josephine busy making flaxseed poultices, with her lips set in a line that betokened she had made up her mind to some disagreeable course of duty.

"Zillah has got pneumonia bad," she said, in reply to Mrs. Tom's inquiries. "The Doctor is here and Mary Bell from the Creek. She'll wait on Zillah, but there'll have to be another woman here to see to the work. I reckon I'll stay. I suppose it's my duty and I don't see who else could be got. You can send Mamie and Jack down to stay at my house until I can go back. I'll run over every day and keep an eye on things."

At the end of a week Zillah was out of danger. Saturday afternoon Josephine went over home to see how Mamie and Jack were getting on. She found Mrs. Tom there, and the latter promptly despatched Jack and Mamie to the post-office that she might have an opportunity to hear Josephine's news.

"I've had an awful week of it, Ida," said Josephine solemnly, as she sat down by the stove and put her feet up on the glowing hearth.

"I suppose Zillah is pretty cranky to wait on," said Mrs. Tom sympathetically.

"Oh, it isn't Zillah. Mary Bell looks after her. No, it's the house. I never lived in such a place of dust and disorder in my born days. I'm sorrier for David Hartley than I ever was for anyone before."

"I suppose he's used to it," said Mrs. Tom with a shrug.

"I don't see how anyone could ever get used to it," groaned Josephine. "And David used to be so particular when he was a boy. The minute I went there the other night I took in that kitchen with a look. I don't believe the paint has even been washed since the house was built. I honestly don't. And I wouldn't like to be called upon to swear when the floor was scrubbed either. The corners were just full of rolls of dust—you could have shovelled it out. I swept it out next day and I thought I'd be choked. As for the pantry—well, the less said about *that* the better. And it's the same all through the house. You could write your name on everything. I couldn't so much as clean up. Zillah was so sick there couldn't be a bit of noise made. I did manage to sweep and dust, and I cleaned out the pantry. And, of course, I saw that the meals were nice and well cooked. You should have seen David's face. He looked as if he couldn't get used to having things clean and tasty. I darned his socks—he hadn't a whole pair to his name—and I've done everything I could to give him a little comfort. Not that I could do much. If Zillah heard me moving round she'd send Mary Bell out to ask what the matter was. When I wanted to go upstairs I'd have to take off my shoes and tiptoe up on my stocking feet, so's she wouldn't know it. And I'll have to stay there another fortnight yet. Zillah won't be able to sit up till then. I don't really know if I can stand it without falling to and scrubbing the house from garret to cellar in spite of her."

Mrs. Tom Sentner did not say much to Josephine. To herself she said complacently:

"She's sorry for David. Well, I've always heard that pity was akin to love. We'll see what comes of this."

Josephine did manage to live through that fortnight. One morning she remarked to David at the breakfast table:

"Well, I think that Mary Bell will be able to attend to the work after today, David. I guess I'll go home tonight."

David's face clouded over.

"Well, I s'pose we oughtn't to keep you any longer, Josephine. I'm sure it's been awful good of you to stay this long. I don't know what we'd have done without you."

"You're welcome," said Josephine shortly.

"Don't go for to walk home," said David; "the snow is too deep. I'll drive you over when you want to go."

"I'll not go before the evening," said Josephine slowly.

David went out to his work gloomily. For three weeks he had been living in comfort. His wants were carefully attended to; his meals were well cooked and served, and everything was bright and clean. And more than all, Josephine had been there, with her cheerful smile and companionable ways. Well, it was all ended now.

Josephine sat at the breakfast table long after David had gone out. She scowled at the sugar-bowl and shook her head savagely at the tea-pot.

"I'll have to do it," she said at last.

"I'm so sorry for him that I can't do anything else."

She got up and went to the window, looking across the snowy field to her own home, nestled between the grove of firs and the orchard.

"It's awful snug and comfortable," she said regretfully, "and I've always felt set on being free and independent. But it's no use. I'd never have a minute's peace of mind again, thinking of David living here in dirt and disorder, and him so particular and tidy by nature. No, it's my duty, plain and clear, to come here and make things pleasant for him—the pointing of Providence, as you might say. The worst of it is, I'll have to tell him so myself. He'll never dare to mention the subject again, after what I said to him that night he proposed last. I wish I hadn't been so dreadful emphatic. Now I've got to say it myself if it is ever said. But I'll not begin by quoting poetry, that's one thing sure!"

Josephine threw back her head, crowned with its shining braids of jet-black hair, and laughed heartily. She bustled back to the stove and poked up the fire.

"I'll have a bit of corned beef and cabbage for dinner," she said, "and I'll make David that pudding he's so fond of. After all, it's kind of nice to have someone to plan and think for. It always did seem like a waste of energy to fuss over cooking things when there was nobody but myself to eat them."

Josephine sang over her work all day, and David went about his with the face of a man who is going to the gallows without benefit of clergy. When he came in to supper at sunset his expression was so woe-begone that Josephine had to dodge into the pantry to keep from laughing outright. She relieved her feelings by pounding the dresser with the potato masher, and then went primly out and took her place at the table.

The meal was not a success from a social point of view. Josephine was nervous and David glum. Mary Bell gobbled down her food with her usual haste, and then went away to carry Zillah hers. Then David said reluctantly:

"If you want to go home now, Josephine, I'll hitch up Red Rob and drive you over."

Josephine began to plait the tablecloth. She wished again that she had not been so emphatic on the occasion of his last proposal. Without replying to David's suggestion she said crossly (Josephine always spoke crossly when she was especially in earnest):

"I want to tell you what I think about Zillah. She's getting better, but she's had a terrible shaking up, and it's my opinion that she won't be good for much all winter. She won't be able to do any hard work, that's certain. If you want my advice, I tell you fair and square that I think she'd better go off for a visit as soon as she's fit. She thinks so herself. Clementine wants her to go and stay a spell with her in town. 'Twould be just the thing for her."

"She can go if she wants to, of course," said David dully. "I can get along by myself for a spell."

"There's no need of your getting along by yourself," said Josephine, more crossly than ever. "I'll—I'll come here and keep house for you if you like."

David looked at her uncomprehendingly.

"Wouldn't people kind of gossip?" he asked hesitatingly. "Not but what—"

"I don't see what they'd have to gossip about," broke in Josephine, "if we were—married."

David sprang to his feet with such haste that he almost upset the table.

"Josephine, do you mean that?" he exclaimed.

"Of course I mean it," she said, in a perfectly savage tone. "Now, for pity's sake, don't say another word about it just now. I can't discuss it for a spell. Go out to your work. I want to be alone for awhile."

For the first and last time David disobeyed her. Instead of going out, he strode around the table, caught Josephine masterfully in his arms, and kissed her. And Josephine, after a second's hesitation, kissed him in return.

Aunt Philippa and the Men

I knew quite well why Father sent me to Prince Edward Island to visit Aunt Philippa that summer. He told me he was sending me there "to learn some sense"; and my stepmother, of whom I was very fond, told me she was sure the sea air would do me a world of good. I did not want to learn sense or be done a world of good; I wanted to stay in Montreal and go on being foolish—and make up my quarrel with Mark Fenwick. Father and Mother did not know anything about this quarrel; they thought I was still on good terms with him—and that is why they sent me to Prince Edward Island.

I was very miserable. I did not want to go to Aunt Philippa's. It was not because I feared it would be dull—for without Mark, Montreal was just as much of a howling wilderness as any other place. But it was so horribly far away. When the time came for Mark to want to make up—as come I knew it would—how could he do it if I were seven hundred miles away?

Nevertheless, I went to Prince Edward Island. In all my eighteen years I had never once disobeyed Father. He is a very hard man to disobey. I knew I should have to make a beginning some time if I wanted to marry Mark, so I saved all my little courage up for that and didn't waste any of it opposing the visit to Aunt Philippa.

I couldn't understand Father's point of view. Of course, he hated old John Fenwick, who had once sued him for libel and won the case. Father had written an indiscreet editorial in the excitement of a red-hot political contest—and was made to understand that there are some things you can't say of another man even at election time. But then, he need not have hated Mark because of that; Mark was not even born when it happened.

Old John Fenwick was not much better pleased about Mark and me than Father was, though he didn't go to the length of forbidding it; he just acted grumpily and disagreeably. Things were unpleasant enough all round without a quarrel between Mark and me; yet quarrel we did—and over next to nothing, too, you understand. And now I had to set out for Prince Edward Island without even seeing him, for he was away in Toronto on business.

When my train reached Copely the next afternoon, Aunt Philippa was waiting for me. There was nobody else in sight, but I would have known her had there been a thousand. Nobody but Aunt Philippa could have that determined mouth, those piercing grey eyes, and that pronounced, unmistakable Goodwin nose. And certainly nobody but Aunt Philippa would have come to meet me arrayed in a wrapper of chocolate print with huge yellow roses scattered over it, and a striped blue-and-white apron!

She welcomed me kindly but absent-mindedly, her thoughts evidently being concentrated on the problem of getting my trunk home. I had only the one, and in Montreal it had seemed to be of moderate size; but on the platform of Copely station, sized up by Aunt Philippa's merciless eye, it certainly looked huge.

"I thought we could a-took it along tied on the back of the buggy," she said disapprovingly, "but I guess we'll have to leave it, and I'll send the hired boy over for it tonight. You can get along without it till then, I s'pose?"

There was a fine irony in her tone. I hastened to assure her meekly that I could, and that it did not matter if my trunk could not be taken up till next day.

"Oh, Jerry can come for it tonight as well as not," said Aunt Philippa, as we climbed into her buggy. "I'd a good notion to send him to meet you, for he isn't doing much today, and I wanted to go to Mrs. Roderick MacAllister's funeral. But my head was aching me so bad I thought I wouldn't enjoy the funeral if I did go. My head is better now, so I kind of wish I had gone. She was a hundred and four years old and I'd always promised myself that I'd go to her funeral."

Aunt Philippa's tone was melancholy. She did not recover her good spirits until we were out on the pretty, grassy, elm-shaded country road, garlanded with its ribbon of buttercups. Then she suddenly turned around and looked me over scrutinizingly.

"You're not as good-looking as I expected from your picture, but them photographs always flatter. That's the reason I never had any took. You're rather thin and brown. But you've good eyes and you look clever. Your father writ me you hadn't much sense, though. He wants me to teach you some, but it's a thankless business. People would rather be fools."

Aunt Philippa struck her steed smartly with the whip and controlled his resultant friskiness with admirable skill.

"Well, you know it's pleasanter," I said, wickedly. "Just think what a doleful world it would be if everybody were sensible."

Aunt Philippa looked at me out of the corner of her eye and disdained any skirmish of flippant epigram.

"So you want to get married?" she said. "You'd better wait till you're grown up."

"How old must a person be before she is grown up?" I asked gravely.

"Humph! That depends. Some are grown up when they're born, and others ain't grown up when they're eighty. That same Mrs. Roderick I was speaking of never grew up. She was as foolish when she was a hundred as when she was ten."

"Perhaps that's why she lived so long," I suggested. All thought of seeking sympathy in Aunt Philippa had vanished. I resolved I would not even mention Mark's name.

"Mebbe 'twas," admitted Aunt Philippa with a grim smile. "*I'd* rather live fifty sensible years than a hundred foolish ones."

Much to my relief, she made no further reference to my affairs. As we rounded a curve in the road where two great over-arching elms met, a buggy wheeled by us, occupied by a young man in clerical costume. He had a pleasant boyish face, and he touched his hat courteously. Aunt Philippa nodded very frostily and gave her horse a quite undeserved cut.

"There's a man you don't want to have much to do with," she said portentously. "He's a Methodist minister."

"Why, Auntie, the Methodists are a very nice denomination," I protested. "My stepmother is a Methodist, you know."

"No, I didn't know, but I'd believe anything of a stepmother. I've no use for Methodists or their ministers. This fellow just came last spring, and it's *my* opinion he smokes. And he thinks every girl who looks at him falls in love with him—as if a Methodist minister was any prize! Don't you take much notice of him, Ursula."

"I'll not be likely to have the chance," I said, with an amused smile.

"Oh, you'll see enough of him. He boards at Mrs. John Callman's, just across the road from us, and he's always out sunning himself on her verandah. Never studies, of course. Last Sunday they say he preached on the iron that floated. If he'd confine himself to the Bible and leave sensational subjects alone it would be better for him and his poor congregation, and so I told Mrs. John Callman to her face. I should think *she* would have had enough of his sex by this time. She married John Callman against her father's will, and he had delirious trembles for years. That's the men for you."

"They're not *all* like that, Aunt Philippa," I protested.

"Most of 'em are. See that house over there? Mrs. Jane Harrison lives there. Her husband took tantrums every few days or so and wouldn't get out of bed. She had to do all the barn work till he'd got over his spell. That's men for you. When he died, people writ her letters of condolence but *I* just sot down and writ her one of congratulation. There's the Presbyterian manse in the hollow. Mr. Bentwell's our minister. He's a good man and he'd be a rather nice one if he didn't think it was his duty to be a little miserable all the time. He won't let his wife wear a fashionable hat, and his daughter can't fix her hair the way she wants to. Even being a minister can't prevent a man from being a crank. Here's Ebenezer Milgrave coming. You take a good look at him. He used to be insane for years. He believed he was dead and used to rage at his wife because she wouldn't bury him. *I'd* a-done it."

Aunt Philippa looked so determinedly grim that I could almost see her with a spade in her hand. I laughed aloud at the picture summoned up.

"Yes, it's funny, but I guess his poor wife didn't find it very humorsome. He's been pretty sane for some years now, but you never can tell when he'll break out again. He's got a brother, Albert Milgrave, who's been married twice. They say he was courting his second wife while his first was dying. Let that be as it may, he used his first wife's wedding ring to marry the second. That's the men for you."

"Don't you know *any* good husbands, Aunt Philippa?" I asked desperately.

"Oh, yes, lots of 'em — over there," said Aunt Philippa sardonically, waving her whip in the direction of a little country graveyard on a distant hill.

"Yes, but *living* — walking about in the flesh?"

"Precious few. Now and again you'll come across a man whose wife won't put up with any nonsense and he *has* to be respectable. But the most of 'em are poor bargains — poor bargains."

"And are all the wives saints?" I persisted.

"Laws, no, but they're too good for the men," retorted Aunt Philippa, as she turned in at her own gate. Her house was close to the road and was painted such a vivid green that the landscape looked faded by contrast. Across the gable end of it was the legend, "Philippa's Farm," emblazoned in huge black letters two feet long. All its surroundings were very neat. On the kitchen doorstep a patchwork cat was making a grave toilet. The groundwork of the cat was white, and its spots were black, yellow, grey, and brown.

"There's Joseph," said Aunt Philippa. "I call him that because his coat is of many colours. But I ain't no lover of cats. They're too much like the men to suit me."

"Cats have always been supposed to be peculiarly feminine," I said, descending.

"'Twas a man that supposed it, then," retorted Aunt Philippa, beckoning to her hired boy. "Here, Jerry, put Prince away. Jerry's a good sort of boy," she confided to me as we went into the house. "I had Jim Spencer last summer and the only good thing about *him* was his appetite. I put up with him till harvest was in, and then one day my patience give out. He upset a churnful of cream in the back yard—and was just as cool as a cowcumber over it—laughed and said it was good for the land. I told him I wasn't in the habit of fertilizing my back yard with cream. But that's the men for you. Come in. I'll have tea ready in no time. I sot the table before I left. There's lemon pie. Mrs. John Cantwell sent it over. I never make lemon pie myself. Ten years ago I took the prize for lemon pies at the county fair, and I've never made any since for fear I'd lose my reputation for them."

The first month of my stay passed not unpleasantly. The summer weather was delightful, and the sea air was certainly splendid. Aunt Philippa's little farm ran right down to the shore, and I spent much of my time there. There were also several families of cousins to be visited in the farmhouses that dotted the pretty, seaward-sloping valley, and they came back to see me at "Philippa's Farm." I picked spruce gum and berries and ferns, and Aunt Philippa taught me to make butter. It was all very idyllic—or would have been if Mark had written. But Mark did not write. I supposed he must be very angry because I had run off to Prince Edward Island without so much as a note of goodbye. But I had been so sure he would understand!

Aunt Philippa never made any further reference to the reason Father had sent me to her, but she allowed no day to pass without holding up to me some horrible example of matrimonial infelicity. The number of unhappy wives who walked or drove past "Philippa's Farm" every afternoon, as we sat on the verandah, was truly pitiable.

We always sat on the verandah in the afternoon, when we were not visiting or being visited. I made a pretence of fancy work, and Aunt Philippa spun diligently on a little old-fashioned spinning-wheel that had been her grandmother's. She always sat before the wood stand which held her flowers, and the gorgeous blots of geranium blossom and big green leaves furnished a pretty background. She always wore her shapeless but clean print wrappers, and her iron-grey hair was always combed neatly down over her ears. Joseph sat between us, sleeping or purring. She spun so expertly that she could keep a close watch on the road as well, and I got the biography of every individual who went by. As for the poor young Methodist minister, who liked to read or walk on the verandah of our neighbour's house, Aunt Philippa never had a good word for him. I had met him once or twice socially and had liked him. I wanted to ask him to call but dared not — Aunt Philippa had vowed he should never enter her house.

"If I was dead and he came to my funeral I'd rise up and order him out," she said.

"I thought he made a very nice prayer at Mrs. Seaman's funeral the other day," I said.

"Oh, I've no doubt he can pray. I never heard anyone make more beautiful prayers than old Simon Kennedy down at the harbour, who was always drunk or hoping to be — and the drunker he was the better he prayed. It ain't no matter how well a man prays if his preaching isn't right. That Methodist man preaches a lot of things that ain't true, and what's worse they ain't sound doctrine. At least, that's what I've heard. I never was in a Methodist church, thank goodness."

"Don't you think Methodists go to heaven as well as Presbyterians, Aunt Philippa?" I asked gravely.

"That ain't for us to decide," said Aunt Philippa solemnly. "It's in higher hands than ours. But I ain't going to associate with them on *earth*, whatever I may have to do in heaven. The folks round here mostly don't make much difference and go to the Methodist church quite often. But *I* say if you are a Presbyterian, *be* a Presbyterian. Of course, if you ain't, it don't matter much what you do. As for that minister man, he has a grand-uncle who was sent to the penitentiary for embezzlement. I found out *that* much."

And evidently Aunt Philippa had taken an unholy joy in finding it out.

"I dare say some of our own ancestors deserved to go to the penitentiary, even if they never did," I remarked. "Who is that woman driving past, Aunt Philippa? She must have been very pretty once."

"She was — and that was all the good it did her. 'Favour is deceitful and beauty is vain,' Ursula. She was Sarah Pyatt and she married Fred Proctor. He was one of your wicked, fascinating men. After she married him he give up being fascinating but he kept on being wicked. *That's* the men for you. Her sister Flora weren't much luckier. *Her* man was that domineering she couldn't call her soul her own. Finally he couldn't get his own way over something and he just suicided by jumping into the well. A good riddance — but of course the well was spoiled. Flora could never abide the thought of using it again, poor thing. *That's* men for you.

"And there's that old Enoch Allan on his way to the station. He's ninety if he's a day. You can't kill some folks with a meat axe. His wife died twenty years ago. He'd been married when he was twenty so they'd lived together for fifty years. She was a faithful, hard-working creature and kept him out of the poorhouse, for he was a shiftless soul, not lazy, exactly, but just too fond of sitting. But he weren't grateful. She had a kind of bitter tongue and they did use to fight scandalous. O' course it was all his fault. Well, she died, and old Enoch and my father drove together to the graveyard. Old Enoch was awful quiet all the way there and back, but just afore they got home, he says solemnly to Father: 'You mayn't believe it, Henry, but this is the happiest day of my life.' *That's* men for you. His brother, Scotty Allan, was the meanest man ever lived in these parts. When his wife died she was buried with a little gold brooch in her collar unbeknownst to him. When he found it out he went one night to the graveyard and opened up the grave and the casket to get that brooch."

"Oh, Aunt Philippa, that is a horrible story," I cried, recoiling with a shiver over the gruesomeness of it.

"'Course it is, but what would you expect of a man?" retorted Aunt Philippa.

Somehow, her stories began to affect me in spite of myself. There were times when I felt very dreary. Perhaps Aunt Philippa was right. Perhaps men possessed neither truth nor constancy. Certainly Mark had forgotten me. I was ashamed of myself because this hurt me so much, but I could not help it. I grew pale and listless. Aunt Philippa sometimes peered at me sharply, but she held her peace. I was grateful for this.

But one day a letter did come from Mark. I dared not read it until I was safely in my own room. Then I opened it with trembling fingers.

The letter was a little stiff. Evidently Mark was feeling sore enough over things. He made no reference to our quarrel or to my sojourn in Prince Edward Island. He wrote that his firm was sending him to South Africa to take charge of their interests there. He would leave in three weeks' time and could not return for five years. If I still cared anything for him, would I meet him in Halifax, marry him, and go to South Africa with him? If I would not, he would understand that I had ceased to love him and that all was over between us.

That, boiled down, was the gist of Mark's letter. When I had read it I cast myself on the bed and wept out all the tears I had refused to let myself shed during my weeks of exile.

For I could not do what Mark asked — I *could not*. I couldn't run away to be married in that desolate, unbefriended fashion. It would be a disgrace. I would feel ashamed of it all my life and be unhappy over it. I thought that Mark was rather unreasonable. He knew what my feelings about run-away marriages were. And was it absolutely necessary for him to go to South

Africa? Of course his father was behind it somewhere, but surely he could have got out of it if he had really tried.

Well, if he went to South Africa he must go alone. But my heart would break.

I cried the whole afternoon, cowering among my pillows. I never wanted to go out of that room again. I never wanted to see anybody again. I hated the thought of facing Aunt Philippa with her cold eyes and her miserable stories that seemed to strip life of all beauty and love of all reality. I could hear her scornful, "That's the men for you," if she heard what was in Mark's letter.

"What is the matter, Ursula?"

Aunt Philippa was standing by my bed. I was too abject to resent her coming in without knocking.

"Nothing," I said spiritlessly.

"If you've been crying for three mortal hours over nothing you want a good spanking and you'll get it," observed Aunt Philippa placidly, sitting down on my trunk. "Get right up off that bed this minute and tell me what the trouble is. I'm bound to know, for I'm in your father's place at present."

"There, then!" I flung her Mark's letter. There wasn't anything in it that it was sacrilege to let another person see. That was one reason why I had been crying.

Aunt Philippa read it over twice. Then she folded it up deliberately and put it back in the envelope.

"What are you going to do?" she asked in a matter-of-fact tone.

"I'm not going to run away to be married," I answered sullenly.

"Well, no, I wouldn't advise you to," said Aunt Philippa reflectively. "It's a kind of low-down thing to do, though there's been a terrible lot of romantic nonsense talked and writ about eloping. It may be a painful necessity sometimes, but it ain't in this case. You write to your young man and tell him to come here and be married respectable under my roof, same as a Goodwin ought to."

I sat up and stared at Aunt Philippa. I was so amazed that it is useless to try to express my amazement.

"Aunt—Philippa," I gasped. "I thought—I thought—"

"You thought I was a hard old customer, and so I am," said Aunt Philippa. "But I don't take my opinions from your father nor anybody else. It didn't prejudice me any against your young man that your father didn't like him. I knew your father of old. I have some other friends in Montreal and I writ to them and asked them what he was like. From what they said I judged he was decent enough as men go. You're too young to be married, but if you let him go off to South Africa he'll slip through your fingers for sure, and I s'pose you're like some of the rest of us—nobody'll do you but the one. So tell him to come here and be married."

"I don't see how I can," I gasped. "I can't get ready to be married in three weeks. I can't—"

"I should think you have enough clothes in that trunk to do you for a spell," said Aunt Philippa sarcastically. "You've more than my mother ever had in all her life. We'll get you a wedding dress of some kind. You can get it made in Charlottetown, if country dressmakers aren't good enough for you, and I'll bake you a wedding cake that'll taste as good as anything you could get in Montreal, even if it won't look so stylish."

"What will Father say?" I questioned.

"Lots o' things," conceded Aunt Philippa grimly. "But I don't see as it matters when neither you nor me'll be there to have our feelings hurt. I'll write a few things to your father. He hasn't got much sense. He ought to be thankful to get a decent young man for his son-in-law in a world where most every man is a wolf in sheep's clothing. But that's the men for you."

And that was Aunt Philippa for you. For the next three weeks she was a blissfully excited, busy woman. I was allowed to choose the material and fashion of my wedding suit and hat myself, but almost everything else was settled by Aunt Philippa. I didn't mind; it was a relief to be rid of all responsibility; I did protest when she declared her intention of having a big wedding and asking all the cousins and semi-cousins on the island, but Aunt Philippa swept my objections lightly aside.

"I'm bound to have one good wedding in this house," she said. "Not likely I'll ever have another chance."

She found time amid all the baking and concocting to warn me frequently not to take it too much to heart if Mark failed to come after all.

"I know a man who jilted a girl on her wedding day. That's the men for you. It's best to be prepared."

But Mark did come, getting there the evening before our wedding day. And then a severe blow fell on Aunt Philippa. Word came from the manse that Mr. Bentwell had been suddenly summoned to Nova Scotia to his mother's deathbed; he had started that night.

"That's the men for you," said Aunt Philippa bitterly. "Never can depend on one of them, not even on a minister. What's to be done now?"

"Get another minister," said Mark easily.

"Where'll you get him?" demanded Aunt Philippa. "The minister at Cliftonville is away on his vacation, and Mercer is vacant, and that leaves none nearer than town. It won't do to depend on a town minister being able to come. No, there's no help for it. You'll have to have that Methodist man."

Aunt Philippa's tone was tragic. Plainly she thought the ceremony would scarcely be legal if that Methodist man married us. But neither Mark nor I cared. We were too happy to be disturbed by any such trifles.

The young Methodist minister married us the next day in the presence of many beaming guests. Aunt Philippa, splendid in black silk and point-lace collar, neither of which lost a whit of dignity or lustre by being made ten years before, was composure itself while the ceremony was going on. But no sooner had the minister pronounced us man and wife than she spoke up.

"Now that's over I want someone to go right out and put out the fire on the kitchen roof. It's been on fire for the last ten minutes."

Minister and bridegroom headed the emergency brigade, and Aunt Philippa pumped the water for them. In a short time the fire was out, all was safe, and we were receiving our deferred congratulations.

"Now, young man," said Aunt Philippa solemnly as she shook hands with Mark, "don't you ever try to get out of this, even if a Methodist minister did marry you."

She insisted on driving us to the train and said goodbye to us as we stood on the car steps. She had caught more of the shower of rice than I had, and as the day was hot and sunny she had tied over her head, atop of that festal silk dress, a huge, home-made, untrimmed straw hat. But she did not look ridiculous. There was a certain dignity about Aunt Philippa in any costume and under any circumstance.

"Aunt Philippa," I said, "tell me this: why have you helped me to be married?"

The train began to move.

"I refused once to run away myself, and I've repented it ever since." Then, as the train gathered speed and the distance between us widened, she shouted after us, "But I s'pose if I had run away I'd have repented of that too."

Bessie's Doll

Tommy Puffer, sauntering up the street, stopped to look at Miss Octavia's geraniums. Tommy never could help stopping to look at Miss Octavia's flowers, much as he hated Miss Octavia. Today they were certainly worth looking at. Miss Octavia had set them all out on her verandah—rows upon rows of them, overflowing down the steps in waves of blossom and colour. Miss Octavia's geraniums were famous in Arundel, and she was very proud of them. But it was her garden which was really the delight of her heart. Miss Octavia always had the prettiest garden in Arundel, especially as far as annuals were concerned. Just now it was like faith—the substance of things hoped for. The poppies and nasturtiums and balsams and morning glories and sweet peas had been sown in the brown beds on the lawn, but they had not yet begun to come up.

Tommy was still feasting his eyes on the geraniums when Miss Octavia herself came around the corner of the house. Her face darkened the minute she saw Tommy. Most people's did. Tommy had the reputation of being a very bad, mischievous boy; he was certainly very poor and ragged, and Miss Octavia disapproved of poverty and rags on principle. Nobody, she argued, not even a boy of twelve, need be poor and ragged if he is willing to work.

"Here, you, get away out of this," she said sharply. "I'm not going to have you hanging over my palings."

"I ain't hurting your old palings," retorted Tommy sullenly. "I was jist a-looking at the flowers."

"Yes, and picking out the next one to throw a stone at," said Miss Octavia sarcastically. "It was you who threw that stone and broke my big scarlet geranium clear off the other day."

"It wasn't—I never chucked a stone at your flowers," said Tommy.

"Don't tell me any falsehoods, Tommy Puffer. It was you. Didn't I catch you firing stones at my cat a dozen times?"

"I might have fired 'em at an old cat, but I wouldn't tech a flower," avowed Tommy boldly—brazenly, Miss Octavia thought.

"You clear out of this or I'll make you," she said warningly.

Tommy had had his ears boxed by Miss Octavia more than once. He had no desire to have the performance repeated, so he stuck his tongue out at Miss Octavia and then marched up the street with his hands in his pockets, whistling jauntily.

"He's the most impudent brat I ever saw in my life," muttered Miss Octavia wrathfully. There was a standing feud between her and all the Arundel small boys, but Tommy was her special object of dislike.

Tommy's heart was full of wrath and bitterness as he marched away. He hated Miss Octavia; he wished something would happen to every one of her flowers; he knew it was Ned Williams who had thrown that stone, and he hoped Ned would throw some more and smash all the flowers. So Tommy raged along the street until he came to Mr. Blacklock's store, and in the window of it he saw something that put Miss Octavia and her disagreeable remarks quite out of his tow-coloured head.

This was nothing more or less than a doll. Now, Tommy was not a judge of dolls and did not take much interest in them, but he felt quite sure that this was a very fine one. It was so big; it was beautifully dressed in blue silk, with a ruffled blue silk hat; it had lovely long golden hair and big brown eyes and pink cheeks; and it stood right up in the showcase and held out its hands winningly.

"Gee, ain't it a beauty!" said Tommy admiringly. "It looks 'sif it was alive, and it's as big as a baby. I must go an' bring Bessie to see it."

Tommy at once hurried away to the shabby little street where what he called "home" was. Tommy's home was a very homeless-looking sort of place. It was the smallest, dingiest, most slatternly house on a street noted for its dingy and slatternly houses. It was occupied by a slatternly mother and a drunken father, as well as by Tommy; and neither the father nor the mother took much notice of Tommy except to scold or nag him. So it is hardly to be wondered at if Tommy was the sort of boy who was frowned upon by respectable citizens.

But one little white blossom of pure affection bloomed in the arid desert of Tommy's existence for all that. In the preceding fall a new family had come to Arundel and moved into the tiny house next to the Puffers'. It was a small, dingy house, just like the others, but before long a great change took place in it. The new family were thrifty, industrious folks, although they were very poor. The little house was white-washed, the paling neatly mended, the bit of a yard cleaned of all its rubbish. Muslin curtains appeared in the windows, and rows of cans, with blossoming plants, adorned the sills.

There were just three people in the Knox family — a thin little mother, who went out scrubbing and took in washing, a boy of ten, who sold newspapers and ran errands — and Bessie.

Bessie was eight years old and walked with a crutch, but she was a smart little lassie and kept the house wonderfully neat and tidy while her mother was away. The very first time she had seen Tommy she had smiled at him sweetly and said, "Good morning." From that moment Tommy was her devoted slave. Nobody had ever spoken like that to him before; nobody had ever smiled so at him. Tommy would have given his useless little life for Bessie, and thenceforth the time he was not devising mischief he spent in bringing little pleasures into her life. It was Tommy's delight to bring that smile to her pale little face and a look of pleasure into her big, patient blue eyes. The other boys on the street tried to tease Bessie at first and shouted "Cripple!" after her when she limped out. But they soon stopped it. Tommy thrashed them all one after another for it, and Bessie was left in peace. She would have had a very lonely life if it had not been for Tommy, for she could not play with the other children. But Tommy was as good as a dozen playmates, and Bessie thought him the best boy in the world. Tommy, whatever he might be with others, was very careful to be good when he was with Bessie. He never said a rude word in her hearing, and he treated her as if she were a little princess. Miss Octavia would have been amazed beyond measure if she had seen how tender and thoughtful and kind and chivalrous that neglected urchin of a Tommy could be when he tried.

Tommy found Bessie sitting by the kitchen window, looking dreamily out of it. For just a moment Tommy thought uneasily that Bessie was looking very pale and thin this spring.

"Bessie, come for a walk up to Mr. Blacklock's store," he said eagerly. "There is something there I want to show you."

"What is it?" Bessie wanted to know. But Tommy only winked mysteriously.

"Ah, I ain't going to tell you. But it's something awful pretty. Just you wait."

Bessie reached for her crutch and the two went up to the store, Tommy carefully suiting his steps to Bessie's slow ones. Just before they reached the store he made her shut her eyes and led her to the window.

"Now—look!" he commanded dramatically.

Bessie looked and Tommy was rewarded. She flushed pinkly with delight and clasped her hands in ecstasy.

"Oh, Tommy, isn't she perfectly beautiful?" she breathed. "Oh, she's the very loveliest dolly I ever saw. Oh, Tommy!"

"I thought you'd like her," said Tommy exultantly. "Don't you wish you had a doll like that of your very own, Bessie?"

Bessie looked almost rebuking, as if Tommy had asked her if she wouldn't like a golden crown or a queen's palace.

"Of course I could never have a dolly like that," she said. "She must cost an awful lot. But it's enough just to look at her. Tommy, will you bring me up here every day just to look at her?"

"'Course," said Tommy.

Bessie talked about the blue-silk doll all the way home and dreamed of her every night. "I'm going to call her Roselle Geraldine," she said. After that she went up to see Roselle Geraldine every day, gazing at her for long moments in silent rapture. Tommy almost grew jealous of her; he thought Bessie liked the doll better than she did him.

"But it don't matter a bit if she does," he thought loyally, crushing down the jealousy. "If she likes to like it better than me, it's all right."

Sometimes, though, Tommy felt uneasy. It was plain to be seen that Bessie had set her heart on that doll. And what would she do when the doll was sold, as would probably happen soon? Tommy thought Bessie would feel awful sad, and he would be responsible for it.

What Tommy feared came to pass. One afternoon, when they went up to Mr. Blacklock's store, the doll was not in the window.

"Oh," cried Bessie, bursting into tears, "she's gone — Roselle Geraldine is gone."

"Perhaps she isn't sold," said Tommy comfortingly. "Maybe they only took her out of the window 'cause the blue silk would fade. I'll go in and ask."

A minute later Tommy came out looking sober.

"Yes, she's sold, Bessie," he said. "Mr. Blacklock sold her to a lady yesterday. Don't cry, Bessie — maybe they'll put another in the window 'fore long."

"It won't be mine," sobbed Bessie. "It won't be Roselle Geraldine. It won't have a blue silk hat and such cunning brown eyes."

Bessie cried quietly all the way home, and Tommy could not comfort her. He wished he had never shown her the doll in the window.

From that day Bessie drooped, and Tommy watched her in agony. She grew paler and thinner. She was too tired to go out walking, and too tired to do the little household tasks she had delighted in. She never spoke about Roselle Geraldine, but Tommy knew she was fretting about her. Mrs. Knox could not think what ailed the child.

"She don't take a bit of interest in nothing," she complained to Mrs. Puffer. "She don't eat enough for a bird. The doctor, he says there ain't nothing the matter with her as he can find out, but she's just pining away."

Tommy heard this, and a queer, big lump came up in his throat. He had a horrible fear that he, Tommy Puffer, was going to cry. To prevent it he began to whistle loudly. But the whistle was a failure, very unlike the real Tommy-whistle. Bessie was sick—and it was all his fault, Tommy believed. If he had never taken her to see that hateful, blue-silk doll, she would never have got so fond of it as to be breaking her heart because it was sold.

"If I was only rich," said Tommy miserably, "I'd buy her a cartload of dolls, all dressed in blue silk and all with brown eyes. But I can't do nothing."

By this time Tommy had reached the paling in front of Miss Octavia's lawn, and from force of habit he stopped to look over it. But there was not much to see this time, only the little green rows and circles in the brown, well-weeded beds, and the long curves of dahlia plants, which Miss Octavia had set out a few days before. All the geraniums were carried in, and the blinds were down. Tommy knew Miss Octavia was away. He had seen her depart on the train that morning, and heard her tell a friend that she was going down to Chelton to visit her brother's folks and wouldn't be back until the next day.

Tommy was still leaning moodily against the paling when Mrs. Jenkins and Mrs. Reid came by, and they too paused to look at the garden.

"Dear me, how cold it is!" shivered Mrs. Reid. "There's going to be a hard frost tonight. Octavia's flowers will be nipped as sure as anything. It's a wonder she'd stay away from them overnight when her heart's so set on them."

"Her brother's wife is sick," said Mrs. Jenkins. "We haven't had any frost this spring, and I suppose Octavia never thought of such a thing. She'll feel awful bad if her flowers get frosted, especially them dahlias. Octavia sets such store by her dahlias."

Mrs. Jenkins and Mrs. Reid moved away, leaving Tommy by the paling. It was cold—there was going to be a hard frost—and Miss Octavia's plants and flowers would certainly be spoiled. Tommy thought he ought to be glad, but he wasn't. He was sorry—not for Miss Octavia, but for her flowers. Tommy had a queer, passionate love for flowers in his twisted little soul. It was a shame that they should be nipped—that all the glory of crimson and purple and gold hidden away in those little green rows and circles should never have a chance to blossom out royally. Tommy could never have put this thought into words, but it was there in his heart. He wished he could save the flowers. And couldn't he? Newspapers spread over the beds and tied around the dahlias would save them, Tommy knew. He had seen Miss Octavia doing it other springs. And he knew there was a big box of newspapers in a little shed in her backyard. Ned Williams had told him there was, and that the shed was never locked.

Tommy hurried home as quickly as he could and got a ball of twine out of his few treasures. Then he went back to Miss Octavia's garden.

The next forenoon Miss Octavia got off the train at the Arundel station with a very grim face. There had been an unusually severe frost for the time of year. All along the road Miss Octavia had seen gardens frosted and spoiled. She knew what she should see when she got to her own—the dahlia stalks drooping and black and limp, the nasturtiums and balsams and poppies and pansies all withered and ruined.

But she didn't. Instead she saw every dahlia carefully tied up in a newspaper, and over all the beds newspapers spread out and held neatly in place with pebbles. Miss Octavia flew into her garden with a radiant face. Everything was safe—nothing was spoiled.

But who could have done it? Miss Octavia was puzzled. On one side of her lived Mrs. Kennedy, who had just moved in and, being a total stranger, would not be likely to think of Miss Octavia's flowers. On the other lived Miss Matheson, who was a "shut-in" and spent all her time on the sofa. But to Miss Matheson Miss Octavia went.

"Rachel, do you know who covered my plants up last night?"

Miss Matheson nodded. "Yes, it was Tommy Puffer. I saw him working away there with papers and twine. I thought you'd told him to do it."

"For the land's sake!" ejaculated Miss Octavia. "Tommy Puffer! Well, wonders will never cease."

Miss Octavia went back to her house feeling rather ashamed of herself when she remembered how she had always treated Tommy Puffer.

"But there must be some good in the child, or he wouldn't have done this," she said to herself. "I've been real mean, but I'll make it up to him."

Miss Octavia did not see Tommy that day, but when he passed the next morning she ran to the door and called him.

"Tommy, Tommy Puffer, come in here!"

Tommy came reluctantly. He didn't like Miss Octavia any better than he had, and he didn't know what she wanted of him. But Miss Octavia soon informed him without loss of words.

"Tommy, Miss Matheson tells me that it was you who saved my flowers from the frost the other night. I'm very much obliged to you indeed. Whatever made you think of doing it?"

"I hated to see the flowers spoiled," muttered Tommy, who was feeling more uncomfortable than he had ever felt in his life.

"Well, it was real thoughtful of you. I'm sorry I've been so hard on you, Tommy, and I believe now you didn't break my scarlet geranium. Is there anything I can do for you — anything you'd like to have? If it's in reason I'll get it for you, just to pay my debt."

Tommy stared at Miss Octavia with a sudden hopeful inspiration. "Oh, Miss Octavia," he cried eagerly, "will you buy a doll and give it to me?"

"Well, for the land's sake!" ejaculated Miss Octavia, unable to believe her ears. "A doll! What on earth do you want of a doll?"

"It's for Bessie," said Tommy eagerly. "You see, it's this way."

Then Tommy told Miss Octavia the whole story. Miss Octavia listened silently, sometimes nodding her head. When he had finished she went out of the room and soon returned, bringing with her the very identical doll that had been in Mr. Blacklock's window.

"I guess this is the doll," she said. "I bought it to give to a small niece of mine, but I can get another for her. You may take this to Bessie."

It would be of no use to try to describe Bessie's joy when Tommy rushed in and put Roselle Geraldine in her arms with a breathless account of the wonderful story. But from that moment Bessie began to pick up again, and soon she was better than she had ever been and the happiest little lassie in Arundel.

When a week had passed, Miss Octavia again called Tommy in; Tommy went more willingly this time. He had begun to like Miss Octavia.

That lady looked him over sharply and somewhat dubiously. He was certainly very ragged and unkempt. But Miss Octavia saw what she had never noticed before — that Tommy's eyes were bright and frank, that Tommy's chin was a good chin, and that Tommy's smile had something very pleasant about it.

"You're fond of flowers, aren't you, Tommy?" she asked.

"You bet," was Tommy's inelegant but heartfelt answer.

"Well," said Miss Octavia slowly, "I have a brother down at Chelton who is a florist. He wants a boy of your age to do handy jobs and run errands about his establishment, and he wants one who is fond of flowers and would like to learn the business. He asked me to recommend him one, and I promised to look out for a suitable boy. Would you like the place, Tommy? And will you promise to be a very good boy and learn to be respectable if I ask my brother to give you a trial and a chance to make something of yourself?"

"Oh, Miss Octavia!" gasped Tommy. He wondered if he were simply having a beautiful dream.

But it was no dream. And it was all arranged later on. No one rejoiced more heartily in Tommy's success than Bessie.

"But I'll miss you dreadfully, Tommy," she said wistfully.

"Oh, I'll be home every Saturday night, and we'll have Sunday together, except when I've got to go to Sunday school. 'Cause Miss Octavia says I must," said Tommy comfortingly. "And the rest of the time you'll have Roselle Geraldine."

"Yes, I know," said Bessie, giving the blue-silk doll a fond kiss, "and she's just lovely. But she ain't as nice as you, Tommy, for all."

Then was Tommy's cup of happiness full.

Charlotte's Ladies

Just as soon as dinner was over at the asylum, Charlotte sped away to the gap in the fence — the northwest corner gap. There was a gap in the southeast corner, too — the asylum fence was in a rather poor condition — but the southeast gap was interesting only after tea, and it was never at any time quite as interesting as the northwest gap.

Charlotte ran as fast as her legs could carry her, for she did not want any of the other orphans to see her. As a rule, Charlotte liked the company of the other orphans and was a favourite with them. But, somehow, she did not want them to know about the gaps. She was sure they would not understand.

Charlotte had discovered the gaps only a week before. They had not been there in the autumn, but the snowdrifts had lain heavily against the fence all winter, and one spring day when Charlotte was creeping through the shrubbery in the northwest corner in search of the little yellow daffodils that always grew there in spring, she found a delightful space where a board had fallen off, whence she could look out on a bit of woodsy road with a little footpath winding along by the fence under the widespreading boughs of the asylum trees. Charlotte felt a wild impulse to slip out and run fast and far down that lovely, sunny, tempting, fenceless road. But that would have been wrong, for it was against the asylum rules, and Charlotte, though she hated most of the asylum rules with all her heart, never disobeyed or broke them. So she subdued the vagrant longing with a sigh and sat down among the daffodils to peer wistfully out of the gap and feast her eyes on this glimpse of a world where there were no brick walls and prim walks and never-varying rules.

Then, as Charlotte watched, the Pretty Lady with the Blue Eyes came along the footpath. Charlotte had never seen her before and hadn't the slightest idea in the world who she was, but that was what she called her as soon as she saw her. The lady was so pretty, with lovely blue eyes that were very sad, although somehow as you looked at them you felt that they ought to be laughing, merry eyes instead. At least Charlotte thought so and wished at once that she knew how to make them laugh. Besides, the Lady had lovely golden hair and the most beautiful pink cheeks, and Charlotte, who had mouse-coloured hair and any number of freckles, had an unbounded admiration for golden locks and roseleaf complexions. The Lady was dressed in black, which Charlotte didn't like, principally because the matron of the asylum wore black and Charlotte didn't—exactly—like the matron.

When the Pretty Lady with the Blue Eyes had gone by, Charlotte drew a long breath.

"If I could pick out a mother I'd pick out one that looked just like her," she said.

Nice things sometimes happen close together, even in an orphan asylum, and that very evening Charlotte discovered the southeast gap and found herself peering into the most beautiful garden you could imagine, a garden where daffodils and tulips grew in great ribbon-like beds, and there were hedges of white and purple lilacs, and winding paths under blossoming trees. It was such a garden as Charlotte had pictured in happy dreams and never expected to see in real life. And yet here it had been all the time, divided from her only by a high board fence.

"I wouldn't have s'posed there could be such a lovely place so near an orphan asylum," mused Charlotte. "It's the very loveliest place I ever saw. Oh, I do wish I could go and walk in it. Well, I do declare! If there isn't a lady in it, too!"

Sure enough, there was a lady, helping an unruly young vine to run in the way it should go over a little arbour. Charlotte instantly named her the Tall Lady with the Black Eyes. She was not nearly so young or so pretty as the Lady with the Blue Eyes, but she looked very kind and jolly.

I'd like her for an aunt, reflected Charlotte. Not for a mother—oh, no, not for a mother, but for an aunt. I know she'd make a splendid aunt. And, oh, just look at her cat!

Charlotte looked at the cat with all her might and main. She loved cats, but cats were not allowed in an orphan asylum, although Charlotte sometimes wondered if there were no orphan kittens in the world which would be appropriate for such an institution.

The Tall Lady's cat was so big and furry, with a splendid tail and elegant stripes. A Very Handsome Cat, Charlotte called him mentally, seeing the capitals as plainly as if they had been printed out. Charlotte's fingers tingled to stroke his glossy coat, but she folded them sternly together.

"You know you can't," she said to herself reproachfully, "so what is the use of wanting to, Charlotte Turner? You ought to be thankful just to see the garden and the Very Handsome Cat."

Charlotte watched the Tall Lady and the Cat until they went away into a fine, big house further up the garden, then she sighed and went back through the cherry trees to the asylum playground, where the other orphans were playing games. But, somehow, games had lost their flavour compared with those fascinating gaps.

It did not take Charlotte long to discover that the Pretty Lady always walked past the northwest gap about one o'clock every day and never at any other time — at least at no other time when Charlotte was free to watch her; and that the Tall Lady was almost always in her garden at five in the afternoon, accompanied by the Very Handsome Cat, pruning and trimming some of her flowers. Charlotte never missed being at the gaps at the proper times, if she could possibly manage it, and her heart was full of dreams about her two Ladies. But the other orphans thought all the fun had gone out of her, and the matron noticed her absent-mindedness and dosed her with sulphur and molasses for it. Charlotte took the dose meekly, as she took everything else. It was all part and parcel with being an orphan in an asylum.

"But if the Pretty Lady with the Blue Eyes was my mother, she wouldn't make me swallow such dreadful stuff," sighed Charlotte. "I don't believe even the Tall Lady with the Black Eyes would — though perhaps she might, aunts not being quite as good as mothers."

"Do you know," said Maggie Brunt, coming up to Charlotte at this moment, "that Lizzie Parker is going to be adopted? A lady is going to adopt her."

"Oh!" cried Charlotte breathlessly. An adoption was always a wonderful event in the asylum, as well as a somewhat rare one. "Oh, how splendid!"

"Yes, isn't it?" said Maggie enviously. "She picked out Lizzie because she was pretty and had curls. I don't think it is fair."

Charlotte sighed. "Nobody will ever want to adopt me, because I've mousy hair and freckles," she said. "But somebody may want you some day, Maggie. You have such lovely black hair."

"But it isn't curly," said Maggie forlornly. "And the matron won't let me put it up in curl papers at night. I just wish I was Lizzie."

Charlotte shook her head. "I don't. I'd love to be adopted, but I wouldn't really like to be anybody but myself, even if I am homely. It's better to be yourself with mousy hair and freckles than somebody else who is ever so beautiful. But I do envy Lizzie, though the matron says it is wicked to envy anyone."

Envy of the fortunate Lizzie did not long possess Charlotte's mind, however, for that very day a wonderful thing happened at noon hour by the northwest gap. Charlotte had always been very careful not to let the Pretty Lady see her, but today, after the Pretty Lady had gone past, Charlotte leaned out of the gap to watch her as far as she could. And just at that very moment the Pretty Lady looked back; and there, peering at her from the asylum fence, was a little scrap of a girl, with mouse-coloured hair and big freckles, and the sweetest, brightest, most winsome little face the Pretty Lady had ever seen. The Pretty Lady smiled right down at Charlotte and for just a moment her eyes looked as Charlotte had always known they ought to look. Charlotte was feeling rather frightened down in her heart but she smiled bravely back.

"Are you thinking of running away?" said the Pretty Lady, and, oh, what a sweet voice she had—sweet and tender, just like a mother's voice ought to be!

"No," said Charlotte, shaking her head gravely. "I should like to run away but it would be of no use, because there is no place to run to."

"Why would you like to run away?" asked the Pretty Lady, still smiling. "Don't you like living here?"

Charlotte opened her big eyes very widely. "Why, it's an orphan asylum!" she exclaimed. "Nobody could like living in an orphan asylum. But, of course, orphans should be very thankful to have any place to live in and I *am* thankful. I'd be thankfuller still if the matron wouldn't make me take sulphur and molasses. If you had a little girl, would you make her take sulphur and molasses?"

"I didn't when I had a little girl," said the Pretty Lady wistfully, and her eyes were sad again.

"Oh, did you really have a little girl once?" asked Charlotte softly.

"Yes, and she died," said the Pretty Lady in a trembling voice.

"Oh, I am sorry," said Charlotte, more softly still. "Did she—did she have lovely golden hair and pink cheeks like yours?"

"No," the Pretty Lady smiled again, though it was a very sad smile. "No, she had mouse-coloured hair and freckles."

"Oh! And weren't you sorry?"

"No, I was glad of it, because it made her look like her father. I've always loved little girls with mouse-coloured hair and freckles ever since. Well, I must hurry along. I'm late now, and schools have a dreadful habit of going in sharp on time. If you should happen to be here tomorrow, I'm going to stop and ask your name."

Of course Charlotte was at the gap the next day and they had a lovely talk. In a week they were the best of friends. Charlotte soon found out that she could make the Pretty Lady's eyes look as they ought to for a little while at least, and she spent all her spare time and lay awake at nights devising speeches to make the Pretty Lady laugh.

Then another wonderful thing happened. One evening when Charlotte went to the southeast gap, the Tall Lady with the Black Eyes was not in the garden—at least, Charlotte thought she wasn't. But the Very Handsome Cat was, sitting gravely under a syringa bush and looking quite proud of himself for being a cat.

"You Very Handsome Cat," said Charlotte, "won't you come here and let me stroke you?"

The Very Handsome Cat did come, just as if he understood English, and he purred with delight when Charlotte took him in her arms and buried her face in his fur. Then—Charlotte thought she would really sink into the ground, for the Tall Lady herself came around a lilac bush and stood before the gap.

"Please, ma'am," stammered Charlotte in an agony of embarrassment, "I wasn't meaning to do any harm to your Very Handsome Cat. I just wanted to pat him. I—I am very fond of cats and they are not allowed in orphan asylums."

"I've always thought asylums weren't run on proper principles," said the Tall Lady briskly. "Bless your heart, child, don't look so scared. You're welcome to pat the cat all you like. Come in and I'll give you some flowers."

"Thank you, but I am not allowed to go off the grounds," said Charlotte firmly, "and I think I'd rather not have any flowers because the matron might want to know where I got them, and then she would have this gap closed up. I live in mortal dread for fear it will be closed anyhow. It's very uncomfortable—living in mortal dread."

The Tall Lady laughed a very jolly laugh. "Yes, I should think it would be," she agreed. "I haven't had that experience."

Then they had a jolly talk, and every evening after that Charlotte went to the gap and stroked the Very Handsome Cat and chatted to the Tall Lady.

"Do you live all alone in that big house?" she asked wonderingly one day.

"All alone," said the Tall Lady.

"Did you always live alone?"

"No. I had a sister living with me once. But I don't want to talk about her. You'll oblige me, Charlotte, by *not* talking about her."

"I won't then," agreed Charlotte. "I can understand why people don't like to have their sisters talked about sometimes. Lily Mitchell has a big sister who was sent to jail for stealing. Of course Lily doesn't like to talk about her."

The Tall Lady laughed a little bitterly. "My sister didn't steal. She married a man I detested, that's all."

"Did he drink?" asked Charlotte gravely. "The matron's husband drank and that was why she left him and took to running an orphan asylum. I think I'd rather put up with a drunken husband than live in an orphan asylum."

"My sister's husband didn't drink," said the Tall Lady grimly. "He was beneath her, that was all. I told her I'd never forgive her and I never shall. He's dead now—he died a year after she married him—and she's working for her living. I dare say she doesn't find it very pleasant. She wasn't brought up to that. Here, Charlotte, is a turnover for you. I made it on purpose for you. Eat it and tell me if you don't think I'm a good cook. I'm dying for a compliment. I never get any now that I've got old. It's a dismal thing to get old and have nobody to love you except a cat, Charlotte."

"I think it is just as bad to be young and have nobody to love you, not *even* a cat," sighed Charlotte, enjoying the turnover, nevertheless.

"I dare say it is," agreed the Tall Lady, looking as if she had been struck by a new and rather startling idea.

I like the tall lady with the Black Eyes ever so much, thought Charlotte that night as she lay in bed, but I love the Pretty Lady. I have more fun with the Tall Lady and the Very Handsome Cat, but I always feel nicer with the Pretty Lady. Oh, I'm so glad her little girl had mouse-coloured hair.

Then the most wonderful thing of all happened. One day a week later the Pretty Lady said, "Would you like to come and live with me, Charlotte?"

Charlotte looked at her. "Are you in earnest?" she asked in a whisper.

"Indeed I am. I want you for my little girl, and if you'd like to come, you shall. I'm poor, Charlotte, really, I'm dreadfully poor, but I can make my salary stretch far enough for two, and we'll love each other enough to cover the thin spots. Will you come?"

"Well, I should just think I will!" said Charlotte emphatically. "Oh, I wish I was sure I'm not dreaming. I do love you so much, and it will be so delightful to be your little girl."

"Very well, sweetheart. I'll come tomorrow afternoon—it is Saturday, so I'll have the whole blessed day off—and see the matron about it. Oh, we'll have lovely times together, dearest. I only wish I'd discovered you long ago."

Charlotte may have eaten and studied and played and kept rules the rest of that day and part of the next, but, if so, she has no recollection of it. She went about like a girl in a dream, and the matron concluded that something more than sulphur and molasses was needed and decided to speak to the doctor about her. But she never did, because a lady came that afternoon and told her she wanted to adopt Charlotte.

Charlotte obeyed the summons to the matron's room in a tingle of excitement. But when she went in, she saw only the matron and the Tall Lady with the Black Eyes. Before Charlotte could look around for the Pretty Lady the matron said, "Charlotte, this lady, Miss Herbert, wishes to adopt you. It is a splendid thing for you, and you ought to be a very thankful little girl."

Charlotte's head fairly whirled. She clasped her hands and the tears brimmed up in her eyes.

"Oh, I like the Tall Lady," she gasped, "but I *love* the Pretty Lady and I promised her I'd be her little girl. I can't break my promise."

"What on earth is the child talking about?" said the mystified matron.

And just then the maid showed in the Pretty Lady. Charlotte flew to her and flung her arms about her.

"Oh, tell them I am your little girl!" she begged. "Tell them I promised you first. I don't want to hurt the Tall Lady's feelings because I truly do like her so very much. But I want to be your little girl."

The Pretty Lady had given one glance at the Tall Lady and flushed red. The Tall Lady, on the contrary, had grown very pale. The matron felt uncomfortable. Everybody knew that Miss Herbert and Mrs. Bond hadn't spoken to each other for years, even if they were sisters and alone in the world except for each other.

Mrs. Bond turned to the matron. "I have come to ask permission to adopt this little girl," she said.

"Oh, I'm very sorry," stammered the matron, "but Miss Herbert has just asked for her, and I have consented."

Charlotte gave a great gulp of disappointment, but the Pretty Lady suddenly wheeled around to face the Tall Lady, with quivering lips and tearful eyes.

"Don't take her from me, Alma," she pleaded humbly. "She—she is so like my own baby and I'm so lonely. Any other child will suit you as well."

"Not at all," said the Tall Lady brusquely. "Not at all, Anna. No other child will suit me at all. And may I ask what you intend to keep her on? I know your salary is barely enough for yourself."

"That is my concern," said the Pretty Lady a little proudly.

"Humph!" The Tall Lady shrugged her shoulders. "Just as independent as ever, Anna, I see. Well, child, what do *you* say? Which of us will you come with? Remember, I have the cat on my side, and Anna can't make half as good turnovers as I can. Remember all this, Charlotte."

"Oh, I—I like you so much," stammered Charlotte, "and I wish I could live with you both. But since I can't, I must go with the Pretty Lady, because I promised, and because I loved her first."

"And best?" queried the Tall Lady.

"And best," admitted Charlotte, bound to be truthful, even at the risk of hurting the Tall Lady's feelings. "But I *do* like you, too—next best. And you really don't need me as much as she does, for you have your Very Handsome Cat and she hasn't anything."

"A cat no longer satisfies the aching void in my soul," said the Tall Lady stubbornly. "Nothing will satisfy it but a little girl with mouse-coloured hair and freckles. No, Anna, I've got to have Charlotte. But I think that with her usual astuteness, she has already solved the problem for us by saying she'd like to live with us both. Why can't she? You just come back home and we'll let bygones be bygones. We both have something to forgive, but I was an obstinate old fool and I've known it for years, though I never confessed it to anybody but the cat."

The Pretty Lady softened, trembled, smiled. She went right up to the Tall Lady and put her arms about her neck.

"Oh, I've wanted so much to be friends with you again," she sobbed. "But I thought you would never relent—and—and—I've been so lonely—"

"There, there," whispered the Tall Lady, "don't cry under the matron's eye. Wait till we get home. I may have some crying to do myself then. Charlotte, go and get your hat and come right over with us. We can sign the necessary papers later on, but we must have you right off. The cat is waiting for you on the back porch, and there is a turnover cooling on the pantry window that is just your size."

"I am so happy," remarked Charlotte, "that I feel like crying myself."

Christmas at Red Butte

"Of course Santa Claus will come," said Jimmy Martin confidently. Jimmy was ten, and at ten it is easy to be confident. "Why, he's *got* to come because it is Christmas Eve, and he always *has* come. You know that, twins."

Yes, the twins knew it and, cheered by Jimmy's superior wisdom, their doubts passed away. There had been one terrible moment when Theodora had sighed and told them they mustn't be too much disappointed if Santa Claus did not come this year because the crops had been poor, and he mightn't have had enough presents to go around.

"That doesn't make any difference to Santa Claus," scoffed Jimmy. "You know as well as I do, Theodora Prentice, that Santa Claus is rich whether the crops fail or not. They failed three years ago, before Father died, but Santa Claus came all the same. Prob'bly you don't remember it, twins, 'cause you were too little, but I do. Of course he'll come, so don't you worry a mite. And he'll bring my skates and your dolls. He knows we're expecting them, Theodora, 'cause we wrote him a letter last week, and threw it up the chimney. And there'll be candy and nuts, of course, and Mother's gone to town to buy a turkey. I tell you we're going to have a ripping Christmas."

"Well, don't use such slangy words about it, Jimmy-boy," sighed Theodora. She couldn't bear to dampen their hopes any further, and perhaps Aunt Elizabeth might manage it if the colt sold well. But Theodora had her painful doubts, and she sighed again as she looked out of the window far down the trail that wound across the prairie, red-lighted by the declining sun of the short wintry afternoon.

"Do people always sigh like that when they get to be sixteen?" asked Jimmy curiously. "You didn't sigh like that when you were only fifteen, Theodora. I wish you wouldn't. It makes me feel funny—and it's not a nice kind of funniness either."

"It's a bad habit I've got into lately," said Theodora, trying to laugh. "Old folks are dull sometimes, you know, Jimmy-boy."

"Sixteen *is* awful old, isn't it?" said Jimmy reflectively. "I'll tell you what *I'm* going to do when I'm sixteen, Theodora. I'm going to pay off the mortgage, and buy mother a silk dress, and a piano for the twins. Won't that be elegant? I'll be able to do that 'cause I'm a man. Of course if I was only a girl I couldn't."

"I hope you'll be a good kind brave man and a real help to your mother," said Theodora softly, sitting down before the cosy fire and lifting the fat little twins into her lap.

"Oh, I'll be good to her, never you fear," assured Jimmy, squatting comfortably down on the little fur rug before the stove—the skin of the coyote his father had killed four years ago. "I believe in being good to your mother when you've only got the one. Now tell us a story, Theodora—a real jolly story, you know, with lots of fighting in it. Only please don't kill anybody. I like to hear about fighting, but I like to have all the people come out alive."

Theodora laughed, and began a story about the Riel Rebellion of '85—a story which had the double merit of being true and exciting at the same time. It was quite dark when she finished, and the twins were nodding, but Jimmy's eyes were wide open and sparkling.

"That was great," he said, drawing a long breath. "Tell us another."

"No, it's bedtime for you all," said Theodora firmly. "One story at a time is my rule, you know."

"But I want to sit up till Mother comes home," objected Jimmy.

"You can't. She may be very late, for she would have to wait to see Mr. Porter. Besides, you don't know what time Santa Claus might come—if he comes at all. If he were to drive along and see you children up instead of being sound asleep in bed, he might go right on and never call at all."

This argument was too much for Jimmy.

"All right, we'll go. But we have to hang up our stockings first. Twins, get yours."

The twins toddled off in great excitement, and brought back their Sunday stockings, which Jimmy proceeded to hang along the edge of the mantel shelf. This done, they all trooped obediently off to bed. Theodora gave another sigh, and seated herself at the window, where she could watch the moonlit prairie for Mrs. Martin's homecoming and knit at the same time.

I am afraid that you will think from all the sighing Theodora was doing that she was a very melancholy and despondent young lady. You couldn't think anything more unlike the real Theodora. She was the jolliest, bravest girl of sixteen in all Saskatchewan, as her shining brown eyes and rosy, dimpled cheeks would have told you; and her sighs were not on her own account, but simply for fear the children were going to be disappointed. She knew that they would be almost heartbroken if Santa Claus did not come, and that this would hurt the patient hardworking little mother more than all else.

Five years before this, Theodora had come to live with Uncle George and Aunt Elizabeth in the little log house at Red Butte. Her own mother had just died, and Theodora had only her big brother Donald left, and Donald had Klondike fever. The Martins were poor, but they had gladly made room for their little niece, and Theodora had lived there ever since, her aunt's right-hand girl and the beloved playmate of the children. They had been very happy until Uncle George's death two years before this Christmas Eve; but since then there had been hard times in the little log house, and though Mrs. Martin and Theodora did their best, it was a woefully hard task to make both ends meet, especially this year when their crops had been poor. Theodora and her aunt had made every sacrifice possible for the children's sake, and at least Jimmy and the twins had not felt the pinch very severely yet.

At seven Mrs. Martins bells jingled at the door and Theodora flew out. "Go right in and get warm, Auntie," she said briskly. "I'll take Ned away and unharness him."

"It's a bitterly cold night," said Mrs. Martin wearily. There was a note of discouragement in her voice that struck dismay to Theodora's heart.

"I'm afraid it means no Christmas for the children tomorrow," she thought sadly, as she led Ned away to the stable. When she returned to the kitchen Mrs. Martin was sitting by the fire, her face in her chilled hand, sobbing convulsively.

"Auntie—oh, Auntie, don't!" exclaimed Theodora impulsively. It was such a rare thing to see her plucky, resolute little aunt in tears. "You're cold and tired—I'll have a nice cup of tea for you in a trice."

"No, it isn't that," said Mrs. Martin brokenly "It was seeing those stockings hanging there. Theodora, I couldn't get a thing for the children—not a single thing. Mr. Porter would only give forty dollars for the colt, and when all the bills were paid there was barely enough left for such necessaries as we must have. I suppose I ought to feel thankful I could get those. But the thought of the children's disappointment tomorrow is more than I can bear. It would have been better to have told them long ago, but I kept building on getting more for the colt. Well, it's weak and foolish to give way like this. We'd better both take a cup of tea and go to bed. It will save fuel."

When Theodora went up to her little room her face was very thoughtful. She took a small box from her table and carried it to the window. In it was a very pretty little gold locket hung on a narrow blue ribbon. Theodora held it tenderly in her fingers, and looked out over the moonlit prairie with a very sober face. Could she give up her dear locket—the locket Donald had given her just before he started for the Klondike? She had never thought she could do such a thing. It was almost the only thing she had to remind her of

Donald—handsome, merry, impulsive, warmhearted Donald, who had gone away four years ago with a smile on his bonny face and splendid hope in his heart.

"Here's a locket for you, Gift o' God," he had said gaily—he had such a dear loving habit of calling her by the beautiful meaning of her name. A lump came into Theodora's throat as she remembered it. "I couldn't afford a chain too, but when I come back I'll bring you a rope of Klondike nuggets for it."

Then he had gone away. For two years letters had come from him regularly. Then he wrote that he had joined a prospecting party to a remote wilderness. After that was silence, deepening into anguish of suspense that finally ended in hopelessness. A rumour came that Donald Prentice was dead. None had returned from the expedition he had joined. Theodora had long ago given up all hope of ever seeing Donald again. Hence her locket was doubly dear to her.

But Aunt Elizabeth had always been so good and loving and kind to her. Could she not make the sacrifice for her sake? Yes, she could and would. Theodora flung up her head with a gesture that meant decision. She took out of the locket the bits of hair—her mother's and Donald's—which it contained (perhaps a tear or two fell as she did so) and then hastily donned her warmest cap and wraps. It was only three miles to Spencer; she could easily walk it in an hour and, as it was Christmas Eve, the shops would be open late. She muse walk, for Ned could not be taken out again, and the mare's foot was sore. Besides, Aunt Elizabeth must not know until it was done.

As stealthily as if she were bound on some nefarious errand, Theodora slipped downstairs and out of the house. The next minute she was hurrying along the trail in the moonlight. The great dazzling prairie was around her, the mystery and splendour of the northern night all about her. It was very calm and cold, but Theodora walked so briskly that she kept warm. The trail from Red Butte to Spencer was a lonely one. Mr. Lurgan's house, halfway to town, was the only dwelling on it.

When Theodora reached Spencer she made her way at once to the only jewellery store the little town contained. Mr. Benson, its owner, had been a friend of her uncle's, and Theodora felt sure that he would buy her locket. Nevertheless her heart beat quickly, and her breath came and went uncomfortably fast as she went in. Suppose he wouldn't buy it. Then there would be no Christmas for the children at Red Butte.

"Good evening, Miss Theodora," said Mr. Benson briskly. "What can I do for you?"

"I'm afraid I'm not a very welcome sort of customer, Mr. Benson," said Theodora, with an uncertain smile. "I want to sell, not buy. Could you—will you buy this locket?"

Mr. Benson pursed up his lips, took up the locket, and examined it. "Well, I don't often buy second-hand stuff," he said, after some reflection, "but I don't mind obliging you, Miss Theodora. I'll give you four dollars for this trinket."

Theodora knew the locket had cost a great deal more than that, but four dollars would get what she wanted, and she dared not ask for more. In a few minutes the locket was in Mr. Benson's possession, and Theodora, with four crisp new bills in her purse, was hurrying to the toy store. Half an hour later she was on her way back to Red Butte, with as many parcels as she could carry — Jimmy's skates, two lovely dolls for the twins, packages of nuts and candy, and a nice plump turkey. Theodora beguiled her lonely tramp by picturing the children's joy in the morning.

About a quarter of a mile past Mr. Lurgan's house the trail curved suddenly about a bluff of poplars. As Theodora rounded the turn she halted in amazement. Almost at her feet the body of a man was lying across the road. He was clad in a big fur coat, and had a fur cap pulled well down over his forehead and ears. Almost all of him that could be seen was a full bushy beard. Theodora had no idea who he was, or where he had come from. But she realized that he was unconscious, and that he would speedily freeze to death if help were not brought. The footprints of a horse galloping across the prairie suggested a fall and a runaway, but Theodora did not waste time in speculation. She ran back at full speed to Mr. Lurgan's, and roused the household. In a few minutes Mr. Lurgan and his son had hitched a horse to a wood-sleigh, and hurried down the trail to the unfortunate man.

Theodora, knowing that her assistance was not needed, and that she ought to get home as quickly as possible, went on her way as soon as she had seen the stranger in safe keeping. When she reached the little log house she crept in, cautiously put the children's gifts in their stockings, placed the turkey on the table where Aunt Elizabeth would see it the first thing in the morning, and then slipped off to bed, a very weary but very happy girl.

The joy that reigned in the little log house the next day more than repaid Theodora for her sacrifice.

"Whoopee, didn't I tell you that Santa Claus would come all right!" shouted the delighted Jimmy. "Oh, what splendid skates!"

The twins hugged their dolls in silent rapture, but Aunt Elizabeth's face was the best of all.

Then the dinner had to be prepared, and everybody had a hand in that. Just as Theodora, after a grave peep into the oven, had announced that the turkey was done, a sleigh dashed around the house. Theodora flew to answer the knock at the door, and there stood Mr. Lurgan and a big, bewhiskered, fur-coated fellow whom Theodora recognized as the stranger she had found on the trail. But—*was* he a stranger? There was something oddly familiar in those merry brown eyes. Theodora felt herself growing dizzy.

"Donald!" she gasped. "Oh, Donald!"

And then she was in the big fellow's arms, laughing and crying at the same time.

Donald it was indeed. And then followed half an hour during which everybody talked at once, and the turkey would have been burned to a crisp had it not been for the presence of mind of Mr. Lurgan who, being the least excited of them all, took it out of the oven, and set it on the back of the stove.

"To think that it was you last night, and that I never dreamed it," exclaimed Theodora. "Oh, Donald, if I hadn't gone to town!"

"I'd have frozen to death, I'm afraid," said Donald soberly. "I got into Spencer on the last train last night. I felt that I must come right out—I couldn't wait till morning. But there wasn't a team to be got for love or money—it was Christmas Eve and all the livery rigs were out. So I came on horseback. Just by that bluff something frightened my horse, and he shied violently. I was half asleep and thinking of my little sister, and I went off like a shot. I suppose I struck my head against a tree. Anyway, I knew nothing more until I came to in Mr. Lurgan's kitchen. I wasn't much hurt—feel none the worse of it except for a sore head and shoulder. But, oh, Gift o' God, how you have grown! I can't realize that you are the little sister I left four years ago. I suppose you have been thinking I was dead?"

"Yes, and, oh, Donald, where *have* you been?"

"Well, I went way up north with a prospecting party. We had a tough time the first year, I can tell you, and some of us never came back. We weren't in a country where post offices were lying round loose either, you see. Then at last, just as we were about giving up in despair, we struck it rich. I've brought a snug little pile home with me, and things are going to look up in this log house, Gift o' God. There'll be no more worrying for you dear people over mortgages."

"I'm so glad—for Auntie's sake," said Theodora, with shining eyes. "But, oh, Donald, it's best of all just to have you back. I'm so perfectly happy that I don't know what to do or say."

"Well, I think you might have dinner," said Jimmy in an injured tone. "The turkey's getting stone cold, and I'm most starving. I just can't stand it another minute."

So, with a laugh, they all sat down to the table and ate the merriest Christmas dinner the little log house had ever known.

How We Went to the Wedding

"If it were to clear up I wouldn't know how to behave, it would seem so unnatural," said Kate. "Do you, by any chance, remember what the sun looks like, Phil?"

"Does the sun ever shine in Saskatchewan anyhow?" I asked with assumed sarcasm, just to make Kate's big, bonny black eyes flash.

They did flash; but Kate laughed immediately after, as she sat down on a chair in front of me and cradled her long, thin, spirited dark face in her palms.

"We have more sunny weather in Saskatchewan than in all the rest of Canada put together, in an average year," she said, clicking her strong, white teeth and snapping her eyes at me. "But I can't blame you for feeling sceptical about it, Phil. If I went to a new country and it rained every day—all day—all night—after I got there for three whole weeks I'd think things not lawful to be uttered about the climate too. So, little cousin, I forgive you. Remember that 'into each life some rain must fall, some days must be dark and dreary.' Oh, if you'd only come to visit me last fall. We had such a bee-yew-tiful September last year. We were drowned in sunshine. This fall we're drowned in water. Old settlers tell of a similar visitation in '72, though they claim even that wasn't quite as bad as this."

I was sitting rather disconsolately by an upper window of Uncle Kenneth Morrison's log house at Arrow Creek. Below was what in dry weather—so, at least, I was told—was merely a pretty, grassy little valley, but which was now a considerable creek of muddy yellow water, rising daily. Beyond was a cheerless prospect of sodden prairie and dripping "bluff."

"It would be a golden, mellow land, with purple hazes over the bluffs, in a normal fall," assured Kate. "Even now if the sun were just to shine out for a day and a good 'chinook' blow you'd see a surprising change. I feel like chanting continually that old rhyme I learned in the first primer,

> 'Rain, rain, go away,Come again some other day:—some other
> day next summer—Phil and Katie want to play.'

Philippa, dear girl, don't look so dismal. It's bound to clear up sometime."

"I wish the 'sometime' would come soon, then," I said, rather grumpily.

"You know it hasn't really rained for three days," protested Kate. "It's been damp and horrid and threatening, but it hasn't rained. I defy you to say that it has actually rained."

"When it's so wet underfoot that you can't stir out without rubber boots it might as well be wet overhead too," I said, still grumpily.

"I believe you're homesick, girl," said Kate anxiously.

"No, I'm not," I answered, laughing, and feeling ashamed of my ungraciousness. "Nobody could be homesick with such a jolly good fellow as you around, Kate. It's only that this weather is getting on my nerves a bit. I'm fit for treasons, stratagems, and spoils. If your chinook doesn't come soon, Kitty, I'll do something quite desperate."

"I feel that way myself," admitted Kate. "Real reckless, Phil. Anyhow, let's put on our despised rubber boots and sally out for a wade."

"Here's Jim Nash coming on horseback down the trail," I said. "Let's wait and see if he's got the mail."

We hurried down, Kate humming, "Somewhere the sun is shining," solely, I believe, because she knew it aggravated me. At any other time I should probably have thrown a pillow at her, but just now I was too eager to see if Jim Nash had brought any mail.

I had come from Ontario, the first of September, to visit Uncle Kenneth Morrison's family. I had been looking forward to the trip for several years. My cousin Kate and I had always corresponded since they had "gone west" ten years before; and Kate, who revelled in the western life, had sung the praises of her adopted land rapturously and constantly. It was quite a joke on her that, when I did finally come to visit her, I should have struck the wettest autumn ever recorded in the history of the west. A wet September in Saskatchewan is no joke, however. The country was almost "flooded out." The trails soon became nearly impassable. All our plans for drives and picnics and inter-neighbour visiting—at that time a neighbour meant a man who lived at least six miles away—had to be given up. Yet I was not lonesome, and I enjoyed my visit in spite of everything. Kate was a host in herself. She was twenty-eight years old—eight years my senior—but the difference in our ages had never been any barrier to our friendship. She was a jolly, companionable, philosophical soul, with a jest for every situation, and a merry solution for every perplexity. The only fault I had to find with her was her tendency to make parodies. Kate's parodies were perfectly awful and always got on my nerves.

She was dreadfully ashamed of the way the Saskatchewan weather was behaving after all her boasting. She was thin at the best of times, but now she grew positively scraggy with the worry of it. I am afraid I took an unholy delight in teasing her, and abused the western weather even more than was necessary.

Jim Nash — the lank youth who was hired to look after the place during Uncle Kenneth's absence on a prolonged threshing expedition — had brought some mail. Kate's share was a letter, postmarked Bothwell, a rising little town about one hundred and twenty miles from Arrow Creek. Kate had several friends there, and one of our plans had been to visit Bothwell and spend a week with them. We had meant to drive, of course, since there was no other way of getting there, and equally of course the plan had been abandoned because of the wet weather.

"Mother," exclaimed Kate, "Mary Taylor is going to be married in a fortnight's time! She wants Phil and me to go up to Bothwell for the wedding."

"What a pity you can't go," remarked Aunt Jennie placidly. Aunt Jennie was always a placid little soul, with a most enviable knack of taking everything easy. Nothing ever worried her greatly, and when she had decided that a thing was inevitable it did not worry her at all.

"But I am going," cried Kate. "I will go — I must go. I positively cannot let Mary Taylor — my own beloved Molly — go and perpetrate matrimony without my being on hand to see it. Yes, I'm going — and if Phil has a spark of the old Blair pioneer spirit in her, she'll go too."

"Of course I'll go if you go," I said.

Aunt Jennie did not think we were in earnest, so she merely laughed at first, and said, "How do you propose to go? Fly — or swim?"

"We'll drive, as usual," said Kate calmly. "I'd feel more at home in that way of locomotion. We'll borrow Jim Nash's father's democrat, and take the ponies. We'll put on old clothes, raincoats, rubber caps and boots, and we'll start tomorrow. In an ordinary time we could easily do it in six days or less, but this fall we'll probably need ten or twelve."

"You don't really mean to go, Kate!" said Aunt Jennie, beginning to perceive that Kate did mean it.

"I do," said Kate, in a convincing tone.

Aunt Jennie felt a little worried — as much as she could feel worried over anything — and she tried her best to dissuade Kate, although she plainly did not have much hope of doing so, having had enough experience with her determined daughter to realize that when Kate said she was going to do a thing she did it. It was rather funny to listen to the ensuing dialogue.

"Kate, you can't do it. It's a crazy idea! The road is one hundred and twenty miles long."

"I've driven it twice, Mother."

"Yes, but not in such a wet year. The trail is impassable in places."

"Oh, there are always plenty of dry spots to be found if you only look hard for them."

"But you don't know where to look for them, and goodness knows what you'll get into while you are looking."

"We'll call at the M.P. barracks and get an Indian to guide us. Indians always know the dry spots."

"The stage driver has decided not to make another trip till the October frosts set in."

"But he always has such a heavy load. It will be quite different with us, you must remember. We'll travel light—just our provisions and a valise containing our wedding garments."

"What will you do if you get mired twenty miles from a human being?"

"But we won't. I'm a good driver and I haven't nerves—but I have nerve. Besides, you forget that we'll have an Indian guide with us."

"There was a company of Hudson Bay freighters ambushed and killed along that very trail by Blackfoot Indians in 1839," said Aunt Jennie dolefully.

"Fifty years ago! Their ghosts must have ceased to haunt it by this time," said Kate flippantly.

"Well, you'll get wet through and catch your deaths of cold," protested Aunt Jennie.

"No fear of it. We'll be cased in rubber. And we'll borrow a good tight tent from the M.P.s. Besides, I'm sure it's not going to rain much more. I know the signs."

"At least wait for a day or two until you're sure that it has cleared up," implored Aunt Jennie.

"Which being interpreted means, 'Wait for a day or two, because then your father may be home and he'll squelch your mad expedition,'" said Kate, with a sly glance at me. "No, no, my mother, your wiles are in vain. We'll hit the trail tomorrow at sunrise. So just be good, darling, and help us pack up some provisions. I'll send Jim for his father's democrat."

Aunt Jennie resigned herself to the inevitable and betook herself to the pantry with the air of a woman who washes her hands of the consequences. I flew upstairs to pack some finery. I was wild with delight over the proposed outing. I did not realize what it actually meant, and I had perfect confidence in Kate, who was an expert driver, an experienced camper out, and an excellent manager. If I could have seen what was ahead of us I would certainly not have been quite so jubilant and reckless, but I would have gone all the same. I would not miss the laughter-provoking memories of that trip out of my life for anything. I have always been glad I went.

We left at sunrise the next morning; there was a sunrise that morning, for a wonder. The sun came up in a pinky-saffron sky and promised us a fine day. Aunt Jennie bade us goodbye and, estimable woman that she was, did not trouble us with advice or forebodings.

Mr. Nash had sent over his "democrat," a light wagon with springs; and Kate's "shaganappies," Tom and Jerry—native ponies, the toughest horse flesh to be found in the world—were hitched to it. Kate and I were properly accoutred for our trip and looked—but I try to forget how we looked! The memory is not flattering.

We drove off in the gayest of spirits. Our difficulties began at the start, for we had to drive a mile before we could find a place to ford the creek. Beyond that, however, we had a passable trail for three miles to the little outpost of the Mounted Police, where five or six men were stationed on detachment duty.

"Sergeant Baker is a friend of mine," said Kate. "He'll be only too glad to lend me all we require."

The sergeant was a friend of Kate's, but he looked at her as if he thought she was crazy when she told him where we were going.

"You'd better take a canoe instead of a team," he said sarcastically. "I've a good notion to arrest you both as horse thieves and prevent you from going on such a mad expedition."

"You know nothing short of arrest would stop me," said Kate, nodding at him with laughing eyes, "and you really won't go to such an extreme, I know. So please be nice, even if it comes hard, and lend us some things. I've come a-borrying."

"I won't lend you a thing," declared the sergeant. "I won't aid and abet you in any such freak as this. Go home now, like a good girl."

"I'm not going home," said Kate. "I'm not a 'good girl'—I'm a wicked old maid, and I'm going to Bothwell. If you won't lend us a tent we'll go without—and sleep in the open—and our deaths will lie forever at your door. I'll come back and haunt you, if you don't lend me a tent. I'll camp on your very threshold and you won't be able to go out of your door without falling over my spook."

"I've more fear of being accountable for your death if I do let you go," said Sergeant Baker dubiously. "However, I see that nothing but physical force will prevent you. What do you want?"

"I want," said Kate, "a cavalry tent, a sheet-iron camp stove, and a good Indian guide — old Peter Crow for choice. He's such a respectable-looking old fellow, and his wife often works for us."

The sergeant gave us the tent and stove, and sent a man down to the Reserve for Peter Crow. Moreover, he vindicated his title of friend by making us take a dozen prairie chickens and a large ham — besides any quantity of advice. We didn't want the advice but we hugely welcomed the ham. Presently our guide appeared — quite a spruce old Indian, as Indians go. I had never been able to shake off my childhood conviction that an Indian was a fearsome creature, hopelessly addicted to scalping knives and tomahawks, and I secretly felt quite horrified at the idea of two defenceless females starting out on a lonely prairie trail with an Indian for guide. Even old Peter Crow's meek appearance did not quite reassure me; but I kept my qualms to myself, for I knew Kate would only laugh at me.

It was ten when we finally got away from the M.P. outpost. Sergeant Baker bade us goodbye in a tone which seemed to intimate that he never expected to see either of us again. What with his dismal predictions and my secret horror of Indians, I was beginning to feel anything but jubilant over our expedition. Kate, however, was as blithe and buoyant as usual. She knew no fear, being one of those enviable folk who can because they think they can. One hundred and twenty miles of half-flooded prairie trail — camping out at night in the solitude of the Great Lone Land — rain — muskegs — Indian guides — nothing had any terror for my dauntless cousin.

For the next three hours, however, we got on beautifully. The trail was fair, though somewhat greasy; the sun shone, though with a somewhat watery gleam, through the mists; and Peter Crow, coiled up on the folded tent behind the seat, slept soundly and snored mellifluously. That snore reassured me greatly. I had never thought of Indians as snoring. Surely one who did couldn't be dreaded greatly.

We stopped at one o'clock and had a cold lunch, sitting in our wagon, while Peter Crow wakened up and watered the ponies. We did not get on so well in the afternoon. The trail descended into low-lying ground where travelling was very difficult. I had to admit old Peter Crow was quite invaluable. He knew, as Kate had foretold, "all the dry spots" — that is to say, spots less wet than others. But, even so, we had to make so many detours that by sunset we were little more than six miles distant from our noon halting place.

"We'd better set camp now, before it gets any darker," said Kate. "There's a capital spot over there, by that bluff of dead poplar. The ground seems pretty dry too. Peter, cut us a set of tent poles and kindle a fire."

"Want my dollar first," said old Peter stolidly.

We had agreed to pay him a dollar a day for the trip, but none of the money was to be paid until we got to Bothwell. Kate told him this. But all the reply she got was a stolid, "Want dollar. No make fire without dollar."

We were getting cold and it was getting dark, so finally Kate, under the law of necessity, paid him his dollar. Then he carried out our orders at his own sweet leisure. In course of time he got a fire lighted, and while we cooked supper he set up the tent and prepared our beds, by cutting piles of brush and covering them with rugs.

Kate and I had a hilarious time cooking that supper. It was my first experience of camping out and, as I had become pretty well convinced that Peter Crow was not the typical Indian of old romance, I enjoyed it all hugely. But we were both very tired, and as soon as we had finished eating we betook ourselves to our tent and found our brush beds much more comfortable than I had expected. Old Peter coiled up on his blanket outside by the fire, and the great silence of a windless prairie enwrapped us. In a few minutes we were sound asleep and never wakened until seven o'clock.

When we arose and lifted the flap of the tent we saw a peculiar sight. The little elevation on which we had pitched our camp seemed to be an island in a vast sea of white mist, dotted here and there with other islands. On every hand to the far horizon stretched that strange, phantasmal ocean, and a hazy sun looked over the shifting billows. I had never seen a western mist before and I thought it extremely beautiful; but Kate, to whom it was no novelty, was more cumbered with breakfast cares.

"I'm ravenous," she said, as she bustled about among our stores. "Camping out always does give one such an appetite. Aren't you hungry, Phil?"

"Comfortably so," I admitted. "But where are our ponies? And where is Peter Crow?"

"Probably the ponies have strayed away looking for pea vines. They love and adore pea vines," said Kate, stirring up the fire from under its blanket of grey ashes. "And Peter Crow has gone to look for them, good old fellow. When you do get a conscientious Indian there is no better guide in the world, but they are rare. Now, Philippa-girl, just pry out the sergeant's ham and shave a few slices off it for our breakfast. Some savoury fried ham always goes well on the prairie."

I went for the ham but could not find it. A thorough search among our effects revealed it not.

"Kate, I can't find the ham," I called out. "It must have fallen out somewhere on the trail."

Kate ceased wrestling with the fire and came to help in the search for the missing delicacy.

"It couldn't have fallen out," she said incredulously. "That is impossible. The tent was fastened securely over everything. Nothing could have jolted out."

"Well, then, where is the ham?" I said.

That question was unanswerable, as Kate discovered after another thorough search. The ham was gone — that much was certain.

"I believe Peter Crow has levanted with the ham," I said decidedly.

"I don't believe Peter Crow could be so dishonest," said Kate rather shortly. "His wife has worked for us for years, and she's as honest as the sunlight."

"Honesty isn't catching," I remarked, but I said nothing more just then, for Kate's black eyes were snapping.

"Anyway, we can't have ham for breakfast," she said, twitching out the frying pan rather viciously. "We'll have to put up with canned chicken — if the cans haven't disappeared too."

They hadn't, and we soon produced a very tolerable breakfast. But neither of us had much appetite.

"Do you suppose Peter Crow has taken the horses as well as the ham?" I asked.

"No," gloomily responded Kate, who had evidently been compelled by the logic of hard facts to believe in Peter's guilt, "he would hardly dare to do that, because he couldn't dispose of them without being found out. They've probably strayed away on their own account when Peter decamped. As soon as this mist lifts I'll have a look for them. They can't have gone far."

We were spared this trouble, however, for when we were washing up the dishes the ponies returned of their own accord. Kate caught them and harnessed them.

"Are we going on?" I asked mildly.

"Of course we're going on," said Kate, her good humour entirely restored. "Do you suppose I'm going to be turned from my purpose by the defection of a miserable old Indian? Oh, wait till he comes round in the winter, begging."

"Will he come?" I asked.

"Will he? Yes, my dear, he will — with a smooth, plausible story to account for his desertion and a bland denial of ever having seen our ham. I shall know how to deal with him then, the old scamp."

"When you do get a conscientious Indian there's no better guide in the world, but they are rare," I remarked with a far-away look.

Kate laughed.

"Don't rub it in, Phil. Come, help me to break camp. We'll have to work harder and hustle for ourselves, that's all."

"But is it safe to go on without a guide?" I inquired dubiously. I hadn't felt very safe with Peter Crow, but I felt still more unsafe without him.

"Safe! Of course, it's safe—perfectly safe. I know the trail, and we'll just have to drive around the wet places. It would have been easier with Peter, and we'd have had less work to do, but we'll get along well enough without him. I don't think I'd have bothered with him at all, only I wanted to set Mother's mind at rest. She'll never know he isn't with us till the trip is over, so that is all right. We're going to have a glorious day. But, oh, for our lost ham! 'The Ham That Was Never Eaten.' There's a subject for a poem, Phil. You write one when we get back to civilization. Methinks I can sniff the savoury odour of that lost ham on all the prairie breezes."

> "Of all sad words of tongue or pen,The saddest are these—it might have been,"

I quoted, beginning to wash the dishes.

> "Saw ye my wee ham, saw ye my ain ham,Saw ye my pork ham down on yon lea?Crossed it the prairie last night in the darknessBorne by an old and unprincipled Cree?"

sang Kate, loosening the tent ropes. Altogether, we got a great deal more fun out of that ham than if we had eaten it.

As Kate had predicted, the day was glorious. The mists rolled away and the sun shone brightly. We drove all day without stopping, save for dinner—when the lost ham figured largely in our conversation—of course. We said so many witty things about it—at least, we thought them witty—that we laughed continuously through the whole meal, which we ate with prodigious appetite.

But with all our driving we were not getting on very fast. The country was exceedingly swampy and we had to make innumerable detours.

"'The longest way round is the shortest way to Bothwell,'" said Kate, when we drove five miles out of our way to avoid a muskeg. By evening we had driven fully twenty-five miles, but we were only ten miles nearer Bothwell than when we had broken camp in the morning.

"We'll have to camp soon," sighed Kate. "I believe around this bluff will be a good place. Oh, Phil, I'm tired—dead tired! My very thoughts are tired. I can't even think anything funny about the ham. And yet we've got to set up the tent ourselves, and attend to the horses; and we'll have to scrape some of the mud off this beautiful vehicle."

"We can leave that till the morning," I suggested.

"No, it will be too hard and dry then. Here we are—and here are two tepees of Indians also!"

There they were, right around the bluff. The inmates were standing in a group before them, looking at us as composedly as if we were not at all an unusual sight.

"I'm going to stay here anyhow," said Kate doggedly.

"Oh, don't," I said in alarm. "They're such a villainous-looking lot—so dirty—and they've got so little clothing on. I wouldn't sleep a wink near them. Look at that awful old squaw with only one eye. They'd steal everything we've got left, Kate. Remember the ham—oh, pray remember the fate of our beautiful ham."

"I shall never forget that ham," said Kate wearily, "but, Phil, we can't drive far enough to be out of their reach if they really want to steal our provisions. But I don't believe they will. I believe they have plenty of food—Indians in tepees mostly have. The men hunt, you know. Their looks are probably the worst of them. Anyhow, you can't judge Indians by appearances. Peter Crow looked respectable—and he was a whited sepulchre. Now, these Indians look as bad as Indians can look—so they may turn out to be angels in disguise."

"Very much disguised, certainly," I acquiesced satirically. "They seem to me to belong to the class of a neighbour of ours down east. Her family is always in rags, because she says, 'a hole is an accident, a patch is a disgrace,' Set camp here if you like, Kate. But I'll not sleep a wink with such neighbours."

I cheerfully ate my words later on. Never were appearances more deceptive than in the case of those Stoneys. There is an old saying that many a kind heart beats behind a ragged coat. The Indians had no coats for their hearts to beat behind—nothing but shirts—some of them hadn't even shirts! But the shirts were certainly ragged enough, and their hearts were kind.

Those Indians were gentlemen. They came forward and unhitched our horses, fed, and watered them; they pitched our tent, and built us a fire, and cut brush for our beds. Kate and I had simply nothing to do except sit on our rugs and tell them what we wanted done. They would have cooked our supper for us if we had allowed it. But, tired as we were, we drew the line at that. Their hearts were pure gold, but their hands! No, Kate and I dragged ourselves up and cooked our own suppers. And while we ate it, those Indians fell to and cleaned all the mud off our democrat for us. To crown all—it is almost unbelievable but it is true, I solemnly avow—they wouldn't take a cent of payment for it all, urge them as we might and did.

"Well," said Kate, as we curled up on our brush beds that night, "there certainly is a special Providence for unprotected females. I'd forgive Peter Crow for deserting us for the sake of those Indians, if he hadn't stolen our lovely ham into the bargain. That was altogether unpardonable."

In the morning the Indians broke camp for us and harnessed our shaganappies. We drove off, waving our hands to them, the delightful creatures. We never saw any of them again. I fear their kind is scarce, but as long as I live I shall remember those Stoneys with gratitude.

We got on fairly well that third day, and made about fifteen miles before dinner time. We ate three of the sergeant's prairie chickens for dinner, and enjoyed them.

"But only think how delicious the ham would have been," said Kate.

Our real troubles began that afternoon. We had not been driving long when the trail swooped down suddenly into a broad depression—a swamp, so full of mud-holes that there didn't seem to be anything but mud-holes. We pulled through six of them—but in the seventh we stuck, hard and fast. Pull as our ponies could and did, they could not pull us out.

"What are we to do?" I said, becoming horribly frightened all at once. It seemed to me that our predicament was a dreadful one.

"Keep cool," said Kate. She calmly took off her shoes and stockings, tucked up her skirt, and waded to the horses' heads.

"Can't I do anything?" I implored.

"Yes, take the whip and spare it not," said Kate. "I'll encourage them here with sundry tugs and inspiring words. You urge them behind with a good lambasting."

Accordingly we encouraged and urged, tugged and lambasted, with a right good will, but all to no effect. Our ponies did their best, but they could not pull the democrat out of that slough.

"Oh, what—" I began, and then I stopped. I resolved that I would not ask that question again in that tone in that scrape. I would be cheerful and courageous like Kate—splendid Kate!

"I shall have to unhitch them, tie one of them to that stump, and ride off on the other for help," said Kate.

"Where to?" I asked.

"Till I find it," grinned Kate, who seemed to think the whole disaster a capital joke. "I may have to go clean back to the tepees—and further. For that matter, I don't believe there were any tepees. Those Indians were too good to be true—they were phantoms of delight—such stuff as dreams are made of. But even if they were real they won't be there now—they'll have folded their tents like the Arabs and as silently stolen away. But I'll find help somewhere."

"I can't stay here alone. You may be gone for hours," I cried, forgetting all my resolutions of courage and cheerfulness in an access of panic.

"Then ride the other pony and come with me," suggested Kate.

"I can't ride bareback," I moaned.

"Then you'll have to stay here," said Kate decidedly. "There's nothing to hurt you, Phil. Sit in the wagon and keep dry. Eat something if you get hungry. I may not be very long."

I realized that there was nothing else to do; and, rather ashamed of my panic, I resigned myself to the inevitable and saw Kate off with a smile of encouragement. Then I waited. I was tired and frightened—horribly frightened. I sat there and imagined scores of gruesome possibilities. It was no use telling myself to be brave. I couldn't be brave. I never was in such a blue funk before or since. Suppose Kate got lost—suppose she couldn't find me again—suppose something happened to her—suppose she couldn't get help—suppose it came on night and I there all alone—suppose Indians—not gentlemanly Stoneys or even Peter Crows, but genuine, old-fashioned Indians—should come along—suppose it began to pour rain!

It did begin to rain, the only one of my suppositions which came true. I hoisted an umbrella and sat there grimly, in that horseless wagon in the mud-hole.

Many a time since have I laughed over the memory of the appearance I must have presented sitting in that mud-hole, but there was nothing in the least funny about it at the time. The worst feature of it all was the uncertainty. I could have waited patiently enough and conquered my fears if I had known that Kate would find help and return within a reasonable time—at least before dark. But everything was doubtful. I was not composed of the stuff out of which heroines are fashioned and I devoutly wished we had never left Arrow Creek.

Shouts—calls—laughter—Kate's dear voice in an encouraging cry from the hill behind me!

"Halloo, honey! Hold the fort a few minutes longer. Here we are. Bless her, hasn't she been a brick to stay here all alone like this—and a tenderfoot at that?"

I could have cried with joy. But I saw that there were men with Kate—two men—white men—and I laughed instead. I had not been brave—I had been an arrant little coward, but I vowed that nobody, not even Kate, should suspect it. Later on Kate told me how she had fared in her search for assistance.

"When I left you, Phil, I felt much more anxious than I wanted to let you see. I had no idea where to go. I knew there were no houses along our trail and I might have to go clean back to the tepees — fifteen miles bareback. I didn't dare try any other trail, for I knew nothing of them and wasn't sure that there were even tepees on them. But when I had gone about six miles I saw a welcome sight — nothing less than a spiral of blue, homely-looking smoke curling up from the prairie far off to my right. I decided to turn off and investigate. I rode two miles and finally I came to a little log shack. There was a bee-yew-tiful big horse in a corral close by. My heart jumped with joy. But suppose the inmates of the shack were half-breeds! You can't realize how relieved I felt when the door opened and two white men came out. In a few minutes everything was explained. They knew who I was and what I wanted, and I knew that they were Mr. Lonsdale and Mr. Hopkins, owners of a big ranch over by Deer Run. They were 'shacking out' to put up some hay and Mrs. Hopkins was keeping house for them. She wanted me to stop and have a cup of tea right off, but I thought of you, Phil, and declined. As soon as they heard of our predicament those lovely men got their two biggest horses and came right with me."

It was not long before our democrat was on solid ground once more, and then our rescuers insisted that we go back to the shack with them for the night. Accordingly we drove back to the shack, attended by our two gallant deliverers on white horses. Mrs. Hopkins was waiting for us, a trim, dark-haired little lady in a very pretty gown, which she had donned in our honour. Kate and I felt like perfect tramps beside her in our muddy old raiment, with our hair dressed by dead reckoning — for we had not included a mirror in our baggage. There was a mirror in the shack, however — small but good — and we quickly made ourselves tidy at least, and Kate even went to the length of curling her bangs — bangs were in style then and Kate had long, thick ones — using the stem of a broken pipe of Mr. Hopkins's for a curler. I was so tired that my vanity was completely crushed out — for the time being — and I simply pinned my bangs back. Later on, when I discovered that Mr. Lonsdale was really the younger son of an English earl, I wished I had curled them, but it was too late then.

He didn't look in the least like a scion of aristocracy. He wore a cowboy rig and had a scrubby beard of a week's growth. But he was very jolly and played the violin beautifully. After tea — and a lovely tea it was, although, as Kate remarked to me later, there was no ham — we had an impromptu concert. Mr. Lonsdale played the violin; Mrs. Hopkins, who sang, was a graduate of a musical conservatory; Mr. Hopkins gave a comic recitation and did a Cree war-dance; Kate gave a spirited account of our adventures since leaving home and mother; and I described — with trimmings — how I felt sitting alone in the democrat in a mud-hole, in a pouring rain on a vast prairie.

Mrs. Hopkins, Kate, and I slept in the one bed the shack boasted, screened off from public view by a calico curtain. Mr. Lonsdale reposed in his accustomed bunk by the stove, but poor Mr. Hopkins had to sleep on the floor. He must have been glad Kate and I stayed only one night.

The fourth morning found us blithely hitting the trail in renewed confidence and spirits. We parted from our kind friends in the shack with mutual regret. Mr. Hopkins gave us a haunch of jumping deer and Mrs. Hopkins gave us a box of home-made cookies. Mr. Lonsdale at first thought he couldn't give us anything, for he said all he had with him was his pipe and his fiddle; but later on he said he felt so badly to see us go without any token of his good will that he felt constrained to ask us to accept a piece of rope that he had tied his outfit together with.

The fourth day we got on so nicely that it was quite monotonous. The sun shone, the chinook blew, our ponies trotted over the trail gallantly. Kate and I sang, told stories, and laughed immoderately over everything. Even a poor joke seems to have a subtle flavour on the prairie. For the first time I began to think Saskatchewan beautiful, with those far-reaching parklike meadows dotted with the white-stemmed poplars, the distant bluffs bannered with the airiest of purple hazes, and the little blue lakes that sparkled and shimmered in the sunlight on every hand.

The only thing approaching an adventure that day happened in the afternoon when we reached a creek which had to be crossed.

"We must investigate," said Kate decidedly. "It would never do to risk getting mired here, for this country is unsettled and we must be twenty miles from another human being."

Kate again removed her shoes and stockings and puddled about that creek until she found a safe fording place. I am afraid I must admit that I laughed most heartlessly at the spectacle she presented while so employed.

"Oh, for a camera, Kate!" I said, between spasms.

Kate grinned. "I don't care what I look like," she said, "but I feel wretchedly unpleasant. This water is simply swarming with wigglers."

"Goodness, what are they?" I exclaimed.

"Oh, they're tiny little things like leeches," responded Kate. "I believe they develop into mosquitoes later on, bad 'cess to them. What Mr. Nash would call my pedal extremities are simply being devoured by the brutes. Ugh! I believe the bottom of this creek is all soft mud. We may have to drive —

no, as I'm a living, wiggler-haunted human being, here's firm bottom. Hurrah, Phil, we're all right!"

In a few minutes we were past the creek and bowling merrily on our way. We had a beautiful camping ground that night—a fairylike little slope of white poplars with a blue lake at its foot. When the sun went down a milk-white mist hung over the prairie, with a young moon kissing it. We boiled some slices of our jumping deer and ate them in the open around a cheery camp-fire. Then we sought our humble couches, where we slept the sleep of just people who had been driving over the prairie all day. Once in the night I wakened. It was very dark. The unearthly stillness of a great prairie was all around me. In that vast silence Kate's soft breathing at my side seemed an intrusion of sound where no sound should be.

"Philippa Blair, can you believe it's yourself?" I said mentally. "Here you are, lying on a brush bed on a western prairie in the middle of the night, at least twenty miles from any human being except another frail creature of your own sex. Yet you're not even frightened. You are very comfy and composed, and you're going right to sleep again."

And right to sleep again I went.

Our fifth day began ominously. We had made an early start and had driven about six miles when the calamity occurred. Kate turned a corner too sharply, to avoid a big boulder; there was a heart-breaking sound.

"The tongue of the wagon is broken," cried Kate in dismay. All too surely it was. We looked at each other blankly.

"What can we do?" I said.

"I'm sure I don't know," said Kate helplessly. When Kate felt helpless I thought things must be desperate indeed. We got out and investigated the damage.

"It's not a clean break," said Kate. "It's a long, slanting break. If we had a piece of rope I believe I could fix it."

"Mr. Lonsdale's piece of rope!" I cried.

"The very thing," said Kate, brightening up.

The rope was found and we set to work. With the aid of some willow withes and that providential rope we contrived to splice the tongue together in some shape.

Although the trail was good we made only twelve miles the rest of the day, so slowly did we have to drive. Besides, we were continually expecting that tongue to give way again, and the strain was bad for our nerves. When we came at sunset to the junction of the Black River trail with ours, Kate resolutely turned the shaganappies down it.

"We'll go and spend the night with the Brewsters," she said. "They live only ten miles down this trail. I went to school in Regina with Hannah Brewster, and though I haven't seen her for ten years I know she'll be glad to see us. She's a lovely person, and her husband is a very nice man. I visited them once after they were married."

We soon arrived at the Brewster place. It was a trim, white-washed little log house in a grove of poplars. But all the blinds were down and we discovered the door was locked. Evidently the Brewsters were not at home.

"Never mind," said Kate cheerfully, "we'll light a fire outside and cook our supper and then we'll spend the night in the barn. A bed of prairie hay will be just the thing."

But the barn was locked too. It was now dark and our plight was rather desperate.

"I'm going to get into the house if I have to break a window," said Kate resolutely. "Hannah would want us to do that. She'd never get over it, if she heard we came to her house and couldn't get in."

Fortunately we did not have to go to the length of breaking into Hannah's house. The kitchen window went up quite easily. We turned the shaganappies loose to forage for themselves, grass and water being abundant. Then we climbed in at the window, lighted our lantern, and found ourselves in a very snug little kitchen. Opening off it on one side was a trim, nicely furnished parlour and on the other a well-stocked pantry.

"We'll light the fire in the stove in a jiffy and have a real good supper," said Kate exultantly. "Here's cold roast beef — and preserves and cookies and cheese and butter."

Before long we had supper ready and we did full justice to the absent Hannah's excellent cheer. After all, it was quite nice to sit down once more to a well-appointed table and eat in civilized fashion.

Then we washed up all the dishes and made everything snug and tidy. I shall never be sufficiently thankful that we did so.

Kate piloted me upstairs to the spare room.

"This is fixed up much nicer than it was when I was here before," she said, looking around. "Of course, Hannah and Ted were just starting out then and they had to be economical. They must have prospered, to be able to afford such furniture as this. Well, turn in, Phil. Won't it be rather jolly to sleep between sheets once more?"

We slept long and soundly until half-past eight the next morning; and dear knows if we would have wakened then of our own accord. But I heard somebody saying in a very harsh, gruff voice, "Here, you two, wake up! I want to know what this means."

We two did wake up, promptly and effectually. I never wakened up so thoroughly in my life before. Standing in our room were three people, one of them a man. He was a big, grey-haired man with a bushy black beard and an angry scowl. Beside him was a woman—a tall, thin, angular personage with red hair and an indescribable bonnet. She looked even crosser and more amazed than the man, if that were possible. In the background was another woman—a tiny old lady who must have been at least eighty. She was, in spite of her tininess, a very striking-looking personage; she was dressed all in black, and had snow-white hair, a dead-white face, and snapping, vivid, coal-black eyes. She looked as amazed as the other two, but she didn't look cross.

I knew something must be wrong—fearfully wrong—but I didn't know what. Even in my confusion, I found time to think that if that disagreeable-looking red-haired woman was Hannah Brewster, Kate must have had a queer taste in school friends. Then the man said, more gruffly than ever, "Come now. Who are you and what business have you here?"

Kate raised herself on one elbow. She looked very wild. I heard the old black-and-white lady in the background chuckle to herself.

"Isn't this Theodore Brewster's place?" gasped Kate.

"No," said the big woman, speaking for the first time. "This place belongs to us. We bought it from the Brewsters in the spring. They moved over to Black River Forks. Our name is Chapman."

Poor Kate fell back on the pillow, quite overcome. "I—I beg your pardon," she said. "I—I thought the Brewsters lived here. Mrs. Brewster is a friend of mine. My cousin and I are on our way to Bothwell and we called here to spend the night with Hannah. When we found everyone away we just came in and made ourselves at home."

"A likely story," said the red woman.

"We weren't born yesterday," said the man.

Madam Black-and-White didn't say anything, but when the other two had made their pretty speeches she doubled up in a silent convulsion of mirth, shaking her head from side to side and beating the air with her hands.

If they had been nice to us, Kate would probably have gone on feeling confused and ashamed. But when they were so disagreeable she quickly regained her self-possession. She sat up again and said in her haughtiest voice, "I do not know when you were born, or where, but it must have been somewhere where very peculiar manners were taught. If you will have the decency to leave our room—this room—until we can get up and dress we will not transgress upon your hospitality" (Kate put a most satirical emphasis on that word) "any longer. And we shall pay you amply for the food we have eaten and the night's lodging we have taken."

The black-and-white apparition went through the motion of clapping her hands, but not a sound did she make. Whether he was cowed by Kate's tone, or appeased by the prospect of payment, I know not, but Mr. Chapman spoke more civilly. "Well, that's fair. If you pay up it's all right."

"They shall do no such thing as pay you," said Madam Black-and-White in a surprisingly clear, resolute, authoritative voice. "If you haven't any shame for yourself, Robert Chapman, you've got a mother-in-law who can be ashamed for you. No strangers shall be charged for food or lodging in any house where Mrs. Matilda Pitman lives. Remember that I've come down in the world, but I haven't forgot all decency for all that. I knew you was a skinflint when Amelia married you and you've made her as bad as yourself. But I'm boss here yet. Here, you, Robert Chapman, take yourself out of here and let those girls get dressed. And you, Amelia, go downstairs and cook a breakfast for them."

I never, in all my life, saw anything like the abject meekness with which those two big people obeyed that mite. They went, and stood not upon the order of their going. As the door closed behind them, Mrs. Matilda Pitman laughed silently, and rocked from side to side in her merriment.

"Ain't it funny?" she said. "I mostly lets them run the length of their tether but sometimes I has to pull them up, and then I does it with a jerk. Now, you can take your time about dressing, my dears, and I'll go down and keep them in order, the mean scalawags."

When we descended the stairs we found a smoking-hot breakfast on the table. Mr. Chapman was nowhere to be seen, and Mrs. Chapman was cutting bread with a sulky air. Mrs. Matilda Pitman was sitting in an armchair, knitting. She still wore her bonnet and her triumphant expression. "Set right in, dears, and make a good breakfast," she said.

"We are not hungry," said Kate, almost pleadingly. "I don't think we can eat anything. And it's time we were on the trail. Please excuse us and let us go on."

Mrs. Matilda Pitman shook a knitting needle playfully at Kate. "Sit down and take your breakfast," she commanded. "Mrs. Matilda Pitman commands you. Everybody obeys Mrs. Matilda Pitman—even Robert and Amelia. You must obey her too."

We did obey her. We sat down and, such was the influence of her mesmeric eyes, we ate a tolerable breakfast. The obedient Amelia never spoke; Mrs.

Matilda Pitman did not speak either, but she knitted furiously and chuckled. When we had finished Mrs. Matilda Pitman rolled up her knitting. "Now, you can go if you want to," she said, "but you don't have to go. You can stay here as long as you like, and I'll make them cook your meals for you."

I never saw Kate so thoroughly cowed.

"Thank you," she said faintly. "You are very kind, but we must go."

"Well, then," said Mrs. Matilda Pitman, throwing open the door, "your team is ready for you. I made Robert catch your ponies and harness them. And I made him fix that broken tongue properly. I enjoy making Robert do things. It's almost the only sport I have left. I'm eighty and most things have lost their flavour, except bossing Robert."

Our democrat and ponies were outside the door, but Robert was nowhere to be seen; in fact, we never saw him again.

"I do wish," said Kate, plucking up what little spirit she had left, "that you would let us—ah—uh"—Kate quailed before Mrs. Matilda Pitman's eye—"recompense you for our entertainment."

"Mrs. Matilda Pitman said before—and meant it—that she doesn't take pay for entertaining strangers, nor let other people where she lives do it, much as their meanness would like to do it."

We got away. The sulky Amelia had vanished, and there was nobody to see us off except Mrs. Matilda Pitman.

"Don't forget to call the next time you come this way," she said cheerfully, waving her knitting at us. "I hope you'll get safe to Bothwell. If I was ten years younger I vow I'd pack a grip and go along with you. I like your spunk. Most of the girls nowadays is such timid, skeery critters. When I was a girl I wasn't afraid of nothing or nobody."

We said and did nothing until we had driven out of sight and earshot. Then Kate laid down the reins and laughed until the tears came.

"Oh, Phil, Phil, will you ever forget this adventure?" she gasped.

"I shall never forget Mrs. Matilda Pitman," I said emphatically.

We had no further adventures that day. Robert Chapman had fixed the tongue so well—probably under Mrs. Matilda Pitman's watchful eyes—that we could drive as fast as we liked; and we made good progress. But when we pitched camp that night Kate scanned the sky with an anxious expression. "I don't like the look of it," she said. "I'm afraid we're going to have a bad day tomorrow."

We had. When we awakened in the morning rain was pouring down. This in itself might not have prevented us from travelling, but the state of the trail did. It had been raining the greater part of the night and the trail was little more than a ditch of slimy, greasy, sticky mud.

If we could have stayed in the tent the whole time it would not have been quite so bad. But we had to go out twice to take the ponies to the nearest pond and water them; moreover, we had to collect pea vines for them, which was not an agreeable occupation in a pouring rain. The day was very cold too, but fortunately there was plenty of dead poplar right by our camp. We kept a good fire on in the camp stove and were quite dry and comfortable as long as we stayed inside. Even when we had to go out we did not get very wet, as we were well protected. But it was a long dreary day. Finally when the dark came down and supper was over Kate grew quite desperate. "Let's have a game of checkers," she suggested.

"Where is your checkerboard?" I asked.

"Oh, I'll soon furnish that," said Kate.

She cut out a square of brown paper, in which a biscuit box had been wrapped, and marked squares off on it with a pencil. Then she produced some red and white high-bush cranberries for men. A cranberry split in two was a king.

We played nine games of checkers by the light of our smoky lantern. Our enjoyment of the game was heightened by the fact that it had ceased raining. Nevertheless, when morning came the trail was so drenched that it was impossible to travel on it.

"We must wait till noon," said Kate.

"That trail won't be dry enough to travel on for a week," I said disconsolately.

"My dear; the chinook is blowing up," said Kate. "You don't know how quickly a trail dries in a chinook. It's like magic."

I did not believe a chinook or anything else could dry up that trail by noon sufficiently for us to travel on. But it did. As Kate said, it seemed like magic. By one o'clock we were on our way again, the chinook blowing merrily against our faces. It was a wind that blew straight from the heart of the wilderness and had in it all the potent lure of the wild. The yellow prairie laughed and glistened in the sun.

We made twenty-five miles that afternoon and, as we were again fortunate enough to find a bluff of dead poplar near which to camp, we built a royal camp-fire which sent its flaming light far and wide over the dark prairie.

We were in jubilant spirits. If the next day were fine and nothing dreadful happened to us, we would reach Bothwell before night.

But our ill luck was not yet at an end. The next morning was beautiful. The sun shone warm and bright; the chinook blew balmily and alluringly; the trail stretched before us dry and level. But we sat moodily before our tent, not even having sufficient heart to play checkers. Tom had gone lame—so lame that there was no use in thinking of trying to travel with him. Kate could not tell what was the matter.

"There is no injury that I can see," she said. "He must have sprained his foot somehow."

Wait we did, with all the patience we could command. But the day was long and wearisome, and at night Tom's foot did not seem a bit better.

We went to bed gloomily, but joy came with the morning. Tom's foot was so much improved that Kate decided we could go on, though we would have to drive slowly.

"There's no chance of making Bothwell today," she said, "but at least we shall be getting a little nearer to it."

"I don't believe there is such a place as Bothwell, or any other town," I said pessimistically. "There's nothing in the world but prairie, and we'll go on driving over it forever, like a couple of female Wandering Jews. It seems years since we left Arrow Creek."

"Well, we've had lots of fun out of it all, you know," said Kate. "Mrs. Matilda Pitman alone was worth it. She will be an amusing memory all our lives. Are you sorry you came?"

"No, I'm not," I concluded, after honest, soul-searching reflection. "No, I'm glad, Kate. But I think we were crazy to attempt it, as Sergeant Baker said. Think of all the might-have-beens."

"Nothing else will happen," said Kate. "I feel in my bones that our troubles are over."

Kate's bones proved true prophets. Nevertheless, that day was a weary one. There was no scenery. We had got into a barren, lakeless, treeless district where the world was one monotonous expanse of grey-brown prairie. We just crawled along. Kate had her hands full driving those ponies. Jerry was in capital fettle and couldn't understand why he mightn't tear ahead at full speed. He was so much disgusted over being compelled to walk that he was very fractious. Poor Tom limped patiently along. But by night his lameness had quite disappeared, and although we were still a good twenty-five miles from Bothwell we could see it quite distinctly far ahead on the level prairie.

"'Tis a sight for sore eyes, isn't it?" said Kate, as we pitched camp.

There is little more to be told. Next day at noon we rattled through the main and only street of Bothwell. Curious sights are frequent in prairie towns, so we did not attract much attention. When we drew up before Mr. Taylor's house Mary Taylor flew out and embraced Kate publicly.

"You darling! I knew you'd get here if anyone could. They telegraphed us you were on the way. You're a brick—two bricks."

"No, I'm not a brick at all, Miss Taylor," I confessed frankly. "I've been an arrant coward and a doubting Thomas and a wet blanket all through the expedition. But Kate is a brick and a genius and an all-round, jolly good fellow."

"Mary," said Kate in a tragic whisper, "have—you—any—ham—in—the—house?"

Jessamine

When the vegetable-man knocked, Jessamine went to the door wearily. She felt quite well acquainted with him. He had been coming all the spring, and his cheery greeting always left a pleasant afterglow behind him. But it was not the vegetable-man after all — at least, not the right one. This one was considerably younger. He was tall and sunburned, with a ruddy, smiling face, and keen, pleasant blue eyes; and he had a spray of honeysuckle pinned on his coat.

"Want any garden stuff this morning?"

Jessamine shook her head. "We always get ours from Mr. Bell. This is his day to come."

"Well, I guess you won't see Mr. Bell for a spell. He fell off a loft out at his place yesterday and broke his leg. I'm his nephew, and I'm going to fill his place till he gets 'round again."

"Oh, I'm so sorry — for Mr. Bell, I mean. Have you any green peas?"

"Yes, heaps of them. I'll bring them in. Anything else?"

"Not today," said Jessamine, with a wistful glance at the honeysuckle.

Mr. Bell, junior, saw it. In an instant the honeysuckle was unpinned and handed to her. "If you like posies, you're welcome to this. I guess you're fond of flowers," he added, as he noted the flash of delight that passed over her pale face.

"Yes, indeed; they put me so in mind of home — of the country. Oh, how sweet this is!"

"You're country-bred, then? Been in the city long?"

"Since last fall. I was born and brought up in the country. I wish I was back. I can't get over being homesick. This honeysuckle seems to bring it right back. We had honeysuckles around our porch at home."

"You don't like the city, then?"

"Oh, no. I sometimes feel as if I should smother here. I shall never feel at home, I am afraid."

"Where did you live before you came here?"

"Up at Middleton. It was an old-fashioned place, but pretty — our house was covered with vines, and there were trees all about it, and great green fields beyond. But I don't know what makes me tell you this. I forgot I was talking to a stranger."

"Pretty little woman," soliloquized Andrew Bell, as he drove away. "She doesn't look happy, though. I suppose she's married some city chap and has to live in town. I guess it don't agree with her. Her eyes had a real hungry look in them over that honeysuckle. She seemed near about crying when she talked of the country."

Jessamine felt more like crying than ever when she went back to her work. Her head ached and she was very tired. The tiny kitchen was hot and stifling. How she longed for the great, roomy kitchen in her old home, with its spotless floors and floods of sunshine streaming in through the maples outside. There was room to live and breathe there, and from the door one looked out over green wind-rippled meadows, under a glorious arch of pure blue sky, away to the purple hills in the distance.

Jessamine Stacy had always lived in the country. When her sister died and the old home had to go, Jessamine could only accept the shelter offered by her brother, John Stacy, who did business in the city.

Of her stylish sister-in-law Jessamine was absolutely in awe. At first Mrs. John was by no means pleased at the necessity of taking a country sister into her family circle. But one day, when the servant girl took a tantrum and left, Mrs. John found it very convenient to have in the house a person who could step into Eliza's place as promptly and efficiently as Jessamine could.

Indeed, she found it so convenient that Eliza never had a successor. Jessamine found herself in the position of maid-of-all-work and kitchen drudge for board and clothes.

She never complained, but she grew thinner and paler as the winter went by. She had worked as hard on the farm, but it was the close confinement and weary routine that told on her. Mrs. John was exacting and querulous. John was absorbed in his business worries and had no time to waste on his sister. Now, when the summer had come, her homesickness was almost unbearable.

The next day Mr. Bell came he handed her a big bunch of sweet-brier roses.

"Here you are," he said heartily. "I took the liberty to bring you these today, seeing you're so fond of posies. The country roads are pink with them now. Why don't you get your husband to bring you out for a drive some day? You'd be as welcome as a lark at my farm."

"I will when he comes along, but I haven't seen him yet."

Mr. Bell gave a prolonged whistle. "Excuse me. I thought you were Mrs. Something-or-other for sure. Aren't you mistress here?"

"Oh, no. My brother's wife is the mistress here. I'm only Jessamine."

She laughed again. She was holding the roses against her face, and her eyes sparkled over them roguishly. The vegetable-man looked at her admiringly.

"You're a country rose yourself, miss, and you ought to be blooming out in the fields, instead of wilting in here."

"I wish I was. Thank you so much for the roses, Mr. — — Mr. — —"

"Bell — Andrew Bell, that's my name. I live out at Pine Pastures. We're all Bells out there — can't throw a stone without hitting one. Glad you like the roses."

After that the vegetable-man brought Jessamine a bouquet every trip. Now it was a big bunch of field-daisies or golden buttercups, now a green glory of spicy ferns, now a cluster of old-fashioned garden flowers.

"They keep life in me," Jessamine told him.

They were great friends by this time. True, she knew little about him but she felt instinctively that he was manly and kind-hearted.

One day when he came Jessamine met him almost gleefully. "No, nothing today. There is no dinner to cook."

"You don't say. Where are the folks?"

"Gone on an excursion. They won't be back until tonight."

"They won't? Well, I'll tell you what to do. You get ready, and when I'm through my rounds we'll go for a drive up the country."

"Oh, Mr. Bell! But won't it be too much bother for you?"

"Well, I reckon not! You want an excursion as well as other folks, and you shall have it."

"Oh, thank you so much. Yes, I'll be ready. You don't know how much it means to me."

"Poor little creature," said Mr. Bell, as he drove away. "It's downright cruelty, that's what it is, to keep her penned up like that. You might as well coop up a lark in a hen-house and expect it to thrive and sing. I'd like to give that brother of hers a piece of my mind."

When he lifted her up to the high seat of his express wagon that afternoon he said, "Now, I want you to do something. Just shut your eyes and don't open them again until I tell you to."

Jessamine laughed and obeyed. Finally she heard him say, "Look."

Jessamine opened her eyes with a little cry. They were on a remote country road, cool and dim and quiet, in the very heart of the beech woods. Long banners of light fell athwart the grey boles. Along the roadsides grew sheets of feathery ferns. Above the sky was gloriously blue. The air was sweet with the wild woodsy smell of the forest.

Jessamine lifted and clasped her hands in rapture. "Oh, how lovely!"

"Do you know where we're going?" said Mr. Bell delightedly. "Out to my farm at Pine Pastures. My aunt keeps house for me, and she'll be real glad to see you. You're just going to have a real good time this afternoon."

They had a delightful drive to begin with, and presently Mr. Bell turned into a wide lane.

"This is Cloverside Farm. I'm proud of it, I'll admit. There isn't a finer place in the county. What do you think of it?"

"Oh, it is lovely — it is like home. Look at those great fields. I'd like to go and lie down in that clover."

Mr. Bell lifted her from the wagon and marched her up a flowery garden path. "You shall do it, and everything else you want to. Here, Aunt, this is the young lady I spoke of. Make her at home while I tend to the horses."

Miss Bell was a pleasant-faced woman with silver hair and kind blue eyes. She took Jessamine's hand in a friendly fashion.

"Come in, dear. You're welcome as a June rose."

When Mr. Bell returned, he found Jessamine standing on the porch with her hands full of honeysuckle and her cheeks pink with excitement.

"I declare, you've got roses already," he exclaimed. "If they'd only stay now, and not bleach out again. What's first now?"

"Oh, I don't know. There are so many things I want to do. Those flowers in the garden are calling me — and I want to go down to that hollow and pick buttercups — and I want to stay right here and look at things."

Mr. Bell laughed. "Come with me to the pasture and see my Jersey calves. They're something worth seeing. Come, Aunt. This way, Miss Stacy."

He led the way down the lane, the two women following together. Jessamine thought she must be in a pleasant dream. The whole afternoon was a feast of delight to her starved heart. When sunset came she sat down, tired out, but radiant, on the porch steps. Her hat had slipped back and her hair was curling around her face. Her dark eyes were aglow; the roses still bloomed in her cheeks.

Mr. Bell looked at her admiringly. "If a man could see that pretty sight every night!" he thought. "And, Great Scott, why can't he? What's to prevent, I'd like to know?"

When the moon rose, Mr. Bell brought his team around and they drove back through the clear night, past the wonderful stillness of the great beech woods and the wide fields. The farmer looked sideways at his companion.

"The little thing wants to be petted and looked after," he thought. "She's just pining away for home and love. And why can't she have it? She's dying by inches in that hole back in town."

Jessamine, quite unsuspecting the farmer's meditations, was living over again in fancy the joys of the afternoon: the ramble in the pasture, the drink of water from the spring under the hillside pines, the bountiful, old-fashioned country supper in the vine-shaded dining-room, the cup of new milk in the dairy at sunset, and all the glory of skies and meadows and trees. How could she go back to her cage again?

The next week Mr. Bell, senior, resumed his visits, and the young farmer came no more to the side door of No. 49. Jessamine missed him greatly. Mr. Bell, senior, never brought her clover or honeysuckle.

But one day his nephew suddenly reappeared. Jessamine opened the door for him, and her face lighted up, but Mr. Bell saw that she had been crying.

"Did you think I had forgotten you?" he asked. "Not a bit of it. Harvest was on and I couldn't get clear before. I've come to ask you when you intend to take another drive to Cloverside Farm. What have you been up to? You look as if you'd been working too hard."

"I—I—haven't felt very well. I'm glad you came today, Mr. Bell. Perhaps I shall not see you again, and I wanted to say goodbye and thank you for all your kindness."

"Goodbye? Why, where are you going?"

"My brother went west a week ago," faltered Jessamine. She could not bring herself to tell the clear-eyed farmer that John Stacy had failed and had been obliged to start for the west without saying goodbye to his creditors. "His wife and I—are going too—next week."

"Oh, Jessamine," exclaimed Mr. Bell in despair, "don't go—you mustn't. I want you at Cloverside Farm. I came today on purpose to ask you. I love you and I'll make you happy if you'll marry me. What do you say, Jessamine?"

Jessamine, by way of answer, sat down on the nearest chair and began to cry.

"Oh, don't," said the wooer in distress. "I didn't want to make you feel bad. If you don't like the idea, I won't mention it again."

"Oh, it isn't that—but I—I thought nobody cared what became of me. You are so kind—I'm afraid I'd only be a bother to you...."

"I'll risk that. You shall have a happy home, little girl. Will you come to it?"

"Ye-e-e-s." It was very indistinct and faltering, but Mr. Bell heard it and considered it a most eloquent answer.

Mrs. John fumed and sulked and chose to consider herself hoodwinked and injured. But Mr. Bell was a resolute man, and a few days later he came for the last time to No. 49 and took his bride away with him.

As they drove through the beech woods he put his arm tenderly around the shy, smiling little woman beside him and said, "You'll never be sorry for this, my dear."

And she never was.

Miss Sally's Letter

Miss Sally peered sharply at Willard Stanley, first through her gold-rimmed glasses and then over them. Willard continued to look very innocent. Joyce got up abruptly and went out of the room.

"So you have bought that queer little house with the absurd name?" said Miss Sally.

"You surely don't call Eden an absurd name," protested Willard.

"I do — for a house. Particularly such a house as that. Eden! There are no Edens on earth. And what are you going to do with it?"

"Live in it."

"Alone?"

Miss Sally looked at him suspiciously.

"No. The truth is, Miss Sally, I am hoping to be married in the fall and I want to fix up Eden for my bride."

"Oh!" Miss Sally drew a long breath, partly it seemed of relief and partly of triumph, and looked at Joyce, who had returned, with an expression that said, "I told you so"; but Joyce, whose eyes were cast down, did not see it.

"And," went on Willard calmly, "I want you to help me fix it up, Miss Sally. I don't know much about such things and you know everything. You will be able to tell me just what to do to make Eden habitable."

Miss Sally looked as pleased as she ever allowed herself to look over anything a man suggested. It was the delight of her heart to plan and decorate and contrive. Her own house was a model of comfort and good taste, and Miss Sally was quite ready for new worlds to conquer. Instantly Eden assumed importance in her eyes. She might be sorry for the misguided bride who was rashly going to trust her life's keeping to a man, but she would see, at least, that the poor thing should have a decent place to begin her martyrdom in.

"I'll be pleased to help you all I can," she said graciously.

Miss Sally could speak very graciously when she chose, even to men. You would not have thought she hated them, but she did. In all sincerity, too. Also, she had brought her niece up to hate and distrust them. Or, she had tried to do so. But at times Miss Sally was troubled with an uncomfortable suspicion that Joyce did not hate and distrust men quite as thoroughly as she ought. The suspicion had recurred several times this summer since Willard Stanley had come to take charge of the biological station at the harbour. Miss Sally did not distrust Willard on his own account. She merely distrusted him on principle and on Joyce's account. Nevertheless, she was rather nice to him. Miss Sally, dear, trim, dainty Miss Sally, with her snow-white curls and her big girlish black eyes, couldn't help being nice, even to a man.

Willard had come a great deal to Miss Sally's. If it were Joyce he were after Miss Sally blocked his schemes with much enjoyment. He never saw Joyce alone — that Miss Sally knew of, at least — and he did not make much apparent headway. But now all danger was removed, Miss Sally thought. He was going to be married to somebody else, and Joyce was safe.

"Thank you," said Willard. "I'll come up tomorrow afternoon, and you and I will take a prowl about Eden and see what must be done. I'm ever so much obliged, Miss Sally."

"I wonder who he is going to marry," said Miss Sally, careless of grammar, after he had gone. "Poor, poor girl!"

"I don't see why you should pity her," said Joyce, not looking up from her embroidery. There was just the merest tremor in her voice. Miss Sally looked at her sharply.

"I pity any woman who is foolish enough to marry," she said solemnly. "No man is to be trusted, Joyce — no man. They are all ready to break a trusting woman's heart for the sport of it. Never you allow any man the chance to break yours, Joyce. I shall never consent to your marrying anybody, so mind you don't take any such notion into your head. There oughtn't to be any danger, for I have instilled correct ideas on this subject into you from childhood. But girls are such fools. I know, because I was one myself once."

"Of course, I would never marry without your consent, Aunt Sally," said Joyce, smiling faintly but affectionately at her aunt. Joyce loved Miss Sally with her whole heart. Everybody did who knew her. There never was a more lovable creature than this pretty little old maid who hated the men so bitterly.

"That's a good girl," said Miss Sally approvingly. "I own that I have been a little afraid that this Willard Stanley was coming here to see you. But my mind is set at rest on that point now, and I shall help him fix up his doll house with a clear conscience. Eden, indeed!"

Miss Sally sniffed and tripped out of the room to hunt up a furniture catalogue. Joyce sighed and let her embroidery slip to the floor.

"Oh, I'm afraid Willard's plan won't succeed," she murmured. "I'm afraid Aunt Sally will never consent to our marriage. And I can't and won't marry him unless she does, for she would never forgive me and I couldn't bear that. I wonder what makes her so bitter against men. She is so sweet and loving, it seems simply unnatural that she should have such a feeling so deeply rooted in her. Oh, what will she say when she finds out—dear little Aunt Sally? I couldn't bear to have her angry with me."

The next day Willard came up from the harbour and took Miss Sally down to see Eden. Eden was a tiny, cornery, gabled grey house just across the road and down a long, twisted windy lane, skirting the edge of a beech wood. Nobody had lived in it for four years, and it had a neglected, out-at-elbow appearance.

"It's rather a box of a place, isn't it?" said Willard slowly. "I'm afraid she will think so. But it is all I can afford just now. I dream of giving her a palace some day, of course. But we'll have to begin humbly. Do you think anything can be made of it?"

Miss Sally was busily engaged in sizing up the possibilities of the place.

"It is pretty small," she said meditatively. "And the yard is small too—and there are far too many trees and shrubs all messed up together. They must be thinned out—and that paling taken down. I think a good deal can be done with it. As for the house—well, let us see the inside."

Willard unlocked the door and showed Miss Sally over the place. Miss Sally poked and pried and sniffed and wrinkled her forehead, and finally stood on the stairs and delivered her ultimatum.

"This house can be done up very nicely. Paint and paper will work wonders. But I wouldn't paint it outside. Leave it that pretty silver weather-grey and plant vines to run over it. Oh, we'll see what we can do. Of course it is small—a kitchen, a dining room, a living room, and two bedrooms. You won't want anything stuffy. You can do the painting yourself, and I'll help you hang the paper. How much money can you spend on it?"

Willard named the sum. It was not a large one.

"But I think it will do," mused Miss Sally. "We'll *make* it do. There's such satisfaction getting as much as you possibly can out of a dollar, and twice as much as anybody else would get. I enjoy that sort of thing. This will be a game, and we'll play it with a right good will. But I do wish you would give the place a sensible name."

"I think Eden is the most appropriate name in the world," laughed Willard. "It will be Eden for me when she comes."

"I suppose you tell her all that and she believes it," said Miss Sally sarcastically. "You'll both find out that there is a good deal more prose than poetry in life."

"But we'll find it out *together*," said Willard tenderly. "Won't that be worth something, Miss Sally? Prose, rightly written and read, is sometimes as beautiful as poetry."

Miss Sally deigned no reply. She carefully gathered up her grey silken skirts from the dusty floor and walked out. "Get Christina Bowes to come up tomorrow and scrub this place out," she said practically. "We can go to town and select paint and paper. I should like the dining room done in pale green and the living room in creamy tones, ranging from white to almost golden brown. But perhaps my taste won't be hers."

"Oh, yes, it will," said Willard with assurance. "I am quite certain she will like everything you like. I can never thank you enough for helping me. If you hadn't consented I should have had to put it into the hands of some outsider whom I couldn't have helped at all. And I *wanted* to help. I wanted to have a finger in everything, because it is for her, you see, Miss Sally. It will be such a delight to fix up this little house, knowing that she is coming to live in it."

"I wonder if you really mean it," said Miss Sally bitterly. "Oh, I dare say you think you do. But *do* you? Perhaps you do. Perhaps you are the exception that proves the rule."

This was a great admission for Miss Sally to make.

For the next two months Miss Sally was happy. Even Willard himself was not more keenly interested in Eden and its development. Miss Sally did wonders with his money. She was an expert at bargain hunting, and her taste was excellent. A score of times she mercilessly nipped Willard's suggestions in the bud. "Lace curtains for the living room — never! They would be horribly out of place in such a house. You don't want curtains at all — just a frill is all that quaint window needs, with a shelf above it for a few bits of pottery. I picked up a love of a brass platter in town yesterday — got it for next to nothing from that old Jew who would really rather *give* you a thing than suffer you to escape without taking something. Oh, I know how to manage them."

"You certainly do," laughed Willard. "It amazes me to see how far you can stretch a dollar."

Willard did the painting under Miss Sally's watchful eye, and they hung the paper together. Together they made trips to town or junketed over the country in search of furniture and dishes of which Miss Sally had heard. Day by day the little house blossomed into a home, and day by day Miss Sally's interest in it grew. She began to have a personal affection for its quaint rooms and their adornments. Moreover, in spite of herself, she felt a growing interest in Willard's bride. He never told her the name of the girl he hoped to bring to Eden, and Miss Sally never asked it. But he talked of her a great deal, in a shy, reverent, tender way.

"He certainly seems to be very much in love with her," Miss Sally told Joyce one evening when she returned from Eden. "I would believe in him if it were possible for me to believe in a man. Anyway, she will have a dear little home. I've almost come to love that Eden house. Why don't you come down and see it, Joyce?"

"Oh, I'll come some day — I hope," said Joyce lightly. "I think I'd rather not see it until it is finished."

"Willard is a nice boy," said Miss Sally suddenly. "I don't think I ever did him justice before. The finer qualities of his character come out in these simple, homely little doings and tasks. He is certainly very thoughtful and kind. Oh, I suppose he'll make a good husband, as husbands go. But he doesn't know the first thing about managing. If his wife isn't a good manager, I don't know what they'll do. And perhaps she won't like the way we've done up Eden. Willard says she will, of course, because he thinks her perfection. But she may have dreadful taste and want the lace curtains and that nightmare of a pink rug Willard admired, and I dare say she'd rather have a new flaunting set of china with rosebuds on it than that dear old dull blue I picked up for a mere song down at the Aldenbury auction. I stood in the rain for two mortal hours to make sure of it, and it was really worth all that Willard has spent on the dining room put together. It will break my heart if she sets to work altering Eden. It's simply perfect as it is — though I suppose I shouldn't say it."

In another week Eden was finished. Miss Sally stood in the tiny hall and looked about her.

"Well, it is done," she said with a sigh. "I'm sorry. I have enjoyed fixing it up tremendously, and now I feel that my occupation is gone. I hope you are satisfied, Willard."

"Satisfied is too mild a word, Miss Sally. I am delighted. I knew you could accomplish wonders, but I never hoped for *this*. Eden is a dream — the dearest, quaintest, sweetest little home that ever waited for a bride. When I bring her here — oh, Miss Sally, do you know what that thought means to me?"

Miss Sally looked curiously at the young man. His face was flushed and his voice trembled a little. There was a far-away shining look in his eyes as if he saw a vision.

"I hope you and she will be happy," said Miss Sally slowly. "When will she be coming, Willard?"

The flush went out of Willard's face, leaving it pale and determined.

"That is for her — and you — to say," he answered steadily.

"Me!" exclaimed Miss Sally. "What have I to do with it?"

"A great deal — for unless you consent she will never come here at all."

"Willard Stanley," said Miss Sally, with ominous calm, "who is the girl you mean to marry?"

"The girl I *hope* to marry is Joyce, Miss Sally. Wait — don't say anything till you hear me out." He came close to her and caught her hands in a boyish grip. "Joyce and I have loved each other ever since we met. But we despaired of winning your consent, and Joyce will not marry me without it. I thought if I could get you to help me fix up my little home that you might get so interested in it — and so well acquainted with me — that you would trust me with Joyce. Please do, Miss Sally. I love her so truly and I know I can make her happy. If you don't, Eden shall never have a mistress. I'll shut it up, just as it is, and leave it sacred to the dead hope of a bride that will never come to it."

"Oh, you wouldn't," protested Miss Sally. "It would be a shame — such a dear little house — and after all the trouble I've taken. But you have tricked me — oh, you men couldn't be straightforward in anything — "

"Wasn't it a fair device for a desperate lover, Miss Sally?" interrupted Willard. "Oh, you mustn't hold spite because of it, dear; And you will give me Joyce, won't you? Because if you don't, I really will shut up Eden forever."

Miss Sally looked wistfully around her. Through the open door on her left she saw the little living room with its quaint, comfortable furniture, its dainty pictures and adornments. Through the front door she saw the trim, velvet-swarded little lawn. Upstairs were two white rooms that only wanted a woman's living presence to make them jewels. And the kitchen on which she had expended so much thought and ingenuity — the kitchen furnished to the last detail, even to the kindling in the range and the match Willard had laid ready to light it! It gave Miss Sally a pang to think of that altar fire never being lighted. It was really the thought of the kitchen that finished Miss Sally.

"You've tricked me," she said again reproachfully. "You've tricked me into loving this house so much that I cannot bear the thought of it never living. You'll have to have Joyce, I suppose. And I believe I'm glad that it isn't a stranger who is to be the mistress of Eden. Joyce won't hanker after pink rugs and lace curtains. And her taste in china is the same as mine. In one way it's a great relief to my mind. But it's a fearful risk — a fearful risk. To think that you may make my dear child miserable!"

"You know you don't think that I will, Miss Sally. I'm not really such a bad fellow, now, am I?"

"You are a man—and I have no confidence whatever in men," declared Miss Sally, wiping some very real tears from her eyes with a very unreal sort of handkerchief—one of the cobwebby affairs of lace her daintiness demanded.

"Miss Sally, why have you such a rooted distrust of men?" demanded Willard curiously. "Somehow, it seems so foreign to your character."

"I suppose you think I am a perfect crank," said Miss Sally, sighing. "Well, I'll tell you why I don't trust men. I have a very good reason for it. A man broke my heart and embittered my life. I've never spoken about it to a living soul, but if you want to hear about it, you shall."

Miss Sally sat down on the second step of the stairs and tucked her wet handkerchief away. She clasped her slender white hands over her knee. In spite of her silvery hair and the little lines on her face she looked girlish and youthful. There was a pink flush on her cheeks, and her big black eyes sparkled with the anger her memories aroused in her.

"I was a young girl of twenty when I met him," she said, "and I was just as foolish as all young girls are—foolish and romantic and sentimental. He was very handsome and I thought him—but there, I won't go into that. It vexes me to recall my folly. But I loved him—yes, I did, with all my heart—with all there was of me to love. He made me love him. He deliberately set himself to win my love. For a whole summer he flirted with me. I didn't know he was flirting—I thought him in earnest. Oh, I was such a little fool—and so happy. Then—he went away. Went away suddenly without even a word of goodbye. But he had been summoned home by his father's serious illness, and I thought he would write—I waited—I hoped. I never heard from him—never saw him again. He had tired of his plaything and flung it aside. That is all," concluded Miss Sally passionately. "I never trusted any man again. When my sister died and gave me her baby, I determined to bring the dear child up safely, training her to avoid the danger I had fallen into. Well, I've failed. But perhaps it will be all right—perhaps there are some men who are true, though Stephen Merritt was false."

"Stephen—who?" demanded Willard abruptly. Miss Sally coloured.

"I didn't mean to tell you his name," she said, getting up. "It was a slip of the tongue. Never mind—forget it and him. He was not worthy of remembrance—and yet I do remember him. I can't forget him—and I hate him all the more for it—for having entered so deeply into my life that I could not cast him out when I knew him unworthy. It is humiliating. There—let us lock up Eden and go home. I suppose you are dying to see Joyce and tell her your precious plot has succeeded."

Willard did not appear to be at all impatient. He had relapsed into a brown study, during which he let Miss Sally lock up the house. Then he walked silently home with her. Miss Sally was silent too. Perhaps she was repenting her confidence—or perhaps she was thinking of her false lover. There was a pathetic droop to her lips, and her black eyes were sad and dreamy.

"Miss Sally," said Willard at last, as they neared her house, "had Stephen Merritt any sisters?"

Miss Sally threw him a puzzled glance.

"He had one—Jean Merritt—whom I disliked and who disliked me," she said crisply. "I don't want to talk of her—she was the only woman I ever hated. I never met any of the other members of his family—his home was in a distant part of the state."

Willard stayed with Joyce so brief a time that Miss Sally viewed his departure with suspicion. This was not very lover-like conduct.

"I dare say he's like all the rest—when his aim is attained the prize loses its value," reflected Miss Sally pessimistically. "Poor Joyce—poor child! But there—there isn't a single inharmonious thing in his house—that is one comfort. I'm so thankful I didn't let Willard buy those brocade chairs he wanted. They would have given Joyce the nightmare."

Meanwhile, Willard rushed down to the biological station and from there drove furiously to the station to catch the evening express. He did not return until three days later, when he appeared at Miss Sally's, dusty and triumphant.

"Joyce is out," said Miss Sally.

"I'm glad of it," said Willard recklessly. "It's you I want to see, Miss Sally. I have something to show you. I've been all the way home to get it."

From his pocketbook Willard drew something folded and creased and yellow that looked like a letter. He opened it carefully and, holding it in his fingers, looked over it at Miss Sally.

"My grandmother's maiden name was Jean Merritt," he said deliberately, "and Stephen Merritt was my great-uncle. I never saw him—he died when I was a child—but I've heard my father speak of him often."

Miss Sally turned very pale. She passed her cobwebby handkerchief across her lips and her hand trembled. Willard went on.

"My uncle never married. He and his sister Jean lived together until her late marriage. I was not very fond of my grandmother. She was a selfish, domineering woman—very unlike the grandmother of tradition. When she died everything she possessed came to me, as my father, her only child, was then dead. In looking over a box of old papers I found a letter—an old love letter. I read it with some interest, wondering whose it could be and how it came among Grandmother's private letters. It was signed 'Stephen,' so that I guessed my great-uncle had been the writer, but I had no idea who the Sally was to whom it was written, until the other day. Then I knew it was you—and I went home to bring you your letter—the letter you should have received long ago. Why you did not receive it I cannot explain. I fear that my grandmother must have been to blame for that—she must have intercepted and kept the letter in order to part her brother and you. In so far as I can I wish to repair the wrong she has done you. I know it can never be repaired—but at least I think this letter will take the bitterness out of the memory of your lover."

He dropped the letter in Miss Sally's lap and went away.

Pale, Miss Sally picked it up and read it. It was from Stephen Merritt to "dearest Sally," and contained a frank, manly avowal of love. Would she be his wife? If she would, let her write and tell him so. But if she did not and could not love him, let her silence reveal the bitter fact; he would wish to spare her the pain of putting her refusal into words, and if she did not write he would understand that she was not for him.

When Willard and Joyce came back into the twilight room they found Miss Sally still sitting by the table, her head leaning pensively on her hand. She had been crying—the cobwebby handkerchief lay beside her, wrecked and ruined forever—but she looked very happy.

"I wonder if you know what you have done for me," she said to Willard. "But no—you can't know—you can't realize it fully. It means everything to me. You have taken away my humiliation and restored to me my pride of womanhood. He really loved me—he was not false—he was what I believed him to be. Nothing else matters to me at all now. Oh, I am very happy—but it would never have been if I had not consented to give you Joyce."

She rose and took their hands in hers, joining them.

"God bless you, dears," she said softly. "I believe you will be happy and that your love for each other will always be true and faithful and tender. Willard, I give you my dear child in perfect trust and confidence."

With her yellowed love letter clasped to her heart, and a raptured shining in her eyes, Miss Sally went out of the room.

My Lady Jane

The boat got into Broughton half an hour after the train had gone. We had been delayed by some small accident to the machinery; hence that lost half-hour, which meant a night's sojourn for me in Broughton. I am ashamed of the things I thought and said. When I think that fate might have taken me at my word and raised up a special train, or some such miracle, by which I might have got away from Broughton that night, I experience a cold chill. Out of gratitude I have never sworn over missing connections since.

At the time, however, I felt thoroughly exasperated. I was in a hurry to get on. Important business engagements would be unhinged by the delay. I was a stranger in Broughton. It looked like a stupid, stuffy little town. I went to a hotel in an atrocious humor. After I had fumed until I wanted a change, it occurred to me that I might as well hunt up Clark Oliver by way of passing the time. I had never been overly fond of Clark Oliver, although he was my cousin. He was a bit of a cad, and stupider than anyone belonging to our family had a right to be. Moreover, he was in politics, and I detest politics. But I rather wanted to see if he looked as much like me as he used to. I hadn't seen him for three years and I hoped that the time might have differentiated us to a saving degree. It was over a year since I had last been blown up by some unknown, excited individual on the ground that I was that scoundrel Oliver — politically speaking. I thought that was a good omen.

I went to Clark's office, found he had left, and followed him to his rooms. The minute I saw him I experienced the same nasty feeling of lost or bewildered individuality which always overcame me in his presence. He was so absurdly like me. I felt as if I were looking into a mirror where my reflection persisted in doing things I didn't do, thereby producing a most uncanny sensation.

Clark pretended he was glad to see me. He really couldn't have been, because his Great Idea hadn't struck him then, and we had always disliked each other.

"Hello, Elliott," he said, shaking me by the hand with a twist he had learned in election campaigns, whereby something like heartiness was simulated. "Glad to see you, old fellow. Gad, you're as like me as ever. Where did you drop from?"

I explained my predicament and we talked amiably and harmlessly for awhile about family gossip. I abhor family gossip, but it is a shade better than politics, and those two subjects are the only ones on which Clark can converse at all. I described Mary Alice's wedding, and Florence's new young man, and Tom-and-Kate's twins. Clark tried to be interested but I saw he had something on what serves him for a mind. After awhile it came out. He looked at his watch with a frown.

"I'm in a bit of a puzzle," he said. "The Mark Kennedys are giving a dinner to-night. You don't know them, of course. They're the big people of Broughton. Kennedy runs the politics of the place, and Mrs. K. makes or mars people socially. It's my first invitation there and it's necessary I should accept it—necessary every way. Mrs. K. would never forgive me if I disappointed her at the last moment. Not that I, personally, am of much account—yet—to her. But it would leave a vacant place. Mrs. K. would never notice me again and, as she bosses Kennedy, I can't afford to offend her. Besides, there's a girl who'll be there. I've met her once. I want to meet her again. She's a beauty and no mistake. Toplofty as they make 'em, though. However, I think I've made an impression on her. It was at the Harvey's dance last week. She was the handsomest woman there, and she never took her eyes off me. I've given Mrs. Kennedy a pretty broad hint that I want to take her in to dinner. If I don't go I'll miss all round."

"Well, what is there to prevent you from going?" I asked, squiffily. I never could endure the way Clark talked about girls and hinted at his conquests.

"Just this. Herbert Bronson came to town this afternoon and is leaving on the 10.30 train to-night. He's sent me word to meet him at his hotel this evening and talk over a mining deal I've been trying to pull off. I simply must go. It's my one chance to corral Bronson. If I lose him it'll be all up, and I'll be thousands out of pocket."

"Well, you *are* in rather a predicament," I agreed, with the philosophical acceptance of the situation that marks the outsider. *I* wasn't hampered by the multiplicity of my business and social engagements that evening, so I could afford to pity Clark. It is always rather nice to be able to pity a person you dislike.

"I should say so. I can't make up my mind what to do. Hang it. I'll *have* to see Bronson. There's no question about that. A man ought to keep an understood substitute on hand to send to dinners when he can't go. By Jove! Elliott!"

Clark's Great Idea had arrived. He bounced up eagerly.

"Elliott, will *you* go to the Kennedys' in my place? They'll never know the difference. Do, now — there's a good fellow!"

"Nonsense!" I said.

"It isn't nonsense. The resemblance between us was foreordained for this hour. I'll lend you my dress suit — it'll fit you — your figure is as much like mine as your face. You've nothing to do with yourself this evening. I offer you a good dinner and an agreeable partner. Come now, to oblige me. You know you owe me a good turn for that Mulhenen business."

The Mulhenen business clinched the matter. Until he mentioned it I had no notion whatever of masquerading as Clark Oliver at the Kennedys' dinner. But, as Clark so delicately put it, he had done me a good turn in that affair and the obligation had rankled ever since. It is beastly to be indebted for a favor to a man you detest. Now was my chance to pay it off and I took it without more ado.

"But," I said doubtfully, "I don't know the Kennedys — nor any of the social stunts that are doing in Broughton; I won't dare to talk about anything, and I'll seem so stupid, even if I don't actually make some irremediable blunder, that the Kennedys will be disgusted with you. It will probably do your prospects more harm than your absence would."

"Not at all. Keep your mouth shut when you can and talk generalities when you can't, and you'll pass. If you take that girl in she's a stranger in Broughton and won't suspect your ignorance of what's going on. Nobody will suspect you. Nobody here knows I have a cousin so like me. Our own mothers haven't always been able to tell us apart. Our very voices are alike. Come now, get into my dinner togs. You haven't much time and Mrs. K. doesn't like late comers."

There seemed to be a number of things that Mrs. Kennedy did not like. I thought my chance of pleasing that critical lady extremely small, especially when I had to live up to Clark Oliver's personality. However, I dressed as expeditiously as possible. The novelty of the adventure rather pleased me. I always liked doing unusual things. Anything was better than lounging away the evening at my hotel. It couldn't do any harm. I owed Clark Oliver a good turn and I would save Mrs. Kennedy the annoyance of a vacant chair.

There was no disputing the fact that I looked most disgustingly like Clark when I got into his clothes. I actually felt a grudge against them for their excellent fit.

"You'll do," said Clark. "Remember you're a Conservative to-night and don't let your rank Liberal views crop out, or you'll queer me for all time with the great and only Mark. He doesn't talk politics at his dinners, though, so you're not likely to have trouble on that score. Mrs. Kennedy has a weakness for beer mugs. Her collection is considered very fine. Scandal whispers that Miss Harvey has a budding interest in settlement work—"

"Miss who?" I said sharply.

"Harvey. Christian name unknown. That's the girl I mentioned. You'll probably take her in. Be nice to her even if you have to make an effort. She's the one I've picked out as your future cousin, you know, so I don't want you to spoil her good opinion of me in any way."

The name had given me a jump. Once, in another world, I had known a Jane Harvey. But Clark's Miss Harvey couldn't be Jane. A month before I had read a newspaper item to the effect that Jane was on the Pacific coast. Moreover, Jane, when I knew her, had certainly no manifest vocation for settlement work. I didn't think two years could have worked such a transformation. Two years! Was it only two years? It seemed more like two centuries.

I went to the Kennedys' in a pleasantly excited frame of mind and a cab. I just missed being late by a hairbreadth. The house was a big one, and everybody pertaining to it was big, except the host. Mark Kennedy was a little, thin man with a bald head. He didn't look like a political power, but that was all the more reason for his being one in a world where things are not what they seem.

Mrs. Kennedy greeted me cordially and told me significantly that she had granted my request. This meant, as my card had already informed me, that I was to take Miss Harvey out. Of course there would be no introduction since Clark Oliver was already acquainted with the lady. I was wondering how I was to locate her when I got a shock that made me dizzy. Jane was over in a corner looking at me.

There was no time to collect my wits. The guests were moving out to the dining-room. I took my nerve in my hand, crossed the room, bowed, and the next moment was walking through the hall with Jane's hand on my arm. The hall was a good long one; I blessed the architect who had planned it. It gave me time to sort out my ideas.

Jane here! Jane going out to dinner with me, believing me to be Clark Oliver! Jane—but it was incredible! The whole thing was a dream—or I had gone crazy!

I looked at her sideways when we had got into our places at the table. She was more beautiful than ever, that tall, brown-haired, disdainful Jane. The settlement work story I was inclined to dismiss as a myth. Settlement work in a beautiful woman generally means crowsfeet or a broken heart. Jane, according to my sight and belief, possessed neither.

Once upon a time I had been engaged to Jane. I had been idiotically in love with her in those days and still more idiotically believed that she loved me. The trouble was that, although I had been cured of the latter phase of my idiocy, the former had become chronic. I had never been able to get over loving Jane. All through those two years I had hugged the fond hope that sometime I might stumble across her in a mild mood and make matters up. There was no such thing as seeking her out or writing to her, since she had icily forbidden me to do so, and Jane had a most detestable habit — in a woman — of meaning what she said. But the deity I had invoked was the god of chance — and this was how he had answered my prayers. I was eating my dinner beside Jane, who supposed me to be Clark Oliver!

What should I do? Confess the truth and plead my cause while she had to sit beside me? That would never do. Someone might overhear us. And, in any case, it would be no passport to Jane's favor that I was a guest in the house under false pretences. She would be certain to disapprove strongly. It was a maddening situation.

Jane, who was calmly eating soup — she was the only woman I had ever seen who could eat soup and look like a goddess at the same time — glanced around and caught me studying her profile. I thought she blushed slightly and I raged inwardly to think that blush was meant for Clark Oliver — Clark Oliver who had told me he thought Jane was smitten on him! Jane! On him!

"Do you know, Mr. Oliver," said Jane slowly, "that you are startlingly like a — a person I used to know? When I first saw you the other night I took you for him."

A *person* you used to know! Oh, Jane, that was the most unkindest cut of all.

"My cousin, Elliott Cameron, I suppose?" I answered as indifferently as I could. "We resemble each other very closely. You were acquainted with Cameron, Miss Harvey?"

"Slightly," said Jane.

"A fine fellow," I said unblushingly.

"A-h," said Jane.

"My favorite relative," I went on brazenly. "He's a thoroughly good sort — rather dull now to what he used to be, though. He had an unfortunate love affair two years ago and has never got over it."

"Indeed?" said Jane coldly, crumbling a bit of bread between her fingers. Her face was expressionless and her voice ditto; but I had heard her criticize nervous people who did things like that at table.

"I fear poor Elliott's life has been completely spoiled," I said, with a sigh. "It's a shame."

"Did he confide the affair to you?" asked Jane, a little scornfully.

"Well, after a fashion. He said enough for me to guess the rest. He never told me the lady's name. She was very beautiful, I understand, and very heartless. Oh, she used him very badly."

"Did he tell you that, too?" asked Jane.

"Not he. He won't listen to a word against her. But a chap can draw his own conclusions, you know."

"What went wrong between them?" asked Jane. She smiled at a lady across the table, as if she were merely asking questions to make conversation, but she went on crumbling bread.

"Simply a very stiff quarrel, I believe. Elliott never went into details. The lady was flirting with somebody else, I fancy."

"People have such different ideas about flirting," said Jane, languidly. "What one would call mere simple friendliness another construes into flirting. Possibly your friend — or is it your cousin? — is one of those men who become insanely jealous over every trifle and attempt to exert authority before they have any to exert. A woman of spirit would hardly fail to resent that."

"Of course Elliott was jealous," I admitted. "But then, you know, Miss Harvey, that jealousy is said to be the measure of a man's love. If he went beyond his rights I am sure he is bitterly sorry for it."

"Does he really care about her still?" asked Jane, eating most industriously, although somehow the contents of her plate did not grow noticeably less. As for me, I didn't pretend to eat. I simply pecked.

"He loves her with all his heart," I answered fervently. "There never has been and never will be any other woman for Elliott Cameron."

"Why doesn't he go and tell her so?" inquired Jane, as if she felt rather bored over the whole subject.

"He doesn't dare to. She forbade him ever to cross her path again. Told him she hated him and always would hate him as long as she lived."

"She must have been an unpleasantly emphatic young woman," commented Jane.

"I'd like to hear anyone say so to Elliott," I responded. "He considers her perfection. I'm sorry for Elliott. His life is wrecked."

"Do you know," said Jane slowly, as if poking about in the recesses of her memory for something half forgotten. "I believe I know the—the girl in question."

"Really?" I said.

"Yes, she is a friend of mine. She—she never told me his name, but putting two and two together, I believe it must have been your cousin. But she—she thinks she was the one to blame."

"Does she?" It was my turn to ask questions now, but my heart thumped so that I could hardly speak.

"Yes, she says she was too hasty and unreasonable. She didn't mean to flirt at all—and she never cared for anyone but—him. But his jealousy irritated her. I suppose she said things to him she didn't really mean. She—she never supposed he was going to take her at her word."

"Do you think she cares for him still?" Considering what was at stake, I think I asked the question very well.

"I think she must," said Jane languidly. "She has never looked at any other man. She devotes most of her time to charitable work, but I feel sure she isn't really happy."

So the settlement story was true. Oh, Jane!

"What would you advise my cousin to do?" I asked. "Do you think he should go boldly to her? Would she listen to him—forgive him?"

"She might," said Jane.

"Have I your permission to tell Elliott Cameron this?" I demanded.

Jane selected and ate an olive with maddening deliberation.

"I suppose you may—if you are really convinced that he wants to hear it," she said at last, as if barely recollecting that I had asked the question two minutes previously.

"I'll tell him as soon as I go home," I said.

I had the satisfaction of startling Jane at last. She turned her head and looked at me. I got a good, square, satisfying gaze into her big, blackish-blue eyes.

"Yes," I said, compelling myself to look away. "He came in on the boat this afternoon too late for his train. Has to stay over till to-morrow night. I left him in my rooms when I came away. Doubtless to-morrow will see him speeding recklessly to his dear divinity. I wonder if he knows where she is at present."

"If he doesn't," said Jane, with the air of dismissing the subject once and forever from her mind, "I can give him the information. You may tell him I'm staying with the Duncan Moores, and shall be leaving day after to-morrow. By the way, have you seen Mrs. Kennedy's collection of steins? It is a remarkably fine one."

Clark Oliver couldn't come to our wedding — or wouldn't. Jane has never met him since, but she cannot understand why I have such an aversion to him, especially when he has such a good opinion of me. She says she thought him charming, and one of the most interesting conversationalists she ever went out to dinner with.

Robert Turner's Revenge

When Robert Turner came to the green, ferny triangle where the station road forked to the right and left under the birches, he hesitated as to which direction he would take. The left led out to the old Turner homestead, where he had spent his boyhood and where his cousin still lived; the right led down to the Cove shore where the Jameson property was situated. Since he had stopped off at Chiswick for the purpose of looking this property over before foreclosing the mortgage on it he concluded that he might as well take the Cove road; he could go around by the shore afterward — he had not forgotten the way even in forty years — and so on up through the old spruce wood in Alec Martin's field — if the spruces were there still and the field still Alec Martin's — to his cousin's place. He would just about have time to make the round before the early country supper hour. Then a brief visit with Tom — Tom had always been a good sort of a fellow although woefully dull and slow-going — and the evening express for Montreal. He swung with a businesslike stride into the Cove road.

As he went on, however, the stride insensibly slackened into an unaccustomed saunter. How well he remembered that old road, although it was forty years since he had last traversed it, a set-lipped boy of fifteen, cast on the world by the indifference of an uncle. The years had made surprisingly little difference in it or in the surrounding scenery. True, the hills and fields and lanes seemed lower and smaller and narrower than he remembered them; there were some new houses along the road, and the belt of woods along the back of the farms had become thinner in most places. But that was all. He had no difficulty in picking out the old familiar spots. There was the big cherry orchard on the Milligan place which had been so famous in his boyhood. It was snow-white with blossoms, as if the trees were possessed of eternal youth; they had been in blossom the last time he had seen them. Well, time had not stood still with him as it had with Luke Milligan's cherry orchard, he reflected grimly. His springtime had long gone by.

The few people he met on the road looked at him curiously, for strangers were not commonplace in Chiswick. He recognized some of the older among them but none of them knew him. He had been an awkward, long-limbed lad with fresh boyish colour and crisp black curls when he had left Chiswick. He returned to it a somewhat portly figure of a man, with close-cropped, grizzled hair, and a face that looked as if it might be carved out of granite, so immobile and unyielding it was — the face of a man who never faltered or wavered, who stuck at nothing that might advance his plans and purposes, a face known and dreaded in the business world where he reigned master. It was a cold, hard, selfish face, but the face of the boy of forty years ago had been neither cold nor hard nor selfish.

Presently the homesteads and orchard lands grew fewer and then ceased altogether. The fields were long and low-lying, sloping down to the misty blue rim of sea. A turn of the road brought him in sudden sight of the Cove, and there below him was the old Jameson homestead, built almost within wave-lap of the pebbly shore and shut away into a lonely grey world of its own by the sea and sands and those long slopes of tenantless fields.

He paused at the sagging gate that opened into the long, deep-rutted lane and, folding his arms on it, looked earnestly and scrutinizingly over the buildings. They were grey and faded, lacking the prosperous appearance that had characterized them once. There was an air of failure about the whole place as if the very land had become disheartened and discouraged.

Long ago, Neil Jameson, senior, had been a well-to-do man. The big Cove farm had been one of the best in Chiswick then. As for Neil Jameson, Junior, Robert Turner's face always grew something grimmer when he recalled him — the one person, boy and man, whom he had really hated in the world. They had been enemies from childhood, and once in a bout of wrestling at the Chiswick school Neil had thrown him by an unfair trick and taunted him continually thereafter on his defeat. Robert had made a compact with himself that some day he would pay Neil Jameson back. He had not forgotten it — he never forgot such things — but he had never seen or heard of Neil Jameson after leaving Chiswick. He might have been dead for anything Robert Turner knew. Then, when John Kesley failed and his effects turned over to his creditors, of whom Robert Turner was the chief, a mortgage on the Cove farm at Chiswick, owned by Neil Jameson, had been found among his assets. Inquiry revealed the fact that Neil Jameson was dead and that the farm was run by his widow. Turner felt a pang of disappointment. What satisfaction was there in wreaking revenge on a dead man? But at least his wife and children should suffer. That debt of his to Jameson for an ill-won victory and many a sneer must be paid in full, if not to him, why, then to his heirs.

His lawyers reported that Mrs. Jameson was two years behind with her interest. Turner instructed them to foreclose the mortgage promptly. Then he took it into his head to revisit Chiswick and have a good look at the Cove farm and other places he knew so well. He had a notion that it might be a decent place to spend a summer month or two in. His wife went to seaside and mountain resorts, but he liked something quieter. There was good fishing at the Cove and in Chiswick pond, as he remembered. If he liked the farm as well as his memory promised him he would do, he would bid it in himself. It would make Neil Jameson turn in his grave if the penniless lad he had jeered at came into the possession of his old ancestral property that had been owned by a Jameson for over one hundred years. There was a flavour in such a revenge that pleased Robert Turner. He smiled one of his occasional grim smiles over it. When Robert Turner smiled, weather prophets of the business sky foretold squalls.

Presently he opened the gate and went through. Halfway down the lane forked, one branch going over to the house, the other slanting across the field to the cove. Turner took the latter and soon found himself on the grey shore where the waves were tumbling in creamy foam just as he remembered them long ago. Nothing about the old cove had changed; he walked around a knobby headland, weather-worn with the wind and spray of years, which cut him off from sight of the Jameson house, and sat down on a rock. He thought himself alone and was annoyed to find a boy sitting on the opposite ledge with a book on his knee.

The lad lifted his eyes and looked Turner over with a clear, direct gaze. He was about twelve years old, tall for his age, slight, with a delicate, clear-cut face — a face that was oddly familiar to Turner, although he was sure he had never seen it before. The boy had oval cheeks, finely tinted with colour, big, shy blue eyes quilled about with long black lashes, and silvery-golden hair lying over his head in soft ringlets like a girl's. What girl's? Something far back in Robert Turner's dreamlike boyhood seemed to call to him like a note of a forgotten melody, sweet yet stirring like a pain. The more he looked at the boy the stronger the impression of a resemblance grew in every feature but the mouth. That was alien to his recollection of the face, yet there was something about it, when taken by itself, that seemed oddly familiar also — yes, and unpleasantly familiar, although the mouth was a good one — finely cut and possessing more firmness than was found in all the other features put together.

"It's a good place for reading, sonny, isn't it?" he inquired, more genially than he had spoken to a child for years. In fact, having no children of his own, he so seldom spoke to a child that his voice and manner when he did so were generally awkward and rusty.

The boy nodded a quick little nod. Somehow, Turner had expected that nod and the glimmer of a smile that accompanied it.

"What book are you reading?" he asked.

The boy held it out; it was an old *Robinson Crusoe*, that classic of boyhood.

"It's splendid," he said. "Billy Martin lent it to me and I have to finish it today because Ned Josephs is to have it next and he's in a hurry for it."

"It's a good while since I read *Robinson Crusoe*," said Turner reflectively. "But when I did it was on this very shore a little further along below the Miller place. There was a Martin and a Josephs in the partnership then too — the fathers, I dare say, of Billy and Ned. What is your name, my boy?"

"Paul Jameson, sir."

The name was a shock to Turner. This boy a Jameson — Neil Jameson's son? Why, yes, he had Neil's mouth. Strange he had nothing else in common with the black-browed, black-haired Jamesons. What business had a Jameson with those blue eyes and silvery-golden curls? It was flagrant forgery on Nature's part to fashion such things and label them Jameson by a mouth.

Hated Neil Jameson's son! Robert Turner's face grew so grey and hard that the boy involuntarily glanced upward to see if a cloud had crossed the sun.

"Your father was Neil Jameson, I suppose?" Turner said abruptly.

Paul nodded. "Yes, but he is dead. He has been dead for eight years. I don't remember him."

"Have you any brothers or sisters?"

"I have a little sister a year younger than I am. The other four are dead. They died long ago. I'm the only boy Mother had. Oh, I do so wish I was bigger and older! If I was I could do something to save the place — I'm sure I could. It is breaking Mother's heart to have to leave it."

"So she has to leave it, has she?" said Turner grimly, with the old hatred stirring in his heart.

"Yes. There is a mortgage on it and we're to be sold out very soon — so the lawyers told us. Mother has tried so hard to make the farm pay but she couldn't. I could if I was bigger — I know I could. If they would only wait a few years! But there is no use hoping for that. Mother cries all the time about it. She has lived at the Cove farm for over thirty years and she says she can't live away from it now. Elsie — that's my sister — and I do all we can to cheer her up, but we can't do much. Oh, if I was only a man!"

The lad shut his lips together — how much his mouth was like his father's — and looked out seaward with troubled blue eyes. Turner smiled another grim smile. Oh, Neil Jameson, your old score was being paid now!

Yet something embittered the sweetness of revenge. That boy's face—he could not hate it as he had accustomed himself to hate the memory of Neil Jameson and all connected with him.

"What was your mother's name before she married your father?" he demanded abruptly.

"Lisbeth Miller," answered the boy, still frowning seaward over his secret thoughts.

Turner started again. Lisbeth Miller! He might have known it. What woman in all the world save Lisbeth Miller could have given her son those eyes and curls? So Lisbeth had married Neil Jameson—little Lisbeth Miller, his schoolboy sweetheart. He had forgotten her—or thought he had; certainly he had not thought of her for years. But the memory of her came back now with a rush.

Little Lisbeth—pretty little Lisbeth—merry little Lisbeth! How clearly he remembered her! The old Miller place had adjoined his uncle's farm. Lisbeth and he had played together from babyhood. How he had worshipped her! When they were six years old they had solemnly promised to marry each other when they grew up, and Lisbeth had let him kiss her as earnest of their compact, made under a bloom-white apple tree in the Miller orchard. Yet she would always blush furiously and deny it ever afterwards; it made her angry to be reminded of it.

He saw himself going to school, carrying her books for her, the envied of all the boys. He remembered how he had fought Tony Josephs because Tony had the presumption to bring her spice apples: he had thrashed him too, so soundly that from that time forth none of the schoolboys presumed to rival him in Lisbeth's affections—roguish little Lisbeth! who grew prettier and saucier every year.

He recalled the keen competition of the old days when to be "head of the class" seemed the highest honour within mortal reach, and was striven after with might and main. He had seldom attained to it because he would never "go up past" Lisbeth. If she missed a word, he, Robert, missed it too, no matter how well he knew it. It was sweet to be thought a dunce for her dear sake. It was all the reward he asked to see her holding her place at the head of the class, her cheeks flushed pink and her eyes starry with her pride of position. And how sweetly she would lecture him on the way home from school about learning his spellings better, and wind up her sermon with the frank avowal, uttered with deliciously downcast lids, that she liked him better than any of the other boys after all, even if he couldn't spell as well as they could. Nothing of success that he had won since had ever thrilled him as that admission of little Lisbeth's!

She had been such a sympathetic little sweetheart too, never weary of listening to his dreams and ambitions, his plans for the future. She had always assured him that she knew he would succeed. Well, he had succeeded—and now one of the uses he was going to make of his success was to turn Lisbeth and her children out of their home by way of squaring matters with a dead man!

Lisbeth had been away from home on a long visit to an aunt when he had left Chiswick. She was growing up and the childish intimacy was fading. Perhaps, under other circumstances, it might have ripened into fruit, but he had gone away and forgotten her; the world had claimed him; he had lost all active remembrance of Lisbeth and, before this late return to Chiswick, he had not even known if she were living. And she was Neil Jameson's widow!

He was silent for a long time, while the waves purred about the base of the big red sandstone rock and the boy returned to his *Crusoe*. Finally Robert Turner roused himself from his reverie.

"I used to know your mother long ago when she was a little girl," he said. "I wonder if she remembers me. Ask her when you go home if she remembers Bobby Turner."

"Won't you come up to the house and see her, sir?" asked Paul politely. "Mother is always glad to see her old friends."

"No, I haven't time today." Robert Turner was not going to tell Neil Jameson's son that he did not care to look for the little Lisbeth of long ago in Neil Jameson's widow. The name spoiled her for him, just as the Jameson mouth spoiled her son for him. "But you may tell her something else. The mortgage will not be foreclosed. I was the power behind the lawyers, but I did not know that the present owner of the Cove farm was my little playmate, Lisbeth Miller. You and she shall have all the time you want. Tell her Bobby Turner does this in return for what she gave him under the big sweeting apple tree on her sixth birthday. I think she will remember and understand. As for you, Paul, be a good boy and good to your mother. I hope you'll succeed in your ambition of making the farm pay when you are old enough to take it in hand. At any rate, you'll not be disturbed in your possession of it."

"Oh, sir! oh, sir!" stammered Paul in an agony of embarrassed gratitude and delight. "Oh, it seems too good to be true. Do you really mean that we're not to be sold out? Oh, won't you come and tell Mother yourself? She'll be so happy—so grateful. Do come and let her thank you."

"Not today. I haven't time. Give her my message, that's all. There, run; the sooner she gets the news the better."

Turner watched the boy as he bounded away, until the headland hid him from sight.

"There goes my revenge—and a fine bit of property eminently suited for a summer residence—all for a bit of old, rusty sentiment," he said with a shrug. "I didn't suppose I was capable of such a mood. But then—little Lisbeth. There never was a sweeter girl. I'm glad I didn't go with the boy to see her. She's an old woman now—and Neil Jameson's widow. I prefer to keep my old memories of her undisturbed—little Lisbeth of the silvery-golden curls and the roguish blue eyes. Little Lisbeth of the old time! I'm glad to be able to have done you the small service of securing your home to you. It is my thanks to you for the friendship and affection you gave my lonely boyhood—my tribute to the memory of my first sweetheart."

He walked away with a smile, whose amusement presently softened to an expression that would have amazed his business cronies. Later on he hummed the air of an old love song as he climbed the steep spruce road to Tom's.

The Fillmore Elderberries

"I expected as much," said Timothy Robinson. His tone brought the blood into Ellis Duncan's face. The lad opened his lips quickly, as if for an angry retort, but as quickly closed them again with a set firmness oddly like Timothy Robinson's own.

"When I heard that lazy, worthless father of yours was dead, I expected you and your mother would be looking to me for help," Timothy Robinson went on harshly. "But you're mistaken if you think I'll give it. You've no claim on me, even if your father was my half-brother—no claim at all. And I'm not noted for charity."

Timothy Robinson smiled grimly. It was very true that he was far from being noted for charity. His neighbours called him "close" and "near." Some even went so far as to call him "a miserly skinflint." But this was not true. It was, however, undeniable that Timothy Robinson kept a tight clutch on his purse-strings, and although he sometimes gave liberally enough to any cause which really appealed to him, such causes were few and far between.

"I am not asking for charity, Uncle Timothy," said Ellis quietly. He passed over the slur at his father in silence, deeply as he felt it, for, alas, he knew that it was only too true. "I expect to support my mother by hard and honest work. And I am not asking you for work on the ground of our relationship. I heard you wanted a hired man, and I have come to you, as I should have gone to any other man about whom I had heard it, to ask you to hire me."

"Yes, I do want a man," said Uncle Timothy drily. "A *man*—not a half-grown boy of fourteen, not worth his salt. I want somebody able and willing to work."

Again Ellis flushed deeply and again he controlled himself. "I am willing to work, Uncle Timothy, and I think you would find me able also if you would try me. I'd work for less than a man's wages at first, of course."

"You won't work for any sort of wages from me," interrupted Timothy Robinson decidedly. "I tell you plainly that I won't hire you. You're the wrong man's son for that. Your father was lazy and incompetent and, worst of all, untrustworthy. I did try to help him once, and all I got was loss and ingratitude. I want none of his kind around my place. I don't believe in you, so you may as well take yourself off, Ellis. I've no more time to waste."

Ellis took himself off, his ears tingling. As he walked homeward his thoughts were very bitter. All Uncle Timothy had said about his father was true, and Ellis realized what a count it was against him in his efforts to obtain employment. Nobody wanted to be bothered with "Old Sam Duncan's son," though nobody had been so brutally outspoken as his Uncle Timothy.

Sam Duncan and Timothy Robinson had been half-brothers. Sam, the older, had been the son of Mrs. Robinson's former marriage. Never were two lads more dissimilar. Sam was a lazy, shiftless fellow, deserving all the hard things that came to be said of him. He would not work and nobody could depend on him, but he was a handsome lad with rather taking ways in his youth, and at first people had liked him better than the close, blunt, industrious Timothy. Their mother had died in their childhood, but Mr. Robinson had been fond of Sam and the boy had a good home. When he was twenty-two and Timothy eighteen, Mr. Robinson had died very suddenly, leaving no will. Everything he possessed went to Timothy. Sam immediately left. He said he would not stay there to be "bossed" by Timothy.

He rented a little house in the village, married a girl "far too good for him," and started in to support himself and his wife by days' work. He had lounged, borrowed, and shirked through life. Once Timothy Robinson, perhaps moved by pity for Sam's wife and baby, had hired him for a year at better wages than most hired men received in Dalrymple. Sam idled through a month of it, then got offended and left in the middle of haying. Timothy Robinson washed his hands of him after that.

When Ellis was fourteen Sam Duncan died, after a lingering illness of a year. During this time the family were kept by the charity of pitying neighbours, for Ellis could not be spared from attendance on his father to make any attempt at earning money. Mrs. Duncan was a fragile little woman, worn out with her hard life, and not strong enough to wait on her husband alone.

When Sam Duncan was dead and buried, Ellis straightened his shoulders and took counsel with himself. He must earn a livelihood for his mother and himself, and he must begin at once. He was tall and strong for his age, and had a fairly good education, his mother having determinedly kept him at school when he had pleaded to be allowed to go to work. He had always been a quiet fellow, and nobody in Dalrymple knew much about him. But they knew all about his father, and nobody would hire Ellis unless he were willing to work for a pittance that would barely clothe him.

Ellis had not gone to his Uncle Timothy until he had lost all hope of getting a place elsewhere. Now this hope too had gone. It was nearly the end of June and everybody who wanted help had secured it. Look where he would, Ellis could see no prospect of employment.

"If I could only get a chance!" he thought miserably. "I know I am not idle or lazy — I know I can work — if I could get a chance to prove it."

He was sitting on the fence of the Fillmore elderberry pasture as he said it, having taken a short cut across the fields. This pasture was rather noted in Dalrymple. Originally a mellow and fertile field, it had been almost ruined by a persistent, luxuriant growth of elderberry bushes. Old Thomas Fillmore had at first tried to conquer them by mowing them down "in the dark of the moon." But the elderberries did not seem to mind either moon or mowing, and flourished alike in all the quarters. For the past two years Old Thomas had given up the contest, and the elderberries had it all their own sweet way.

Thomas Fillmore, a bent old man with a shrewd, nutcracker face, came through the bushes while Ellis was sitting on the fence.

"Howdy, Ellis. Seen anything of my spotted calves? I've been looking for 'em for over an hour."

"No, I haven't seen any calves — but a good many might be in this pasture without being visible to the naked eye," said Ellis, with a smile.

Old Thomas shook his head ruefully. "Them elders have been too many for me," he said. "Did you ever see a worse-looking place? You'd hardly believe that twenty years ago there wasn't a better piece of land in Dalrymple than this lot, would ye? Such grass as grew here!"

"The soil must be as good as ever if anything had a chance to grow on it," said Ellis. "Couldn't those elders be rooted out?"

"It'd be a back-breaking job, but I reckon it could be done if anyone had the muscle and patience and time to tackle it. I haven't the first at my age, and my hired man hasn't the last. And nobody would do it for what I could afford to pay."

"What will you give me if I undertake to clean the elders out of this field for you, Mr. Fillmore?" asked Ellis quietly.

Old Thomas looked at him with a surprised face, which gradually reverted to its original shrewdness when he saw that Ellis was in earnest. "You must be hard up for a job," he said.

"I am," was Ellis's laconic answer.

"Well, lemme see." Old Thomas calculated carefully. He never paid a cent more for anything than he could help, and was noted for hard bargaining. "I'll give ye sixteen dollars if you clean out the whole field," he said at length.

Ellis looked at the pasture. He knew something about cleaning out elderberry brush, and he also knew that sixteen dollars would be very poor pay for it. Most of the elders were higher than a man's head, with big roots, thicker than his wrist, running deep into the ground.

"It's worth more, Mr. Fillmore," he said.

"Not to me," responded Old Thomas drily. "I've plenty more land and I'm an old fellow without any sons. I ain't going to pay out money for the benefit of some stranger who'll come after me. You can take it or leave it at sixteen dollars."

Ellis shrugged his shoulders. He had no prospect of anything else, and sixteen dollars were better than nothing. "Very well, I'll take it," he said.

"Well, now, look here," said Old Thomas shrewdly, "I'll expect you to do the work thoroughly, young man. Them roots ain't to be cut off, remember; they'll have to be dug out. And I'll expect you to finish the job if you undertake it too, and not drop it halfway through if you get a chance for a better one."

"I'll finish with your elderberries before I leave them," promised Ellis.

Ellis went to work the next day. His first move was to chop down all the brush and cart it into heaps for burning. This took two days and was comparatively easy work. The third day Ellis tackled the roots. By the end of the forenoon he had discovered just what cleaning out an elderberry pasture meant, but he set his teeth and resolutely persevered. During the afternoon Timothy Robinson, whose farm adjoined the Fillmore place, wandered by and halted with a look of astonishment at the sight of Ellis, busily engaged in digging and tearing out huge, tough, stubborn elder roots. The boy did not see his uncle, but worked away with a vim and vigour that were not lost on the latter.

"He never got that muscle from Sam," reflected Timothy. "Sam would have fainted at the mere thought of stumping elders. Perhaps I've been mistaken in the boy. Well, well, we'll see if he holds out."

Ellis did hold out. The elderberries tried to hold out too, but they were no match for the lad's perseverance. It was a hard piece of work, however, and Ellis never forgot it. Week after week he toiled in the hot summer sun, digging, cutting, and dragging out roots. The job seemed endless, and his progress each day was discouragingly slow. He had expected to get through in a month, but he soon found it would take two. Frequently Timothy Robinson wandered by and looked at the increasing pile of roots and the slowly extending stretch of cleared land. But he never spoke to Ellis and made no comment on the matter to anybody.

One evening, when the field was about half done, Ellis went home more than usually tired. It had been a very hot day. Every bone and muscle in him ached. He wondered dismally if he would ever get to the end of that wretched elderberry field. When he reached home Jacob Green from Westdale was there. Jacob lost no time in announcing his errand.

"My hired boy's broke his leg, and I must fill his place right off. Somebody referred me to you. Guess I'll try you. Twelve dollars a month, board, and lodging. What say?"

For a moment Ellis's face flushed with delight. Twelve dollars a month and permanent employment! Then he remembered his promise to Mr. Fillmore. For a moment he struggled with the temptation. Then he mastered it. Perhaps the discipline of his many encounters with those elderberry roots helped him to do so.

"I'm sorry, Mr. Green," he said reluctantly. "I'd like to go, but I can't. I promised Mr. Fillmore that I'd finish cleaning up his elderberry pasture when I'd once begun it, and I shan't be through for a month yet."

"Well, I'd see myself turning down a good offer for Old Tom Fillmore," said Jacob Green.

"It isn't for Mr. Fillmore — it's for myself," said Ellis steadily. "I promised and I must keep my word."

Jacob drove away grumblingly. On the road he met Timothy Robinson and stopped to relate his grievances.

It must be admitted that there were times during the next month when Ellis was tempted to repent having refused Jacob Green's offer. But at the end of the month the work was done and the Fillmore elderberry pasture was an elderberry pasture no longer. All that remained of the elders, root and branch, was piled into a huge heap ready for burning.

"And I'll come up and set fire to it when it's dry enough," Ellis told Mr. Fillmore. "I claim the satisfaction of that."

"You've done the job thoroughly," said Old Thomas. "There's your sixteen dollars, and every cent of it was earned, if ever money was, I'll say that much for you. There ain't a lazy bone in your body. If you ever want a recommendation just you come to me."

As Ellis passed Timothy Robinson's place on the way home that worthy himself appeared, strolling down his lane. "Ah, Ellis," he said, speaking to his nephew for the first time since their interview two months before, "so you've finished with your job?"

"Yes, sir."

"Got your sixteen dollars, I suppose? It was worth four times that. Old Tom cheated you. You were foolish not to have gone to Green when you had the chance."

"I'd promised Mr. Fillmore to finish with his pasture, sir!"

"Humph! Well, what are you going to do now?"

"I don't know. Harvest will be on next week. I may get in somewhere as an extra hand for a spell."

"Ellis," said his uncle abruptly, after a moment's silence, "I'm going to discharge my man. He's no earthly good. Will you take his place? I'll give you fifteen dollars a month and found."

Ellis stared at Timothy Robinson. "I thought you told me that you had no place for my father's son," he said slowly.

"I've changed my mind. I've seen how you went at that elderberry job. Great snakes, there couldn't be a better test for anybody than rooting out them things. I know you can work. When Jacob Green told me why you'd refused his offer I knew you could be depended on. You come to me and I'll do well by you. I've no kith or kin of my own except you. And look here, Ellis. I'm tired of hired housekeepers. Will your mother come up and live with us and look after things a bit? I've a good girl, and she won't have to work hard, but there must be somebody at the head of a household. She must have a good headpiece—for you have inherited good qualities from someone, and goodness knows it wasn't from your father."

"Uncle Timothy," said Ellis respectfully but firmly, "I'll accept your offer gratefully, and I am sure Mother will too. But there is one thing I must say. Perhaps my father deserves all you say of him—but he is dead—and if I come to you it must be with the understanding that nothing more is ever to be said against him."

Timothy Robinson smiled—a queer, twisted smile that yet had a hint of affection and comprehension in it. "Very well," he said. "I'll never cast his shortcomings up to you again. Come to me—and if I find you always as industrious and reliable as you've proved yourself to be negotiating them elders, I'll most likely forget that you ain't my own son some of these days."

The Finished Story

She always sat in a corner of the west veranda at the hotel, knitting something white and fluffy, or pink and fluffy, or pale blue and fluffy — always fluffy, at least, and always dainty. Shawls and scarfs and hoods the things were, I believe. When she finished one she gave it to some girl and began another. Every girl at Harbour Light that summer wore some distracting thing that had been fashioned by Miss Sylvia's slim, tireless, white fingers.

She was old, with that beautiful, serene old age which is as beautiful in its way as youth. Her girlhood and womanhood must have been very lovely to have ripened into such a beauty of sixty years. It was a surprise to everyone who heard her called *Miss* Sylvia. She looked so like a woman who ought to have stalwart, grown sons and dimpled little grandchildren.

For the first two days after the arrival at the hotel she sat in her corner alone. There was always a circle of young people around her; old folks and middle-aged people would have liked to join it, but Miss Sylvia, while she was gracious to all, let it be distinctly understood that her sympathies were with youth. She sat among the boys and girls, young men and maidens, like a fine white queen. Her dress was always the same and somewhat old-fashioned, but nothing else would have suited her half so well; she wore a lace cap on her snowy hair and a heliotrope shawl over her black silk shoulders. She knitted continually and talked a good deal, but listened more. We sat around her at all hours of the day and told her everything.

When you were first introduced to her you called her Miss Stanleymain. Her endurance of that was limited to twenty-four hours. Then she begged you to call her Miss Sylvia, and as Miss Sylvia you spoke and thought of her forevermore.

Miss Sylvia liked us all, but I was her favourite. She told us so frankly and let it be understood that when I was talking to her and her heliotrope shawl was allowed to slip under one arm it was a sign that we were not to be interrupted. I was as vain of her favour as any lovelorn suitor whose lady had honoured him, not knowing, as I came to know later, the reason for it.

Although Miss Sylvia had an unlimited capacity for receiving confidences, she never gave any. We were all sure that there must be some romance in her life, but our efforts to discover it were unsuccessful. Miss Sylvia parried tentative questions so skilfully that we knew she had something to defend. But one evening, when I had known her a month, as time is reckoned, and long years as affection and understanding are computed, she told me her story—at least, what there was to tell of it. The last chapter was missing.

We were sitting together on the veranda at sunset. Most of the hotel people had gone for a harbour sail; a few forlorn mortals prowled about the grounds and eyed our corner wistfully, but by the sign of the heliotrope shawl knew it was not for them.

I was reading one of my stories to Miss Sylvia. In my own excuse I must allege that she tempted me to do it. I did not go around with manuscripts under my arm, inflicting them on defenceless females. But Miss Sylvia had discovered that I was a magazine scribbler, and moreover, that I had shut myself up in my room that very morning and perpetrated a short story. Nothing would do but that I read it to her.

It was a rather sad little story. The hero loved the heroine, and she loved him. There was no reason why he should not love her, but there was a reason why he could not marry her. When he found that he loved her he knew that he must go away. But might he not, at least, tell her his love? Might he not, at least, find out for his consolation if she cared for him? There was a struggle; he won, and went away without a word, believing it to be the more manly course. When I began to read Miss Sylvia was knitting, a pale green something this time, of the tender hue of young leaves in May. But after a little her knitting slipped unheeded to her lap and her hands folded idly above it. It was the most subtle compliment I had ever received.

When I turned the last page of the manuscript and looked up, Miss Sylvia's soft brown eyes were full of tears. She lifted her hands, clasped them together and said in an agitated voice:

"Oh, no, no; don't let him go away without telling her—just telling her. Don't let him do it!"

"But, you see, Miss Sylvia," I explained, flattered beyond measure that my characters had seemed so real to her, "that would spoil the story. It would have no reason for existence then. Its *motif* is simply his mastery over self. He believes it to be the nobler course."

"No, no, it wasn't—if he loved her he should have told her. Think of her shame and humiliation—she loved him, and he went without a word and she could never know he cared for her. Oh, you must change it—you must, indeed! I cannot bear to think of her suffering what I have suffered."

Miss Sylvia broke down and sobbed. To appease her, I promised that I would remodel the story, although I knew that the doing so would leave it absolutely pointless.

"Oh, I'm so glad," said Miss Sylvia, her eyes shining through her tears. "You see, I know it would make her happier—I know it. I'm going to tell you my poor little story to convince you. But you—you must not tell it to any of the others."

"I am sorry you think the admonition necessary," I said reproachfully.

"Oh, I do not, indeed I do not," she hastened to assure me. "I know I can trust you. But it's such a poor little story. You mustn't laugh at it—it is all the romance I had. Years ago—forty years ago—when I was a young girl of twenty, I—learned to care very much for somebody. I met him at a summer resort like this. I was there with my aunt and he was there with his mother, who was delicate. We saw a great deal of each other for a little while. He was—oh, he was like no other man I had ever seen. You remind me of him somehow. That is partly why I like you so much. I noticed the resemblance the first time I saw you. I don't know in just what it consists—in your expression and the way you carry your head, I think. He was not strong—he coughed a good deal. Then one day he went away—suddenly. I had thought he cared for me, but he never said so—just went away. Oh, the shame of it! After a time I heard that he had been ordered to California for his health. And he died out there the next spring. My heart broke then, I never cared for anybody again—I couldn't. I have always loved him. But it would have been so much easier to bear if I had only known that he loved me—oh, it would have made all the difference in the world. And the sting of it has been there all these years. I can't even permit myself the joy of dwelling on his memory because of the thought that perhaps he did not care."

"He must have cared," I said warmly. "He couldn't have helped it, Miss Sylvia."

Miss Sylvia shook her head with a sad smile.

"I cannot be sure. Sometimes I think he did. But then the doubt creeps back again. I would give almost anything to know that he did—to know that I have not lavished all the love of my life on a man who did not want it. And I never can know, never—I can hope and almost believe, but I can never know. Oh, you don't understand—a man couldn't fully understand what my pain has been over it. You see now why I want you to change the story. I am sorry for that poor girl, but if you only let her know that he really loves her she will not mind all the rest so very much; she will be able to bear the pain of even life-long separation if she only knows."

Miss Sylvia picked up her knitting and went away. As for me, I thought savagely of the dead man she loved and called him a cad, or at best, a fool.

Next day Miss Sylvia was her serene, smiling self once more, and she did not again make any reference to what she had told me. A fortnight later she returned home and I went my way back to the world. During the following winter I wrote several letters to Miss Sylvia and received replies from her. Her letters were very like herself. When I sent her the third-rate magazine containing my story — nothing but a third-rate magazine would take it in its rewritten form — she wrote to say that she was so glad that I had let the poor girl know.

Early in April I received a letter from an aunt of mine in the country, saying that she intended to sell her place and come to the city to live. She asked me to go out to Sweetwater for a few weeks and assist her in the business of settling up the estate and disposing of such things as she did not wish to take with her.

When I arrived at Sweetwater I found it moist and chill with the sunny moisture and teasing chill of our Canadian springs. They are long and fickle and reluctant, these springs of ours, but, oh, the unnamable charm of them! There was something even in the red buds of the maples at Sweetwater and in the long, smoking stretches of hillside fields that sent a thrill through my veins, finer and subtler than any given by old wine.

A week after my arrival, when we had got the larger affairs pretty well straightened out, Aunt Mary suggested that I had better overhaul Uncle Alan's room.

"The things there have never been meddled with since he died," she said. "In particular, there's an old trunk full of his letters and his papers. It was brought home from California after his death. I've never examined them. I don't suppose there is anything of any importance among them. But I'm not going to carry all that old rubbish to town. So I wish you would look over them and see if there is anything that should be kept. The rest may be burned."

I felt no particular interest in the task. My Uncle Alan Blair was a mere name to me. He was my mother's eldest brother and had died years before I was born. I had heard that he had been very clever and that great things had been expected of him. But I anticipated no pleasure from exploring musty old letters and papers of forty neglected years.

I went up to Uncle Alan's room at dusk that night. We had been having a day of warm spring rain, but it had cleared away and the bare maple boughs outside the window were strung with glistening drops. The room looked to the north and was always dim by reason of the close-growing Sweetwater pines. A gap had been cut through them to the northwest, and in it I had a glimpse of the sea Uncle Alan had loved, and above it a wondrous sunset sky fleeced over with little clouds, pale and pink and golden and green, that suddenly reminded me of Miss Sylvia and her fluffy knitting. It was with the thought of her in my mind that I lighted a lamp and began the task of grubbing into Uncle Alan's trunkful of papers. Most of these were bundles of yellowed letters, of no present interest, from his family and college friends. There were several college theses and essays, and a lot of loose miscellania pertaining to boyish school days. I went through the collection rapidly, until at the bottom of the trunk, I came to a small book bound in dark-green leather. It proved to be a sort of journal, and I began to glance over it with a languid interest.

It had been begun in the spring after he had graduated from college. Although suspected only by himself, the disease which was to end his life had already fastened upon him. The entries were those of a doomed man, who, feeling the curse fall on him like a frost, blighting all the fair hopes and promises of life, seeks some help and consolation in the outward self-communing of a journal. There was nothing morbid, nothing unmanly in the record. As I read, I found myself liking Uncle Alan, wishing that he might have lived and been my friend.

His mother had not been well that summer and the doctor ordered her to the seashore. Alan accompanied her. Here occurred a hiatus in the journal. No leaves had been torn out, but a quire or so of them had apparently become loosened from the threads that held them in place. I found them later on in the trunk, but at the time I passed to the next page. It began abruptly:

> This girl is the sweetest thing that God ever made. I had not known a woman could be so fair and sweet. Her beauty awes me, the purity of her soul shines so clearly through it like an illuminating lamp. I love her with all my power of loving and I am thankful that it is so. It would have been hard to die without having known love. I am glad that it has come to me, even if its price is unspeakable bitterness. A man has not lived for nothing who has known and loved Sylvia Stanleymain.
>
> I must not seek her love—that is denied me. If I were well and strong I should win it; yes, I believe I could win it, and nothing in the world would prevent me from trying, but, as things are, it would be the part of a coward to try. Yet I cannot resist the delight of being with her, of talking to her, of watching her wonderful face. She is in my thoughts day and night, she dwells in my dreams. O, Sylvia, I love you, my sweet!

A week later there was another entry:

> July Seventeenth.
>
> I am afraid. To-day I met Sylvia's eyes. In them was a look which at first stirred my heart to its deeps with tumultuous delight, and then I remembered. I must spare her that suffering, at whatever cost to myself. I must not let myself dwell on the dangerous sweetness of the thought that her heart is turning to me. What would be the crowning joy to another man could be only added sorrow to me.

Then:

> July Eighteenth.
>
> This morning I took the train to the city. I was determined to know the worst once for all. The time had come when I must. My doctor at home had put me off with vague hopes and perhapses. So I went to a noted physician in the city. I told him I wanted the whole truth—I made him tell it. Stripped of all softening verbiage it is this: I have perhaps eight months or a year to live—no more!
>
> I had expected it, although not quite so soon. Yet the certainty was none the less bitter. But this is no time for self-pity. It is of Sylvia I must think now. I shall go away at once, before the sweet fancy which is possibly budding in her virgin heart shall have bloomed into a flower that might poison some of her fair years.
>
> July Nineteenth.
>
> It is over. I said good-bye to her to-day before others, for I dared not trust myself to see her alone. She looked hurt and startled, as if someone had struck her. But she will soon forget, even if I have not been mistaken in the reading of her eyes. As for me, the bitterness of death is already over in that parting. All that now remains is to play the man to the end.

From further entries in the journal I learned that Alan Blair had returned to Sweetwater and later on had been ordered to California. The entries during his sojourn there were few and far between. In all of them he spoke of Sylvia. Finally, after a long silence, he had written:

> I think the end is not far off now. I am not sorry for my suffering has been great of late. Last night I was easier. I slept and dreamed that I saw Sylvia. Once or twice I thought that I would arrange to have this book sent to her after my death. But I have decided that it would be unwise. It would only pain her, so I shall destroy it when I feel the time has come.
>
> It is sunset in this wonderful summer land. At home in Sweetwater it is only early spring as yet, with snow lingering along the edges of the woods. The sunsets there will be creamy-yellow and pale red now. If I could but see them once more! And Sylvia—

There was a little blot where the pen had fallen. Evidently the end had been nearer than Alan Blair had thought. At least, there were no more entries, and the little green book had not been destroyed. I was glad that it had not been; and I felt glad that it was thus put in my power to write the last chapter of Miss Sylvia's story for her.

As soon as I could leave Sweetwater I went to the city, three hundred miles away, where Miss Sylvia lived. I found her in her library, in her black silk dress and heliotrope shawl, knitting up cream wool, for all the world as if she had just been transplanted from the veranda corner of Harbour Light.

"My dear boy!" she said.

"Do you know why I have come?" I asked.

"I am vain enough to think it was because you wanted to see me," she smiled.

"I did want to see you; but I would have waited until summer if it had not been that I wished to bring you the missing chapter of your story, dear lady."

"I—I—don't understand," said Miss Sylvia, starting slightly.

"I had an uncle, Alan Blair, who died forty years ago in California," I said quietly. "Recently I have had occasion to examine some of his papers. I found a journal among them and I have brought it to you because I think that you have the best right to it."

I dropped the parcel in her lap. She was silent with surprise and bewilderment.

"And now," I added, "I am going away. You won't want to see me or anyone for a while after you have read this book. But I will come up to see you to-morrow."

When I went the next day Miss Sylvia herself met me at the door. She caught my hand and drew me into the hall. Her eyes were softly radiant.

"Oh, you have made me so happy!" she said tremulously. "Oh, you can never know how happy! Nothing hurts now—nothing ever can hurt, because I know he did care."

She laid her face down on my shoulder, as a girl might have nestled to her lover, and I bent and kissed her for Uncle Alan.

The Garden of Spices

Jims tried the door of the blue room. Yes, it was locked. He had hoped Aunt Augusta *might* have forgotten to lock it; but when did Aunt Augusta forget anything? Except, perhaps, that little boys were not born grown-ups — and *that* was something she never remembered. To be sure, she was only a half-aunt. Whole aunts probably had more convenient memories.

Jims turned and stood with his back against the door. It was better that way; he could not imagine things behind him then. And the blue room was so big and dim that a dreadful number of things could be imagined in it. All the windows were shuttered but one, and that one was so darkened by a big pine tree branching right across it that it did not let in much light.

Jims looked very small and lost and lonely as he shrank back against the door — so small and lonely that one might have thought that even the sternest of half-aunts should have thought twice before shutting him up in that room and telling him he must stay there the whole afternoon instead of going out for a promised ride. Jims hated being shut up alone — especially in the blue room. Its bigness and dimness and silence filled his sensitive little soul with vague horror. Sometimes he became almost sick with fear in it. To do Aunt Augusta justice, she never suspected this. If she had she would not have decreed this particular punishment, because she knew Jims was delicate and must not be subjected to any great physical or mental strain. That was why she shut him up instead of whipping him. But how was she to know it? Aunt Augusta was one of those people who never know anything unless it is told them in plain language and then hammered into their heads. There was no one to tell her but Jims, and Jims would have died the death before he would have told Aunt Augusta, with her cold, spectacled eyes and thin, smileless mouth, that he was desperately frightened when he was shut in the blue room. So he was always shut in it for punishment; and the punishments came very often, for Jims was always doing things that Aunt Augusta considered naughty. At first, this time, Jims did not feel quite so frightened as usual because he was very angry. As he put it, he was very mad at Aunt Augusta. He hadn't *meant* to spill his pudding over the floor and the tablecloth and his clothes; and how such a little bit of pudding — Aunt Augusta was mean with desserts — could ever have spread itself over so much territory Jims could not understand. But he had made a terrible mess and Aunt Augusta had been very angry and had said he must be cured of such carelessness. She said he must spend the afternoon in the blue room instead of going for a ride with Mrs. Loring in her new car.

Jims was bitterly disappointed. If Uncle Walter had been home Jims would have appealed to him — for when Uncle Walter could be really wakened up to a realization of his small nephew's presence in his home, he was very kind and indulgent. But it was so hard to waken him up that Jims seldom attempted it. He liked Uncle Walter, but as far as being acquainted with him went he might as well have been the inhabitant of a star in the Milky Way. Jims was just a lonely, solitary little creature, and sometimes he felt so friendless that his eyes smarted, and several sobs had to be swallowed.

There were no sobs just now, though — Jims was still too angry. It wasn't fair. It was so seldom he got a car ride. Uncle Walter was always too busy, attending to sick children all over the town, to take him. It was only once in a blue moon Mrs. Loring asked him to go out with her. But she always ended up with ice cream or a movie, and to-day Jims had had strong hopes that both were on the programme.

"I hate Aunt Augusta," he said aloud; and then the sound of his voice in that huge, still room scared him so that he only thought the rest. "I won't have any fun — and she won't feed my gobbler, either."

Jims had shrieked "Feed my gobbler," to the old servant as he had been hauled upstairs. But he didn't think Nancy Jane had heard him, and nobody, not even Jims, could imagine Aunt Augusta feeding the gobbler. It was always a wonder to him that she ate, herself. It seemed really too human a thing for her to do.

"I wish I had spilled that pudding *on purpose*," Jims said vindictively, and with the saying his anger evaporated — Jims never could stay angry long — and left him merely a scared little fellow, with velvety, nut-brown eyes full of fear that should have no place in a child's eyes. He looked so small and helpless as he crouched against the door that one might have wondered if even Aunt Augusta would not have relented had she seen him.

How that window at the far end of the room rattled! It sounded terribly as if somebody — or *something* — were trying to get in. Jims looked desperately at the unshuttered window. He must get to it; once there, he could curl up in the window seat, his back to the wall, and forget the shadows by looking out into the sunshine and loveliness of the garden over the wall. Jims would have likely have been found dead of fright in that blue room some time had it not been for the garden over the wall.

But to get to the window Jims must cross the room and pass by the bed. Jims held that bed in special dread. It was the oldest fashioned thing in the old-fashioned, old-furnitured house. It was high and rigid, and hung with gloomy blue curtains. *Anything* might jump out of such a bed.

Jims gave a gasp and ran madly across the room. He reached the window and flung himself upon the seat. With a sigh of relief he curled down in the corner. Outside, over the high brick wall, was a world where his imagination could roam, though his slender little body was pent a prisoner in the blue room.

Jims had loved that garden from his first sight of it. He called it the Garden of Spices and wove all sorts of yarns in fancy — yarns gay and tragic — about it. He had only known it for a few weeks. Before that, they had lived in a much smaller house away at the other side of the town. Then Uncle Walter's uncle — who had brought him up just as he was bringing up Jims — had died, and they had all come to live in Uncle Walter's old home. Somehow, Jims had an idea that Uncle Walter wasn't very glad to come back there. But he had to, according to great-uncle's will. Jims himself didn't mind much. He liked the smaller rooms in their former home better, but the Garden of Spices made up for all.

It was such a beautiful spot. Just inside the wall was a row of aspen poplars that always talked in silvery whispers and shook their dainty, heart-shaped leaves at him. Beyond them, under scattered pines, was a rockery where ferns and wild things grew. It was almost as good as a bit of woods — and Jims loved the woods, though he scarcely ever saw them. Then, past the pines, were roses just breaking into June bloom — roses in such profusion as Jims hadn't known existed, with dear little paths twisting about among the bushes. It seemed to be a garden where no frost could blight or rough wind blow. When rain fell it must fall very gently. Past the roses one saw a green lawn, sprinkled over now with the white ghosts of dandelions, and dotted with ornamental trees. The trees grew so thickly that they almost hid the house to which the garden pertained. It was a large one of grey-black stone, with stacks of huge chimneys. Jims had no idea who lived there. He had asked Aunt Augusta and Aunt Augusta had frowned and told him it did not matter who lived there and that he must never, on any account, mention the next house or its occupant to Uncle Walter. Jims would never have thought of mentioning them to Uncle Walter. But the prohibition filled him with an unholy and unsubduable curiosity. He was devoured by the desire to find out who the folks in that tabooed house were.

And he longed to have the freedom of that garden. Jims loved gardens. There had been a garden at the little house but there was none here — nothing but an old lawn that had been fine once but was now badly run to seed. Jims had heard Uncle Walter say that he was going to have it attended to but nothing had been done yet. And meanwhile here was a beautiful garden over the wall which looked as if it should be full of children. But no children were ever in it — or anybody else apparently. And so, in spite of its beauty, it had a lonely look that hurt Jims. He *wanted* his Garden of Spices to be full of laughter. He pictured himself running in it with imaginary playmates — and there was a mother in it — or a big sister — or, at the least, a whole aunt who would let you hug her and would never dream of shutting you up in chilly, shadowy, horrible blue rooms.

"It seems to me," said Jims, flattening his nose against the pane, "that I must get into that garden or bust."

Aunt Augusta would have said icily, "We do not use such expressions, James," but Aunt Augusta was not there to hear.

"I'm afraid the Very Handsome Cat isn't coming to-day," sighed Jims. Then he brightened up; the Very Handsome Cat was coming across the lawn. He was the only living thing, barring birds and butterflies, that Jims ever saw in the garden. Jims worshipped that cat. He was jet black, with white paws and dickey, and he had as much dignity as ten cats. Jims' fingers tingled to stroke him. Jims had never been allowed to have even a kitten because Aunt Augusta had a horror of cats. And you cannot stroke gobblers!

The Very Handsome Cat came through the rose garden paths on his beautiful paws, ambled daintily around the rockery, and sat down in a shady spot under a pine tree, right where Jims could see him, through a gap in the little poplars. He looked straight up at Jims and winked. At least, Jims always believed and declared he did. And that wink said, or seemed to say, plainly:

"Be a sport. Come down here and play with me. A fig for your Aunt Augusta!"

A wild, daring, absurd idea flashed into Jims' brain. Could he? He could! He would! He knew it would be easy. He had thought it all out many times, although until now he had never dreamed of really doing it. To unhook the window and swing it open, to step out on the pine bough and from it to another that hung over the wall and dropped nearly to the ground, to spring from it to the velvet sward under the poplars — why, it was all the work of a minute. With a careful, repressed whoop Jims ran towards the Very Handsome Cat.

The cat rose and retreated in deliberate haste; Jims ran after him. The cat dodged through the rose paths and eluded Jims' eager hands, just keeping tantalizingly out of reach. Jims had forgotten everything except that he must catch the cat. He was full of a fearful joy, with an elfin delight running through it. He had escaped from the blue room and its ghosts; he was in his Garden of Spices; he had got the better of mean old Aunt Augusta. But he *must* catch the cat.

The cat ran over the lawn and Jims pursued it through the green gloom of the thickly clustering trees. Beyond them came a pool of sunshine in which the old stone house basked like a huge grey cat itself. More garden was before it and beyond it, wonderful with blossom. Under a huge spreading beech tree in the centre of it was a little tea table; sitting by the table reading was a lady in a black dress.

The cat, having lured Jims to where he wanted him, sat down and began to lick his paws. He was quite willing to be caught now; but Jims had no longer any idea of catching him. He stood very still, looking at the lady. She did not see him then and Jims could only see her profile, which he thought very beautiful. She had wonderful ropes of blue-black hair wound around her head. She looked so sweet that Jims' heart beat. Then she lifted her head and turned her face and saw him. Jims felt something of a shock. She was not pretty after all. One side of her face was marked by a dreadful red scar. It quite spoilt her good looks, which Jims thought a great pity; but nothing could spoil the sweetness of her face or the loveliness of her peculiar soft, grey-blue eyes. Jims couldn't remember his mother and had no idea what she looked like, but the thought came into his head that he would have liked her to have eyes like that. After the first moment Jims did not mind the scar at all.

But perhaps that first moment had revealed itself in his face, for a look of pain came into the lady's eyes and, almost involuntarily it seemed, she put her hand up to hide the scar. Then she pulled it away again and sat looking at Jims half defiantly, half piteously. Jims thought she must be angry because he had chased her cat.

"I beg your pardon," he said gravely, "I didn't mean to hurt your cat. I just wanted to play with him. He is *such* a very handsome cat."

"But where did you come from?" said the lady. "It is so long since I saw a child in this garden," she added, as if to herself. Her voice was as sweet as her face. Jims thought he was mistaken in thinking her angry and plucked up heart of grace. Shyness was no fault of Jims.

"I came from the house over the wall," he said. "My name is James Brander Churchill. Aunt Augusta shut me up in the blue room because I spilled my pudding at dinner. I hate to be shut up. And I was to have had a ride this afternoon — and ice cream — and *maybe* a movie. So I was mad. And when your Very Handsome Cat came and looked at me I just got out and climbed down."

He looked straight at her and smiled. Jims had a very dear little smile. It seemed a pity there was no mother alive to revel in it. The lady smiled back.

"I think you did right," she said.

"*You* wouldn't shut a little boy up if you had one, would you?" said Jims.

"No—no, dear heart, I wouldn't," said the lady. She said it as if something hurt her horribly. She smiled again gallantly.

"Will you come here and sit down?" she added, pulling a chair out from the table.

"Thank you. I'd rather sit here," said Jims, plumping down on the grass at her feet. "Then maybe your cat will come to me."

The cat came over promptly and rubbed his head against Jims' knee. Jims stroked him delightedly; how lovely his soft fur felt and his round velvety head.

"I like cats," explained Jims, "and I have nothing but a gobbler. This is such a Very Handsome Cat. What is his name, please?"

"Black Prince. He loves me," said the lady. "He always comes to my bed in the morning and wakes me by patting my face with his paw. *He* doesn't mind my being ugly."

She spoke with a bitterness Jims couldn't understand.

"But you are not ugly," he said.

"Oh, I *am* ugly—I *am* ugly," she cried. "Just look at me—right at me. Doesn't it hurt you to look at me?"

Jims looked at her gravely and dispassionately.

"No, it doesn't," he said. "Not a bit," he added, after some further exploration of his consciousness.

Suddenly the lady laughed beautifully. A faint rosy flush came into her unscarred cheek.

"James, I believe you mean it."

"Of course I mean it. And, if you don't mind, please call me Jims. Nobody calls me James but Aunt Augusta. She isn't my whole aunt. She is just Uncle Walter's half-sister. *He* is my whole uncle."

"What does he call you?" asked the lady. She looked away as she asked it.

"Oh, Jims, when he thinks about me. He doesn't often think about me. He has too many sick children to think about. Sick children are all Uncle Walter cares about. He's the greatest children's doctor in the Dominion, Mr. Burroughs says. But he is a woman-hater."

"How do you know that?"

"Oh, I heard Mr. Burroughs say it. Mr. Burroughs is my tutor, you know. I study with him from nine till one. I'm not allowed to go to the public school.

I'd like to, but Uncle Walter thinks I'm not strong enough yet. I'm going next year, though, when I'm ten. I have holidays now. Mr. Burroughs always goes away the first of June."

"How came he to tell you your uncle was a woman-hater?" persisted the lady.

"Oh, he didn't tell me. He was talking to a friend of his. He thought I was reading my book. So I was — but I heard it all. It was more interesting than my book. Uncle Walter was engaged to a lady, long, long ago, when he was a young man. She was devilishly pretty."

"Oh, Jims!"

"Mr. Burroughs said so. I'm only quoting," said Jims easily. "And Uncle Walter just worshipped her. And all at once she just jilted him without a word of explanation, Mr. Burroughs said. So that is why he hates women. It isn't any wonder, is it?"

"I suppose not," said the lady with a sigh. "Jims, are you hungry?"

"Yes, I am. You see, the pudding was spilled. But how did you know?"

"Oh, boys always used to be hungry when I knew them long ago. I thought they hadn't changed. I shall tell Martha to bring out something to eat and we'll have it here under this tree. You sit here — I'll sit there. Jims, it's so long since I talked to a little boy that I'm not sure that I know how."

"You know how, all right," Jims assured her. "But what am I to call you, please?"

"My name is Miss Garland," said the lady a little hesitatingly. But she saw the name meant nothing to Jims. "I would like you to call me Miss Avery. Avery is my first name and I never hear it nowadays. Now for a jamboree! I can't offer you a movie — and I'm afraid there isn't any ice cream either. I could have had some if I'd known you were coming. But I think Martha will be able to find something good."

A very old woman, who looked at Jims with great amazement, came out to set the table. Jims thought she must be as old as Methusaleh. But he did not mind her. He ran races with Black Prince while tea was being prepared, and rolled the delighted cat over and over in the grass. And he discovered a fragrant herb-garden in a far corner and was delighted. Now it was truly a garden of spices.

"Oh, it is so beautiful here," he told Miss Avery, who sat and looked at his revels with a hungry expression in her lovely eyes. "I wish I could come often."

"Why can't you?" said Miss Avery.

The two looked at each other with sly intelligence.

"I could come whenever Aunt Augusta shuts me up in the blue room," said Jims.

"Yes," said Miss Avery. Then she laughed and held out her arms. Jims flew into them. He put his arms about her neck and kissed her scarred face.

"Oh, I wish *you* were my aunt," he said.

Miss Avery suddenly pushed him away. Jims was horribly afraid he had offended her. But she took his hand.

"We'll just be chums, Jims," she said. "That's really better than being relations, after all. Come and have tea."

Over that glorious tea-table they became life-long friends. They had always known each other and always would. The Black Prince sat between them and was fed tit-bits. There was such a lot of good things on the table and nobody to say "You have had enough, James." James ate until *he* thought he had enough. Aunt Augusta would have thought he was doomed, could she have seen him.

"I suppose I must go back," said Jims with a sigh. "It will be our supper time in half an hour and Aunt Augusta will come to take me out."

"But you'll come again?"

"Yes, the first time she shuts me up. And if she doesn't shut me up pretty soon I'll be so bad she'll have to shut me up."

"I'll always set a place for you at the tea-table after this, Jims. And when you're not here I'll pretend you are. And when you can't come here write me a letter and bring it when you do come."

"Good-bye," said Jims. He took her hand and kissed it. He had read of a young knight doing that and had always thought he would like to try it if he ever got a chance. But who could dream of kissing Aunt Augusta's hands?

"You dear, funny thing," said Miss Avery. "Have you thought of how you are to get back? Can you reach that pine bough from the ground?"

"Maybe I can jump," said Jims dubiously.

"I'm afraid not. I'll give you a stool and you can stand on it. Just leave it there for future use. Good-bye, Jims. Jims, two hours ago I didn't know there was such a person in the world as you — and now I love you — I love you."

Jims' heart filled with a great warm gush of gladness. He had always wanted to be loved. And no living creature, he felt sure, loved him, except his gobbler — and a gobbler's love is not very satisfying, though it is better than nothing. He was blissfully happy as he carried his stool across the lawn. He climbed his pine and went in at the window and curled up on the seat in a maze of delight. The blue room was more shadowy than ever but that did not matter. Over in the Garden of Spices was friendship and laughter and romance galore. The whole world was transformed for Jims.

From that time Jims lived a shamelessly double life. Whenever he was shut in the blue room he escaped to the Garden of Spices—and he was shut in very often, for, Mr. Burroughs being away, he got into a good deal of what Aunt Augusta called mischief. Besides, it is a sad truth that Jims didn't try very hard to be good now. He thought it paid better to be bad and be shut up. To be sure there was always a fly in the ointment. He was haunted by a vague fear that Aunt Augusta might relent and come to the blue room before supper time to let him out.

"And *then* the fat would be in the fire," said Jims.

But he had a glorious summer and throve so well on his new diet of love and companionship that one day Uncle Walter, with fewer sick children to think about than usual, looked at him curiously and said:

"Augusta, that boy seems to be growing much stronger. He has a good color and his eyes are getting to look more like a boy's eyes should. We'll make a man of you yet, Jims."

"He may be getting stronger but he's getting naughtier, too," said Aunt Augusta, grimly. "I am sorry to say, Walter, that he behaves very badly."

"We were all young once," said Uncle Walter indulgently.

"Were *you*?" asked Jims in blank amazement.

Uncle Walter laughed.

"Do you think me an antediluvian, Jims?"

"I don't know what *that* is. But your hair is gray and your eyes are tired," said Jims uncompromisingly.

Uncle Walter laughed again, tossed Jims a quarter, and went out.

"Your uncle is only forty-five and in his prime," said Aunt Augusta dourly.

Jims deliberately ran across the room to the window and, under pretence of looking out, knocked down a flower pot. So he was exiled to the blue room and got into his beloved Garden of Spices where Miss Avery's beautiful eyes looked love into his and the Black Prince was a jolly playmate and old Martha petted and spoiled him to her heart's content.

Jims never asked questions but he was a wide-awake chap, and, taking one thing with another, he found out a good deal about the occupants of the old stone house. Miss Avery never went anywhere and no one ever went there. She lived all alone with two old servants, man and maid. Except these two and Jims nobody had ever seen her for twenty years. Jims didn't know why, but he thought it must be because of the scar on her face.

He never referred to it, but one day Miss Avery told him what caused it.

"I dropped a lamp and my dress caught fire and burned my face, Jims. It made me hideous. I was beautiful before that—very beautiful. Everybody said so. Come in and I will show you my picture."

She took him into her big parlor and showed him the picture hanging on the wall between the two high windows. It was of a young girl in white. She certainly was very lovely, with her rose-leaf skin and laughing eyes. Jims looked at the pictured face gravely, with his hands in his pockets and his head on one side. Then he looked at Miss Avery.

"You were prettier then—yes," he said, judicially, "but I like your face ever so much better now."

"Oh, Jims, you can't," she protested.

"Yes, I do," persisted Jims. "You look kinder and—nicer now."

It was the nearest Jims could get to expressing what he felt as he looked at the picture. The young girl was beautiful, but her face was a little hard. There was pride and vanity and something of the insolence of great beauty in it. There was nothing of that in Miss Avery's face now—nothing but sweetness and tenderness, and a motherly yearning to which every fibre of Jims' small being responded. How they loved each other, those two! And how they understood each other! To *love* is easy, and therefore common; but to *understand*—how rare that is! And oh! such good times as they had! They made taffy. Jims had always longed to make taffy, but Aunt Augusta's immaculate kitchen and saucepans might not be so desecrated. They read fairy tales together. Mr. Burroughs had disapproved of fairy tales. They blew soap-bubbles out on the lawn and let them float away over the garden and the orchard like fairy balloons. They had glorious afternoon teas under the beech tree. They made ice cream themselves. Jims even slid down the bannisters when he wanted to. And he could try out a slang word or two occasionally without anybody dying of horror. Miss Avery did not seem to mind it a bit.

At first Miss Avery always wore dark sombre dresses. But one day Jims found her in a pretty gown of pale primrose silk. It was very old and old-fashioned, but Jims did not know that. He capered round her in delight.

"You like me better in this?" she asked, wistfully.

"I like you just as well, no matter what you wear," said Jims, "but that dress is awfully pretty."

"Would you like me to wear bright colors, Jims?"

"You bet I would," said Jims emphatically.

After that she always wore them—pink and primrose and blue and white; and she let Jims wreathe flowers in her splendid hair. He had quite a knack of it. She never wore any jewelry except, always, a little gold ring with a design of two clasped hands.

"A friend gave that to me long ago when we were boy and girl together at school," she told Jims once. "I never take it off, night or day. When I die it is to be buried with me."

"You mustn't die till I do," said Jims in dismay.

"Oh, Jims, if we could only *live* together nothing else would matter," she said hungrily. "Jims—Jims—I see so little of you really—and some day soon you'll be going to school—and I'll lose you."

"I've got to think of some way to prevent it," cried Jims. "I won't have it. I won't—I won't."

But his heart sank notwithstanding.

One day Jims slipped from the blue room, down the pine and across the lawn with a tear-stained face.

"Aunt Augusta is going to kill my gobbler," he sobbed in Miss Avery's arms. "She says she isn't going to bother with him any longer—and he's getting old—and he's to be killed. And that gobbler is the only friend I have in the world except you. Oh, I can't *stand* it, Miss Avery."

Next day Aunt Augusta told him the gobbler had been sold and taken away. And Jims flew into a passion of tears and protest about it and was promptly incarcerated in the blue room. A few minutes later a sobbing boy plunged through the trees—and stopped abruptly. Miss Avery was reading under the beech and the Black Prince was snoozing on her knee—and a big, magnificent, bronze turkey was parading about on the lawn, twisting his huge fan of a tail this way and that.

"*My* gobbler!" cried Jims.

"Yes. Martha went to your uncle's house and bought him. Oh, she didn't betray you. She told Nancy Jane she wanted a gobbler and, having seen one over there, thought perhaps she could get him. See, here's your pet, Jims, and here he shall live till he dies of old age. And I have something else for you— Edward and Martha went across the river yesterday to the Murray Kennels and got it for you."

"Not a dog?" exclaimed Jims.

"Yes—a dear little bull pup. He shall be your very own, Jims, and I only stipulate that you reconcile the Black Prince to him."

It was something of a task but Jims succeeded. Then followed a month of perfect happiness. At least three afternoons a week they contrived to be together. It was all too good to be true, Jims felt. Something would happen soon to spoil it. Just *suppose* Aunt Augusta grew tender-hearted and ceased to punish! Or suppose she suddenly discovered that he was growing too big to be shut up! Jims began to stint himself in eating lest he grew too fast. And then Aunt Augusta worried about his loss of appetite and suggested to Uncle Walter that he should be sent to the country till the hot weather was over. Jims didn't want to go to the country now because his heart was elsewhere. He must eat again, if he grew like a weed. It was all very harassing.

Uncle Walter looked at him keenly.

"It seems to me you're looking pretty fit, Jims. Do you want to go to the country?"

"No, please."

"Are you happy, Jims?"

"Sometimes."

"A boy should be happy all the time, Jims."

"If I had a mother and someone to play with I would be."

"I have tried to be a mother to you, Jims," said Aunt Augusta, in an offended tone. Then she addressed Uncle Walter. "A younger woman would probably understand him better. And I feel that the care of this big place is too much for me. I would prefer to go to my own old home. If you had married long ago, as you should, Walter, James would have had a mother and some cousins to play with. I have always been of this opinion."

Uncle Walter frowned and got up.

"Just because one woman played you false is no good reason for spoiling your life," went on Aunt Augusta severely. "I have kept silence all these years but now I am going to speak—and speak plainly. You should marry, Walter. You are young enough yet and you owe it to your name."

"Listen, Augusta," said Uncle Walter sternly. "I loved a woman once. I believed she loved me. She sent me back my ring one day and with it a message saying she had ceased to care for me and bidding me never to try to look upon her face again. Well, I have obeyed her, that is all."

"There was something strange about all that, Walter. The life she has since led proves that. So you should not let it embitter you against all women."

"I haven't. It's nonsense to say I'm a woman-hater, Augusta. But that experience has robbed me of the power to care for another woman."

"Well, this isn't a proper conversation for a child to hear," said Aunt Augusta, recollecting herself. "Jims, go out."

Jims would have given one of his ears to stay and listen with the other. But he went obediently.

And then, the very next day, the dreaded something happened.

It was the first of August and very, very hot. Jims was late coming to dinner and Aunt Augusta reproved him and Jims, deliberately, and with malice aforethought, told her he thought she was a nasty old woman. He had never been saucy to Aunt Augusta before. But it was three days since he had seen Miss Avery and the Black Prince and Nip and he was desperate. Aunt Augusta crimsoned with anger and doomed Jims to an afternoon in the blue room for impertinence.

"And I shall tell your uncle when he comes home," she added.

That rankled, for Jims didn't want Uncle Walter to think him impertinent. But he forgot all his worries as he scampered through the Garden of Spices to the beech tree. And there Jims stopped as if he had been shot. Prone on the grass under the beech tree, white and cold and still, lay his Miss Avery—dead, stone dead!

At least Jims drought she was dead. He flew into the house like a mad thing, shrieking for Martha. Nobody answered. Jims recollected, with a rush of sickening dread, that Miss Avery had told him Martha and Edward were going away that day to visit a sister. He rushed blindly across the lawn again, through the little side gate he had never passed before and down the street home. Uncle Walter was just opening the door of his car.

"Uncle Walter—come—come," sobbed Jims, clutching frantically at his hand. "Miss Avery's dead—dead—oh, come quick."

"*Who* is dead?"

"Miss Avery—Miss Avery Garland. She's lying on the grass over there in her garden. And I love her so—and I'll die, too—oh, Uncle Walter, *come*."

Uncle Walter looked as if he wanted to ask some questions, but he said nothing. With a strange face he hurried after Jims. Miss Avery was still lying there. As Uncle Walter bent over her he saw the broad red scar and started back with an exclamation.

"She is dead?" gasped Jims.

"No," said Uncle Walter, bending down again—"no, she has only fainted, Jims—overcome by the heat, I suppose. I want help. Go and call somebody."

"There's no one home here to-day," said Jims, in a spasm of joy so great that it shook him like a leaf.

"Then go home and telephone over to Mr. Loring's. Tell them I want the nurse who is there to come here for a few minutes."

Jims did his errand. Uncle Walter and the nurse carried Miss Avery into the house and then Jims went back to the blue room. He was so unhappy he didn't care where he went. He wished something *would* jump at him out of the bed and put an end to him. Everything was discovered now and he would never see Miss Avery again. Jims lay very still on the window seat. He did not even cry. He had come to one of the griefs that lie too deep for tears.

"I think I must have been put under a curse at birth," thought poor Jims.

Over at the stone house Miss Avery was lying on the couch in her room. The nurse had gone away and Dr. Walter was sitting looking at her. He leaned forward and pulled away the hand with which she was hiding the scar on her face. He looked first at the little gold ring on the hand and then at the scar.

"Don't," she said piteously.

"Avery — why did you do it? — *why* did you do it?"

"Oh, you know — you must know now, Walter."

"Avery, did you break my heart and spoil my life — and your own — simply because your face was scarred?"

"I couldn't bear to have you see me hideous," she moaned. "You had been so proud of my beauty. I — I — thought you couldn't love me any more — I couldn't bear the thought of looking in your eyes and seeing aversion there."

Walter Grant leaned forward.

"Look in my eyes, Avery. Do you see any aversion?"

Avery forced herself to look. What she saw covered her face with a hot blush.

"Did you think my love such a poor and superficial thing, Avery," he said sternly, "that it must vanish because a blemish came on your fairness? Do you think *that* would change me? Was your own love for me so slight?"

"No — no," she sobbed. "I have loved you every moment of my life, Walter. Oh, don't look at me so sternly."

"If you had even told me," he said. "You said I was never to try to look on your face again — and they told me you had gone away. You sent me back my ring."

"I kept the old one," she interrupted, holding out her hand, "the first one you ever gave me — do you remember, Walter? When we were boy and girl."

"You robbed me of all that made life worth while, Avery. Do you wonder that I've been a bitter man?"

"I was wrong—I was wrong," she sobbed. "I should have believed in you. But don't you think I've paid, too? Forgive me, Walter—it's too late to atone—but forgive me."

"*Is* it too late?" he asked gravely.

She pointed to the scar.

"Could you endure seeing this opposite to you every day at your table?" she asked bitterly.

"Yes—if I could see your sweet eyes and your beloved smile with it, Avery," he answered passionately. "Oh, Avery, it was *you* I loved—not your outward favor. Oh, how foolish you were—foolish and morbid! You always put too high a value on beauty, Avery. If I had dreamed of the true state of the case—if I had known you were here all these years—why I heard a rumor long ago that you had married, Avery—but if I had known I would have come to you and *made* you be—sensible."

She gave a little laugh at his lame conclusion. That was so like the old Walter. Then her eyes filled with tears as he took her in his arms.

The door of the blue room opened. Jims did not look up. It was Aunt Augusta, of course—and she had heard the whole story.

"Jims, boy."

Jims lifted his miserable eyes. It was Uncle Walter—but a different Uncle Walter—an Uncle Walter with laughing eyes and a strange radiance of youth about him.

"Poor, lonely little fellow," said Uncle Walter unexpectedly. "Jims, would you like Miss Avery to come *here*—and live with us always—and be your real aunt?"

"Great snakes!" said Jims, transformed in a second. "Is there any chance of *that*?"

"There is a certainty, thanks to you," said Uncle Walter. "You can go over to see her for a little while. Don't talk her to death—she's weak yet—and attend to that menagerie of yours over there—she's worrying because the bull dog and gobbler weren't fed—and Jims—"

But Jims had swung down through the pine and was tearing across the Garden of Spices.

The Girl and the Photograph

When I heard that Peter Austin was in Vancouver I hunted him up. I had met Peter ten years before when I had gone east to visit my father's people and had spent a few weeks with an uncle in Croyden. The Austins lived across the street from Uncle Tom, and Peter and I had struck up a friendship, although he was a hobbledehoy of awkward sixteen and I, at twenty-two, was older and wiser and more dignified than I've ever been since or ever expect to be again. Peter was a jolly little round freckled chap. He was all right when no girls were around; when they were he retired within himself like a misanthropic oyster, and was about as interesting. This was the one point upon which we always disagreed. Peter couldn't endure girls; I was devoted to them by the wholesale. The Croyden girls were pretty and vivacious. I had a score of flirtations during my brief sojourn among them.

But when I went away the face I carried in my memory was not that of any girl with whom I had walked and driven and played the game of hearts.

It was ten years ago, but I had never been quite able to forget that girl's face. Yet I had seen it but once and then only for a moment. I had gone for a solitary ramble in the woods over the river and, in a lonely little valley dim with pines, where I thought myself alone, I had come suddenly upon her, standing ankle-deep in fern on the bank of a brook, the late evening sunshine falling yellowly on her uncovered dark hair. She was very young—no more than sixteen; yet the face and eyes were already those of a woman. Such a face! Beautiful? Yes, but I thought of that afterward, when I was alone. With that face before my eyes I thought only of its purity and sweetness, of the lovely soul and rich mind looking out of the great, greyish-blue eyes which, in the dimness of the pine shadows, looked almost black. There was something in the face of that child-woman I had never seen before and was destined never to see again in any other face. Careless boy though I was, it stirred me to the deeps. I felt that she must have been waiting forever in that pine valley for me and that, in finding her, I had found all of good that life could offer me.

I would have spoken to her, but before I could shape my greeting into words that should not seem rude or presumptuous, she had turned and gone, stepping lightly across the brook and vanishing in the maple copse beyond.

For no more than ten seconds had I gazed into her face, and the soul of her, the real woman behind the fair outwardness, had looked back into my eyes; but I had never been able to forget it.

When I returned home I questioned my cousins diplomatically as to who she might be. I felt strangely reluctant to do so—it seemed in some way sacrilege; yet only by so doing could I hope to discover her. They could tell me nothing; nor did I meet her again during the remainder of my stay in Croyden, although I never went anywhere without looking for her, and haunted the pine valley daily, in the hope of seeing her again. My disappointment was so bitter that I laughed at myself.

I thought I was a fool to feel thus about a girl I had met for a moment in a chance ramble—a mere child at that, with her hair still hanging in its long glossy schoolgirl braid. But when I remembered her eyes, my wisdom forgave me.

Well, that was ten years ago; in those ten years the memory had, I must confess, grown dimmer. In our busy western life a man had not much time for sentimental recollections. Yet I had never been able to care for another woman. I wanted to; I wanted to marry and settle down. I had come to the time of life when a man wearies of drifting and begins to hanker for a calm anchorage in some snug haven of his own. But, somehow, I shirked the matter. It seemed rather easier to let things slide.

At this stage Peter came west. He was something in a bank, and was as round and jolly as ever; but he had evidently changed his attitude towards girls, for his rooms were full of their photos. They were stuck around everywhere and they were all pretty. Either Peter had excellent taste, or the Croyden photographers knew how to flatter. But there was one on the mantel which attracted my attention especially. If the photo were to be trusted the girl was quite the prettiest I had ever seen.

"Peter, what pretty girl's picture is this on your mantel?" I called out to Peter, who was in his bedroom, donning evening dress for some function.

"That's my cousin, Marian Lindsay," he answered. "She *is* rather nice-looking, isn't she. Lives in Croyden now—used to live up the river at Chiselhurst. Didn't you ever chance across her when you were in Croyden?"

"No," I said. "If I had I wouldn't have forgotten her face."

"Well, she'd be only a kid then, of course. She's twenty-six now. Marian is a mighty nice girl, but she's bound to be an old maid. She's got notions—ideals, she calls 'em. All the Croyden fellows have been in love with her at one time or another but they might as well have made up to a statue. Marian really hasn't a spark of feeling or sentiment in her. Her looks are the best part of her, although she's confoundedly clever."

Peter spoke rather squiffily. I suspected that he had been one of the smitten swains himself. I looked at the photo for a few minutes longer, admiring it more every minute and, when I heard Peter coming out, I did an unjustifiable thing—I took that photo and put it in my pocket.

I expected Peter would make a fuss when he missed it, but that very night the house in which he lived was burned to the ground. Peter escaped with the most important of his goods and chattels, but all the counterfeit presentments of his dear divinities went up in smoke. If he ever thought particularly of Marian Lindsay's photograph he must have supposed that it shared the fate of the others.

As for me, I propped my ill-gotten treasure up on my mantel and worshipped it for a fortnight. At the end of that time I went boldly to Peter and told him I wanted him to introduce me by letter to his dear cousin and ask her to agree to a friendly correspondence with me.

Oddly enough, I did not do this without some reluctance, in spite of the fact that I was as much in love with Marian Lindsay as it was possible to be through the medium of a picture. I thought of the girl I had seen in the pine wood and felt an inward shrinking from a step that might divide me from her forever. But I rated myself for this nonsense. It was in the highest degree unlikely that I should ever meet the girl of the pines again. If she were still living she was probably some other man's wife. I would think no more about it.

Peter whistled when he heard what I had to say.

"Of course I'll do it, old man," he said obligingly. "But I warn you I don't think it will be much use. Marian isn't the sort of girl to open up a correspondence in such a fashion. However, I'll do the best I can for you."

"Do. Tell her I'm a respectable fellow with no violent bad habits and all that. I'm in earnest, Peter. I want to make that girl's acquaintance, and this seems the only way at present. I can't get off just now for a trip east. Explain all this, and use your cousinly influence in my behalf if you possess any."

Peter grinned.

"It's not the most graceful job in the world you are putting on me, Curtis," he said. "I don't mind owning up now that I was pretty far gone on Marian myself two years ago. It's all over now, but it was bad while it lasted. Perhaps Marian will consider your request more favourably if I put it in the light of a favour to myself. She must feel that she owes me something for wrecking my life."

Peter grinned again and looked at the one photo he had contrived to rescue from the fire. It was a pretty, snub-nosed little girl. She would never have consoled me for the loss of Marian Lindsay, but every man to his taste.

In due time Peter sought me out to give me his cousin's answer.

"Congratulations, Curtis. You've out-Caesared Caesar. You've conquered without even going and seeing. Marian agrees to a friendly correspondence with you. I am amazed, I admit—even though I did paint you up as a sort of Sir Galahad and Lancelot combined. I'm not used to seeing proud Marian do stunts like that, and it rather takes my breath."

I wrote to Marian Lindsay after one farewell dream of the girl under the pines. When Marian's letters began to come regularly I forgot the other one altogether.

Such letters—such witty, sparkling, clever, womanly, delightful letters! They completed the conquest her picture had begun. Before we had corresponded six months I was besottedly in love with this woman whom I had never seen. Finally, I wrote and told her so, and I asked her to be my wife.

A fortnight later her answer came. She said frankly that she believed she had learned to care for me during our correspondence, but that she thought we should meet in person, before coming to any definite understanding. Could I not arrange to visit Croyden in the summer? Until then we would better continue on our present footing.

I agreed to this, but I considered myself practically engaged, with the personal meeting merely to be regarded as a sop to the Cerberus of conventionality. I permitted myself to use a decidedly lover-like tone in my letters henceforth, and I hailed it as a favourable omen that I was not rebuked for this, although Marian's own letters still retained their pleasant, simple friendliness.

Peter had at first tormented me mercilessly about the affair, but when he saw I did not like his chaff he stopped it. Peter was always a good fellow. He realized that I regarded the matter seriously, and he saw me off when I left for the east with a grin tempered by honest sympathy and understanding.

"Good luck to you," he said. "If you win Marian Lindsay you'll win a pearl among women. I haven't been able to grasp her taking to you in this fashion, though. It's so unlike Marian. But, since she undoubtedly has, you are a lucky man."

I arrived in Croyden at dusk and went to Uncle Tom's. There I found them busy with preparations for a party to be given that night in honour of a girl friend who was visiting my cousin Edna. I was secretly annoyed, for I wanted to hasten at once to Marian. But I couldn't decently get away, and on second thoughts I was consoled by the reflection that she would probably come to the party. I knew she belonged to the same social set as Uncle Tom's girls. I should, however, have preferred our meeting to have been under different circumstances.

From my stand behind the palms in a corner I eagerly scanned the guests as they arrived. Suddenly my heart gave a bound. Marian Lindsay had just come in.

I recognized her at once from her photograph. It had not flattered her in the least; indeed, it had not done her justice, for her exquisite colouring of hair and complexion were quite lost in it. She was, moreover, gowned with a taste and smartness eminently admirable in the future Mrs. Eric Curtis. I felt a thrill of proprietary pride as I stepped out from behind the palms. She was talking to Aunt Grace; but her eyes fell on me. I expected a little start of recognition, for I had sent her an excellent photograph of myself; but her gaze was one of blankest unconsciousness.

I felt something like disappointment at her non-recognition, but I consoled myself by the reflection that people often fail to recognize other people whom they have seen only in photographs, no matter how good the likeness may be. I waylaid Edna, who was passing at that time, and said, "Edna I want you to introduce me to the girl who is talking to your mother."

Edna laughed.

"So you have succumbed at first sight to our Croyden beauty? Of course I'll introduce you, but I warn you beforehand that she is the most incorrigible flirt in Croyden or out of it. So take care."

It jarred on me to hear Marian called a flirt. It seemed so out of keeping with her letters and the womanly delicacy and fineness revealed in them. But I reflected that women sometimes find it hard to forgive another woman who absorbs more than her share of lovers, and generally take their revenge by dubbing her a flirt, whether she deserves the name or not.

We had crossed the room during this reflection. Marian turned and stood before us, smiling at Edna, but evincing no recognition whatever of myself. It is a piquant experience to find yourself awaiting an introduction to a girl to whom you are virtually engaged.

"Dorothy dear," said Edna, "this is my cousin, Mr. Curtis, from Vancouver. Eric, this is Miss Armstrong."

I suppose I bowed. Habit carries us mechanically through many impossible situations. I don't know what I looked like or what I said, if I said anything. I don't suppose I betrayed my dire confusion, for Edna went off unconcernedly without another glance at me.

Dorothy Armstrong! Gracious powers—who—where—why? If this girl was Dorothy Armstrong who was Marian Lindsay? To whom was I engaged? There was some awful mistake somewhere, for it could not be possible that there were two girls in Croyden who looked exactly like the photograph reposing in my valise at that very moment. I stammered like a schoolboy.

"I—oh—I—your face seems familiar to me, Miss Armstrong. I—I—think I must have seen your photograph somewhere."

"Probably in Peter Austin's collection," smiled Miss Armstrong. "He had one of mine before he was burned out. How is he?"

"Peter? Oh, he's well," I replied vaguely. I was thinking a hundred words to the second, but my thoughts arrived nowhere. I was staring at Miss Armstrong like a man bewitched. She must have thought me a veritable booby. "Oh, by the way—can you tell me—do you know a Miss Lindsay in Croyden?"

Miss Armstrong looked surprised and a little bored. Evidently she was not used to having newly introduced young men inquiring about another girl.

"Marian Lindsay? Oh, yes."

"Is she here tonight?" I said.

"No, Marian is not going to parties just now, owing to the recent death of her aunt, who lived with them."

"Does she—oh—does she look like you at all?" I inquired idiotically.

Amusement glimmered but over Miss Armstrong's boredom. She probably concluded that I was some harmless lunatic.

"Like me? Not at all. There couldn't be two people more dissimilar. Marian is quite dark. I am fair. And our features are altogether unlike. Why, good evening, Jack. Yes, I believe I did promise you this dance."

She bowed to me and skimmed away with Jack. I saw Aunt Grace bearing down upon me and fled incontinently. In my own room I flung myself on a chair and tried to think the matter out. Where did the mistake come in? How had it happened? I shut my eyes and conjured up the vision of Peter's room that day. I remembered vaguely that, when I had picked up Dorothy Armstrong's picture, I had noticed another photograph that had fallen face downward beside it. That must have been Marian Lindsay's, and Peter had thought I meant it.

And now what a position I was in! I was conscious of bitter disappointment. I had fallen in love with Dorothy Armstrong's photograph. As far as external semblance goes it was she whom I loved. I was practically engaged to another woman—a woman who, in spite of our correspondence, seemed to me now, in the shock of this discovery, a stranger. It was useless to tell myself that it was the mind and soul revealed in those letters that I loved, and that that mind and soul were Marian Lindsay's. It was useless to remember that Peter had said she was pretty. Exteriorly, she was a stranger to me; hers was not the face which had risen before me for nearly a year as the face of the woman I loved. Was ever unlucky wretch in such a predicament before?

Well, there was only one thing to do. I must stand by my word. Marian Lindsay was the woman I had asked to marry me, whose answer I must shortly go to receive. If that answer were "yes" I must accept the situation and banish all thought of Dorothy Armstrong's pretty face.

Next evening at sunset I went to "Glenwood," the Lindsay place. Doubtless, an eager lover might have gone earlier, but an eager lover I certainly was not. Probably Marian was expecting me and had given orders concerning me, for the maid who came to the door conveyed me to a little room behind the stairs—a room which, as I felt as soon as I entered it, was a woman's pet domain. In its books and pictures and flowers it spoke eloquently of dainty femininity. Somehow, it suited the letters. I did not feel quite so much the stranger as I had felt. Nevertheless, when I heard a light footfall on the stairs my heart beat painfully. I stood up and turned to the door, but I could not look up. The footsteps came nearer; I knew that a white hand swept aside the *portière* at the entrance; I knew that she had entered the room and was standing before me.

With an effort I raised my eyes and looked at her. She stood, tall and gracious, in a ruby splendour of sunset falling through the window beside her. The light quivered like living radiance over a dark proud head, a white throat, and a face before whose perfect loveliness the memory of Dorothy Armstrong's laughing prettiness faded like a star in the sunrise, nevermore in the fullness of the day to be remembered. Yet it was not of her beauty I thought as I stood spellbound before her. I seemed to see a dim little valley full of whispering pines, and a girl standing under their shadows, looking at me with the same great, greyish-blue eyes which gazed upon me now from Marian Lindsay's face—the same face, matured into gracious womanhood, that I had seen ten years ago; and loved—aye, loved—ever since. I took an unsteady step forward.

"Marian?" I said.

When I got home that night I burned Dorothy Armstrong's photograph. The next day I went to my cousin Tom, who owns the fashionable studio of Croyden and, binding him over to secrecy, sought one of Marian's latest photographs from him. It is the only secret I have ever kept from my wife.

Before we were married Marian told me something.

"I always remembered you as you looked that day under the pines," she said. "I was only a child, but I think I loved you then and ever afterwards. When I dreamed my girl's dream of love your face rose up before me. I had the advantage of you that I knew your name — I had heard of you. When Peter wrote about you I knew who you were. That was why I agreed to correspond with you. I was afraid it was a forward — an unwomanly thing to do. But it seemed my chance for happiness and I took it. I am glad I did."

I did not answer in words, but lovers will know how I did answer.

The Gossip of Valley View

It was the first of April, and Julius Barrett, aged fourteen, perched on his father's gatepost, watched ruefully the low descending sun, and counted that day lost. He had not succeeded in "fooling" a single person, although he had tried repeatedly. One and all, old and young, of his intended victims had been too wary for Julius. Hence, Julius was disgusted and ready for anything in the way of a stratagem or a spoil.

The Barrett gatepost topped the highest hill in Valley View. Julius could see the entire settlement, from "Young" Thomas Everett's farm, a mile to the west, to Adelia Williams's weather-grey little house on a moonrise slope to the east. He was gazing moodily down the muddy road when Dan Chester, homeward bound from the post office, came riding sloppily along on his grey mare and pulled up by the Barrett gate to hand a paper to Julius.

Dan was a young man who took life and himself very seriously. He seldom smiled, never joked, and had a Washingtonian reputation for veracity. Dan had never told a conscious falsehood in his life; he never even exaggerated.

Julius, beholding Dan's solemn face, was seized with a perfectly irresistible desire to "fool" him. At the same moment his eye caught the dazzling reflection of the setting sun on the windows of Adelia Williams's house, and he had an inspiration little short of diabolical. "Have you heard the news, Dan?" he asked.

"No, what is it?" asked Dan.

"I dunno's I ought to tell it," said Julius reflectively. "It's kind of a family affair, but then Adelia didn't say not to, and anyway it'll be all over the place soon. So I'll tell you, Dan, if you'll promise never to tell who told you. Adelia Williams and Young Thomas Everett are going to be married."

Julius delivered himself of this tremendous lie with a transparently earnest countenance. Yet Dan, credulous as he was, could not believe it all at once.

"Git out," he said.

"It's true, 'pon my word," protested Julius. "Adelia was up last night and told Ma all about it. Ma's her cousin, you know. The wedding is to be in June, and Adelia asked Ma to help her get her quilts and things ready."

Julius reeled all this off so glibly that Dan finally believed the story, despite the fact that the people thus coupled together in prospective matrimony were the very last people in Valley View who could have been expected to marry each other. Young Thomas was a confirmed bachelor of fifty, and Adelia Williams was forty; they were not supposed to be even well acquainted, as the Everetts and the Williamses had never been very friendly, although no open feud existed between them.

Nevertheless, in view of Julius's circumstantial statements, the amazing news must be true, and Dan was instantly agog to carry it further. Julius watched Dan and the grey mare out of sight, fairly writhing with ecstasy. Oh, but Dan had been easy! The story would be all over Valley View in twenty-four hours. Julius laughed until he came near to falling off the gatepost.

At this point Julius and Danny drop out of our story, and Young Thomas enters.

It was two days later when Young Thomas heard that he was to be married to Adelia Williams in June. Eben Clark, the blacksmith, told him when he went to the forge to get his horse shod. Young Thomas laughed his big jolly laugh. Valley View gossip had been marrying him off for the last thirty years, although never before to Adelia Williams.

"It's news to me," he said tolerantly.

Eben grinned broadly. "Ah, you can't bluff it off like that, Tom," he said. "The news came too straight this time. Well, I was glad to hear it, although I was mighty surprised. I never thought of you and Adelia. But she's a fine little woman and will make you a capital wife."

Young Thomas grunted and drove away. He had a good deal of business to do that day, involving calls at various places—the store for molasses, the mill for flour, Jim Bentley's for seed grain, the doctor's for toothache drops for his housekeeper, the post office for mail—and at each and every place he was joked about his approaching marriage. In the end it rather annoyed Young Thomas. He drove home at last in what was for him something of a temper. How on earth had that fool story started? With such detailed circumstantiality of rugs and quilts, too? Adelia Williams must be going to marry somebody, and the Valley View gossips, unable to locate the man, had guessed Young Thomas.

When he reached home, tired, mud-bespattered, and hungry, his housekeeper, who was also his hired man's wife, asked him if it was true that he was going to be married. Young Thomas, taking in at a glance the ill-prepared, half-cold supper on the table, felt more annoyed than ever, and said it wasn't, with a strong expression—not quite an oath—for Young Thomas never swore, unless swearing be as much a matter of intonation as of words.

Mrs. Dunn sighed, patted her swelled face, and said she was sorry; she had hoped it was true, for her man had decided to go west. They were to go in a month's time. Young Thomas sat down to his supper with the prospect of having to look up another housekeeper and hired man before planting to destroy his appetite.

Next day, three people who came to see Young Thomas on business congratulated him on his approaching marriage. Young Thomas, who had recovered his usual good humour, merely laughed. There was no use in being too earnest in denial, he thought. He knew that his unusual fit of petulance with his housekeeper had only convinced her that the story was true. It would die away in time, as other similar stories had died, he thought. Valley View gossip was imaginative.

Young Thomas looked rather serious, however, when the minister and his wife called that evening and referred to the report. Young Thomas gravely said that it was unfounded. The minister looked graver still and said he was sorry — he had hoped it was true. His wife glanced significantly about Young Thomas's big, untidy sitting-room, where there were cobwebs on the ceiling and fluff in the corners and dust on the mop-board, and said nothing, but looked volumes.

"Dang it all," said Young Thomas, as they drove away, "they'll marry me yet in spite of myself."

The gossip made him think about Adelia Williams. He had never thought about her before; he was barely acquainted with her. Now he remembered that she was a plump, jolly-looking little woman, noted for being a good housekeeper. Then Young Thomas groaned, remembering that he must start out looking for a housekeeper soon; and housekeepers were not easily found, as Young Thomas had discovered several times since his mother's death ten years before.

Next Sunday in church Young Thomas looked at Adelia Williams. He caught Adelia looking at him. Adelia blushed and looked guiltily away.

"Dang it all," reflected Young Thomas, forgetting that he was in church. "I suppose she has heard that fool story too. I'd like to know the person who started it; man or woman, I'd punch their head."

Nevertheless, Young Thomas went on looking at Adelia by fits and starts, although he did not again catch Adelia looking at him. He noticed that she had round rosy cheeks and twinkling brown eyes. She did not look like an old maid, and Young Thomas wondered that she had been allowed to become one. Sarah Barnett, now, to whom report had married him a year ago, looked like a dried sour apple.

For the next four weeks the story haunted Young Thomas like a spectre. Down it would not. Everywhere he went he was joked about it. It gathered fresh detail every week. Adelia was getting her clothes ready; she was to be married in seal-brown cashmere; Vinnie Lawrence at Valley Centre was making it for her; she had got a new hat with a long ostrich plume; some said white, some said grey.

Young Thomas kept wondering who the man could be, for he was convinced that Adelia was going to marry somebody. More than that, once he caught himself wondering enviously. Adelia was a nice-looking woman, and he had not so far heard of any probable housekeeper.

"Dang it all," said Young Thomas to himself in desperation. "I wouldn't care if it was true."

His married sister from Carlisle heard the story and came over to investigate. Young Thomas denied it shortly, and his sister scolded. She had devoutly hoped it was true, she said, and it would have been a great weight off her mind.

"This house is in a disgraceful condition, Thomas," she said severely. "It would break Mother's heart if she could rise out of her grave to see it. And Adelia Williams is a perfect housekeeper."

"You didn't use to think so much of the Williams crowd," said Young Thomas drily.

"Oh, some of them don't amount to much," admitted Maria, "but Adelia is all right."

Catching sight of an odd look on Young Thomas's face, she added hastily, "Thomas Everett, I believe it's true after all. Now, is it? For mercy's sake don't be so sly. You might tell me, your own and only sister, if it is."

"Oh, shut up," was Young Thomas's unfeeling reply to his own and only sister.

Young Thomas told himself that night that Valley View gossip would drive him into an asylum yet if it didn't let up. He also wondered if Adelia was as much persecuted as himself. No doubt she was. He never could catch her eye in church now, but he would have been surprised had he realized how many times he tried to.

The climax came the third week in May, when Young Thomas, who had been keeping house for himself for three weeks, received a letter and an express box from his cousin, Charles Everett, out in Manitoba. Charles and he had been chums in their boyhood. They corresponded occasionally still, although it was twenty years since Charles had gone west.

The letter was to congratulate Young Thomas on his approaching marriage. Charles had heard of it through some Valley View correspondents of his wife. He was much pleased; he had always liked Adelia, he said—had been an old beau of hers, in fact. Thomas might give her a kiss for him if he liked. He forwarded a wedding present by express and hoped they would be very happy, etc.

The present was an elaborate hatrack of polished buffalo horns, mounted on red plush, with an inset mirror. Young Thomas set it up on the kitchen table and scowled moodily at his reflection in the mirror. If wedding presents were beginning to come, it was high time something was done. The matter was past being a joke. This affair of the present would certainly get out — things always got out in Valley View, dang it all—and he would never hear the last of it.

"I'll marry," said Young Thomas decisively. "If Adelia Williams won't have me, I'll marry the first woman who will, if it's Sarah Barnett herself."

Young Thomas shaved and put on his Sunday suit. As soon as it was safely dark, he hied him away to Adelia Williams. He felt very doubtful about his reception, but the remembrance of the twinkle in Adelia's brown eyes comforted him. She looked like a woman who had a sense of humour; she might not take him, but she would not feel offended or insulted because he asked her.

"Dang it all, though, I hope she will take me," said Young Thomas. "I'm in for getting married now and no mistake. And I can't get Adelia out of my head. I've been thinking of her steady ever since that confounded gossip began."

When he knocked at Adelia's door he discovered that his face was wet with perspiration. Adelia opened the door and started when she saw him; then she turned very red and stiffly asked him in. Young Thomas went in and sat down, wondering if all men felt so horribly uncomfortable when they went courting.

Adelia stooped low over the woodbox to put a stick of wood in the stove, for the May evening was chilly. Her shoulders were shaking; the shaking grew worse; suddenly Adelia laughed hysterically and, sitting down on the woodbox, continued to laugh. Young Thomas eyed her with a friendly grin.

"Oh, do excuse me," gasped poor Adelia, wiping tears from her eyes. "This is—dreadful—I didn't mean to laugh—I don't know why I'm laughing—but—I—can't help it."

She laughed helplessly again. Young Thomas laughed too. His embarrassment vanished in the mellowness of that laughter. Presently Adelia composed herself and removed from the woodbox to a chair, but there was still a suspicious twitching about the corners of her mouth.

"I suppose," said Young Thomas, determined to have it over with before the ice could form again, "I suppose, Adelia, you've heard the story that's been going about you and me of late?"

Adelia nodded. "I've been persecuted to the verge of insanity with it," she said. "Every soul I've seen has tormented me about it, and people have written me about it. I've denied it till I was black in the face, but nobody believed me. I can't find out how it started. I hope you believe, Mr. Everett, that it couldn't possibly have arisen from anything I said. I've felt dreadfully worried for fear you might think it did. I heard that my cousin, Lucilla Barrett, said I told her, but Lucilla vowed to me that she never said such a thing or even dreamed of it. I've felt dreadful bad over the whole affair. I even gave up the idea of making a quilt after a lovely new pattern I've got because they made such a talk about my brown dress."

"I've been kind of supposing that you must be going to marry somebody, and folks just guessed it was me," said Young Thomas — he said it anxiously.

"No, I'm not going to be married to anybody," said Adelia with a laugh, taking up her knitting.

"I'm glad of that," said Young Thomas gravely. "I mean," he hastened to add, seeing the look of astonishment on Adelia's face, "that I'm glad there isn't any other man because — because I want you myself, Adelia."

Adelia laid down her knitting and blushed crimson. But she looked at Young Thomas squarely and reproachfully.

"You needn't think you are bound to say that because of the gossip, Mr. Everett," she said quietly.

"Oh, I don't," said Young Thomas earnestly. "But the truth is, the story set me to thinking about you, and from that I got to wishing it was true — honest, I did — I couldn't get you out of my head, and at last I didn't want to. It just seemed to me that you were the very woman for me if you'd only take me. Will you, Adelia? I've got a good farm and house, and I'll try to make you happy."

It was not a very romantic wooing, perhaps. But Adelia was forty and had never been a romantic little body even in the heyday of youth. She was a practical woman, and Young Thomas was a fine looking man of his age with abundance of worldly goods. Besides, she liked him, and the gossip had made her think a good deal about him of late. Indeed, in a moment of candour she had owned to herself the very last Sunday in church that she wouldn't mind if the story were true.

"I'll — I'll think of it," she said.

This was practically an acceptance, and Young Thomas so understood it. Without loss of time he crossed the kitchen, sat down beside Adelia, and put his arms about her plump waist.

"Here's a kiss Charlie sent me to give you," he said, giving it.

The Letters

Just before the letter was brought to me that evening I was watching the red November sunset from the library window. It was a stormy, unrestful sunset, gleaming angrily through the dark fir boughs that were now and again tossed suddenly and distressfully in a fitful gust of wind. Below, in the garden, it was quite dark, and I could only see dimly the dead leaves that were whirling and dancing uncannily over the roseless paths. The poor dead leaves — yet not quite dead! There was still enough unquiet life left in them to make them restless and forlorn. They hearkened yet to every call of the wind, who cared for them no longer but only played freakishly with them and broke their rest. I felt sorry for the leaves as I watched them in that dull, weird twilight, and angry — in a petulant fashion that almost made me laugh — with the wind that would not leave them in peace. Why should they — and I — be vexed with these transient breaths of desire for a life that had passed us by?

I was in the grip of a bitter loneliness that evening — so bitter and so insistent that I felt I could not face the future at all, even with such poor fragments of courage as I had gathered about me after Father's death, hoping that they would, at least, suffice for my endurance, if not for my content. But now they fell away from me at sight of the emptiness of life.

The emptiness! Ah, it was from that I shrank. I could have faced pain and anxiety and heartbreak undauntedly, but I could not face that terrible, yawning, barren emptiness. I put my hands over my eyes to shut it out, but it pressed in upon my consciousness insistently, and would not be ignored longer.

The moment when a woman realizes that she has nothing to live for — neither love nor purpose nor duty — holds for her the bitterness of death. She is a brave woman indeed who can look upon such a prospect unquailingly, and I was not brave. I was weak and timid. Had not Father often laughed mockingly at me because of it?

It was three weeks since Father had died — my proud, handsome, unrelenting old father, whom I had loved so intensely and who had never loved me. I had always accepted this fact unresentfully and unquestioningly, but it had steeped my whole life in its tincture of bitterness. Father had never forgiven me for two things. I had cost my mother's life and I was not a son to perpetuate the old name and carry on the family feud with the Frasers.

I was a very lonely child, with no playmates or companions of any sort, and my girlhood was lonelier still. The only passion in my life was my love for my father. I would have done and suffered anything to win his affection in return. But all I ever did win was an amused tolerance — and I was grateful for that — almost content. It was much to have something to love and be permitted to love it.

If I had been a beautiful and spirited girl I think Father might have loved me, but I was neither. At first I did not think or care about my lack of beauty; then one day I was alone in the beech wood; I was trying to disentangle my skirt which had caught on some thorny underbrush. A young man came around the curve of the path and, seeing my predicament, bent with murmured apology to help me. He had to kneel to do it, and I saw a ray of sunshine falling through the beeches above us strike like a lance of light athwart the thick brown hair that pushed out from under his cap. Before I thought I put out my hand and touched it softly, then I blushed crimson with shame over what I had done. But he did not know — he never knew.

When he had released my dress he rose and our eyes met for a moment as I timidly thanked him. I saw that he was good to look upon — tall and straight, with broad, stalwart shoulders and a dark, clean-cut face. He had a firm, sensitive mouth and kindly, pleasant, dark blue eyes. I never quite forgot the look in those eyes. It made my heart beat strangely, but it was only for a moment, and the next he had lifted his cap and passed on.

As I went homeward I wondered who he might be. He must be a stranger, I thought — probably a visitor in some of our few neighbouring families. I wondered too if I should meet him again, and found the thought very pleasant.

I knew few men and they were all old, like Father, or at least elderly. They were the only people who ever came to our house, and they either teased me or overlooked me. None of them was at all like this young man I had met in the beech wood, nor ever could have been, I thought.

When I reached home I stopped before the big mirror that hung in the hall and did what I had never done before in my life — looked at myself very scrutinizingly and wondered if I had any beauty. I could only sorrowfully conclude that I had not — I was so slight and pale, and the thick black hair and dark eyes that might have been pretty in another woman seemed only to accentuate the lack of spirit and regularity in my features. I was still standing there, gazing wistfully at my mirrored face with a strange sinking of spirit, when Father came through the hall, his riding whip in his hand. Seeing me, he laughed.

"Don't waste your time gazing into mirrors, Isobel," he said carelessly. "That might have been excusable in former ladies of Shirley whose beauty might pardon and even adorn vanity, but with you it is only absurd. The needle and the cookbook are all that you need concern yourself with."

I was accustomed to such speeches from him, but they had never hurt me so cruelly before. At that moment I would have given all the world only to be beautiful.

The next Sunday I looked across the church, and in the Fraser pew I saw the young man I had met in the wood. He was looking at me with his arms folded over his breast and on his brow a little frown that seemed somehow indicative of pain and surprise. I felt a miserable sense of disappointment. If he were the Frasers' guest I could not expect to meet him again. Father hated the Frasers, all the Shirleys hated them; it was an old feud, bitter and lasting, that had been as much our inheritance for generations as land and money. The only thing Father had ever taken pains to teach me was detestation of the Frasers and all their works. I accepted this as I accepted all the other traditions of my race. I thought it did not matter much. The Frasers were not likely to come my way, and hatred was a good satisfying passion in the lack of all else. I think I rather took a pride in hating them as became my blood.

I did not look at the Fraser pew again, but outside, under the elms, we met him, standing in the dappling light and shadow. He looked very handsome and a little sad. I could not help glancing back over my shoulder as Father and I walked to the gate, and I saw him looking after us with that little frown which again made me think something had hurt him. I liked better the smile he had worn in the beech wood, but I had an odd liking for the frown too, and I think I had a foolish longing to go back to him, put up my fingers and smooth it away.

"So Alan Fraser has come home," said my father.

"Alan Fraser?" I repeated, with a strange, horrible feeling of coldness and chill coming over me like a shadow on a bright day. Alan Fraser, the son of old Malcolm Fraser of Glenellyn! The son of our enemy! He had been living since childhood with his dead mother's people, so much I knew. And this was he! Something stung and smarted in my eyes. I think the sting and smart might have turned to tears if Father had not been looking down at me.

"Yes. Didn't you see him in his father's pew? But I forgot. You are too demure to be looking at the young men in preaching — or out of it, Isobel. You are a model young woman. Odd that the men never like the model young women! Curse old Malcolm Fraser! What right has he to have a son like that when I have nothing but a puling girl? Remember, Isobel, that if you ever meet that young man you are not to speak to or look at him, or even intimate that you are aware of his existence. He is your enemy and the enemy of your race. You will show him that you realize this."

Of course that ended it all—though just what there had been to end would have been hard to say. Not long afterwards I met Alan Fraser again, when I was out for a canter on my mare. He was strolling through the beech wood with a couple of big collies, and he stopped short as I drew near. I had to do it—Father had decreed—my Shirley pride demanded—that I should do it. I looked him unseeingly in the face, struck my mare a blow with my whip, and dashed past him. I even felt angry, I think, that a Fraser should have the power to make me feel so badly in doing my duty.

After that I had forgotten. There was nothing to make me remember, for I never met Alan Fraser again. The years slipped by, one by one, so like each other in their colourlessness that I forgot to take account of them. I only knew that I grew older and that it did not matter since there was nobody to care. One day they brought Father in, white-lipped and groaning. His mare had thrown him, and he was never to walk again, although he lived for five years. Those five years had been the happiest of my life. For the first time I was necessary to someone—there was something for me to do which nobody else could do so well. I was Father's nurse and companion; and I found my pleasure in tending him and amusing him, soothing his hours of pain and brightening his hours of ease. People said I "did my duty" toward him. I had never liked that word "duty," since the day I had ridden past Alan Fraser in the beech wood. I could not connect it with what I did for Father. It was my delight because I loved him. I did not mind the moods and the irritable outbursts that drove others from him.

But now he was dead, and I sat in the sullen dusk, wishing that I need not go on with life either. The loneliness of the big echoing house weighed on my spirit. I was solitary, without companionship. I looked out on the outside world where the only sign of human habitation visible to my eyes was the light twinkling out from the library window of Glenellyn on the dark fir hill two miles away. By that light I knew Alan Fraser must have returned from his long sojourn abroad, for it only shone when he was at Glenellyn. He still lived there, something of a hermit, people said; he had never married, and he cared nothing for society. His companions were books and dogs and horses; he was given to scientific researches and wrote much for the reviews; he travelled a great deal. So much I knew in a vague way. I even saw him occasionally in church, and never thought the years had changed him much, save that his face was sadder and sterner than of old and his hair had become iron-grey. People said that he had inherited and cherished the old hatred of the Shirleys—that he was very bitter against us. I believed it. He had the face of a good hater—or lover—a man who could play with no emotion but must take it in all earnestness and intensity.

When it was quite dark the housekeeper brought in the lights and handed me a letter which, she said, a man had just brought up from the village post office. I looked at it curiously before I opened it, wondering from whom it was. It was postmarked from a city several miles away, and the firm, decided, rather peculiar handwriting was strange to me. I had no correspondents. After Father's death I had received a few perfunctory notes of condolence from distant relatives and family friends. They had hurt me cruelly, for they seemed to exhale a subtle spirit of congratulation on my being released from a long and unpleasant martyrdom of attendance on an invalid, that quite overrode the decorous phrases of conventional sympathy in which they were expressed. I hated those letters for their implied injustice. I was not thankful for my "release." I missed Father miserably and longed passionately for the very tasks and vigils that had evoked their pity.

This letter did not seem like one of those. I opened it and took out some stiff, blackly written sheets. They were undated and, turning to the last, I saw that they were unsigned. With a not unpleasant tingling of interest I sat down by my desk to read. The letter began abruptly:

> You will not know by whom this is written. Do not seek to know—now or ever. It is only from behind the veil of your ignorance of my identity that I can ever write to you fully and freely as I wish to write—can say what I wish to say in words denied to a formal and conventional expression of sympathy. Dear lady, let me say to you thus what is in my heart.
>
> I know what your sorrow is, and I think I know what your loneliness must be—the sorrow of a broken tie, the loneliness of a life thrown emptily back on itself. I know how you loved your father—how you must have loved him if those eyes and brow and mouth speak truth, for they tell of a nature divinely rich and deep, giving of its wealth and tenderness ungrudgingly to those who are so happy as to be the objects of its affection. To such a nature bereavement must bring a depth and an agony of grief unknown to shallower souls.
>
> I know what your father's helplessness and need of you meant to you. I know that now life must seem to you a broken and embittered thing and, knowing this, I venture to send this greeting across the gulf of strangerhood between us, telling you that my understanding sympathy is fully and freely yours, and bidding you take heart for the future, which now, it may be, looks so heartless and hopeless to you.
>
> Believe me, dear lady, it will be neither. Courage will come to you with the kind days. You will find noble tasks to do, beautiful and

gracious duties waiting along your path. The pain and suffering of the world never dies, and while it lives there will be work for such as you to do, and in the doing of it you will find comfort and strength and the highest joy of living. I believe in you. I believe you will make of your life a beautiful and worthy thing. I give you Godspeed for the years to come. Out of my own loneliness I, an unknown friend, who has never clasped your hand, send this message to you. I understand—I have always understood—and I say to you: "Be of good cheer."

To say that this strange letter was a mystery to me seems an inadequate way of stating the matter. I was completely bewildered, nor could I even guess who the writer might be, think and ponder as I might.

The letter itself implied that the writer was a stranger. The handwriting was evidently that of a man, and I knew no man who could or would have sent such a letter to me.

The very mystery stung me to interest. As for the letter itself, it brought me an uplift of hope and inspiration such as I would not have believed possible an hour earlier. It rang so truly and sincerely, and the mere thought that somewhere I had a friend who cared enough to write it, even in such odd fashion, was so sweet that I was half ashamed of the difference it made in my outlook. Sitting there, I took courage and made a compact with myself that I would justify the writer's faith in me—that I would take up my life as something to be worthily lived for all good, to the disregard of my own selfish sorrow and shrinking. I would seek for something to do—for interests which would bind me to my fellow-creatures—for tasks which would lessen the pains and perils of humankind. An hour before, this would not have seemed to me possible; now it seemed the right and natural thing to do.

A week later another letter came. I welcomed it with an eagerness which I feared was almost childish. It was a much longer letter than the first and was written in quite a different strain. There was no apology for or explanation of the motive for writing. It was as if the letter were merely one of a permitted and established correspondence between old friends. It began with a witty, sparkling review of a new book the writer had just read, and passed from this to crisp comments on the great events, political, scientific, artistic, of the day. The whole letter was pungent, interesting, delightful—an impersonal essay on a dozen vital topics of life and thought. Only at the end was a personal note struck.

"Are you interested in these things?" ran the last paragraph. "In what is being done and suffered and attained in the great busy world? I think you must be—for I have seen you and read what is written in your face. I believe you care for these things as I do—that your being thrills to the 'still, sad music of humanity' — that the songs of the poets I love find an echo in your spirit and the aspirations of all struggling souls a sympathy in your heart. Believing this, I have written freely to you, taking a keen pleasure in thus revealing my thoughts and visions to one who will understand. For I too am friendless, in the sense of one standing alone, shut out from the sweet, intimate communion of feeling and opinion that may be held with the heart's friends. Shall you have read this as a friend, I wonder — a candid, uncritical, understanding friend? Let me hope it, dear lady."

I was expecting the third letter when it came — but not until it did come did I realize what my disappointment would have been if it had not. After that every week brought me a letter; soon those letters were the greatest interest in my life. I had given up all attempts to solve the mystery of their coming and was content to enjoy them for themselves alone. From week to week I looked forward to them with an eagerness that I would hardly confess, even to myself.

And such letters as they were, growing longer and fuller and freer as time went on — such wise, witty, brilliant, pungent letters, stimulating all my torpid life into tingling zest! I had begun to look abroad in my small world for worthy work and found plenty to do. My unknown friend evidently kept track of my expanding efforts, for he commented and criticized, encouraged and advised freely. There was a humour in his letters that I liked; it leavened them with its sanity and reacted on me most wholesomely, counteracting many of the morbid tendencies and influences of my life. I found myself striving to live up to the writer's ideal of philosophy and ambition, as pictured, often unconsciously, in his letters.

They were an intellectual stimulant as well. To understand them fully I found it necessary to acquaint myself thoroughly with the literature and art, the science and the politics they touched upon. After every letter there was something new for me to hunt out and learn and assimilate, until my old narrow mental attitude had so broadened and deepened, sweeping out into circles of thought I had never known or imagined, that I hardly knew myself.

They had been coming for a year before I began to reply to them. I had often wished to do so — there were so many things I wanted to say and discuss, but it seemed foolish to write letters that could not be sent. One day a letter came that kindled my imagination and stirred my heart and soul so deeply that they insistently demanded answering expression. I sat down at my desk and wrote a full reply to it. Safe in the belief that the mysterious friend to whom it was written would never see it, I wrote with a perfect freedom and a total lack of self-consciousness that I could never have attained otherwise. The writing of that letter gave me a pleasure second only to that which the reading of his brought. For the first time I discovered the delight of revealing my thought unhindered by the conventions. Also, I understood better why the writer of those letters had written them. Doubtless he had enjoyed doing so and was not impelled thereto simply by a purely philanthropic wish to help me.

When my letter was finished I sealed it up and locked it away in my desk with a smile at my middle-aged folly. What, I wondered, would all my sedate, serious friends, my associates of mission and hospital committees think if they knew. Well, everybody has, or should have, a pet nonsense in her life. I did not think mine was any sillier than some others I knew, and to myself I admitted that it was very sweet. I knew if those letters ceased to come all savour would go out of my life.

After that I wrote a reply to every letter I received and kept them all locked up together. It was delightful. I wrote out all my doings and perplexities and hopes and plans and wishes—yes, and my dreams. The secret romance of it all made me look on existence with joyous, contented eyes.

Gradually a change crept over the letters I received. Without ever affording the slightest clue to the identity of their writer they grew more intimate and personal. A subtle, caressing note of tenderness breathed from them and thrilled my heart curiously. I felt as if I were being drawn into the writer's life, admitted into the most sacred recesses of his thoughts and feelings. Yet it was all done so subtly, so delicately, that I was unconscious of the change until I discovered it in reading over the older letters and comparing them with the later ones.

Finally a letter came—my first love letter, and surely never was a love letter received under stranger circumstances. It began abruptly as all the letters had begun, plunging into the middle of the writer's strain of thought without any preface. The first words drove the blood to my heart and then sent it flying hotly all over my face.

> I love you. I must say it at last. Have you not guessed it before? It has trembled on my pen in every line I have written to you—yet I have never dared to shape it into words before. I know not how I dare now. I only know that I must. What a delight to write it out and know that you will read it. Tonight the mood is on me to tell it to you recklessly and lavishly, never pausing to stint or weigh words. Sweetheart, I love you—love you—love you—dear true, faithful woman soul, I love you with all the heart of a man.
>
> Ever since I first saw you I have loved you. I can never come to tell you so in spoken words; I can only love you from afar and tell my love under the guise of impersonal friendship. It matters not to you, but it matters more than all else in life to me. I am glad that I love you, dear—glad, glad, glad.

There was much more, for it was a long letter. When I had read it I buried my burning face in my hands, trembling with happiness. This strange confession of love meant so much to me; my heart leaped forth to meet it with answering love. What mattered it that we could never meet—that I could not even guess who my lover was? Somewhere in the world was a love that was mine alone and mine wholly and mine forever. What mattered his name or his station, or the mysterious barrier between us? Spirit leaped to spirit unhindered over the fettering bounds of matter and time. I loved and was beloved. Nothing else mattered.

I wrote my answer to his letter. I wrote it fearlessly and unstintedly. Perhaps I could not have written so freely if the letter were to have been read by him; as it was, I poured out the riches of my love as fully as he had done. I kept nothing back, and across the gulf between us I vowed a faithful and enduring love in response to his.

The next day I went to town on business with my lawyers. Neither of the members of the firm was in when I called, but I was an old client, and one of the clerks showed me into the private office to wait. As I sat down my eyes fell on a folded letter lying on the table beside me. With a shock of surprise I recognized the writing. I could not be mistaken—I should have recognized it anywhere.

The letter was lying by its envelope, so folded that only the middle third of the page was visible. An irresistible impulse swept over me. Before I could reflect that I had no business to touch the letter, that perhaps it was unfair to my unknown friend to seek to discover his identity when he wished to hide it, I had turned the letter over and seen the signature.

I laid it down again and stood up, dizzy, breathless, unseeing. Like a woman in a dream I walked through the outer office and into the street. I must have walked on for blocks before I became conscious of my surroundings. The name I had seen signed to that letter was Alan Fraser!

No doubt the reader has long ago guessed it—has wondered why I had not. The fact remains that I had not. Out of the whole world Alan Fraser was the last man whom I should have suspected to be the writer of those letters—Alan Fraser, my hereditary enemy, who, I had been told, cherished the old feud so faithfully and bitterly, and hated our very name.

And yet I now wondered at my long blindness. No one else could have written those letters—no one but him. I read them over one by one when I reached home and, now that I possessed the key, he revealed himself in every line, expression, thought. And he loved me!

I thought of the old feud and hatred; I thought of my pride and traditions. They seemed like the dust and ashes of outworn things—things to be smiled at and cast aside. I took out all the letters I had written—all except the last one—sealed them up in a parcel and directed it to Alan Fraser. Then, summoning my groom, I bade him ride to Glenellyn with it. His look of amazement almost made me laugh, but after he was gone I felt dizzy and frightened at my own daring.

When the autumn darkness came down I went to my room and dressed as the woman dresses who awaits the one man of all the world. I hardly knew what I hoped or expected, but I was all athrill with a nameless, inexplicable happiness. I admit I looked very eagerly into the mirror when I was done, and I thought that the result was not unpleasing. Beauty had never been mine, but a faint reflection of it came over me in the tremulous flush and excitement of the moment. Then the maid came up to tell me that Alan Fraser was in the library.

I went down with my cold hands tightly clasped behind me. He was standing by the library table, a tall, broad-shouldered man, with the light striking upward on his dark, sensitive face and iron-grey hair. When he saw me he came quickly forward.

"So you know—and you are not angry—your letters told me so much. I have loved you since that day in the beech wood, Isobel—Isobel."

His eyes were kindling into mine. He held my hands in a close, impetuous clasp. His voice was infinitely caressing as he pronounced my name. I had never heard it since Father died—I had never heard it at all so musically and tenderly uttered. My ancestors might have turned in their graves just then—but it mattered not. Living love had driven out dead hatred.

"Isobel," he went on, "there was *one* letter unanswered—the last."

I went to my desk, took out the last letter I had written and gave it to him in silence. While he read it I stood in a shadowy corner and watched him, wondering if life could always be as sweet as this. When he had finished he turned to me and held out his arms. I went to them as a bird to her nest, and with his lips against mine the old feud was blotted out forever.

The Life-Book of Uncle Jesse

Uncle Jesse! The name calls up the vision of him as I saw him so often in those two enchanted summers at Golden Gate; as I saw him the first time, when he stood in the open doorway of the little low-eaved cottage on the harbour shore, welcoming us to our new domicile with the gentle, unconscious courtesy that became him so well. A tall, ungainly figure, somewhat stooped, yet suggestive of great strength and endurance; a clean-shaven old face deeply lined and bronzed; a thick mane of iron-grey hair falling quite to his shoulders; and a pair of remarkably blue, deep-set eyes, which sometimes twinkled and sometimes dreamed, but oftener looked out seaward with a wistful question in them, as of one seeking something precious and lost. I was to learn one day what it was for which Uncle Jesse looked.

It cannot be denied that Uncle Jesse was a homely man. His spare jaws, rugged mouth, and square brow were not fashioned on the lines of beauty, but though at first sight you thought him plain you never thought anything more about it—the spirit shining through that rugged tenement beautified it so wholly.

Uncle Jesse was quite keenly aware of his lack of outward comeliness and lamented it, for he was a passionate worshipper of beauty in everything. He told Mother once that he'd rather like to be made over again and made handsome.

"Folks say I'm good," he remarked whimsically, "but I sometimes wish the Lord had made me only half as good and put the rest of it into looks. But I reckon He knew what He was about, as a good Captain should. Some of us have to be homely or the purty ones—like Miss Mary there—wouldn't show up so well."

I was not in the least pretty but Uncle Jesse was always telling me I was—and I loved him for it. He told the fib so prettily and sincerely that he almost made me believe it for the time being, and I really think he believed it himself. All women were lovely and of good report in his eyes, because of one he had loved. The only time I ever saw Uncle Jesse really angered was when someone in his hearing cast an aspersion on the character of a shore girl. The wretched man who did it fairly cringed when Uncle Jesse turned on him with lightning of eye and thundercloud of brow. At that moment I no longer found it hard to reconcile Uncle Jesse's simple, kindly personality with the wild, adventurous life he had lived.

We went to Golden Gate in the spring. Mother's health had not been good and her doctor recommended sea air and quiet. Uncle James, when he heard it, proposed that we take possession of a small cottage at Golden Gate, to which he had recently fallen heir by the death of an old aunt who had lived in it.

"I haven't been up to see it," he said, "but it is just as Aunt Elizabeth left it and she was the pink of neatness. The key is in the possession of an old sailor living nearby — Jesse Boyd is the name, I think. I imagine you can be very comfortable in it. It is built right on the harbour shore, inside the bar, and it is within five minutes' walk of the outside shore."

Uncle James's offer fitted in very opportunely with our limp family purse, and we straightway betook ourselves to Golden Gate. We telegraphed to Jesse Boyd to have the house opened for us and, one crisp spring day, when a rollicking wind was scudding over the harbour and the dunes, whipping the water into white caps and washing the sandshore with long lines of silvery breakers, we alighted at the little station and walked the half mile to our new home, leaving our goods and chattels to be carted over in the evening by an obliging station agent's boy.

Our first glimpse of Aunt Elizabeth's cottage was a delight to soul and sense; it looked so like a big grey seashell stranded on the shore. Between it and the harbour was only a narrow strip of shingle, and behind it was a gnarled and battered fir wood where the winds were in the habit of harping all sorts of weird and haunting music. Inside, it was to prove even yet more quaint and delightful, with its low, dark-beamed ceilings and square, deep-set windows by which, whether open or shut, sea breezes entered at their own sweet will. The view from our door was magnificent, taking in the big harbour and sweeps of purple hills beyond. The entrance of the harbour gave it its name — a deep, narrow channel between the bar of sand dunes on the one side and a steep, high, frowning red sandstone cliff on the other. We appreciated its significance the first time we saw a splendid golden sunrise flooding it, coming out of the wonderful sea and sky beyond and billowing through that narrow passage in waves of light. Truly, it was a golden gate through which one might sail to "faerie lands forlorn."

As we went along the path to our little house we were agreeably surprised to see a blue spiral of smoke curling up from its big, square chimney, and the next moment Uncle Jesse (we were calling him Uncle Jesse half an hour after we met him, so it seems scarcely worthwhile to begin with anything else) came to the door.

"Welcome, ladies," he said, holding out a big, hard, but scrupulously clean hand. "I thought you'd be feeling a bit tired and hungry, maybe, so when I came over to open up I put on a fire and brewed you up a cup of tea. I just delight in being neighbourly and 'tain't often I have the chance."

We found that Uncle Jesse's "cup of tea" meant a veritable spread. He had aired the little dining room, set out the table daintily with Aunt Elizabeth's china and linen—"knowed jest where to put my hands on 'em—often and often helped old Miss Kennedy wash 'em. We were cronies, her and me. I miss her terrible"—and adorned it with mayflowers which, as we afterwards discovered, he had tramped several miles to gather. There was good bread and butter, "store" biscuits, a dish of tea fit for the gods on high Olympus, and a platter of the most delicious sea trout, done to a turn.

"Thought they'd be tasty after travelling," said Uncle Jesse. "They're fresh as trout can be, ma'am. Two hours ago they was swimming in Johnson's pond yander. I caught 'em—yes, ma'am. It's about all I'm good for now, catching trout and cod occasional. But 'tweren't always so—not by no manner of means. I used to do other things, as you'd admit if you saw my life-book."

I was so hungry and tired that I did not then "rise to the bait" of Uncle Jesse's "life-book." I simply wanted to begin on those trout. Mother insisted that Uncle Jesse sit down and help us eat the repast he had prepared, and he assented without undue coaxing.

"Thank ye kindly. 'Twill be a real treat. I mostly has to eat my meals alone, with the reflection of my ugly old phiz in a looking glass opposite for company. 'Tisn't often I have the chance to sit down with two such sweet purty ladies."

Uncle Jesse's compliments look bald enough on paper, but he paid them with such gracious, gentle deference of tone and look that the woman who received them felt that she was being offered a queen's gift in kingly fashion.

He broke bread with us and from that moment we were all friends together and forever. After we had eaten all we could, we sat at our table for an hour and listened to Uncle Jesse telling us stories of his life.

"If I talk too much you must jest check me," he said seriously, but with a twinkle in his eyes. "When I do get a chance to talk to anyone I'm apt to run on terrible."

He had been a sailor from the time he was ten years old, and some of his adventures had such a marvellous edge that I secretly wondered if Uncle Jesse were not drawing a rather long bow at our credulous expense. But in this, as I found later, I did him injustice. His tales were all literally true, and Uncle Jesse had the gift of the born story-teller, whereby "unhappy, far-off things" can be brought vividly before the hearer and made to live again in all their pristine poignancy.

Mother and I laughed and shivered over Uncle Jesse's tales, and once we found ourselves crying. Uncle Jesse surveyed our tears with pleasure shining out through his face like an illuminating lamp.

"I like to make folks cry that way," he remarked. "It's a compliment. But I can't do justice to the things I've seen and helped do. I've got 'em all jotted down in my life-book but I haven't got the knack of writing them out properly. If I had, I could make a great book, if I had the knack of hitting on just the right words and stringing everything together proper on paper. But I can't. It's in this poor human critter," Uncle Jesse patted his breast sorrowfully, "but he can't get it out."

When Uncle Jesse went home that evening Mother asked him to come often to see us.

"I wonder if you'd give that invitation if you knew how likely I'd be to accept it," he remarked whimsically.

"Which is another way of saying you wonder if I meant it," smiled Mother. "I do, most heartily and sincerely."

"Then I'll come. You'll likely be pestered with me at any hour. And I'd be proud to have you drop over to visit me now and then too. I live on that point yander. Neither me nor my house is worth coming to see. It's only got one room and a loft and a stovepipe sticking out of the roof for a chimney. But I've got a few little things lying around that I picked up in the queer corners I used to be poking my nose into. Mebbe they'd interest you."

Uncle Jesse's "few little things" turned out to be the most interesting collection of curios I had ever seen. His one neat little living room was full of them—beautiful, hideous or quaint as the case might be, and almost all having some weird or exciting story attached.

Mother and I had a beautiful summer at Golden Gate. We lived the life of two children with Uncle Jesse as a playmate. Our housekeeping was of the simplest description and we spent our hours rambling along the shores, reading on the rocks or sailing over the harbour in Uncle Jesse's trim little boat. Every day we loved the simple-souled, true, manly old sailor more and more. He was as refreshing as a sea breeze, as interesting as some ancient chronicle. We never tired of listening to his stories, and his quaint remarks and comments were a continual delight to us. Uncle Jesse was one of those interesting and rare people who, in the picturesque phraseology of the shore folks, "never speak but they say something." The milk of human kindness and the wisdom of the serpent were mingled in Uncle Jesse's composition in delightful proportions.

One day he was absent all day and returned at nightfall.

"Took a tramp back yander." "Back yander" with Uncle Jesse might mean the station hamlet or the city a hundred miles away or any place between — "to carry Mr. Kimball a mess of trout. He likes one occasional and it's all I can do for a kindness he did me once. I stayed all day to talk to him. He likes to talk to me, though he's an eddicated man, because he's one of the folks that's *got* to talk or they're miserable, and he finds listeners scarce 'round here. The folks fight shy of him because they think he's an infidel. He ain't *that* far gone exactly — few men is, I reckon — but he's what you might call a heretic. Heretics are wicked but they're mighty interesting. It's just that they've got sorter lost looking for God, being under the impression that He's hard to find — which He ain't, never. Most of 'em blunder to Him after a while I guess. I don't think listening to Mr. Kimball's arguments is likely to do *me* much harm. Mind you, I believe what I was brought up to believe. It saves a vast of trouble — and back of it all, God is good. The trouble with Mr. Kimball is, he's a leetle *too* clever. He thinks he's bound to live up to his cleverness and that it's smarter to thrash out some new way of getting to heaven than to go by the old track the common, ignorant folks is travelling. But he'll get there sometime all right and then he'll laugh at himself."

Nothing ever seemed to put Uncle Jesse out or depress him in any way.

"I've kind of contracted a habit of enjoying things," he remarked once, when Mother had commented on his invariable cheerfulness. "It's got so chronic that I believe I even enjoy the disagreeable things. It's great fun thinking they can't last. 'Old rheumatiz,' I says, when it grips me hard, 'you've *got* to stop aching sometime. The worse you are the sooner you'll stop, perhaps. I'm bound to get the better of you in the long run, whether in the body or out of the body.'"

Uncle Jesse seldom came to our house without bringing us something, even if it were only a bunch of sweet grass.

"I favour the smell of sweet grass," he said. "It always makes me think of my mother."

"She was fond of it?"

"Not that I knows on. Dunno's she ever saw any sweet grass. No, it's because it has a kind of motherly perfume — not too young, you understand — something kind of seasoned and wholesome and dependable — just like a mother."

Uncle Jesse was a very early riser. He seldom missed a sunrise.

"I've seen all kinds of sunrises come in through that there Gate," he said dreamily one morning when I myself had made a heroic effort at early rising and joined him on the rocks halfway between his house and ours. "I've been all over the world and, take it all in all, I've never seen a finer sight than a summer sunrise out there beyant the Gate. A man can't pick his time for dying, Mary—jest got to go when the Captain gives his sailing orders. But if I could I'd go out when the morning comes in there at the Gate. I've watched it a many times and thought what a thing it would be to pass out through that great white glory to whatever was waiting beyant, on a sea that ain't mapped out on any airthly chart. I think, Mary, I'd find lost Margaret there."

He had already told me the story of "lost Margaret," as he always called her. He rarely spoke of her, but when he did his love for her trembled in every tone—a love that had never grown faint or forgetful. Uncle Jesse was seventy; it was fifty years since lost Margaret had fallen asleep one day in her father's dory and drifted—as was supposed, for nothing was ever known certainly of her fate—across the harbour and out of the Gate, to perish in the black thunder squall that had come up suddenly that long-ago afternoon. But to Uncle Jesse those fifty years were but as yesterday when it is past.

"I walked the shore for months after that," he said sadly, "looking to find her dear, sweet little body, but the sea never gave her back to me. But I'll find her sometime. I wisht I could tell you just how she looked but I can't. I've seen a fine silvery mist hanging over the Gate at sunrise that seemed like her—and then again I've seen a white birch in the woods back yander that made me think of her. She had pale brown hair and a little white face, and long slender fingers like yours, Mary, only browner, for she was a shore girl. Sometimes I wake up in the night and hear the sea calling to me in the old way and it seems as if lost Margaret called in it. And when there's a storm and the waves are sobbing and moaning I hear her lamenting among them. And when they laugh on a gay day it's *her* laugh—lost Margaret's sweet little laugh. The sea took her from me but some day I'll find her, Mary. It can't keep us apart forever."

I had not been long at Golden Gate before I saw Uncle Jesse's "life-book," as he quaintly called it. He needed no coaxing to show it and he proudly gave it to me to read. It was an old leather-bound book filled with the record of his voyages and adventures. I thought what a veritable treasure trove it would be to a writer. Every sentence was a nugget. In itself the book had no literary merit; Uncle Jesse's charm of story-telling failed him when he came to pen and ink; he could only jot down roughly the outlines of his famous tales, and both spelling and grammar were sadly askew. But I felt that if anyone possessing the gift could take that simple record of a brave, adventurous life, reading between the bald lines the tale of dangers staunchly faced and duties manfully done, a wonderful story might be made from it. Pure comedy and thrilling tragedy were both lying hidden in Uncle Jesse's "life-book," waiting for the touch of the magician's hand to waken the laughter and grief and horror of thousands. I thought of my cousin, Robert Kennedy, who juggled with words in a masterly fashion, but complained that he found it hard to create incidents or characters. Here were both ready to his hand, but Robert was in Japan in the interests of his paper.

In the fall, when the harbour lay black and sullen under November skies, Mother and I went back to town, parting with Uncle Jesse regretfully. We wanted him to visit us in town during the winter but he shook his head.

"It's too far away, Mary. If lost Margaret called me I mightn't hear her there. I must be here when my time comes. It can't be very far off now."

I wrote often to Uncle Jesse through the winter and sent him books and magazines. He enjoyed them but he thought—and truly enough—that none of them came up to his life-book for real interest.

"If my life-book could be took and writ by someone that knowed how, it would beat them holler," he wrote in one of his few letters to me.

In the spring we returned joyfully to Golden Gate. It was as golden as ever and the harbour as blue; the winds still rollicked as gaily and sweetly and the breakers boomed outside the bar as of yore. All was unchanged save Uncle Jesse. He had aged greatly and seemed frail and bent. After he had gone home from his first call on us, Mother cried.

"Uncle Jesse will soon be going to seek lost Margaret," she said.

In June Robert came. I took him promptly over to see Uncle Jesse, who was very much excited when he found that Robert was a "real writing man."

"Robert wants to hear some of your stories, Uncle Jesse," I said. "Tell him the one about the captain who went crazy and imagined he was the Flying Dutchman."

This was Uncle Jesse's best story. It was a compound of humour and horror, and though I had heard it several times, I laughed as heartily and shivered as fearsomely over it as Robert did. Other tales followed; Uncle Jesse told how his vessel had been run down by a steamer, how he had been boarded by Malay pirates, how his ship had caught fire, how he had helped a political prisoner escape from a South American republic. He never said a boastful word, but it was impossible to help seeing what a hero the man had been—brave, true, resourceful, unselfish, skilful. He sat there in his poor little room and made those things live again for us. By a lift of the eyebrow, a twist of the lip, a gesture, a word, he painted some whole scene or character so that we saw it as it was.

Finally, he lent Robert his life-book. Robert sat up all night reading it and came to the breakfast table in great excitement.

"Mary, this is a wonderful book. If I could take it and garb it properly — work it up into a systematic whole and string it on the thread of Uncle Jesse's romance of lost Margaret, it would be the novel of the year. Do you suppose he would let me do it?"

"Let you! I think he would be delighted," I answered.

And he was. He was as excited as a schoolboy over it. At last his cherished dream was to be realized and his life-book given to the world.

"We'll collaborate," said Robert. "You will give the soul and I the body. Oh, we'll write a famous book between us, Uncle Jesse. And we'll get right to work."

Uncle Jesse was a happy man that summer. He looked upon the little back room we gave up to Robert for a study as a sacred shrine. Robert talked everything over with Uncle Jesse but would not let him see the manuscript. "You must wait till it is published," he said. "Then you'll get it all at once in its best shape."

Robert delved into the treasures of the life-book and used them freely. He dreamed and brooded over lost Margaret until she became a vivid reality to him and lived in his pages. As the book progressed it took possession of him and he worked at it with feverish eagerness. He let me read the manuscript and criticize it; and the concluding chapter of the book, which the critics later on were pleased to call idyllic, was modelled after my suggestions, so that I felt as if I had a share in it too.

It was autumn when the book was finished. Robert went back to town, but Mother and I decided to stay at Golden Gate all winter. We loved the spot and, besides, I wished to remain for Uncle Jesse's sake. He was failing all the time, and after Robert went and the excitement of the book-making was past, he failed still more rapidly. His tramping expeditions were over and he seldom went out in his boat. Neither did he talk a great deal. He liked to come over and sit silently for hours at our seaward window, looking out wistfully toward the Gate with his swiftly whitening head leaning on his hand. The only keen interest he still had was in Robert's book. He waited and watched impatiently for its publication.

"I want to live till I see it," he said, "just that long — then I'll be ready to go. He said it would be out in the spring — I must hang on till it comes, Mary."

There were times when I doubted sadly if he would "hang on." As the winter wore away he grew frailer and frailer. But ever he looked forward to the coming of spring and "the book," *his* book, transformed and glorified.

One day in young April the book came at last. Uncle Jesse had gone to the post office faithfully every day for a month, expecting it, but this day he was too feeble to go and I went for him. The book was there. It was called simply, *The Life-Book of Jesse Boyd*, and on the title page the names of Robert Kennedy and Jesse Boyd were printed as collaborators.

I shall never forget Uncle Jesse's face as I handed it to him. I came away and left him reading it, oblivious to all else. All night the light burned in his window, and I looked out across the sands to it and pictured the delight of the old man poring over the printed pages whereon his own life was portrayed. I wondered how he would like the ending—the ending I had suggested. I was never to know.

After breakfast I went over to Uncle Jesse's house, taking some little delicacy Mother had cooked for him. It was an exquisite morning, full of delicate spring tints and sounds. The harbour was sparkling and dimpling like a girl, the winds were playing hide and seek roguishly among the stunted firs, and the silver-flashing gulls were soaring over the bar. Beyond the Gate was a shining, wonderful sea.

When I reached the little house on the point I saw the lamp still burning wanly in the window. A quick alarm struck at my heart. Without waiting to knock, I lifted the latch, and entered.

Uncle Jesse was lying on the old sofa by the window, with the book clasped to his heart. His eyes were closed and on his face was a look of the most perfect peace and happiness—the look of one who has long sought and found at last.

We could not know at what hour he had died, but somehow I think he had his wish and went out when the morning came in through the Golden Gate. Out on that shining tide his spirit drifted, over the sunrise sea of pearl and silver, to the haven where lost Margaret waited beyond the storms and calms.

The Little Black Doll

Everybody in the Marshall household was excited on the evening of the concert at the Harbour Light Hotel—everybody, even to Little Joyce, who couldn't go to the concert because there wasn't anybody else to stay with Denise. Perhaps Denise was the most excited of them all—Denise, who was slowly dying of consumption in the Marshall kitchen chamber because there was no other place in the world for her to die in, or anybody to trouble about her. Mrs. Roderick Marshall thought it very good of herself to do so much for Denise. To be sure, Denise was not much bother, and Little Joyce did most of the waiting on her.

At the tea table nothing was talked of but the concert; for was not Madame Laurin, the great French Canadian prima donna, at the hotel, and was she not going to sing? It was the opportunity of a lifetime—the Marshalls would not have missed it for anything. Stately, handsome old Grandmother Marshall was going, and Uncle Roderick and Aunt Isabella, and of course Chrissie, who was always taken everywhere because she was pretty and graceful, and everything that Little Joyce was not.

Little Joyce would have liked to go to the concert, for she was very fond of music; and, besides, she wanted to be able to tell Denise all about it. But when you are shy and homely and thin and awkward, your grandmother never takes you anywhere. At least, such was Little Joyce's belief.

Little Joyce knew quite well that Grandmother Marshall did not like her. She thought it was because she was so plain and awkward—and in part it was. Grandmother Marshall cared very little for granddaughters who did not do her credit. But Little Joyce's mother had married a poor man in the face of her family's disapproval, and then both she and her husband had been inconsiderate enough to die and leave a small orphan without a penny to support her. Grandmother Marshall fed and clothed the child, but who could make anything of such a shy creature with no gifts or graces whatever? Grandmother Marshall had no intention of trying. Chrissie, the golden-haired and pink-cheeked, was Grandmother Marshall's pet.

Little Joyce knew this. She did not envy Chrissie but, oh, how she wished Grandmother Marshall would love her a little, too! Nobody loved her but

Denise and the little black doll. And Little Joyce was beginning to understand that Denise would not be in the kitchen chamber very much longer, and the little black doll couldn't *tell* you she loved you—although she did, of course. Little Joyce had no doubt at all on this point.

Little Joyce sighed so deeply over this thought that Uncle Roderick smiled at her. Uncle Roderick *did* smile at her sometimes.

"What is the matter, Little Joyce?" he asked.

"I was thinking about my black doll," said Little Joyce timidly.

"Ah, your black doll. If Madame Laurin were to see it, she'd likely want it. She makes a hobby of collecting dolls all over the world, but I doubt if she has in her collection a doll that served to amuse a little girl four thousand years ago in the court of the Pharaohs."

"I think Joyce's black doll is very ugly," said Chrissie. "My wax doll with the yellow hair is ever so much prettier."

"My black doll isn't ugly," cried Little Joyce indignantly. She could endure to be called ugly herself, but she could not bear to have her darling black doll called ugly. In her excitement she upset her cup of tea over the tablecloth. Aunt Isabella looked angry, and Grandmother Marshall said sharply: "Joyce, leave the table. You grow more awkward and careless every day."

Little Joyce, on the verge of tears, crept away and went up the kitchen stairs to Denise to be comforted. But Denise herself had been crying. She lay on her little bed by the low window, where the glow of the sunset was coming in; her hollow cheeks were scarlet with fever.

"Oh! I want so much to hear Madame Laurin sing," she sobbed. "I feel lak I could die easier if I hear her sing just one leetle song. She is Frenchwoman, too, and she sing all de ole French songs—de ole songs my mudder sing long 'go. Oh! I so want to hear Madame Laurin sing."

"But you can't, dear Denise," said Little Joyce very softly, stroking Denise's hot forehead with her cool, slender hand. Little Joyce had very pretty hands, only nobody had ever noticed them. "You are not strong enough to go to the concert. I'll sing for you, if you like. Of course, I can't sing very well, but I'll do my best."

"You sing lak a sweet bird, but you are not Madame Laurin," said Denise restlessly. "It is de great Madame I want to hear. I haf not long to live. Oh, I know, Leetle Joyce—I know what de doctor look lak—and I want to hear Madame Laurin sing 'fore I die. I know it is impossible—but I long for it so—just one leetle song."

Denise put her thin hands over her face and sobbed again. Little Joyce went and sat down by the window, looking out into the white birches. Her heart ached bitterly. Dear Denise was going to die soon—oh, very soon! Little Joyce, wise and knowing beyond her years, saw that. And Denise wanted to hear Madame Laurin sing. It seemed a foolish thing to think of, but Little Joyce thought hard about it; and when she had finished thinking, she got her little black doll and took it to bed with her, and there she cried herself to sleep.

At the breakfast table next morning the Marshalls talked about the concert and the wonderful Madame Laurin. Little Joyce listened in her usual silence; her crying the night before had not improved her looks any. Never, thought handsome Grandmother Marshall, had she appeared so sallow and homely. Really, Grandmother Marshall could not have the patience to look at her. She decided that she would not take Joyce driving with her and Chrissie that afternoon, as she had thought of, after all.

In the forenoon it was discovered that Denise was much worse, and the doctor was sent for. He came, and shook his head, that being really all he could do under the circumstances. When he went away, he was waylaid at the back door by a small gypsy with big, black, serious eyes and long black hair.

"Is Denise going to die?" Little Joyce asked in the blunt, straightforward fashion Grandmother Marshall found so trying.

The doctor looked at her from under his shaggy brows and decided that here was one of the people to whom you might as well tell the truth first as last, because they are bound to have it.

"Yes," he said.

"Soon?"

"Very soon, I'm afraid. In a few days at most."

"Thank you," said Little Joyce gravely.

She went to her room and did something with the black doll. She did not cry, but if you could have seen her face you would have wished she would cry.

After dinner Grandmother Marshall and Chrissie drove away, and Uncle Roderick and Aunt Isabella went away, too. Little Joyce crept up to the kitchen chamber. Denise was lying in an uneasy sleep, with tear stains on her face. Then Little Joyce tiptoed down and sped away to the hotel.

She did not know just what she would say or do when she got there, but she thought hard all the way to the end of the shore road. When she came out to the shore, a lady was sitting alone on a big rock—a lady with a dark, beautiful face and wonderful eyes. Little Joyce stopped before her and looked at her meditatively. Perhaps it would be well to ask advice of this lady.

"If you please," said Little Joyce, who was never shy with strangers, for whose opinion she didn't care at all, "I want to see Madame Laurin at the hotel and ask her to do me a very great favour. Will you tell me the best way to go about seeing her? I shall be much obliged to you."

"What is the favour you want to ask of Madame Laurin?" inquired the lady, smiling.

"I want to ask her if she will come and sing for Denise before she dies — before Denise dies, I mean. Denise is our French girl, and the doctor says she cannot live very long, and she wishes with all her heart to hear Madame Laurin sing. It is very bitter, you know, to be dying and want something very much and not be able to get it."

"Do you think Madame Laurin will go?" asked the lady.

"I don't know. I am going to offer her my little black doll. If she will not come for that, there is nothing else I can do."

A flash of interest lighted up the lady's brown eyes. She bent forward.

"Is it your doll you have in that box? Will you let me see it?"

Little Joyce nodded. Mutely she opened the box and took out the black doll. The lady gave an exclamation of amazed delight and almost snatched it from Little Joyce. It was a very peculiar little doll indeed, carved out of some black polished wood.

"Child, where in the world did you get this?" she cried.

"Father got it out of a grave in Egypt," said Little Joyce. "It was buried with the mummy of a little girl who lived four thousand years ago, Uncle Roderick says. She must have loved her doll very much to have had it buried with her, mustn't she? But she could not have loved it any more than I do."

"And yet you are going to give it away?" said the lady, looking at her keenly.

"For Denise's sake," explained Little Joyce. "I would do anything for Denise because I love her and she loves me. When the only person in the world who loves you is going to die, there is nothing you would not do for her if you could. Denise was so good to me before she took sick. She used to kiss me and play with me and make little cakes for me and tell me beautiful stories."

The lady put the little black doll back in the box. Then she stood up and held out her hand.

"Come," she said. "I am Madame Laurin, and I shall go and sing for Denise."

Little Joyce piloted Madame Laurin home and into the kitchen and up the back stairs to the kitchen chamber—a proceeding which would have filled Aunt Isabella with horror if she had known. But Madame Laurin did not seem to mind, and Little Joyce never thought about it at all. It was Little Joyce's awkward, unMarshall-like fashion to go to a place by the shortest way there, even if it was up the kitchen stairs.

Madame Laurin stood in the bare little room and looked pityingly at the wasted, wistful face on the pillow.

"This is Madame Laurin, and she is going to sing for you, Denise," whispered Little Joyce.

Denise's face lighted up, and she clasped her hands.

"If you please," she said faintly. "A French song, Madame—de ole French song dey sing long 'go."

Then did Madame Laurin sing. Never had that kitchen chamber been so filled with glorious melody. Song after song she sang—the old folklore songs of the *habitant*, the songs perhaps that Evangeline listened to in her childhood.

Little Joyce knelt by the bed, her eyes on the singer like one entranced. Denise lay with her face full of joy and rapture—such joy and rapture! Little Joyce did not regret the sacrifice of her black doll—never could regret it, as long as she remembered Denise's look.

"T'ank you, Madame," said Denise brokenly, when Madame ceased. "Dat was so beautiful—de angel, dey cannot sing more sweet. I love music so much, Madame. Leetle Joyce, she sing to me often and often—she sing sweet, but not lak you—oh, not lak you."

"Little Joyce must sing for me," said Madame, smiling, as she sat down by the window. "I always like to hear fresh, childish voices. Will you, Little Joyce?"

"Oh, yes." Little Joyce was quite unembarrassed and perfectly willing to do anything she could for this wonderful woman who had brought that look to Denise's face. "I will sing as well as I can for you. Of course, I can't sing very well and I don't know anything but hymns. I always sing hymns for Denise, although she is a Catholic and the hymns are Protestant. But her priest told her it was all right, because all music was of God. Denise's priest is a very nice man, and I like him. He thought my little black doll—*your* little black doll— was splendid. I'll sing 'Lead, Kindly Light.' That is Denise's favourite hymn."

Then Little Joyce, slipping her hand into Denise's, began to sing. At the first note Madame Laurin, who had been gazing out of the window with a rather listless smile, turned quickly and looked at Little Joyce with amazed eyes. Delight followed amazement, and when Little Joyce had finished, the great Madame rose impulsively, her face and eyes glowing, stepped swiftly to Little Joyce and took the thin dark face between her gemmed hands.

"Child, do you know what a wonderful voice you have—what a marvellous voice? It is—it is—I never heard such a voice in a child of your age. Mine was nothing to it—nothing at all. You will be a great singer some day—far greater than I—yes. But you must have the training. Where are your parents? I must see them."

"I have no parents," said the bewildered Little Joyce. "I belong to Grandmother Marshall, and she is out driving."

"Then I shall wait until your Grandmother Marshall comes home from her drive," said Madame Laurin decidedly.

Half an hour later a very much surprised old lady was listening to Madame Laurin's enthusiastic statements.

"How is it I have never heard you sing, if you can sing so well?" asked Grandmother Marshall, looking at Little Joyce with something in her eyes that had never been in them before—as Little Joyce instantly felt to the core of her sensitive soul. But Little Joyce hung her head. It had never occurred to her to sing in Grandmother Marshall's presence.

"This child must be trained by-and-by," said Madame Laurin. "If you cannot afford it, Mrs. Marshall, I will see to it. Such a voice must not be wasted."

"Thank you, Madame Laurin," said Grandmother Marshall with a gracious dignity, "but I am quite able to give my granddaughter all the necessary advantages for the development of her gift. And I thank you very much for telling me of it."

Madame Laurin bent and kissed Little Joyce's brown cheek.

"Little gypsy, good-by. But come every day to this hotel to see me. And next summer I shall be back. I like you—because some day you will be a great singer and because today you are a loving, unselfish baby."

"You have forgotten the little black doll, Madame," said Little Joyce gravely.

Madame threw up her hands, laughing. "No, no, I shall not take your little black doll of the four thousand years. Keep it for a mascot. A great singer always needs a mascot. But do not, I command you, take it out of the box till I am gone, for if I were to see it again, I might not be able to resist the temptation. Some day I shall show you *my* dolls, but there is not such a gem among them."

When Madame Laurin had gone, Grandmother Marshall looked at Little Joyce.

"Come to my room, Joyce. I want to see if we cannot find a more becoming way of arranging your hair. It has grown so thick and long. I had no idea how thick and long. Yes, we must certainly find a better way than that stiff braid. Come!"

Little Joyce, taking Grandmother Marshall's extended hand, felt very happy. She realized that this strange, stately old lady, who never liked little girls unless they were pretty or graceful or clever, was beginning to love her at last.

The Man on the Train

When the telegram came from William George, Grandma Sheldon was all alone with Cyrus and Louise. And Cyrus and Louise, aged respectively twelve and eleven, were not very much good, Grandma thought, when it came to advising what was to be done. Grandma was "all in a flutter, dear, oh dear," as she said.

The telegram said that Delia, William George's wife, was seriously ill down at Green Village, and William George wanted Samuel to bring Grandma down immediately. Delia had always thought there was nobody like Grandma when it came to nursing sick folks.

But Samuel and his wife were both away—had been away for two days and intended to be away for five more. They had driven to Sinclair, twenty miles away, to visit with Mrs. Samuel's folks for a week.

"Dear, oh dear, what shall I do?" said Grandma.

"Go right to Green Village on the evening train," said Cyrus briskly.

"Dear, oh dear, and leave you two alone!" cried Grandma.

"Louise and I will do very well until tomorrow," said Cyrus sturdily. "We will send word to Sinclair by today's mail, and Father and Mother will be home by tomorrow night."

"But I never was on the cars in my life," protested Grandma nervously. "I'm—I'm so frightened to start alone. And you never know what kind of people you may meet on the train."

"You'll be all right, Grandma. I'll drive you to the station, get you your ticket, and put you on the train. Then you'll have nothing to do until the train gets to Green Village. I'll send a telegram to Uncle William George to meet you."

"I shall fall and break my neck getting off the train," said Grandma pessimistically. But she was wondering at the same time whether she had better take the black valise or the yellow, and whether William George would be likely to have plenty of flaxseed in the house.

It was six miles to the station, and Cyrus drove Grandma over in time to catch a train that reached Green Village at nine o'clock.

"Dear, oh dear," said Grandma, "what if William George's folks ain't there to meet me? It's all very well, Cyrus, to say that they will be there, but you don't know. And it's all very well to say not to be nervous because everything will be all right. If you were seventy-five years old and had never set foot on the cars in your life you'd be nervous too, and you can't be sure that everything will be all right. You never know what sort of people you'll meet on the train. I may get on the wrong train or lose my ticket or get carried past Green Village or get my pocket picked. Well, no, I won't do that, for not one cent will I carry with me. You shall take back home all the money you don't need to get my ticket. Then I shall be easier in my mind. Dear, oh dear, if it wasn't that Delia is so seriously ill I wouldn't go one step."

"Oh, you'll be all right, Grandma," assured Cyrus.

He got Grandma's ticket for her and Grandma tied it up in the corner of her handkerchief. Then the train came in and Grandma, clinging closely to Cyrus, was put on it. Cyrus found a comfortable seat for her and shook hands cheerily.

"Good-bye, Grandma. Don't be frightened. Here's the *Weekly Argus*. I got it at the store. You may like to look over it."

Then Cyrus was gone, and in a minute the station house and platform began to glide away.

Dear, oh dear, what has happened to it? thought Grandma in dismay. The next moment she exclaimed aloud, "Why, it's us that's moving, not it!"

Some of the passengers smiled pleasantly at Grandma. She was the variety of old lady at which people do smile pleasantly; a grandma with round, pink cheeks, soft, brown eyes, and lovely snow-white curls is a nice person to look at wherever she is found.

After a while Grandma, to her amazement, discovered that she liked riding on the cars. It was not at all the disagreeable experience she had expected it to be. Why, she was just as comfortable as if she were in her own rocking chair at home! And there was such a lot of people to look at, and many of the ladies had such beautiful dresses and hats. After all, the people you met on a train, thought Grandma, are surprisingly like the people you meet off it. If it had not been for wondering how she would get off at Green Village, Grandma would have enjoyed herself thoroughly.

Four or five stations farther on the train halted at a lonely-looking place consisting of the station house and a barn, surrounded by scrub woods and blueberry barrens. One passenger got on and, finding only one vacant seat in the crowded car, sat right down beside Grandma Sheldon.

Grandma Sheldon held her breath while she looked him over. Was he a pickpocket? He didn't appear like one, but you can never be sure of the people you meet on the train. Grandma remembered with a sigh of thankfulness that she had no money.

Besides, he seemed really very respectable and harmless. He was quietly dressed in a suit of dark-blue serge with a black overcoat. He wore his hat well down on his forehead and was clean shaven. His hair was very black, but his eyes were blue—nice eyes, Grandma thought. She always felt great confidence in a man who had bright, open, blue eyes. Grandpa Sheldon, who had died so long ago, four years after their marriage, had had bright blue eyes.

To be sure, he had fair hair, reflected Grandma. It's real odd to see such black hair with such light blue eyes. Well, he's real nice looking, and I don't believe there's a mite of harm in him.

The early autumn night had now fallen and Grandma could not amuse herself by watching the scenery. She bethought herself of the paper Cyrus had given her and took it out of her basket. It was an old weekly a fortnight back. On the first page was a long account of a murder case with scare heads, and into this Grandma plunged eagerly. Sweet old Grandma Sheldon, who would not have harmed a fly and hated to see even a mousetrap set, simply revelled in the newspaper accounts of murders. And the more shocking and cold-blooded they were, the more eagerly did Grandma read of them.

This murder story was particularly good from Grandma's point of view; it was full of "thrills." A man had been shot down, apparently in cold blood, and his supposed murderer was still at large and had eluded all the efforts of justice to capture him. His name was Mark Hartwell, and he was described as a tall, fair man, with full auburn beard and curly, light hair.

"What a shocking thing!" said Grandma aloud.

Her companion looked at her with a kindly, amused smile.

"What is it?" he asked.

"Why, this murder at Charlotteville," answered Grandma, forgetting, in her excitement, that it was not safe to talk to people you meet on the train. "It just makes my blood run cold to read about it. And to think that the man who did it is still around the country somewhere—plotting other murders, I haven't a doubt. What is the good of the police?"

"They're dull fellows," agreed the dark man.

"But I don't envy that man his conscience," said Grandma solemnly—and somewhat inconsistently, in view of her statement about the other murders that were being plotted. "What must a man feel like who has the blood of a fellow creature on his hands? Depend upon it, his punishment has begun already, caught or not."

"That is true," said the dark man quietly.

"Such a good-looking man too," said Grandma, looking wistfully at the murderer's picture. "It doesn't seem possible that he can have killed anybody. But the paper says there isn't a doubt."

"He is probably guilty," said the dark man, "but nothing is known of his provocation. The affair may not have been so cold-blooded as the accounts state. Those newspaper fellows never err on the side of undercolouring."

"I really think," said Grandma slowly, "that I would like to see a murderer—just one. Whenever I say anything like that, Adelaide—Adelaide is Samuel's wife—looks at me as if she thought there was something wrong about me. And perhaps there is, but I do, all the same. When I was a little girl, there was a man in our settlement who was suspected of poisoning his wife. She died very suddenly. I used to look at him with such interest. But it wasn't satisfactory, because you could never be sure whether he was really guilty or not. I never could believe that he was, because he was such a nice man in some ways and so good and kind to children. I don't believe a man who was bad enough to poison his wife could have any good in him."

"Perhaps not," agreed the dark man. He had absent-mindedly folded up Grandma's old copy of the *Argus* and put it in his pocket. Grandma did not like to ask him for it, although she would have liked to see if there were any more murder stories in it. Besides, just at that moment the conductor came around for tickets.

Grandma looked in the basket for her handkerchief. It was not there. She looked on the floor and on the seat and under the seat. It was not there. She stood up and shook herself—still no handkerchief.

"Dear, oh dear," exclaimed Grandma wildly, "I've lost my ticket—I always knew I would—I told Cyrus I would! Oh, where can it be?"

The conductor scowled unsympathetically. The dark man got up and helped Grandma search, but no ticket was to be found.

"You'll have to pay the money then, and something extra," said the conductor gruffly.

"I can't—I haven't a cent of money," wailed Grandma. "I gave it all to Cyrus because I was afraid my pocket would be picked. Oh, what shall I do?"

"Don't worry. I'll make it all right," said the dark man. He took out his pocketbook and handed the conductor a bill. That functionary grumblingly made the change and marched onward, while Grandma, pale with excitement and relief, sank back into her seat.

"I can't tell you how much I am obliged to you, sir," she said tremulously. "I don't know what I should have done. Would he have put me off right here in the snow?"

"I hardly think he would have gone to such lengths," said the dark man with a smile. "But he's a cranky, disobliging fellow enough—I know him of old. And you must not feel overly grateful to me. I am glad of the opportunity to help you. I had an old grandmother myself once," he added with a sigh.

"You must give me your name and address, of course," said Grandma, "and my son—Samuel Sheldon of Midverne—will see that the money is returned to you. Well, this is a lesson to me! I'll never trust myself on a train again, and all I wish is that I was safely off this one. This fuss has worked my nerves all up again."

"Don't worry, Grandma. I'll see you safely off the train when we get to Green Village."

"Will you, though? Will you, now?" said Grandma eagerly. "I'll be real easy in my mind, then," she added with a returning smile. "I feel as if I could trust you for anything—and I'm a real suspicious person too."

They had a long talk after that—or, rather, Grandma talked and the dark man listened and smiled. She told him all about William George and Delia and their baby and about Samuel and Adelaide and Cyrus and Louise and the three cats and the parrot. He seemed to enjoy her accounts of them too.

When they reached Green Village station he gathered up Grandma's parcels and helped her tenderly off the train.

"Anybody here to meet Mrs. Sheldon?" he asked of the station master.

The latter shook his head. "Don't think so. Haven't seen anybody here to meet anybody tonight."

"Dear, oh dear," said poor Grandma. "This is just what I expected. They've never got Cyrus's telegram. Well, I might have known it. What shall I do?"

"How far is it to your son's?" asked the dark man.

"Only half a mile—just over the hill there. But I'll never get there alone this dark night."

"Of course not. But I'll go with you. The road is good—we'll do finely."

"But that train won't wait for you," gasped Grandma, half in protest.

"It doesn't matter. The Starmont freight passes here in half an hour and I'll go on her. Come along, Grandma."

"Oh, but you're good," said Grandma. "Some woman is proud to have you for a son."

The man did not answer. He had not answered any of the personal remarks Grandma had made to him in her conversation.

They were not long in reaching William George Sheldon's house, for the village road was good and Grandma was smart on her feet. She was welcomed with eagerness and surprise.

"To think that there was no one to meet you!" exclaimed William George. "But I never dreamed of your coming by train, knowing how you were set against it. Telegram? No, I got no telegram. S'pose Cyrus forgot to send it. I'm most heartily obliged to you, sir, for looking after my mother so kindly."

"It was a pleasure," said the dark man courteously. He had taken off his hat, and they saw a curious scar, shaped like a large, red butterfly, high up on his forehead under his hair. "I am delighted to have been of any assistance to her."

He would not wait for supper — the next train would be in and he must not miss it.

"There are people looking for me," he said with his curious smile. "They will be much disappointed if they do not find me."

He had gone, and the whistle of the Starmont freight had blown before Grandma remembered that he had not given her his name and address.

"Dear, oh dear, how are we ever going to send that money to him?" she exclaimed. "And he so nice and goodhearted!"

Grandma worried over this for a week in the intervals of looking after Delia. One day William George came in with a large city daily in his hands. He looked curiously at Grandma and then showed her the front-page picture of a man, clean-shaven, with an oddly shaped scar high up on his forehead.

"Did you ever see that man, Mother?" he asked.

"Of course I did," said Grandma excitedly. "Why, it's the man I met on the train. Who is he? What is his name? Now, we'll know where to send —"

"That is Mark Hartwell, who shot Amos Gray at Charlotteville three weeks ago," said William George quietly.

Grandma looked at him blankly for a moment.

"It couldn't be," she gasped at last. "That man a murderer! I'll never believe it!"

"It's true enough, Mother. The whole story is here. He had shaved his beard and dyed his hair and came near getting clear out of the country. They were on his trail the day he came down in the train with you and lost it because of his getting off to bring you here. His disguise was so perfect that there was little fear of his being recognized so long as he hid that scar. But it was seen in Montreal and he was run to earth there. He has made a full confession."

"I don't care," cried Grandma valiantly. "I'll never believe he was all bad—a man who would do what he did for a poor old woman like me, when he was flying for his life too. No, no, there was good in him even if he did kill that man. And I'm sure he must feel terrible over it."

In this view Grandma persisted. She never would say or listen to a word against Mark Hartwell, and she had only pity for him whom everyone else condemned. With her own trembling hands she wrote him a letter to accompany the money Samuel sent before Hartwell was taken to the penitentiary for life. She thanked him again for his kindness to her and assured him that she knew he was sorry for what he had done and that she would pray for him every night of her life. Mark Hartwell had been hard and defiant enough, but the prison officials told that he cried like a child over Grandma Sheldon's little letter.

"There's nobody all bad," says Grandma when she relates the story. "I used to believe a murderer must be, but I know better now. I think of that poor man often and often. He was so kind and gentle to me—he must have been a good boy once. I write him a letter every Christmas and I send him tracts and papers. He's my own little charity. But I've never been on the cars since and I never will be again. You never can tell what will happen to you or what sort of people you'll meet if you trust yourself on a train."

The Romance of Jedediah

Jedediah was not a name that savoured of romance. His last name was Crane, which is little better. And it would be no use to call this story "Mattie Adams's Romance" because Mattie Adams is not a romantic name either. But names have really nothing to do with romance. The most exciting and tragic affair I ever knew was between a man named Silas Putdammer and a woman named Kezia Cullen — which has nothing to do with the present story.

Jedediah, to all outward seeming, did not appear to be any more romantic than his name. He looked distinctly commonplace as he rode comfortably along the winding country road that was dreaming in the haze and sunshine of a midsummer afternoon. He was perched on the seat of a bright red pedlar's wagon, above and behind a dusty, ambling, red pony of that peculiar gait and appearance pertaining to the ponies of country pedlars — a certain placid, unhasting leanness, as of a nag that has encountered troubles of his own and has lived them down by sheer patience and staying power. From the bright red wagon proceeded a certain metallic rumbling and clinking as it bowled along, and two or three nests of tin pans on its flat rope-encircled top flashed back the light so dazzlingly that Jedediah seemed the beaming sun of a little planetary system all his own. A new broom sticking up aggressively at each of the four corners gave the wagon a resemblance to a triumphal chariot.

Jedediah himself had not been in the tin-peddling business long enough to acquire the apologetic, out-at-elbows appearance which distinguishes a tin pedlar from other kinds of pedlars. In fact, this was his maiden venture in this line; hence he still looked plump and self-respecting. He had a round red face under his plug hat, twinkling blue eyes, and a little pursed-up mouth, the shape of which was partly due to nature and partly to much whistling. Jedediah's pudgy body was clothed in a suit of large, light checks, and he wore a bright pink necktie and an amethyst pin. Will I still be believed when I assert that, in spite of all this, Jedediah was full of, and bubbling over with, romance?

Romance cares not for appearances and apparently delights in contradictions. The homely shambling man you pass unnoticed on the street may have, tucked away in his past, a story more exciting and thrilling than anything you have ever read in fiction. So it was, in a measure, with Jedediah; poor, unknown to fame, afflicted with a double chin and bald spot, reduced to driving a tin-wagon for a living, he yet had his romance and he was still romantic.

As Jedediah rode through Amberley he looked about him with interest. He knew it well, although it was fifteen years since he had seen it. He had been born and brought up in Amberley; he had left it at the age of twenty-five to make his fortune. But Amberley was Amberley still. Jedediah found it hard to believe that it or himself was fifteen years older.

"There's the Stanton place," he said. "Charlie has painted the house yellow — it used to be white; and Bob Hollman has cut the trees down behind the blacksmith forge. Bob never had any poetry in his soul — no romance, as you might say. He was what you might call a plodder — you might call him that. Get up, my nag, get up. There's the old Harkness place — seems to be spruced up considerable. Folks used to say if ye wanted to see how the world looked the morning after the flood just go into George Harkness's barn-yard on a rainy day. The pond and the old hills ain't changed any. Get up, my nag, get up. There's the Adams homestead. Do I really behold it again?"

Jedediah thought the moment deliciously romantic. He revelled in it and, to match his exhilarated mood, he touched the pony with his whip and went clinking and glittering down the hill under the poplars at a dashing rate. He had not intended to offer his wares in Amberley that day. He meant to break the ice in Occidental, the village beyond. But he could not pass the Adams place. When he came to the open gate he turned in under the willows and drove down the wide, shady lane, girt on both sides with a trim white paling smothered in lavish sweetbriar bushes that were gay with bloom. Jedediah's heart was beating furiously under his checks.

"What a fool you are, Jed Crane," he told himself. "You used to be a young fool, and now you're an old one. Sad, that! Get up, my nag, get up. It's a poor lookout for a man of your years, Jed. Don't get excited. It ain't the least likely that Mattie Adams is here yet. She's married and gone years ago, no doubt. It's probable there's no Adamses here at all now. But it's romantic, yes, it's romantic. It's splendid. Get up, my nag, get up."

The Adams place itself was not unromantic. The house was a large, old-fashioned white one, with green shutters and a front porch with Grecian columns. These were thought very elegant in Amberley. Mrs. Carmody said they gave a house such a classical air. In this instance the classical effect was somewhat smothered in honeysuckle, which rioted over the whole porch and hung in pale yellow, fragrant festoons over the rows of potted scarlet geraniums that flanked the green steps. Beyond the house a low-boughed orchard covered the slope between it and the main road, and behind it there was a revel of colour betokening a flower garden.

Jedediah climbed down from his lofty seat and walked dubiously to a side door that looked more friendly, despite its prim screen, than the classical front porch. As he drew near he saw a woman sitting behind the screen—a woman who rose as he approached and opened the door. Jedediah's heart had been beating a wild tattoo as he crossed the yard. It now stopped altogether—at least he declared in later years it did.

The woman was Mattie Adams—Mattie Adams fifteen years older than when he had seen her last, plumper, rosier, somewhat broader-faced, but still unmistakably Mattie Adams. Jedediah felt that the situation was delicious.

"Mattie," he said, holding out his hand.

"Why, Jed, how are you?" said Mattie, as if they had parted the week before. It had always taken a great deal to disturb Mattie. Whatever happened she was calm. Even an old lover, and the only one she had ever possessed at that, dropping, so to speak, from the skies, after fifteen years' disappearance, did not ruffle her placidity.

"I didn't suppose you'd know me, Mattie," said Jedediah, still holding her hand foolishly.

"I knew you the minute I set eyes on you," returned Mattie. "You're some fatter and older—like myself—but you're Jed still. Where have you been all these years?"

"Pretty near everywhere, Mattie—pretty near everywhere. And ye see what it's come to—here I be driving a tin-wagon for Boone Brothers. Business is business—don't you want to buy some new tinware?"

To himself, Jed thought it was romantic, asking a woman whom he had loved all his life to buy tins on the occasion of their first meeting after fifteen years' separation.

"I don't know but I do want a quart measure," said Mattie, in her sweet, unchanged voice, "but all in good time. You must stay and have tea with me, Jed. I'm all alone now—Mother and Father have gone. Unhitch your horse and put him in the third stall in the stable."

Jed hesitated.

"I ought to be getting on, I s'pose," he said wistfully. "I hain't done much today—"

"You must stay to tea," interrupted Mattie. "Why, Jed, there's ever so much to tell and ask. And we can't stand here in the yard and talk. Look at Selena. There she is, watching us from the kitchen window. She'll watch as long as we stand here."

Jed swung himself around. Over the little valley below the Adams homestead was a steep, treeless hill, and on its crest was perched a bare farmhouse with windows stuck lavishly all over it. At one of them a long, pale face was visible.

"Has Selena been pasted up at that window ever since the last time we stood here and talked, Mattie?" asked Jed, half resentfully, half amusedly. It was characteristic of Mattie to laugh first at the question, and then blush over the memory it revived.

"Most of the time, I guess," she said shortly. "But come—come in. I never could talk under Selena's eyes, even if they were four hundred yards away."

Jed went in and stayed to tea. The old Adams pantry had not failed, nor apparently the Adams skill in cooking. After tea Jed hung around till sunset and drove away with a warm invitation from Mattie to call every time his rounds took him through Amberley. As he went, Selena's face appeared at the window of the house over the valley.

When he had gone Mattie went around to the classical porch and sat herself down under the honeysuckle festoons that dangled above her smooth braids of fawn-coloured hair. She knew Selena would be down posthaste presently, agog with curiosity to find out who the pedlar was whom Mattie had delighted to honour with an invitation to tea. Mattie preferred to meet Selena out of doors. It was easier to thrust and parry there. Meanwhile, she wanted to think over things.

Fifteen years before Jedediah Crane had been Mattie Adams's beau. Jedediah was romantic even then, but, as he was a slim young fellow at the time, with an abundance of fair, curly hair and innocent blue eyes, his romance was rather an attraction than not. At least the then young and pretty Mattie had found it so.

The Adamses looked with no favour on the match. They were a thrifty, well-to-do folk. As for the Cranes—well, they were lazy and shiftless, for the most part. It would be a *mésalliance* for an Adams to marry a Crane. Still, it would doubtless have happened—for Mattie, though a meek-looking damsel, had a mind of her own—had it not been for Selena Ford, Mattie's older sister.

Selena, people said, had married James Ford for no other reason than that his house commanded a view of nearly every dooryard in Amberley. This may or may not have been sheer malice. Certainly nothing that went on in the Adams yard escaped Selena.

She watched Mattie and Jed in the moonlight one night. She saw Jed kiss Mattie. It was the first time he had ever done so—and the last, poor fellow. For Selena swooped down on her parents the next day. Such a storm did she brew up that Mattie was forbidden to speak to Jed again. Selena herself gave Jed a piece of her mind. Jed usually was not afflicted with undue sensitiveness. But he had some slumbering pride at the basis of his character and it was very stubborn when roused. Selena roused it. Jed vowed he would never creep and crawl at the feet of the Adamses, and he went west forthwith, determined, as aforesaid, to make his fortune and hurl Selena's scorn back in her face.

And now he had come home, driving a tin-wagon. Mattie smiled to think of it. She bore Jed no ill will for his failure. She felt sorry for him and inclined to think that fate had used him hardly — fate and Selena together. Mattie had never had another beau. People thought she was engaged to Jed Crane until her time for beaus went by. Mattie did not mind; she had never liked anybody so well as Jed. To be sure, she had not thought of him for years. It was strange he should come back like this — "romantic," as he said himself.

Mattie's reverie was interrupted by Selena. Angular, pale-eyed Mrs. Ford was as unlike the plump, rosy Mattie as a sister could be. Perhaps her chronic curiosity, which would not let her rest, was accountable for her excessive leanness.

"Who was that pedlar that was here this afternoon, Mattie?" she demanded as soon as she arrived.

Mattie smiled. "Jed Crane," she said. "He's home from the West and driving a tin-wagon for the Boones."

Selena gave a little gasp. She sat down on the lowest step and untied her bonnet strings.

"Mattie Adams! And you kept him hanging about the whole afternoon."

"Why not?" said Mattie wickedly. She liked to alarm Selena. "Jed and I were always beaus, you know."

"Mattie Adams! You don't mean to say you're going to make a fool of yourself over Jed Crane again? A woman of your age!"

"Don't get excited, Selena," implored Mattie. In the old days Selena could cow her, but that time was past. "I never saw the like of you for getting stirred up over nothing."

"I'm not excited. I'm perfectly calm. But I might well be excited over your folly, Mattie Adams. The idea of your taking up again with old Jed Crane!"

"He's fifteen years younger than Jim," said Mattie, giving thrust for thrust.

When Selena had come over Mattie had not the slightest idea of resuming her former relationship with the romantic Jedediah. She had merely shown him kindness for old friendship's sake. But so well did the unconscious Selena work in Jed's behalf that when she flounced off home in a pet Mattie was resolved that she would take Jed back if he wanted to come. She wasn't going to put up with Selena's everlasting interference. She would show her that she was independent.

When a week had passed Jed came again. He sold Mattie a stew-pan and he would not go in to tea this time, but they stood and talked in the yard for the best part of an hour, while Selena glared at them from her kitchen window. Their conversation was most innocent and harmless, being mainly gossip about what had come and gone during Jed's exile. But Mattie knew that Selena thought that she and Jed were making love to each other in this shameless, public fashion. When Jed went, Mattie, more for Selena's benefit than his, broke off some sprays of honeysuckle and pinned them on his coat. The fragrance went with Jedediah as he drove through Amberley, and pleasant thoughts were born of it.

"It's romantic," he told the pony. "Blessed if it ain't romantic! Not that Mattie cares anything about me now. I know she don't. But it's just her kind way. She wants to cheer me up and let me know I've a friend still. Get up, my nag, get up. I ain't one to persoom on her kindness neither; I know my place. But still, say what you will, it's romantic — this sitooation. This is it. Here I be, loving the ground she walks on, as I've always done, and I can't let on that I do because I'm a poor ne'er-do-well as ain't fit to look at her, an independent woman with property. And she's a-showing kindness to me for old times' sake, and piercing my heart all the time, not knowing. Why, it's romance with a vengeance, that's what it is. Get up, my nag, get up."

Thereafter Jed called at the Adams place every week. Generally he stayed to tea. Mattie always bought something of him to colour an excuse. Her kitchen fairly glittered with new tinware. She gave Selena the overflow by way of heaping coals of fire.

After every visit Jedediah held stern counsel with himself and decided that he must not call to see Mattie again — at least, not for a long time; then he must not stay to tea. He would struggle with himself all the way down the poplar hill — not without a comforting sense of the romance of the struggle — but it always ended the same way. He turned in under the willows and clinked musically into Mattie's yard. At least, the rattle of the tin-wagon sounded musically to Mattie.

Meanwhile, Selena watched from her window and raged.

Amberley people shrugged their shoulders when gossip noised the matter abroad. But, being good-humoured in the main, they forebore to do more than say that Mattie Adams was free to make a goose of herself if it pleased her, and that Jed Crane wasn't such a fool as he looked. The Adams farm was one of the best in Amberley, and it had not grown any poorer under Mattie's management.

"If Jed walks in there and hangs up his hat he'll have done well for himself after all."

This was Selena's view of it also, barring the good nature. She was furious at the whole affair, and she did her best to make Mattie's life a burden to her with slurs and thrusts. But they all misjudged Jed. He had no intention of "walking in and hanging up his hat" — or trying to. Romantic as he was, it never occurred to him that Mattie might be as romantic as himself. She did not care for him, and anyhow he, Jed, had a little too much pride to ask her, a rich woman, to marry him, a poor man who had lost all caste he ever possessed by taking up tin-peddling. Jed was determined not to "persoom." And, oh, how deliciously romantic it all was! He hugged himself with sorrowful delight over it.

As the summer waned and the long yellow leaves began to fall thickly from the willows in the Adams lane Jed began to talk of going out west again. Tin-peddling was not possible in winter, and he didn't think he would try it another summer. Mattie listened with dismay in her heart. All summer she had made much of Jed, by way of tormenting Selena. But now she realized what he really meant to her. The old love had wakened to life in her heart; she could not let Jed go out of her life again, leaving her to the old loneliness. If Jed went away everything would be flat, stale, and unprofitable.

She knew him to be at heart the kindest, most gentle of human beings, and the mere fact of his having been unsuccessful, even what some of his old neighbours might call stupid, did not change her feelings toward him in the least. He was Jed — that was sufficient for her, and she had business capability enough for both, when it came to that.

Mattie began to drop hints. But Jed would not take them. True, once or twice he thought that perhaps Mattie did care a little for him yet. But it would not do for him to take advantage of that.

"No, I just couldn't do that," he told the pony. "I worship the ground that woman treads on, but it ain't for the likes of me to tell her so, not now. Get up, my nag, get up. This has been a mighty pleasant summer with that visit to look forward to every week. But it's about over now and you must tramp, Jed."

Jed sighed. He remembered that it was more romantic than ever, but all at once this failed to comfort him. Romance up to a certain point was food; beyond that it palled, so to speak. Jed's romance failed him just when he needed it most.

Mattie, meanwhile, was forced to the dismal conclusion that her hints were thrown away. Jed was plainly determined not to speak. Mattie felt half angry with him. She did not choose to make a martyr of herself to romance, and surely the man didn't expect her to ask him to marry her.

"I'm sure and certain he's as fond of me as ever he was," she mused. "I suppose he's got some ridiculous notion about being too poor to aspire to me. Jed always had more pride than a Crane could carry. Well, I've done all I can — all I'm going to do. If Jed's determined to go, he must go, I s'pose."

Mattie would not let herself cry, although she felt like it. She went out and picked apples instead.

Mattie might have remained so and Jedediah's romance might never have reached a better ending, if it had not been for Selena, who came over just then to help Mattie pick the golden russets. Fate had evidently destined her as Jed's best helper. All summer she had been fairly goading Mattie into love with Jedediah and now she was moved to add the last spur.

"Jed Crane's going away, I hear," she said maliciously. "Seems to me you're bound to be jilted again, Mattie."

Mattie had no answer ready. Selena went on undauntedly.

"You've made a nice fool of yourself all summer, I vow. Throwing yourself at Jed's head — and he doesn't want you, even with all your property."

"He does want me," said Mattie calmly. Her lips were very firm and her cheeks scarlet. "He is not going away. We are to be married about Christmas, and Jed will take charge of the farm for me."

"Matilda Adams!" said Selena. It was all she was capable of saying.

The rest of the golden russets were picked in a dead silence, Mattie working with an unusually high colour in her cheeks, while Selena's thin lips were pressed so closely together as to be little else than a hair line.

After Selena had gone home, sulking, Mattie picked on with a very determined face. The die was cast; she could not bear Selena's slurs and she would not. And she had not told a lie either. Her words were true; she would make them true. All the Adams determination — and that was not a little — was roused in her.

"If Jed jilts me, he'll do it to my face, clean and clever," she said viciously.

When Jed came again he was very solemn. He thought it would be his last visit, but Mattie felt differently. She had dressed herself with unusual care and crimped her hair. Her cheeks were scarlet and her eyes bright. Jed thought she looked younger and prettier than ever. The thought that this was the last time he would see her for many a long day to come grew more and more unbearable, yet he firmly determined he would let no presuming word pass his lips. Mattie had been so kind to him. It was only honourable of him in return not to let her throw herself away on a poor failure like himself.

"I suppose this is your last round with the wagon," she said. She had taken him out into the garden to say it. The garden was out of view from the Ford place. Propose she must, but she drew the line at proposing under Selena's eyes.

Jed nodded dully. "Yes, and then I must toddle off and look for something else to do. You see, I haven't much of a gift so to speak for business, Mattie, and it takes me so long to get worked into an understanding of a business or trade that I'm generally asked to quit before you might say I've really commenced. It's been a mighty happy summer for me, though I can't say I've done much in the selling line except to you, Mattie. What with your kindness and these little visits you've been good enough to let me make every week, I feel I may say it's been the happiest summer of my life, and I'm never going to forget it, but as I said, it's time for me to be moving on elsewhere and finding something else to do."

"There is something for you to do right here—if you will do it," said Mattie faintly. For a moment she felt as if she could not go on; Jed and the garden and the scarf of late asters whirled around her dizzily. She held by the sweet-pea trellis to steady herself.

"I—I said a terrible thing to Selena the other day. I—I don't know what I'll do about it if—if—you don't help me out, Jed."

"I'll do anything I can," said Jed, with hearty sympathy. "You know that, Mattie. What is the trouble?"

His kindly voice and the good will and affection beaming in his honest blue eyes gave Mattie renewed courage to go on with her self-imposed and most embarrassing task, although before she ended her voice shook and dwindled away to such a low whisper that Jed had to bend his head close to hers to hear what she was saying.

"I—I said—she goaded me into saying it, Jed—slighting and slurring—jeering at me because you were going away. I just got mad, Jed—and I told her you weren't going—that you and I—that we were to be—married."

"Mattie, did you mean that?" he cried. "If you did, I'm the happiest man alive. I didn't dare persoom—I didn't s'pose you thought anything of me. But if you do—and if you want me—here's all there is of me, heart and soul and body, forever and ever, as I've been all my life."

Thinking over this speech afterwards Jed was dissatisfied with it. He thought he might have made it much more eloquent and romantic than it was. But it served the purpose very well. It was convincing—it came straight from his honest, stupid heart, and Mattie knew it. She held out her hands and Jed gathered her into his arms.

It was certainly a most fortunate circumstance that the garden was well out of the range of Selena's vision, or the sight of her sister and the remaining member of the despised Crane family repeating their foolish performance, which many years previous had resulted in Jed's long banishment, might have caused her to commit almost any unheard-of act of spite as an outlet for her jealous anger. But only the few remaining garden flowers were witness to the lovers' indiscretion, and they kept their own counsel after the manner of flowers, so Selena's feelings were mercifully spared this further outrage.

That evening Jed drove slowly away through the twilight, mounted for the last time on the tin-wagon. He was so happy that he bore no grudge against even Selena Ford. As the pony climbed the poplar hill Jed drew a long breath and freed his mind to the surrounding landscape and to his faithful and slow-plodding steed that had been one of the main factors in this love affair, having patiently carried him to and from the abode of his lady-love throughout the summer just passed. Jedediah was as brimful of happiness as mortal man could be, and his rosy thoughts flowed forth in a kind of triumphant chant which would have driven Selena stark distracted had she been within hearing distance. What he said too was but a poor expression of what he thought, but to the trees and fields and pony he chanted,

"Well, this *is* romance. What else would you call it now? Me, poor, scared to speak — and Mattie ups and does it for me, bless her. Yes, I've been longing for romance all my life, and I've got it at last. None of your commonplace courtships for me, I always said. Them was my very words. And I guess this has been a little uncommon — I guess it has. Anyhow, I'm uncommon happy. I never felt so romantic before. Get up, my nag, get up."

The Tryst of the White Lady

"I wisht ye'd git married, Roger," said Catherine Ames. "I'm gitting too old to work—seventy last April—and who's going to look after ye when I'm gone. Git married, b'y—git married."

Roger Temple winced. His aunt's harsh, disagreeable voice always jarred horribly on his sensitive nerves. He was fond of her after a fashion, but always that voice made him wonder if there could be anything harder to endure.

Then he gave a bitter little laugh.

"Who'd have me, Aunt Catherine?" he asked.

Catherine Ames looked at him critically across the supper table. She loved him in her way, with all her heart, but she was not in the least blind to his defects. She did not mince matters with herself or with other people. Roger was a sallow, plain-featured fellow, small and insignificant looking. And, as if this were not bad enough, he walked with a slight limp and had one thin shoulder a little higher than the other—"Jarback" Temple he had been called in school, and the name still clung to him. To be sure, he had very fine grey eyes, but their dreamy brilliance gave his dull face an uncanny look which girls did not like, and so made matters rather worse than better. Of course looks didn't matter so much in the case of a man; Steve Millar was homely enough, and all marked up with smallpox to boot, yet he had got for wife the prettiest and smartest girl in South Bay. But Steve was rich. Roger was poor and always would be. He worked his stony little farm, from which his father and grandfather had wrested a fair living, after a fashion, but Nature had not cut him out for a successful farmer. He hadn't the strength for it and his heart wasn't in it. He'd rather be hanging over a book. Catherine secretly thought Roger's matrimonial chances very poor, but it would not do to discourage the b'y. What he needed was spurring on.

"Ye'll git someone if ye don't fly too high," she announced loudly and cheerfully. "Thar's always a gal or two here and thar that's glad to marry for a home. 'Tain't no use for *you* to be settin' your thoughts on anyone young and pretty. Ye wouldn't git her and ye'd be worse off if ye did. Your grandfather married for looks, and a nice useless wife he got—sick half her time. Git a good strong girl that ain't afraid of work, that'll hold things together when ye're reading po'try—that's as much as you kin expect. And the sooner the better. I'm done—last winter's rheumatiz has about finished *me*. An' we can't afford hired help."

Roger felt as if his raw, quivering soul were being seared. He looked at his aunt curiously—at her broad, flat face with the mole on the end of her dumpy nose, the bristling hairs on her chin, the wrinkled yellow neck, the pale, protruding eyes, the coarse, good-humoured mouth. She was so extremely ugly—and he had seen her across the table all his life. For twenty-five years he had looked at her so. Must he continue to go on looking at ugliness in the shape of a wife all the rest of his life—he, who worshipped beauty in everything?

"Did my mother look like you, Aunt Catherine?" he asked abruptly.

His aunt stared—and snorted. Her snort was meant to express kindly amusement, but it sounded like derision and contempt.

"Yer ma wasn't so humly as me," she said cheerfully, "but she wan't no beauty either. None of the Temples was ever better lookin' than was necessary. We was *workers*. Yer pa wa'n't bad looking. You're humlier than either of 'em. Some ways ye take after yer grandma—though *she* was counted pretty at one time. She was yaller and spindlin' like you, and you've got her eyes. What yer so int'rested in yer ma's looks all at once fer?"

"I was wondering," said Roger coolly, "if Father ever looked at her across the table and wished she were prettier."

Catherine giggled. Her giggle was ugly and disagreeable like everything else about her—everything except a certain odd, loving, loyal old heart buried deep in her bosom, for the sake of which Roger endured the giggle and all the rest.

"Dessay he did—dessay he did. Men al'ays has a hankerin' for good looks. But ye've got to cut yer coat 'cording to yer cloth. As for yer poor ma, she didn't live long enough to git as ugly as me. When I come here to keep house for yer pa, folks said as it wouldn't be long 'fore he married me. *I* wouldn't a-minded. But yer pa never hinted it. S'pose he'd had enough of ugly women likely."

Catherine snorted amiably again. Roger got up—he couldn't endure any more just then. He must escape.

"Now you think over what I've said," his aunt called after him. "Ye've gotter git a wife soon, however ye manage it. 'Twon't be so hard if ye're reasonable. Don't stay out as late as ye did last night. Ye coughed all night. Where was ye—down at the shore?"

"No," said Roger, who always answered her questions even when he hated to. "I was down at Aunt Isabel's grave."

"Till eleven o'clock! Ye ain't wise! I dunno what hankering ye have after that unchancy place. *I* ain't been near it for twenty year. I wonder ye ain't scairt. What'd ye think ye'd do if ye saw her ghost?"

Catherine looked curiously at Roger. She was very superstitious and she believed firmly in ghosts, and saw no absurdity in her question.

"I wish I *could* see it," said Roger, his great eyes flashing. He believed in ghosts too, at least in Isabel Temple's ghost. His uncle had seen it; his grandfather had seen it; he believed he would see it — the beautiful, bewitching, mocking, luring ghost of lovely Isabel Temple.

"Don't wish such stuff," said Catherine. "Nobody ain't never the same after they've seen her."

"Was Uncle different?" Roger had come back into the kitchen and was looking curiously at his aunt.

"Diff'rent? He was another man. He didn't even *look* the same. Sich eyes! Al'ays looking past ye at something behind ye. They'd give anyone creeps. He never had any notion of flesh-and-blood women after that — said a man wouldn't, after seeing Isabel. His life was plumb ruined. Lucky he died young. I hated to be in the same room with him — he wa'n't canny, that was all there was to it. *You* keep away from that grave — *you* don't want to look odder than ye are by nature. And when ye git married, ye'll have to give up roamin' about half the night in graveyards. A wife wouldn't put up with it, as I've done."

"I'll never get as good a wife as you, Aunt Catherine," said Roger with a little whimsical smile that gave him the look of an amused gnome.

"Dessay you won't. But someone ye have to have. Why'n't ye try 'Liza Adams. She *might* have ye — she's gittin' on."

"'Liza ... Adams!"

"That's what I said. Ye needn't repeat it — 'Liza ... Adams — 's if I'd mentioned a hippopotamus. I git out of patience with ye. I b'lieve in my heart ye think ye ought to git a wife that'd look like a picter."

"I do, Aunt Catherine. That's just the kind of wife I want — grace and beauty and charm. Nothing less than that will ever content me."

Roger laughed bitterly again and went out. It was sunset. There was no work to do that night except to milk the cows, and his little home boy could do that. He felt a glad freedom. He put his hand in his pocket to see if his beloved Wordsworth was there and then he took his way across the fields, under a sky of purple and amber, walking quickly despite his limp. He wanted to get to some solitary place where he could forget Aunt Catherine and her abominable suggestions and escape into the world of dreams where he habitually lived and where he found the loveliness he had not found nor could hope to find in his real world.

Roger's mother had died when he was three and his father when he was eight. His little, old, bedridden grandmother had lived until he was twelve. He had loved her passionately. She had not been pretty in his remembrance—a tiny, shrunken, wrinkled thing—but she had beautiful grey eyes that never grew old and a soft, gentle voice—the only woman's voice he had ever heard with pleasure. He was very critical as regards women's voices and very sensitive to them. Nothing hurt him quite so much as an unlovely voice—not even unloveliness of face. Her death had left him desolate. She was the only human being who had ever understood him. He could never, he thought, have got through his tortured school days without her. After she died he would not go to school. He was not in any sense educated. His father and grandfather had been illiterate men and he had inherited their underdeveloped brain cells. But he loved poetry and read all he could get of it. It overlaid his primitive nature with a curious iridescence of fancy and furnished him with ideals and hungers his environment could never satisfy. He loved beauty in everything. Moonrises hurt him with their loveliness and he could sit for hours gazing at a white narcissus—much to his aunt's exasperation. He was solitary by nature. He felt horribly alone in a crowded building but never in the woods or in the wild places along the shore. It was because of this that his aunt could not get him to go to church—which was a horror to her orthodox soul. He told her he would like to go to church if it were empty but he could not bear it when it was full—full of smug, ugly people. Most people, he thought, were ugly— though not so ugly as he was—and ugliness made him sick with repulsion. Now and then he saw a pretty girl at whom he liked to look but he never saw one that wholly pleased him. To him, the homely, crippled, poverty-stricken Roger Temple whom they all would have scorned, there was always a certain subtle something wanting, and the lack of it kept him heartwhole. He knew that this probably saved him from much suffering, but for all that he regretted it. He wanted to love, even vainly; he wanted to experience this passion of which the poets sang so much. Without it he felt he lacked the key to a world of wonder. He even tried to fall in love; he went to church for several Sundays and sat where he could see beautiful Elsa Carey. She was lovely—it gave him pleasure to look at her; the gold of her hair was so bright and living; the pink of her cheek so pure, the curve of her neck so flawless, the lashes of her eyes so dark and silken. But he looked at her as at a picture. When he tried to think and dream of her, it bored him. Besides, he knew she had a rather nasal voice. He used to laugh sarcastically to himself over Elsa's feelings if she had known how desperately he was trying to fall in love with her and failing — Elsa the queen of hearts, who believed she had only to look to reign. He gave up trying at last, but he still longed to love. He knew he would never marry; he could not marry plainness, and beauty would have none of him; but he did not want to miss everything and he had moments when he was very bitter and rebellious because he felt he must miss it forever.

He went straight to Isabel Temple's grave in the remote shore field of his farm. Isabel Temple had lived and died eighty years ago. She had been very lovely, very wilful, very fond of playing with the hearts of men. She had married William Temple, the brother of his great-grandfather, and as she stood in her white dress beside her bridegroom, at the conclusion of the wedding ceremony, a jilted lover, crazed by despair, had entered the house and shot her dead. She had been buried in the shore field, where a square space had been dyked off in the centre for a burial lot because the church was then so far away. With the passage of years the lot had grown up so thickly with fir and birch and wild cherry that it looked like a compact grove. A winding path led through it to its heart where Isabel Temple's grave was, thickly overgrown with long, silken, pale green grass. Roger hurried along the path and sat down on the big grey boulder by the grave, looking about him with a long breath of delight. How lovely — and witching — and unearthly it was here. Little ferns were growing in the hollows and cracks of the big boulder where clay had lodged. Over Isabel Temple's crooked, lichened gravestone hung a young wild cherry in its delicate bloom. Above it, in a little space of sky left by the slender tree tops, was a young moon. It was too dark here after all to read Wordsworth, but that did not matter. The place, with its moist air, its tang of fir balsam, was like a perfumed room where a man might dream dreams and see visions. There was a soft murmur of wind in the boughs over him, and the faraway moan of the sea on the bar crept in. Roger surrendered himself utterly to the charm of the place. When he entered that grove, he had left behind the realm of daylight and things known and come into the realm of shadow and mystery and enchantment. Anything might happen — anything might be true.

Eighty long years had come and gone, but Isabel Temple, thus cruelly torn from life at the moment when it had promised her most, did not even yet rest calmly in her grave; such at least was the story, and Roger believed it. It was in his blood to believe it. The Temples were a superstitious family, and there was nothing in Roger's upbringing to correct the tendency. His was not a sceptical or scientific mind. He was ignorant and poetical and credulous. He had always accepted unquestioningly the tale that Isabel Temple had been seen on earth long after the red clay was heaped over her murdered body. Her bridegroom had seen her, when he went to visit her on the eve of his second and unhappy marriage; his grandfather had seen her. His grandmother, who had told him Isabel's story, had told him this too, and believed it. She had added, with a bitterness foreign to his idea of her, that her husband had never been the same to her afterwards; his uncle had seen her—and had lived and died a haunted man. It was only to men the lovely, restless ghost appeared, and her appearance boded no good to him who saw. Roger knew this, but he had a curious longing to see her. He had never avoided her grave as others of his tribe did. He loved the spot, and he believed that some time he would see Isabel Temple there. She came, so the story went, to one in each generation of the family.

He gazed down at her sunken grave; a little wind, that came stealing along the floor of the grove, raised and swayed the long, hair-like grass on it, giving the curious suggestion of something prisoned under it trying to draw a long breath and float upward.

Then, when he lifted his eyes again, he saw her!

She was standing behind the gravestone, under the cherry tree, whose long white branches touched her head; standing there, with her head drooping a little, but looking steadily at him. It was just between dusk and dark now, but he saw her very plainly. She was dressed in white, with some filmy scarf over her head, and her hair hung in a dark heavy braid over her shoulder. Her face was small and ivory-white, and her eyes were very large and dark. Roger looked straight into them and they did something to him—drew something out of him that was never to be his again—his heart? his soul? He did not know. He only knew that lovely Isabel Temple had now come to him and that he was hers forever.

For a few moments that seemed years he looked at her—looked till the lure of her eyes drew him to his feet as a man rises in sleep-walking. As he slowly stood up, the low-hanging bough of a fir tree pushed his cap down over his face and blinded him. When he snatched it off, she was gone.

Roger Temple did not go home that night till the spring dawn was in the sky. Catherine was sleepless with anxiety about him. When she heard him come up the stairs, she opened her door and peeped out. Roger went along the hall without seeing her. His brilliant eyes stared straight before him, and there was something in his face that made Catherine steal back to her bed with a little shiver of fear. He looked like his uncle. She did not ask him, when they met at breakfast, where or how he had spent the night. He had been dreading the question and was relieved beyond measure when it was not asked. But, apart from that, he was hardly conscious of her presence. He ate and drank mechanically and voicelessly. When he had gone out, Catherine wagged her uncomely grey head ominously.

"He's bewitched," she muttered. "I know the signs. He's seen her—drat her! It's time she gave up that kind of work. Well, I dunno what to do—thar ain't anything I can do, I reckon. He'll never marry now—I'm as sure of that as of any mortal thing. He's in love with a ghost."

It had not yet occurred to Roger that he was in love. He thought of nothing but Isabel Temple—her lovely, lovely face, sweeter than any picture he had ever seen or any ideal he had dreamed, her long dark hair, her slim form and, more than all, her compelling eyes. He saw them wherever he looked—they drew him—he would have followed them to the end of the world, heedless of all else.

He longed for night, that he might again steal to the grave in the haunted grove. She might come again—who knew? He felt no fear, nothing but a terrible hunger to see her again. But she did not come that night—nor the next—nor the next. Two weeks went by and he had not seen her. Perhaps he would never see her again—the thought filled him with anguish not to be borne. He knew now that he loved her—Isabel Temple, dead for eighty years. This was love—this searing, torturing, intolerably sweet thing—this possession of body and soul and spirit. The poets had sung but weakly of it. He could tell them better if he could find words. Could other men have loved at all—could any man love those blowzy, common girls of earth? It seemed impossible—absurd. There was only one thing that could be loved—that white spirit. No wonder his uncle had died. He, Roger Temple, would soon die too. That would be well. Only the dead could woo Isabel. Meanwhile he revelled in his torment and his happiness—so madly commingled that he never knew whether he was in heaven or hell. It was beautiful—and dreadful—and wonderful—and exquisite—oh, so exquisite. Mortal love could never be so exquisite. He had never lived before—now he lived in every fibre of his being.

He was glad Aunt Catherine did not worry him with questions. He had feared she would. But she never asked any questions now and she was afraid of Roger, as she had been afraid of his uncle. She dared not ask questions. It was a thing that must not be tampered with. Who knew what she might hear if she asked him questions? She was very unhappy. Something dreadful had happened to her poor boy—he had been bewitched by that hussy—he would die as his uncle had died.

"Mebbe it's best," she muttered. "He's the last of the Temples, so mebbe she'll rest in her grave when she's killed 'em all. I dunno what she's sich a spite at *them* for—there'd be more sense if she'd haunt the Mortons, seein' as a Morton killed her. Well, I'm mighty old and tired and worn out. It don't seem that it's been much use, the way I've slaved and fussed to bring that b'y up and keep things together for him—and now the ghost's got him. I might as well have let him die when he was a sickly baby."

If this had been said to Roger he would have retorted that it was worthwhile to have lived long enough to feel what he was feeling now. He would not have missed it for a score of other men's lives. He had drunk of some immortal wine and was as a god. Even if she never came again, he had seen her once, and she had taught him life's great secret in that one unforgettable exchange of eyes. She was his—his in spite of his ugliness and his crooked shoulder. No man could ever take her from him.

But she did come again. One evening, when the darkening grove was full of magic in the light of the rising yellow moon shining across the level field, Roger sat on the big boulder by the grave. The evening was very still; there was no sound save the echoes of noisy laughter that seemed to come up from the bay shore—drunken fishermen, likely as not. Roger resented the intrusion of such a sound in such a place—it was a sacrilege. When he came here to dream of her, only the loveliest of muted sounds should be heard—the faintest whisper of trees, the half-heard, half-felt moan of surf, the airiest sigh of wind. He never read Wordsworth now or any other book. He only sat there and thought of her, his great eyes alight, his pale face flushed with the wonder of his love.

She slipped through the dark boughs like a moonbeam and stood by the stone. Again he saw her quite plainly—saw and drank her in with his eyes. He did not feel surprise—something in him had known she would come again. He would not move a muscle lest he lose her as he had lost her before. They looked at each other—for how long? He did not know; and then—a horrible thing happened. Into that place of wonder and revelation and mystery reeled a hiccoughing, laughing creature, a drunken sailor from a harbour ship, with a leering face and desecrating breath.

"Oh, you're here, my dear—I thought I'd catch you yet," he said.

He caught hold of her. She screamed. Roger sprang forward and struck him in the face. In his fury of sudden rage the strength of ten seemed to animate his slender body and pass into his blow. The sailor reeled back and put up his hands. He was a coward—and even a brave man might have been daunted by that terrible white face and those blazing eyes. He backed down the path.

"Shorry—shorry," he muttered. "Didn't know she was your girl—shorry I butted in. Shentlemans never butt in—shorry—shir—shorry."

He kept repeating his ridiculous "shorry" until he was out of the grove. Then he turned and ran stumblingly across the field. Roger did not follow; he went back to Isabel Temple's grave. The girl was lying across it; he thought she was unconscious. He stooped and picked her up—she was light and small, but she was warm flesh and blood; she clung uncertainly to him for a moment and he felt her breath on his face. He did not speak—he was too sick at heart. She did not speak either. He did not think this strange until afterwards. He was incapable of thinking just then; he was dazed, wretched, lost. Presently he became aware that she was timidly pulling his arm. It seemed that she wanted him to go with her—she was evidently frightened of that brute—he must take her to safety. And then—

She moved on down the little path and he followed. Out in the moonlit field he saw her clearly. With her drooping head, her flowing dark hair, her great brown eyes, she looked like the nymph of a wood-brook, a haunter of shadows, a creature sprung from the wild. But she was mortal maid, and he—what a fool he had been! Presently he would laugh at himself, when this dazed agony should clear away from his brain. He followed her down the long field to the bay shore. Now and then she paused and looked back to see if he were coming, but she never spoke. When she reached the shore road she turned and went along it until they came to an old grey house fronting the calm grey harbour. At its gate she paused. Roger knew now who she was. Catherine had told him about her a month ago.

She was Lilith Barr, a girl of eighteen, who had come to live with her uncle and aunt. Her father had died some months before. She was absolutely deaf as the result of some accident in childhood, and she was, as his own eyes told him, exquisitely lovely in her white, haunting style. But she was not Isabel Temple; he had tricked himself—he had lived in a fool's paradise—oh, he must get away and laugh at himself. He left her at her gate, disregarding the little hand she put timidly out—but he did not laugh at himself. He went back to Isabel Temple's grave and flung himself down on it and cried like a boy. He wept his stormy, anguished soul out on it; and when he rose and went away, he believed it was forever. He thought he could never, never go there again.

Catherine looked at him curiously the next morning. He looked wretched—haggard and hollow-eyed. She knew he had not come in till the summer dawn. But he had lost the rapt, uncanny look she hated; suddenly she no longer felt afraid of him. With this, she began to ask questions again.

"What kept ye out so late again last night, b'y?" she said reproachfully.

Roger looked at her in her morning ugliness. He had not really seen her for weeks. Now she smote on his tortured senses, so long drugged with beauty, like a physical blow. He suddenly burst into a laughter that frightened her.

"Preserve's, b'y, have ye gone mad? Or," she added, "have ye seen Isabel Temple's ghost?"

"No," said Roger loudly and explosively. "Don't talk any more about that damned ghost. Nobody ever saw it. The whole story is balderdash."

He got up and went violently out, leaving Catherine aghast. Was it possible Roger had sworn? What on earth had come over the b'y? But come what had or come what would, he no longer looked *fey*—there was that much to be thankful for. Even an occasional oath was better than that. Catherine went stiffly about her dish-washing, resolving to have 'Liza Adams to supper some night.

For a week Roger lived in agony—an agony of shame and humiliation and self-contempt. Then, when the edge of his bitter disappointment wore away, he made another dreadful discovery. He still loved her and longed for her just as keenly as before. He wanted madly to see her—her flower-like face, her great, asking eyes, the sleek, braided flow of her hair. Ghost or woman—spirit or flesh—it mattered not. He could not live without her. At last his hunger for her drew him to the old grey house on the bay shore. He knew he was a fool—she would never look at him; he was only feeding the flame that must consume him. But go he must and did, seeking for his lost paradise.

He did not see her when he went in, but Mrs. Barr received him kindly and talked about her in a pleasant garrulous fashion which jarred on Roger, yet he listened greedily. Lilith, her aunt told him, had been made deaf by the accidental explosion of a gun when she was eight years old. She could not hear a sound but she could talk.

"A little, that is—not much, but enough to get along with. But she don't like talking somehow—dunno why. She's shy—and we think maybe she don't like to talk much because she can't hear her own voice. She don't ever speak except just when she has to. But she's been trained to lip-reading something wonderful—she can understand anything that's said when she can see the person that's talking. Still, it's a terrible drawback for the poor child—she's never had any real girl-life and she's dreadful sensitive and retiring. We can't get her to go out anywhere, only for lonely walks along shore by herself. We're much obliged for what you did the other night. It ain't safe for her to wander about alone as she does, but it ain't often anybody from the harbour gets up this far. She was dreadful upset about it—hasn't got over her scare yet."

When Lilith came in, her ivory-white face went scarlet all over at the sight of Roger. She sat down in a shadowy corner. Mrs. Barr got up and went out. Roger was mute; he could find nothing to say. He could have talked glibly enough to Isabel Temple's ghost in some unearthly tryst by her grave, but he could not find a word to say to this slip of flesh and blood. He felt very foolish and absurd, and very conscious of his twisted shoulder. What a fool he had been to come!

Then Lilith looked up at him—and smiled. A little shy, friendly smile. Roger suddenly saw her not as the tantalizing, unreal, mystic thing of the twilit grove, but as a little human creature, exquisitely pretty in her young-moon beauty, longing for companionship. He got up, forgetting his ugliness, and went across the room to her.

"Will you come for a walk," he said eagerly. He held out his hand like a child; as a child she stood up and took it; like two children they went out and down the sunset shore. Roger was again incredibly happy. It was not the same happiness as had been his in that vanished fortnight; it was a homelier happiness with its feet on the earth. The amazing thing was that he felt she was happy too—happy because she was walking with *him*, "Jarback" Temple, whom no girl had even thought about. A certain secret well-spring of fancy that had seemed dry welled up in him sparklingly again.

Through the summer weeks the odd courtship went on. Roger talked to her as he had never talked to anyone. He did not find it in the least hard to talk to her, though her necessity of watching his face so closely while he talked bothered him occasionally. He felt that her intent gaze was reading his soul as well as his lips. She never talked much herself; what she did say she spoke so low that it was hardly above a whisper, but she had a voice as lovely as her face—sweet, cadenced, haunting. Roger was quite mad about her, and he was horribly afraid that he could never get up enough courage to ask her to marry him. And he was afraid that if he did, she would never consent. In spite of her shy, eager welcomes he could not believe she could care for him—for *him*. She liked him, she was sorry for him, but it was unthinkable that she, white, exquisite Lilith, could marry him and sit at his table and his hearth. He was a fool to dream of it.

To the existence of romance and glamour in which he lived, no gossip of the countryside penetrated. Yet much gossip there was, and at last it came blundering in on Roger to destroy his fairy world a second time. He came downstairs one night in the twilight, ready to go to Lilith. His aunt and an old crony were talking in the kitchen; the crony was old, and Catherine, supposing Roger was out of the house, was talking loudly in that horrible voice of hers with still more horrible zest and satisfaction.

"Yes, I'm guessing it'll be a match as ye say. Oh the b'y's doing well. He ain't for every market, as I'm bound to admit. Ef she wan't deaf she wouldn't look at him, no doubt. But she has scads of money—they won't need to do a tap of work unless they like—and she's a good housekeeper too her aunt tells me. She's pretty enough to suit him—he's as particular as never was—and he wan't crooked and she wan't deaf when they was born, so it's likely their children will be all right. I'm that proud when I think of the match."

Roger fled out of the house, white of face and sick of heart. He went, not to the bay shore, but to Isabel Temple's grave. He had never been there since the night when he had rescued Lilith, but now he rushed to it in his new agony. His aunt's horrible practicalities had filled him with disgust—they dragged his love in the dust of sordid things. And Lilith was rich; he had never known that—never suspected it. He could never ask her to marry him now; he must never see her again. For the second time he had lost her, and this second losing could not be borne.

He sat down on the big boulder by the grave and dropped his poor grey face in his hands, moaning in anguish. Nothing was left him, not even dreams. He hoped he could soon die.

He did not know how long he sat there—he did not know when she came. But when he lifted his miserable eyes, he saw her, sitting just a little way from him on the big stone and looking at him with something in her face that made his heart beat madly. He forgot Aunt Catherine's sacrilege—he forgot that he was a presumptuous fool. He bent forward and kissed her lips for the first time. The wonder of it loosed his bound tongue.

"Lilith," he gasped, "I love you."

She put her hand into his and nestled closer to him.

"I thought you would have told me that long ago," she said.

Uncle Richard's New Year's Dinner

Prissy Baker was in Oscar Miller's store New Year's morning, buying matches—for New Year's was not kept as a business holiday in Quincy—when her uncle, Richard Baker, came in. He did not look at Prissy, nor did she wish him a happy New Year; she would not have dared. Uncle Richard had not been on speaking terms with her or her father, his only brother, for eight years.

He was a big, ruddy, prosperous-looking man—an uncle to be proud of, Prissy thought wistfully, if only he were like other people's uncles, or, indeed, like what he used to be himself. He was the only uncle Prissy had, and when she had been a little girl they had been great friends; but that was before the quarrel, in which Prissy had had no share, to be sure, although Uncle Richard seemed to include her in his rancour.

Richard Baker, so he informed Mr. Miller, was on his way to Navarre with a load of pork.

"I didn't intend going over until the afternoon," he said, "but Joe Hemming sent word yesterday he wouldn't be buying pork after twelve today. So I have to tote my hogs over at once. I don't care about doing business New Year's morning."

"Should think New Year's would be pretty much the same as any other day to you," said Mr. Miller, for Richard Baker was a bachelor, with only old Mrs. Janeway to keep house for him.

"Well, I always like a good dinner on New Year's," said Richard Baker. "It's about the only way I can celebrate. Mrs. Janeway wanted to spend the day with her son's family over at Oriental, so I was laying out to cook my own dinner. I got everything ready in the pantry last night, 'fore I got word about the pork. I won't get back from Navarre before one o'clock, so I reckon I'll have to put up with a cold bite."

After her Uncle Richard had driven away, Prissy walked thoughtfully home. She had planned to spend a nice, lazy holiday with the new book her father had given her at Christmas and a box of candy. She did not even mean to cook a dinner, for her father had had to go to town that morning to meet a friend and would be gone the whole day. There was nobody else to cook dinner for. Prissy's mother had died when Prissy was a baby. She was her father's housekeeper, and they had jolly times together.

But as she walked home, she could not help thinking about Uncle Richard. He would certainly have cold New Year cheer, enough to chill the whole coming year. She felt sorry for him, picturing him returning from Navarre, cold and hungry, to find a fireless house and an uncooked dinner in the pantry.

Suddenly an idea popped into Prissy's head. Dared she? Oh, she never could! But he would never know — there would be plenty of time — she would!

Prissy hurried home, put her matches away, took a regretful peep at her unopened book, then locked the door and started up the road to Uncle Richard's house half a mile away. She meant to go and cook Uncle Richard's dinner for him, get it all beautifully ready, then slip away before he came home. He would never suspect her of it. Prissy would not have him suspect for the world; she thought he would be more likely to throw a dinner of her cooking out of doors than to eat it.

Eight years before this, when Prissy had been nine years old, Richard and Irving Baker had quarrelled over the division of a piece of property. The fault had been mainly on Richard's side, and that very fact made him all the more unrelenting and stubborn. He had never spoken to his brother since, and he declared he never would. Prissy and her father felt very badly over it, but Uncle Richard did not seem to feel badly at all. To all appearance he had completely forgotten that there were such people in the world as his brother Irving and his niece Prissy.

Prissy had no trouble in breaking into Uncle Richard's house, for the woodshed door was unfastened. She tripped into the hostile kitchen with rosy cheeks and mischief sparkling in her eyes. This was an adventure — this was fun! She would tell her father all about it when he came home at night and what a laugh they would have!

There was still a good fire in the stove, and in the pantry Prissy found the dinner in its raw state — a fine roast of fresh pork, potatoes, cabbage, turnips and the ingredients of a raisin pudding, for Richard Baker was fond of raisin puddings, and could make them as well as Mrs. Janeway could, if that was anything to boast of.

In a short time the kitchen was full of bubbling and hissings and appetizing odours. Prissy enjoyed herself hugely, and the raisin pudding, which she rather doubtfully mixed up, behaved itself beautifully.

"Uncle Richard said he'd be home by one," said Prissy to herself, as the clock struck twelve, "so I'll set the table now, dish up the dinner, and leave it where it will keep warm until he gets here. Then I'll slip away home. I'd like to see his face when he steps in. I suppose he'll think one of the Jenner girls across the street has cooked his dinner."

Prissy soon had the table set, and she was just peppering the turnips when a gruff voice behind her said:

"Well, well, what does this mean?"

Prissy whirled around as if she had been shot, and there stood Uncle Richard in the woodshed door!

Poor Prissy! She could not have looked or felt more guilty if Uncle Richard had caught her robbing his desk. She did not drop the turnips for a wonder; but she was too confused to set them down, so she stood there holding them, her face crimson, her heart thumping, and a horrible choking in her throat.

"I—I—came up to cook your dinner for you, Uncle Richard," she stammered. "I heard you say—in the store—that Mrs. Janeway had gone home and that you had nobody to cook your New Year's dinner for you. So I thought I'd come and do it, but I meant to slip away before you came home."

Poor Prissy felt that she would never get to the end of her explanation. Would Uncle Richard be angry? Would he order her from the house?

"It was very kind of you," said Uncle Richard drily. "It's a wonder your father let you come."

"Father was not home, but I am sure he would not have prevented me if he had been. Father has no hard feelings against you, Uncle Richard."

"Humph!" said Uncle Richard. "Well, since you've cooked the dinner you must stop and help me eat it. It smells good, I must say. Mrs. Janeway always burns pork when she roasts it. Sit down, Prissy. I'm hungry."

They sat down. Prissy felt quite giddy and breathless, and could hardly eat for excitement; but Uncle Richard had evidently brought home a good appetite from Navarre, and he did full justice to his New Year's dinner. He talked to Prissy too, quite kindly and politely, and when the meal was over he said slowly:

"I'm much obliged to you, Prissy, and I don't mind owning to you that I'm sorry for my share in the quarrel, and have wanted for a long time to be friends with your father again, but I was too ashamed and proud to make the first advance. You can tell him so for me, if you like. And if he's willing to let bygones be bygones, tell him I'd like him to come up here with you tonight when he gets home and spend the evening with me."

"Oh, he will come, I know!" cried Prissy joyfully. "He has felt so badly about not being friendly with you, Uncle Richard. I'm as glad as can be."

Prissy ran impulsively around the table and kissed Uncle Richard. He looked up at his tall, girlish niece with a smile of pleasure.

"You're a good girl, Prissy, and a kind-hearted one too, or you'd never have come up here to cook a dinner for a crabbed old uncle who deserved to eat cold dinners for his stubbornness. It made me cross today when folks wished me a happy New Year. It seemed like mockery when I hadn't a soul belonging to me to make it happy. But it has brought me happiness already, and I believe it will be a happy year all the way through."

"Indeed it will!" laughed Prissy. "I'm so happy now I could sing. I believe it was an inspiration—my idea of coming up here to cook your dinner for you."

"You must promise to come and cook my New Year's dinner for me every New Year we live near enough together," said Uncle Richard.

And Prissy promised.

White Magic

One September afternoon in the year of grace 1840 Avery and Janet Sparhallow were picking apples in their Uncle Daniel Sparhallow's big orchard. It was an afternoon of mellow sunshine; about them, beyond the orchard, were old harvest fields, mellowly bright and serene, and beyond the fields the sapphire curve of the St. Lawrence Gulf was visible through the groves of spruce and birch. There was a soft whisper of wind in the trees, and the pale purple asters that feathered the orchard grass swayed gently towards each other. Janet Sparhallow, who loved the outdoor world and its beauty, was, for the time being at least, very happy, as her little brown face, with its fine, satiny skin, plainly showed. Avery Sparhallow did not seem so happy. She worked rather abstractedly and frowned oftener than she smiled.

Avery Sparhallow was conceded to be a beauty, and had no rival in Burnley Beach. She was very pretty, with the obvious, indisputable prettiness of rich black hair, vivid, certain colour, and laughing, brilliant eyes. Nobody ever called Janet a beauty, or even thought her pretty. She was only seventeen — five years younger than Avery — and was rather lanky and weedy, with a rope of straight dark-brown hair, long, narrow, shining brown eyes and very black lashes, and a crooked, clever little mouth. She had visitations of beauty when excited, because then she flushed deeply, and colour made all the difference in the world to her; but she had never happened to look in the glass when excited, so that she had never seen herself beautiful; and hardly anybody else had ever seen her so, because she was always too shy and awkward and tongue-tied in company to feel excited over anything. Yet very little could bring that transforming flush to her face: a wind off the gulf, a sudden glimpse of blue upland, a flame-red poppy, a baby's laugh, a certain footstep. As for Avery Sparhallow, she never got excited over anything — not even her wedding dress, which had come from Charlottetown that day, and was incomparably beyond anything that had ever been seen in Burnley Beach before. For it was made of an apple-green silk, sprayed over with tiny rosebuds, which had been specially sent for to England, where Aunt Matilda Sparhallow had a brother in the silk trade. Avery Sparhallow's wedding dress was making far more of a sensation in Burnley Beach than her wedding itself was making. For Randall Burnley had been dangling after her for three years, and everybody knew that there was nobody for a Sparhallow to marry except a Burnley and nobody for a Burnley to marry except a Sparhallow.

"Only one silk dress—and I want a dozen," Avery had said scornfully.

"What would you do with a dozen silk dresses on a farm?" Janet asked wonderingly.

"Oh—what indeed?" agreed Avery, with an impatient laugh.

"Randall will think just as much of you in drugget as in silk," said Janet, meaning to comfort.

Again Avery laughed.

"That is true. Randall never notices what a woman has on. I like a man who does notice—and tells me about it. I like a man who likes me better in silk than in drugget. I will wear this rosebud silk when I'm married, and it will be supposed to last me the rest of my life and be worn on all state occasions, and in time become an heirloom like Aunt Matilda's hideous blue satin. I want a new silk dress every month."

Janet paid little attention to this kind of raving. Avery had always been more or less discontented. She would be contented enough after she was married. Nobody could be discontented who was Randall Burnley's wife. Janet was sure of that.

Janet liked picking apples; Avery did not like it; but Aunt Matilda had decreed that the red apples should be picked that afternoon, and Aunt Matilda's word was law at the Sparhallow farm, even for wilful Avery. So they worked and talked as they worked—of Avery's wedding, which was to be as soon as Bruce Gordon should arrive from Scotland.

"I wonder what Bruce will be like," said Avery. "It is eight years since he went home to Scotland. He was sixteen then—he will be twenty-four now. He went away a boy—he will come back a man."

"I don't remember much about him," said Janet. "I was only nine when he went away. He used to tease me—I do remember that." There was a little resentment in her voice. Janet had never liked being teased. Avery laughed.

"You were so touchy, Janet. Touchy people always get teased. Bruce was very handsome—and as nice as he was handsome. Those two years he was here were the nicest, gayest time I ever had. I wish he had stayed in Canada. But of course he wouldn't do that. His father was a rich man and Bruce was ambitious. Oh, Janet, I wish I could live in the old land. That would be life."

Janet had heard all this before and could not understand it. She had no hankering for either Scotland or England. She loved the new land and its wild, virgin beauty. She yearned to the future, never to the past.

"I'm tired of Burnley Beach," Avery went on passionately, shaking apples wildly off a laden bough by way of emphasis. "I know all the people — what they are — what they can be. It's like reading a book for the twentieth time. I know where I was born and who I'll marry — and where I'll be buried. That's knowing too much. All my days will be alike when I marry Randall. There will never be anything unexpected or surprising about them. I tell you Janet," Avery seized another bough and shook it with a vengeance, "I hate the very thought of it."

"The thought of — what?" said Janet in bewilderment.

"Of marrying Randall Burnley — or marrying anybody down here — and settling down on a farm for life."

Then Avery sat down on the rung of her ladder and laughed at Janet's face.

"You look stunned, Janet. Did you really think I wanted to marry Randall?"

Janet was stunned, and she did think that. How could any girl not want to marry Randall Burnley if she had the chance?

"Don't you love him?" she asked stupidly.

Avery bit into a nut-sweet apple.

"No," she said frankly. "Oh, I don't hate him, of course. I like him well enough. I like him very well. But we'll quarrel all our lives."

"Then what are you marrying him for?" asked Janet.

"Why, I'm getting on — twenty-two — all the girls of my age are married already. I won't be an old maid, and there's nobody but Randall. Nobody good enough for a Sparhallow, that is. You wouldn't want me to marry Ned Adams or John Buchanan, would you?"

"No," said Janet, who had her full share of the Sparhallow pride.

"Well, then, of course I must marry Randall. That's settled and there's no use making faces over the notion. I'm not making faces, but I'm tired of hearing you talk as if you thought I adored him and must be in the seventh heaven because I was going to marry him, you romantic child."

"Does Randall know you feel like this?" asked Janet in a low tone.

"No. Randall is like all men — vain and self-satisfied — and believes I'm crazy about him. It's just as well to let him think so, until we're safely married anyhow. Randall has some romantic notions too, and I'm not sure that he'd marry me if he knew, in spite of his three years' devotion. And I have no intention of being jilted three weeks before my wedding day."

Avery laughed again, and tossed away the core of her apple.

Janet, who had been very pale, went crimson and lovely. She could not endure hearing Randall criticized. "Vain and self-satisfied" — when there was never a man less so! She was horrified to feel that she almost hated Avery — Avery who did not love Randall.

"What a pity Randall didn't take a fancy to you instead of me, Janet," said Avery teasingly. "Wouldn't you like to marry him, Janet? Wouldn't you now?"

"No," cried Janet angrily. "I just like Randall, I've liked him ever since that day when I was a little thing and he came here and saved me from being shut up all day in that dreadful dark closet because I broke Aunt Matilda's blue cup — when I hadn't meant to break it. He wouldn't let her shut me up! He is like that — he understands! I want you to marry him because he wants you, and it isn't fair that you — that you — "

"Nothing is fair in this world, child. Is it fair that I, who am so pretty — you know I am pretty, Janet — and who love life and excitement, should have to be buried on a P.E. Island farm all my days? Or else be an old maid because a Sparhallow mustn't marry beneath her? Come, Janet, don't look so woebegone. I wouldn't have told you if I'd thought you'd take it so much to heart. I'll be a good wife to Randall, never fear, and I'll keep him up to the notch of prosperity much better than if I thought him a little lower than the angels. It doesn't do to think a man perfection, Janet, because he thinks so too, and when he finds someone who agrees with him he is inclined to rest on his oars."

"At any rate, you don't care for anyone else," said Janet hopefully.

"Not I. I like Randall as well as I like anybody."

"Randall won't be satisfied with that," muttered Janet. But Avery did not hear her, having picked up her basket of apples and gone. Janet sat down on the lower rung of the ladder and gave herself up to an unpleasant reverie. Oh, how the world had changed in half an hour! She had never been so worried in her life. She was so fond of Randall — she had always been fond of him — why, he was just like a brother to her! She couldn't possibly love a brother more. And Avery was going to hurt him; it would hurt him horribly when he found out she did not love him. Janet could not bear the thought of Randall being hurt; it made her fairly savage. He must not be hurt — Avery must love him. Janet could not understand why she did not.

Surely everyone must love Randall. It had never occurred to Janet to ask herself, as Avery had asked, if she would like to marry Randall. Randall could never fancy her — a little plain, brown thing, only half grown. Nobody could think of her beside beautiful, rose-faced Avery. Janet accepted this fact unquestioningly. She had never been jealous. She only felt that she wanted

Randall to have everything he wanted — to be perfectly happy. Why, it would be dreadful if he did not marry Avery — if he went and married some other girl. She would never see him then, never have any more delightful talks with him about all the things they both loved so much — winds and delicate dawns, mysterious woods in moonlight and starry midnights, silver-white sails going out of the harbour in the magic of morning, and the grey of gulf storms. There would be nothing in life; it would just be one great, unbearable emptiness; for she, herself, would never marry. There was nobody for her to marry — and she didn't care. If she could have Randall for a real brother, she would not mind a bit being an old maid. And there was that beautiful new frame house Randall had built for his bride, which she, Janet, had helped him build, because Avery would not condescend to details of pantry and linen closet and cupboards. Janet and Randall had had such fun over the cupboards. No stranger must ever come to be mistress of that house. Randall must marry Avery, and she must love him. Could anything be done to make her love him?

"I believe I'll go and see Granny Thomas," said Janet desperately.

She thought this was a silly idea, but it still haunted her and would not be shaken off. Granny Thomas was a very old woman who lived at Burnley Cove and was reputed to be something of a witch. That is, people who were not Sparhallows or Burnleys gave her that name. Sparhallows or Burnleys, of course, were above believing in such nonsense. Janet was above believing it; but still — the sailors along shore were careful to "keep on the good side" of Granny Thomas, lest she brew an unfavourable wind for them, and there was much talk of love potions. Janet knew that people said Peggy Buchanan would never have got Jack McLeod if Granny had not given her a love potion. Jack had never looked at Peggy, though she was after him for years; and then, all at once, he was quite mad about her — and married her — and wore her life out with jealousy. And Peggy, the homeliest of all the Buchanan girls! There must be something in it. Janet made a sudden desperate resolve. She would go to Granny and ask her for a love potion to make Avery love Randall. If Granny couldn't do any good, she couldn't do any harm. Janet was a little afraid of her, and had never been near her house, but what wouldn't she do for Randall?

Janet never lost much time in carrying out any resolution she made. The next afternoon she slipped away to visit Granny Thomas. She put on her longest dress and did her hair up for the first time. Granny must not think her a child. She rowed herself down the long pond to the row of golden-brown sand dunes that parted it from the gulf. It was a wonderful autumn day. There were wild growths and colours and scents in sweet procession all around the pond. Every curve in it revealed some little whim of loveliness. On the left bank, in a grove of birch, was Randall's new house, waiting to be sanctified by love and joy and birth. Janet loved to be alone thus with the delightful day. She was sorry when she had walked over the stretch of windy weedy sea fields and reached Granny's little tumbledown house at the Cove — sorry and a little frightened as well. But only a little; there was good stuff in Janet; she lifted the latch boldly and walked in when Granny bade. Granny was curled up on a stool by her fireplace, and if ever anybody did look like a witch, she did. She waved her pipe at another stool, and Janet sat down, gazing a little curiously at Granny, whom she had never seen at such close quarters before.

Will I look like that when I am very old? she thought, beholding Granny's wizened, marvellously wrinkled face. I wonder if anybody will be sorry when you die.

"Staring wasn't thought good manners in my time," said Granny. Then, as Janet blushed crimson under the rebuke, she added, "Keep red like that instead o' white, and you won't need no love ointment."

Janet felt a little cold thrill. How did Granny know what she had come for? Was she a real witch after all? For a moment she wished she hadn't come. Perhaps it was not right to tamper with the powers of darkness. Peggy Buchanan was notoriously unhappy. If Janet had known how to get herself away, she would have gone without asking for anything.

Then a sound came from the lean-to behind the house.

"S-s-h. I hear the devil grunting like a pig," muttered Granny, looking very impish.

But Janet smiled a little contemptuously. She knew it was a pig and no devil. Granny Thomas was only an old fraud. Her awe passed away and left her cool Sparhallow.

"Can you," she said with her own directness, "make a — a person care for another person — care — very much?"

Granny removed her pipe and chuckled.

"What you want is toad ointment," she said.

Toad ointment! Janet shuddered. That did not sound very nice. Granny noticed the shudder.

"Nothing like it," she said, nodding her crone-like old grey head. "There's other things, but noan so sure. Put a li'l bit — oh, such a li'l bit — on his eyelids, and he's yourn for life. You need something powerful — you're noan so pretty — only when you're blushing."

Janet was blushing again. So Granny thought she wanted the charm for herself! Well, what did it matter? Randall was the only one to be considered.

"Is it very—expensive?" she faltered. She had not much money. Money was no plentiful thing on a P.E.I. farm in 1840.

"Oh, noa—oh, noa," Granny leered. "I don't sell it. I gives it. I like to see young folks happy. You don't need much, as I've said—just a li'l smootch and you'll have your man, and send old Granny a bite o' the wedding cake and fig o' baccy for luck, and a bid to the fir-r-st christening! Doan't forget that, dearie."

Janet was cold again with anger. She hated old Granny Thomas. She would never come near her again.

"I'd rather pay you its worth," she said coldly.

"You couldn't, dearie. What money could be eno' for such a treasure? But that's the Sparhallow pride. Well, go, see if the Sparhallow pride and the Sparhallow money will buy you your lad's love."

Granny looked so angry that Janet hastened to appease her.

"Oh, please forgive me—I meant no offence. Only—it must have cost you much trouble to make it."

Granny chuckled again. She was vastly pleased to see a Sparhallow suing to her—a Sparhallow!

"Toads am cheap," she said. "It's all in the knowing how and the time o' the moon. Here, take this li'l pill box—there's eno' in it—and put a li'l bit on his eyelids when you've getten the chance—and when he looks at you, he'll love you. Mind you, though, that he looks at no other first—it's the first one he sees that he'll love. That's the way it works."

"Thank you." Janet took the little box. She wished she dared to go at once. But perhaps this would anger Granny. Granny looked at her with a twinkle in her little, incredibly old eyes.

"Be off," she said. "You're in a hurry to go—you're as proud as any of the proud Sparhallows. But I bear you no grudge. I likes proud people—when they have to come to me to get help."

Janet found herself outside with a relieved heart in her bosom and her little box in her hand. For a moment she was tempted to throw it away. But no—Randall would be so unhappy if he found out Avery didn't love him! She would try the ointment at least—she would try to forget about the toads and not let herself think how it was made—something might come of it.

Janet hurried home along the shore, where a silvery wave broke in a little lovely silvery curve on the sand. She was so happy that her cheeks burned, and Randall Burnley, who was sitting on the edge of her flat when she reached the pond, looked at her with admiration. Janet dropped her box into her pocket stealthily when she saw him. What with her guilty secret, she hardly knew whether she was glad or not when he said he was going to row her up the pond.

"I saw you go down an hour ago and I've been waiting ever since," he said. "Where have you been?"

"Oh—I just—wanted a walk—this lovely day," said Janet miserably. She felt that she was telling an untruth and this hurt her horribly—especially when it was to Randall. This was what came of truck with witches—you were led into falsehood and deception straightaway. Again Janet was tempted to drop Granny's pill box into the depths of Burnley Pond—and again she decided not to because she saw Randall Burnley's deep-set, blue-grey eyes, that could look tender or sorrowful or passionate or whimsical as he willed, and thought how they would look when he found Avery did not love him.

So Janet drowned the voice of conscience and was brazenly happy— happy because Randall Burnley rowed her up the pond—happy because he walked halfway home with her over the autumnal fields—happy because he talked of the day and the sea and the golden weather, as only Randall could talk. But she thought she was happy because she had in her pocket what might make Avery love him.

Randall went as far as the stile in the birch wood between the Burnley and the Sparhallow land—and he kept her there talking for another half-hour—and though he talked only of a book he had read and a new puppy he was training, Janet listened with her soul in her ears. She talked too—quite freely; she was never in the least shy or tongue-tied or awkward in Randall's company. There she was always at her best, with a delightful feeling of being understood. She wondered if he noticed she had her hair done up. Her eyes shone and her brown face was full of rosy, kissable hues. When he finally turned away homeward, life went flat. Janet decided she was very tired after her long walk and her trying interview. But it did not matter, since she had her love potion. That was so much nicer a name than toad ointment.

That night Janet rubbed mutton tallow on her hands. She had never done that before—she had thought it vain and foolish—though Avery did it every night. But that afternoon on the pond Randall had said something about the beautiful shape of her pretty slender hands. He had never paid her a compliment before. Her hands were brown and a little hard—not soft and white like Avery's. So Janet resorted to the mutton tallow. If one had a scrap of beauty, if only in one's hands, one might as well take care of it.

Having got her ointment, the next thing was to make use of it. This was not so easy—because, in the first place, it must not be done when there was any danger of Avery's seeing some other than Randall first—and it must be done without Avery's knowing it. The two problems combined were almost too much for Janet. She bided her chance like a watchful cat—but it did not come. Two weeks went by and it had not come. Janet was getting very desperate. The wedding day was only a week away. The bride's cake was made and the turkeys fattened. The invitations were sent out. Janet's own bridesmaid dress was ready. And still the little pill box in the till of Janet's blue chest was unopened. She had never even opened it, lest virtue escape.

Then her chance came at last, unexpectedly. One evening at dusk, when Janet was crossing the little dark upstairs hall, Aunt Matilda called up to her.

"Janet, send Avery down. There is a young man wanting to see her."

Aunt Matilda was laughing a little—as she always did when Randall came. It was a habit with her, hanging over from the early days of Randall's courtship. Janet went on into their room to tell Avery. And lo, Avery was lying asleep on her bed, tired out from her busy day. Janet, after one glance, flew to her chest. She took out her pill box and opened it, a little fearfully. The toad ointment was there, dark and unpleasant enough to view. Janet tiptoed breathlessly to the bed and gingerly scraped the tip of her finger in the ointment.

She said so little would be enough—oh, I hope I'm not doing wrong.

Trembling with excitement, she brushed lightly the white lids of Avery's eyes. Avery stirred and opened them. Janet guiltily thrust her pill box behind her.

"Randall is downstairs asking for you, Avery."

Avery sat up, looking annoyed. She had not expected Randall that evening and would greatly have preferred a continuance of her nap. She went down crossly enough, but looking very lovely, flushed from sleep. Janet stood in their room, clasping her cold hands nervously over her breast. Would the charm work? Oh, she must know—she must know. She could not wait. After a few moments that seemed like years she crept down the stairs and out into the dusk of the June-warm September night. Like a shadow she slipped up to the open parlour window and looked cautiously in between the white muslin curtains. The next minute she had fallen on her knees in the mint bed. She wished she could die then and there.

The young man in the parlour was not Randall Burnley. He was dark and smart and handsome; he was sitting on the sofa by Avery's side, holding her hands in his, smiling into her rosy, delighted, excited face. And he was Bruce Gordon—no doubt of that. Bruce Gordon, the expected cousin from Scotland!

"Oh, what have I done? What have I done?" moaned poor Janet, wringing her hands. She had seen Avery's face quite plainly—had seen the look in her eyes. Avery had never looked at Randall Burnley like that. Granny Thomas' abominable ointment had worked all right—and Avery had fallen in love with the wrong man.

Janet, cold with horror and remorse, dragged herself up to the window again and listened. She must know—she must be sure. She could hear only a word here and there, but that word was enough.

"I thought you promised to wait for me, Avery," Bruce said reproachfully.

"You were so long in coming back—I thought you had forgotten me," cried Avery.

"I think I did forget a little, Avery. I was such a boy. But now—well, thank Heaven, I haven't come too late."

There was a silence, and shameless Janet, peering above the window sill, saw what she saw. It was enough. She crept away upstairs to her room. She was lying there across the bed when Avery swept in—a splendid, transfigured Avery, flushed triumphant. Janet sat up, pallid, tear-stained, and looked at her.

"Janet," said Avery, "I am going to marry Bruce Gordon next Wednesday night instead of Randall Burnley."

Janet sprang forward and caught Avery's hand.

"You must not," she cried wildly. "It's all my fault—oh, if I could only die—I got the love ointment from Granny Thomas to rub on your eyes to make you love the first man you would see. I meant it to be Randall—I thought it was Randall—oh, Avery!"

Avery had been listening, between amazement and anger. Now anger mastered amazement.

"Janet Sparhallow," she cried, "are you crazy? Or do you mean that you went to Granny Thomas—you, a Sparhallow!—and asked her for a love philtre to make me love Randall Burnley?"

"I didn't tell her it was for you—she thought I wanted it for myself," moaned Janet. "Oh, we must undo it—I'll go to her again—no doubt she knows of some way to undo the spell—"

Avery, whose rages never lasted long, threw back her dark head and laughed ringingly.

"Janet Sparhallow, you talk as if you lived in the dark ages! The idea of supposing that horrid old woman could give you love philtres! Why, girl, I've always loved Bruce—always. But I thought he'd forgotten me. And tonight when he came I found he hadn't. There's the whole thing in a nutshell. I'm going to marry him and go home with him to Scotland."

"And what about Randall?" said Janet, corpse-white.

"Oh, Randall—pooh! Do you suppose I'm worrying about Randall? But you must go to him tomorrow and tell him for me, Janet."

"I will not—I will not."

"Then I'll tell him myself—and I'll tell him about you going to Granny," said Avery cruelly. "Janet, don't stand there looking like that. I've no patience with you. I shall be perfectly happy with Bruce—I would have been miserable with Randall. I know I shan't sleep a wink tonight—I'm so excited. Why, Janet, I'll be Mrs. Gordon of Gordon Brae—and I'll have everything heart can desire and the man of my heart to boot. What has lanky Randall Burnley with his little six-roomed house to set against that?"

If Avery did not sleep, neither did Janet. She lay awake till dawn, suffering such misery as she had never endured in her life before. She knew she must go to Randall Burnley tomorrow and break his heart. If she did not, Avery would tell him—tell him what Janet had done. And he must not know that—he must not. Janet could not bear that thought.

It was a pallid, dull-eyed Janet who went through the birch wood to the Burnley farm next afternoon, leaving behind her an excited household where the sudden change of bridegrooms, as announced by Avery, had rather upset everybody. Janet found Randall working in the garden of his new house—setting out rosebushes for Avery—Avery, who was to jilt him at the very altar, so to speak. He came over to open the gate for Janet, smiling his dear smile. It was a dear smile—Janet caught her breath over the dearness of it—and she was going to blot it off his face.

She spoke out, with plainness and directness. When you had to deal a mortal blow, why try to lighten it?

"Avery sent me to tell you that she is going to marry Bruce Gordon instead of you. He came last night—and she says that she has always liked him best."

A very curious change came over Randall's face—but not the change Janet had expected to see. Instead of turning pale Randall flushed; and instead of a sharp cry of pain and incredulity, Randall said in no uncertain tones, "Thank God!"

Janet wondered if she were dreaming. Granny Thomas' love potion seemed to have turned the world upside down. For Randall's arms were about her and Randall was pressing his lean bronzed cheek to hers and Randall was saying:

"Now I can tell you, Janet, how much I love you."

"Me? Me!" choked Janet.

"You. Why, you're in the very core of my heart, girl. Don't tell me you can't love me—you can—you must—why, Janet," for his eyes had caught and locked with hers for a minute, "you do!"

There were five minutes about which nobody can tell anything, for even Randall and Janet never knew clearly just what happened in those five minutes. Then Janet, feeling somehow as if she had died and then come back to life, found her tongue.

"Three years ago you came courting Avery," she said reproachfully.

"Three years ago you were a child. I did not think about you. I wanted a wife—and Avery was pretty. I thought I was in love with her. Then you grew up all at once—and we were such good friends—I never could talk to Avery—she wasn't interested in anything I said—and you have eyes that catch a man—I've always thought of your eyes. But I was honour-bound to Avery—I didn't dream you cared. You must marry me next Wednesday, Janet—we'll have a double wedding. You won't mind—being married—so soon?"

"Oh, no—I won't—mind," said Janet dazedly. "Only—oh, Randall—I must tell you—I didn't mean to tell you—I'd have rather died—but now—I must tell you about it now—because I can't bear anything hidden between us. I went to old Granny Thomas—and got a love ointment from her—to make Avery love you, because I knew she didn't—and I wanted you to be happy—Randall, don't—I can't talk when you do that! Do you think Granny's ointment could have made her care for Bruce?"

Randall laughed—the little, low laugh of the triumphant lover.

"If it did, I'm glad of it. But I need no such ointment on my eyes to make me love you—you carry your philtre in that elfin little face of yours, Janet."